BLOODBONDED

Amy Rose Davis

amy rose davis

Bloodbonded

ISBN: 978-1-945557-91-0

First Edition

ACKNOWLEDGMENTS

This has been a long slog.

The seeds of *Bloodbonded* were there back in 2009 when I first wrote *Raven-marked* during NaNoWriMo. A draft of *Bloodbonded* went to beta readers in 2012 while an agent tried to convince big publishing that my series was worth reading. That same draft languished on my hard drive for 18 months when I worked out a crisis of faith. And it's been calling, beckoning, whispering, sometimes shouting, always begging for completion ever since I dipped a toe back into the waters of writing and publishing in 2015.

And through it all, my threes of fans have waited.

There are many people to thank. Linda Kincaid once again drew maps for me. Robin Ludwig designed the cover back in 2012 when I thought I'd be able to publish this book in a reasonable amount of time. Aleta Sanstrum, Laurel Kriegler, Jane Wells, Kelly McCrady Schaub, Lisa Nowak, Nathan Hodgdon, Michal Ingraham, and Ellen Samek beta read for me. Too many people to name gave me pep talks, but I must recognize Kathleen Peters specifically as she spoke several very true things into my world at just the right moments. And my husband, Bryce, continued to tolerate the mood swings, anxiety, and general crazy-making of living with a writer.

But I think this book really belongs to you. The readers. My threes of fans.

You have offered patient encouragement, gentle prodding, and wise words of kindness at all the right moments over the last four years. You have given me reason to hope that this series might reach some people. You have been a balm to my spirit. I cannot begin to express how much I appreciate you.

So readers, *Bloodbonded* belongs to you.

I hope it was worth the wait.

TAURA

Galoch Sea

Ragged Isles

Sacred Isle
(Wisdomkeeper)

Starling's Cross

Salmon Springs

Firth of Mullen

Brae Sidh Village

Fox Hill

Kiern

Wolf Tribe

Tribal Territory

Stone Coast

Macha Tor

Cuhall's Channel

Hound Tribe

Torlach

N

Herons Rest

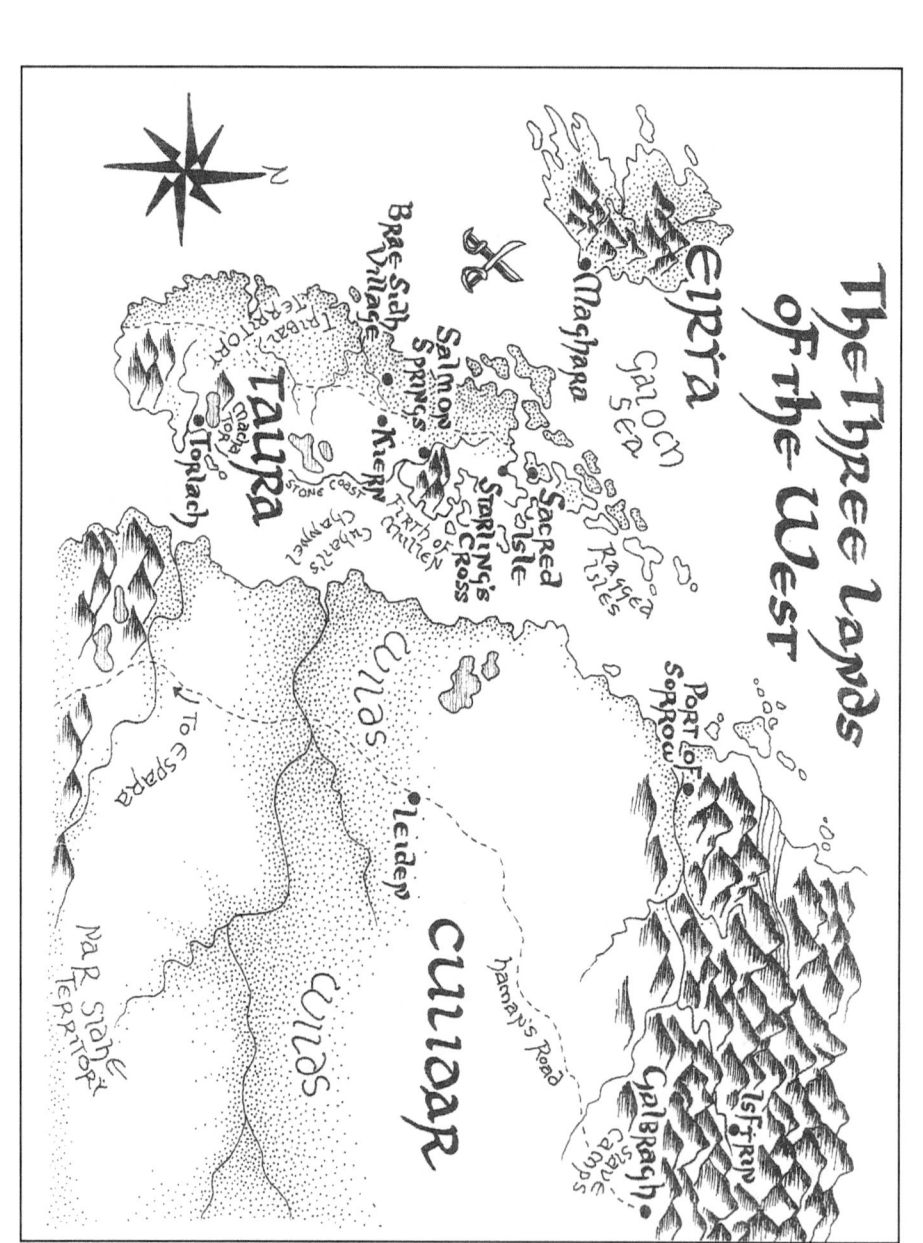

PROLOGUE

When the Forbidden rise, the Deliverer will come.
— Prophecy of the lion tribe

The Mac Mahon estates were in controlled chaos when Emrys arrived at the front gate. He reined in near the guardhouse, keeping his face shielded with a hood. "I need to see your master."

A guard approached, one hand on his sword. Emrys sensed the archers in the towers above him; at least two had arrows trained on him. "The master'll want to know wha' it's about," the guard said.

"Tell him I have a proposal for him. Tell him ..." He paused and flipped the guard a coin. "Tell him it will help him expand his business."

The guard caught the coin and turned it over in his hand a few times. He gestured with his chin. "Wait in th' yard."

The gate opened. Emrys rode into the courtyard and dismounted to await further instructions. Men in matching livery patrolled the estate in well-formed lines, unlike the rough, haphazard order of Allyn's estate. The slaves were housed in camps some distance away, and the estate itself suggested only wealth, not the method of its acquisition. Alasdair Mac Mahon counted himself as noble as the Prince of Galbragh. *And who could gainsay him? There is little difference between them.*

The guard returned from consulting a livery-clad steward at the front door of the manor house. "My master says he'll see you, but you'll leave all your weapons here."

"Of course." *One must appreciate the false security of a man who doesn't know his soul is in danger.* He removed his sword and several daggers and followed the guard to the house.

The steward led Emrys through a house filled with the finest of carpets, artwork, and furnishings from around the world. Uniformed servants carried out the thousand mindless tasks of domestics who have served rich men throughout time—polishing furniture, lighting candles and sconces, delivering trays of food and drink. The sound of stringed music floated down the estate corridor, and when the steward opened an ornately carved oak door, Emrys saw a young, dark-haired girl in a silk dress playing a lyre.

Nearby, an aging man reclined on a chaise. The man wore a long robe over silk trousers and slippers, his shoulder-length graying hair tied back at his neck. He gestured toward Emrys for silence, and the girl played for several more moments.

Emrys surveyed the room. Music, art, imports from the East—*he thinks himself an aesthete.* The silks were printed with patterns unknown in the frigid northern climate. *He's traded with the Tal'Amuni slavers.* The décor of the room revealed other trading relationships. *Ebony from Friqqur. Woolen tapestries from the Middle Isles. And if I'm not mistaken, that carafe most assuredly contains Esparan wine.* He suppressed a smile. *There is no man more corruptible than one who loves his comforts.*

When the echo of the lyre died away, the man clapped and stood. "Wonderful, my dear, simply lovely." He held out his hand, and she took it and stood. The man bent and kissed the girl's cheek. "You improve every day."

She curtsied. "Thank you, my lord. Will you have further need of me?"

"You may wait in my chambers. I'll attend you as soon as I'm done with this appointment."

Red crept up her cheeks. "As you wish, my lord."

He lifted her chin and tsked. "Dear, you mustn't look so ashamed. Take pride in your work."

"Yes, my lord. I will."

He rang a bell, and a Tal'Amuni eunuch came forward to take the girl's arm and led her away.

The man turned to Emrys and clapped his hands together. "Well, now I feel refreshed and ready to tackle new business."

Emrys inclined his head. "I fear the nature of my business with you requires a certain amount of anonymity for the moment."

Mac Mahon's eyes narrowed. "You may go," he said to the guard. A servant poured wine. Mac Mahon lifted two goblets, offering one to Emrys. "Anonymity," Mac Mahon said. "You'll understand, I'm sure, if I'm a bit skeptical of any stranger who shows up at my door with promises of grandeur and wealth on the guarantee of silence on my part."

"Tell your servants to leave."

Mac Mahon gestured, and men and women disappeared through side doors. When the room was silent again, Mac Mahon sat. "You have my attention."

Emrys lowered his hood and sat across from the slaver. "You've done well for yourself."

"Cattle, Tal'Amuni silks, and steel are good businesses."

"So are courtesans."

Mac Mahon lifted his goblet. "You've heard of my particular talents for training girls."

"I have. I'm quite impressed." He nodded toward the door where the harper had disappeared. "Is that one a new girl?"

"Not new, but she is a particular favorite of mine. I found her in a group of villagers. Now that she's maturing, her training in the arts of the courtesan is progressing nicely." Mac Mahon sipped his wine. "I don't think you came here to discuss my particular business dealings—or perhaps I misunderstand your need for anonymity?"

"I understand you had a visit from Prince Henry."

Mac Mahon leaned forward and put down his goblet. "He's an idiot. Seems he lost a girl who was in his care, and now he wants to blame me for it. He claims some clues led him to my door. I told him—no one matching his ward's description has come through here in weeks. I look at every girl we bring in, and if she was as beautiful as he says, I would have seen her. Besides, why would I want to anger Henry? It's his habit of looking the other way that keeps me in business."

Emrys drank from his goblet. *Tasteless.* "Seamus Allyn planted those clues."

"You have proof?"

"I do, but it doesn't matter. He's dead. His whole empire will be in shambles by nightfall."

A smile curled the edges of Mac Mahon's mouth. "Oh, this is delightful. I'll swoop down and take his empire today, before the Tal'Amuni have time—"

"They'll be leaving as well—returning to Tal'Amun."

"You're certain?"

"Yes. One of their chief eunuchs left the camp this morning. The rest are packing to return east."

Mac Mahon frowned. "Abandoning their trade here? What would drive them away?"

"I don't know." *Tal'Amuni wards are stronger than I thought.*

Mac Mahon stood and walked to the window. "I can have the entire northern plain," he said, his voice strained with the rough desire for power.

"And with the entire slaving empire in your control, you can crush Henry, take Galbragh, and set yourself up as the only authority here."

The man stood with his back to Emrys, his body taut. "King—no, *Emperor* Alasdair has a lovely ring to it, doesn't it?" He turned. "But surely you didn't come here just to deliver news I would have discovered on my own in a day or two."

"No." Emrys set his goblet down. *Tread carefully.* "How would you like to expand your business venture into precious metals and gemstones?"

Mac Mahon sat down and leaned closer to Emrys. "Tell me."

"There is a tribe in the mountains beyond the river. They sit on untold wealth, but they refuse to deal with anyone from the plains."

Mac Mahon waved a dismissive hand. "Rumors and legends. I've heard this fairy story before."

Emrys reached into a pocket and drew out a handful of silver nuggets. He scattered them on a table. "It's not a story. The mountains hold vast deposits of silver, gold, gems. But the tribe does not like outlanders on its mountain. The people have pushed back slavers once before, decades ago. If you don't go about this properly, your entire empire will come crashing down."

Mac Mahon's eyes never left the silver. "What do you suggest?"

"If you promise me men, I can show you how to find the riches the mountain holds."

Mac Mahon rubbed his chin. "How many men?"

"Three thousand. More, if possible."

Mac Mahon snorted a laugh. "*Three thousand men?* Impossible. I don't even have that many directly in my employ."

"Recruit them. Find them among your slaves, if you wish. Go through the villages and conscript them."

Mac Mahon waved a hand in frustration. "Men won't just flock to my banner. They'll want something."

Emrys gestured to the silver. "Promise them spoils—land and gems. Soon, you'll have plenty to hand out."

"Still, three thousand is a large number."

Emrys fought back rising anger. *But for human cowardice, I could rule the world. I could take his soul—I could consume him now. I could gain much strength from this man. But would it be enough to fight the raven? I can't risk it—not until the raven is weakened. Better to let Mac Mahon weaken him for me.* "I will bring you some. Five hundred, at least. You will provide the rest."

"One thousand. You provide one thousand, and I will conscript and capture the rest."

Emrys returned the nuggets to his pocket. He lifted his goblet in agreement. "It is done."

The slaver turned toward the window again, his fingers tracing the rim of his goblet in slow, thoughtful consideration. "And you? What do you want in return?"

Emrys' hands tightened around the goblet. "Destroy the tribe. Utterly and completely. Leave none alive. Should you leave them alive, they will recover one day and defeat you."

"Destroy people I could use or sell?"

"Promise me that much, or I will not tell you the secret to finding them and the treasures of the mountain."

"Very well. And Henry? What of Galbragh?"

"Let it sit. Galbragh is not going anywhere. Build your empire in the north and then take Galbragh from a position of strength."

Alasdair Mac Mahon laughed. "Oh, this is wonderful. *Wonderful!* Such a day—my enemies routed and the aroma of empire in the air. This calls for a celebration." Mac Mahon rang the bell, and the eunuch returned. "Take our friend to the east wing. Let him choose his courtesan for the night."

"That's not necessary."

Mac Mahon held up a hand. "Gratis, my friend. Just a sampling—a taste of the pleasures I've taught these fine ladies." He smiled. "You might be in the market for a long-term companion one day. Use this chance to sample my ladies."

"Thank you, but no."

"I insist." Mac Mahon's face turned stony.

Emrys again considered finishing him. *Consuming a soul that dark would make me more powerful in one night than if I consumed hundreds— thousands—of simple thieves. But I need him still, and he needs to think he owns me.* He finally inclined his head. "Thank you."

Emrys followed the eunuch to a wing where courtesans lounged in the pursuit of all manner of activities suitable for noblewomen—embroidery, music, reading, painting. In one far corner, a pretty blonde woman sat at a desk, scratching out words on parchment. "Her," Emrys said.

The eunuch bowed and went to the woman. She put away her things and stood. "My lord," she said. "Shall we adjourn to my room?"

He took her arm. "What were you writing?"

"Poetry, my lord. Would you like to hear it?"

He removed one glove. "Another time."

When they reached her room, he turned and put a hand on her throat. She choked and gasped, her face paling with lack of air. He drew as much of her soul into himself as he dared—enough to have a taste, but not kill her. He let her go, and she collapsed onto the floor, her green silk gown puddling around her. He crouched. "You'll recover," he said, pulling his glove on. "You have most of your soul left. But if I ever hear that you've told your master anything but that you entertained me in every way you knew how, I'll come back and finish what I started. Do you understand?"

Vacant eyes stared up. "I . . . understand . . . ."

"Good." He straightened. "Do not leave this room until morning."

He slipped between the elements and went south.

CHAPTER ONE

The lion awakens. The mountain bleeds.
— Tribal prophecy

Mairead pulled her knees up to her chest and burrowed against Connor's shoulder. He adjusted the blanket over them and tightened his arm around her. "Cold?" he asked.

"No." She stifled a yawn, but it came out as more of a sigh. "I think I'm finally warm."

He pressed his lips to her head. "Try to sleep. I'll keep watch."

"Remember when we started this journey, and I wouldn't even let you put an arm around me?"

"This probably isn't entirely proper, is it?"

"Not in the least."

He chuckled. "Don't worry. I'll behave myself. I'll wait until we're wed."

Married. Could he really mean it? I'm not ready to think about that. How can I trust him? But he's here now, and I do love him. She draped one arm over his middle and tucked her head against his chest again. She tried to sort out the memories of the previous week. She remembered Melik's blood on the snow after he sold her to the slavers and the sting of the snakebite on her arm when they subdued her with the venom. She pictured the twisted anger on Allyn's face when he tried to rape her, and she heard the gurgle of his last breaths when he fell to her dagger in his side. She shuddered. *It was justice. He'll never hurt another woman again.*

There were other memories, too—the hesitant defiance of a slave woman, the promise of escape with the Tal'Amuni eunuch, the surprising conviction that she was meant to free Culidar from its enslavement. *And Connor.* The sight of Connor in the corridor, the feel of his arm pulling her close once the slavers were dead, the scent of the jerkin she clung to as they galloped away— it was more than she'd dared hope or dream of in the week after he left Prince Henry's palace. *He came for me, he loves me, he wants me. And he'll be recognized as a duke. His name is no longer tainted. But what does it mean for us? Does he have to go back to Taura? I can't go back. I belong here.*

The air around them moved, and Queen Maeve alit, the braids of air dissolving around her. Her lips tightened when she saw them huddled near a tree. She gave her head a small shake and folded her hands before her. "I found Henry. He's been roaming the northern plains looking for Mairead. I told him where you were, and he promised to ride to meet you at first light." She addressed Mairead. "You are well?"

Mairead stood. "Very well, thank you, your majesty. Your healers did excellent work."

Maeve, however, did not look pleased. Her mouth tightened into a thin line again. "A word, Mairead? Alone?"

"Mother ...."

"Connor," Mairead said, one hand on his arm. "It's all right."

He hesitated. "I'll make sure we're secure here. Mother, behave yourself." He stepped into the trees.

Maeve watched him go. "It would appear you have what you wanted," she said when he was out of earshot. "My son is clearly in love with you."

"He says as much."

"And you? What are your intentions toward him?"

I don't know. "I do love him, that much is true." *As for the rest ....*

Maeve spoke in a low, fierce whisper. "I warned you," she said. "I told you that he would ruin you and leave you."

Mairead crossed her arms. "Are you angry that he might wish to do more than bed me? Or are you angry that I pose a threat to your plans for him?"

The wind stirred the trees above them, and Mairead felt the Sidh braids tease the hair on her arms. Maeve took a deep breath. The braids faded. "He has responsibilities," she said. "To our people."

"I will ensure that he fulfills them," Mairead said. "I have no wish to alienate the Sidh. I wish to restore the alliance between your people and the Taurin throne." *If you can stomach the woman who wishes to share your son.*

Maeve bit off a laugh. "You have no idea what you are committing to," she said.

"I don't under—"

"I need his blood," Maeve said, voice rising, a hint of desperation behind it. "I need him to give me an heir. I cannot have more children, and there has never been a girl child born with all three talents outside my direct line. Connor is, right now, the strongest Sidh alive. He is even stronger than I am." She took a deep breath. When she spoke again, her voice was calm, resigned, even tired. "I do not enjoy this. I wish things were different. I don't want to risk introducing human blood—or even tribal earth magic—into our line. I do not wish to rely on his half-human blood to provide me with a fully Sidh heir. I certainly don't wish to be reduced to a bitter old woman whose only concern is bloodlines. But I fear I have no other choice. I cannot reign forever. I need an heir, or my people will die."

"Can no one else—"

"No. There is no other Sidh woman who even comes close to my strength in the elements. When I die, the *codagha* will die, and the Sidh will die, unless another with the binding magic takes control of the web. I examine every Sidh child born, and I have never found anyone who could come close to my power or Connor's, and none with the binding magic. Connor is the best option to sire an heir for me." She closed her eyes and shook her head. "I am sorry, Mairead. But I must ask. Please, for the Sidh, for my people—please, give him up for a time. Send him home. I will not require him to wed, but I need his blood."

Mairead understood. *Give him up so he can bed a Sidh girl—let him sire a child on another woman so his mother can have her heir. How could I share him that way? But can the world survive if the Sidh do not?* "I can promise he and I will discuss it. And should he choose it, I will not stop him. But he is his own man."

"No one knows that better than I," Maeve said. In the distance, the Ferimin screeched, and Maeve shivered. "They are bolder each night. I can't keep making these trips."

Connor stepped back into the clearing, hand on his sword. "You're all right?"

"Yes," Mairead said. "It wasn't that close."

"They won't stay away for long," Maeve said.

"We'll be fine," Connor said. "Go home, Mother. I'll be in touch."

Maeve called up green and blue braids to take her back to Taura.

"Water," Mairead said. "Not air."

"She travels in the snow to hide her scent."

"The Ferimin can smell the Sidh?"

"They have very good senses. We aren't sure how they can detect us, but we know they can. They have killed the Sidh before."

"Do they see the braids?"

"I don't think so. I think only those with the elemental magic—Brae Sidh and Nar Sidhe—can see the braids. But there must be something they can detect." He frowned. "I wish she'd travel in the earth braids. Even if they could detect her, they wouldn't be able to attack her if she were in the ground. I think she feels too confined that way." He watched the sky until the braids were gone and the screeching of the Ferimin had faded.

Mairead put a hand on his arm. "Connor?"

He startled. "I'm fine," he said. He rubbed a hand over his eyes. He looked at the ground where their blankets lay and frowned in concentration, and in a moment, braids in a dozen shades of orange wove through the patch of ground. When they faded, he gestured. "Try it."

"What is it?"

"Warming stones—or rather, stone talent to warm the ground. I've seen her do it a hundred times. Try it."

Mairead sat down, and the heat spread through her legs. "It's wonderful. It's like sitting in a warm bath."

He sat down next to her and pulled the blanket over them both. "What did she want to talk with you about?"

Mairead chewed her lip. *He should know what's expected of him.* "Do you remember how you told me that you thought your mother wanted you to settle down and have children with some Sidh girl?"

He sighed. "She told you to send me home, didn't she?"

"She only wants what's best for her people."

He leaned his head against the tree. "Well, at least a conversation about my mother should ensure your chastity."

"What?"

"Nothing. My mother is complicated. She wants what she wants, but she doesn't always understand the impact of her desires." He stroked her cheek with one hand. "You know what I want, and you know what my mother wants. Perhaps the question is, 'what do you want?'"

"I want you to stay here."

"Then I'll stay here."

She put her hand over his. "As easy as that?"

"As easy as that." He lifted her chin. "As long as I have a chance to build a life with you, I could never be with another woman, Mairead. The only woman I want is you."

A life with him. A family. A home. Does he realize what he's saying? Committing to that kind of life—is he capable of that? She took his hand from her chin and held it in her lap. "But it's not just about us," she said.

"Why not?"

"Because your mother is right. We don't belong to each other, Connor. We belong to bigger things. We both have a calling, and we can't be certain our callings overlap." She put a hand on his arm. "I do love you, and I don't want to lose you, but how can we be certain that our marriage would be the right thing for Taura or the Sidh?"

The silence weighed on the clearing. "You're afraid."

"Of what?"

"Of going to bed with me. You have to know, Mairead—I would never abuse you the way Allyn did."

"I won't deny that, right now, the idea of going to bed with you isn't very appealing. But that will pass. What Allyn did was his sin, not mine. He didn't take my chastity, and I won't allow him to steal anything else from me, either. And I had my justice."

"Then my mother threatened you with something."

"That's not her way." *At least, I don't think it's her way.* "But if the Sidh die, where would that leave Taura? Or even the world?"

"The Sidh aren't going anywhere. My mother will find her heir, and the child won't be mine." He paused. "If you aren't afraid of bedding and my mother didn't threaten you, then the only other reason is that you don't trust me."

"Of course I don't trust you. You left me."

His voice rose. "For your good." He dropped her hands and stood, resolute, staring down at her. "I can't make you trust me, and I can't make you believe that I only wanted to save you. I can only wait for that. But as for the rest, what my mother wants is not what I want. The only way my mother is going to get what she wants is to compel me, and I am willing to gamble that she won't do that. I have sworn my heart to you for all of your days, and even if you won't take me as your lover or your husband, I will still serve you and your descendants until the day I die." He stood. "I need to walk. Get some sleep."

She started to stand. "Connor—"

"I'll be close if you need me." He scrubbed a hand through his hair and walked into the trees.

Mairead lay down and watched him until she couldn't keep her eyes open. *Alshada, give me wisdom.*

She woke in the night to tense silence. The braids around her bed were gone, and the fire had died down to a few gray coals. She sat up. "Connor?"

He touched her elbow and leaned close to her ear. "Someone's near."

Slavers. Mairead's heart hammered against her ribs. She reached for a knife, realized she didn't have one, and jumped to her feet. The clouds had cleared enough for the waxing moon to cast thin light into the clearing. She blinked herself awake, clearing the sleep from her eyes. "A wolf?"

Connor slipped a dagger into her hand. "No. Maybe." Soft hoofbeats closed in on their camp and stopped. Someone dismounted. "I can smell him," Connor said, barely above a whisper. "Them. Men, a couple of horses, and something else."

"What?"

"Don't know." Connor leapt toward the trees and swung his sword. Steel glinted on steel in the faint light, and Mairead heard the swords meet. Connor swung again and stepped back. "Who are you?"

"We're here for her."

Mairead's heart raced. A warm tingle erupted in her palm, and she cried out and dropped her dagger. Blue light glowed from the scar where she'd cut herself the night she left the sayada. "Connor—"

But Connor was swinging again, his blow met by another parry. "You'll have to get through me first."

"We're here to protect her."

Connor snarled. "I protect her."

The stranger stepped farther into the clearing. *He's tribal.* "Stop!" Mairead stepped toward them. "Connor, look at him."

The man stepped closer. In the faint moonlight and the glow of Mairead's hand, she saw leathers and fur sashes, a head full of braids, and tattooed arms.

"Who are you?" Connor asked.

"I'm Gareth. I'm one of hers. We are bloodbonded." He looked at Mairead. "Are you all right? Is this man friend or foe?"

"You can talk to me," Connor said. "She's my charge."

Gareth ignored him. "Are you all right?" he asked Mairead again.

"I'm fine. This man guards me."

Gareth didn't put the blade away. "Forgive me, traitha—I would kneel, but I fear your guard would take my head if I tried."

Connor frowned. "Traitha? She's not a chieftain."

"She is our chieftain. She called us through the bloodbond."

CHAPTER TWO

The earth demands the blood of kings.
— Third Book of the Wisdomkeepers

The frenzied activity of the Mac Niall estate was not enough to help Braedan shake off his exhaustion. He suppressed a yawn, rubbed his temples, and adjusted his riding gloves. *I'd pay for a decent night's sleep. A night in my own bed, with Igraine.* He grinned. *On second thought, that might not prove conducive to sleep.*

It had been two weeks since Braedan had helped Edgar defend his village and the Brae Sidh against Duke Mac Rian and his daughter, Olwyn. In the aftermath of the battle, he'd spent most of his time working with the staff and townspeople of both Kiern and neighboring Fox Hill to combine the administration of the two estates, begin repairs on buildings the Mac Rians had neglected, and write out the legal documents necessary to transfer ownership of the estate to Connor Mac Niall and give him the full rights of a Taurin duke. Sleep had been a precious and all-too-infrequent commodity. Between coaxing the residents of both estates into renewed cooperation and establishing some peace with the tribes, he'd had little time for dallying in his bed. *And there are the nightmares ....*

He sensed rather than heard Edgar approach from behind. "Come to see me off?"

"Come to speak sense to you," the chieftain said. He stood next to Braedan and watched the men in the courtyard. "It's too soon. The estates aren't ready to govern themselves."

Braedan grimaced. *I know. But what choice do I have?* "If it were possible, I would stay longer. But there is trouble in Salmon Springs now, and I still would like to be home before winter hits. As it is, I'll barely make it."

"What trouble is this?"

The word had come just the day before. Ronan Kerry wrote to tell Braedan that one of the northern dukes, Duke Fingall of Salmon Springs, had rescinded his support of Braedan's ascension and intended to seek a dissolution of the monarchy. Kerry suggested that Braedan ride to Salmon Springs with his forces to put down any simmering revolt. *The rumbling begins. Fingall was on my side in Torlach. What's happened to change his mind?* "I can't say. It doesn't concern the tribes." He paused. "I am only taking thirty men with me.

The rest will remain here until spring. They can help govern and restore the estates."

Edgar grunted in acknowledgment. "There is the other issue."

Braedan suppressed a flinch, hoping Edgar didn't notice. The chieftain had been warning him since the battle that Braedan's tribal blade would exact control over him, give him horrific, potentially prophetic dreams, and even possibly drive him to madness. *But it can't be the blade. I'm just tired—it's just exhaustion.* "I am well, Edgar. I've had nary a single dream since the battle—not even the simplest terror of walking into a banquet without clothes." He put a hand on the traitha's shoulder. "Your concern is appreciated, but unfounded. I am well."

"The earthspirit is going to give you nothing but trouble until you deal with her."

"She hasn't yet."

"She bides her time."

Braedan spread his hands. "What would you have me do? Stay here until some mysterious force draws me further away from my duties? From my princess? I'm the King of Taura. I came here to settle a dispute. It's settled. And in the process, a duke and his daughter are dead. There will be repercussions. I can't idle here and—"

"You can go wherever you wish," Edgar said. "But you can't escape this blade—this spirit." He cut off Braedan's response with a sharp gesture. "I am done arguing my position. This is not why I came. Someone has requested to meet you. Come."

"I'm needed here."

"Don't you trust your men? Give me an hour."

An hour. For peace between us. It is a small price. He gestured to Malcolm. "I'm going to the tribe."

"Alone?"

"No, with Edgar."

"Sire—"

"Do not question me, or I will see you with forty lashes in the courtyard."

Malcolm snapped to attention and bowed. "Yes, your majesty."

I am becoming my father—foul-tempered, tyrannical, and capricious. He spun around and walked away.

Edgar's long stride matched his own. "Harsh words for a man who seeks only to protect you."

"Do you mother hen your tribesmen? Do you let them mother hen you?"

"No. But we are tribesmen."

Braedan bit off a retort. "He is too protective. He worries that—" He stopped.

Edgar turned back.

Braedan gestured to the trees. "We are missing some men. Some Taurins."

Edgar waited.

"They went missing after the battle. A dozen or so. We haven't seen them since."

"And you waited two weeks to tell me?"

"We don't think they went into the forest. We're fairly certain they deserted into Taura." He paused as Edgar stared in appraisal. "It happens. Men desert in all battles."

"Not tribesmen."

"Did you fetch me to debate the value of tribesmen against Taurins?"

Edgar raised an eyebrow. "You say you've had nary a single dream, but you are short-tempered as a hungry bobcat. Men who enjoy plenty of dreamless rest are not so irritable."

He'll figure out that I'm lying to him if I can't control my tongue. "I have not had enough sleep to dream. I've been too busy."

Edgar crossed his arms. "Hmm."

Braedan rubbed the bridge of his nose. He considered how to respond, and when he did, he controlled his voice with effort. "We're looking, all right? And it's a dozen or so deserters. No match for tribesmen. If you find them, will you take them to the estate?"

"If that's what you wish," Edgar said. "Your guard—he worries that these men are more than deserters?"

Braedan shifted his feet. "They were men from Stone Coast. My uncle's men."

"Your uncle's men."

"You see why I need to be back in Torlach sooner rather than later."

Edgar grunted. "I also see why you're in a foul temper. Come."

At least that much threw him off the scent of the blade and the dreams. Braedan fell in step behind him.

The Taurin soldiers on the Mac Niall estate gave Braedan a wide berth as he stormed toward tribal territory with Edgar next to him. *I had a vision,* he thought. *I wanted people to love me enough to follow me. Now, they follow me from fear. And this is just one estate and two weeks. In the meantime, what is my uncle doing in Torlach? And Igraine?*

They continued their course deep into the heart of the forest, where only a few livestock pens offered visible evidence of the nearby tribal village. Sentries nodded toward Edgar when he acknowledged them, and while they cast distrustful glances toward Braedan, a few did manage to incline their heads with some amount of respect.

At last, they reached a small clearing near a massive oak tree. Braedan shivered and rubbed his arms. At his hip, the tribal blade warmed. "What is this place?"

"An earth shrine. The guardians use it for our rites. But it's also near something else."

The air shifted, and a small breeze stirred the leaves. The breeze grew stronger, coalescing into an eddy of dust and leaves on the forest floor, and a woman melted out of the air in front of Braedan the way someone might remove a cloak in one fluid movement.

On instinct, Braedan stepped back and started to draw his sword. "Aldora's dugs, Edgar."

The woman—a petite, dark beauty with black curls that fell to her waist—raised her eyebrows. "Not the welcome I hoped for from another royal," she said. She folded her hands before her and tipped her head to one side. "You aren't what I expected, your majesty."

Braedan didn't know how to answer. He could only stare, breathless before the ethereal beauty of the woman before him. She wore a gown of deepest red, made from some kind of vaguely translucent fabric that shifted color in the light without ever revealing more than the lady would wish to reveal. The circlet on her brow was an intricate design of three strands of silver that looped in and out of each other in knots he knew he could never follow to their ends. From the very center of the circlet, a murky teardrop stone lay against the lady's dark skin. Her dark brown eyes were familiar, and he thought he'd seen a similar grin somewhere, but at the same time, he was certain he would have remembered meeting such a woman.

Edgar grinned. "That was quite an entrance, your majesty."

"I thought the young man could use a little taste of Sidh talent."

Edgar took the woman's hand, bowed, and kissed her knuckles. "King Braedan Mac Corin of Taura, may I introduce you to Maeve SilverAir, Queen of the Brae Sidh and Keeper of the Holy Relics?" He lowered his voice. "You can close your mouth now, Braedan."

Braedan felt his lips join and realized he truly had been gaping. "Majesty," he said, remembering too late that he should have offered her at least a passing bow. "It's a pleasure."

"As for me," she answered. "You're taller than your father was. Thinner. You have your mother's face and skin."

He mouthed words that couldn't come. "I'm to believe you knew my mother? Forgive me, your majesty, but you only look old enough to be my younger sister."

"She has more . . . ah, life experience than you and I put together, prince-ling," Edgar said.

The queen shot Edgar a dark look, which he answered with a grin. "The Sidh have unusually long lifespans," she said, still looking at Edgar with a mixture of amusement and irritation. "I haven't counted my years since before you were born, I'm certain. Yes, I knew your mother. She was a lovely woman, and a good friend to the Brae Sidh. Her death was a painful blow to me."

Braedan flinched. He'd realized years before that no amount of drinking could erase the memory of the day when the guards wouldn't allow him to see his mother, when they took him to his father's rooms instead, and his father had told him, without emotion, that his mother had taken her own life. It stung to think of the moment again—for this strange woman to know more than he did about his own mother's death. He'd gone to Stone Coast shortly after that to live with his uncle, Ronan Kerry, and he'd only seen his father on rare occasions when the regent would request Braedan's presence for some affair, or when Kerry would visit his wife's family in Espara and send Braedan home. "How do you know so much about my family? How could you—"

"I was there. I knew your father—I met him early in his reign, but it quick-ly became clear that he had no desire to work with the Sidh as his father had."

She knew my father and grandfather. How old is this woman? "How long has the government known about you? How long has this been going on?"

"Generations. Each time a new regent or king came to the throne, the Sidh queen introduced herself. Long ago, long before even my mother ruled the Sidh, Taurin kings and regents attended the coronations of the Sidh queens, and we attended their coronations and installations with the Table of Counci-lors. Time passed, more visitors came to Taura, and the Sidh retreated into the forest. Still, we were able to have good relationships with most of the regents. Those we couldn't trust had their—" She paused. "The Sidh healers have some interesting abilities when it comes to memory. We've controlled what the regents remember of us very tightly." She smiled. "I must say, you're reacting far better than your father did when he met me."

"My father never handled surprises very well."

Maeve chuckled. "He very nearly took my head off. Fortunately, I had a fierce tribal guard and a Taurin duke to stand for me that day. We had the healers remove his memories, but not before your mother came in the room.

She knew what I was right away, and we were able to have a long talk about her role in the kingdom and her influence behind the throne. It was the first of many." A sad look passed over her fine features. "We were even with child close to the same time, although my son was born earlier." Edgar put a hand on her shoulder, and she covered it with her own.

Braedan frowned. "A tribal guard and a Taurin duke to stand for you." He looked at Edgar. "You were her tribal guard, weren't you?"

"It was before I was traitha, before her son was born, but yes—thirty years ago, I traveled as a guard to Torlach with this woman and her Taurin duke to meet your father," Edgar said.

"Her Taurin duke—Duke Culain Mac Niall," Braedan said. Edgar and Maeve stared at him without blinking. "You're Connor Mac Niall's mother." *That's why the eyes and mouth are so familiar.*

"I can have healers here in a moment. If you value your memories, if you can work with me and not against me, I will let you keep your wits."

"Are you his mother?"

"I am. And I want to know from you: what are your intentions regarding my son?"

"Intentions?"

"What do you intend for his estate? For his title?"

Mothers are all the same. "Your son, Connor Mac Niall, is, as of the moment I signed the proclamation yesterday, fully invested with all of the privileges and responsibilities of a Duke of Taura. I have also signed a separate proclamation absolving Culain Mac Niall of any wrongdoing against the crown, and I have restored the Mac Niall name to full honor and standing on the Table of Councilors."

She let out a very slow breath. Edgar reached for her, but she held up a hand. "It's just been so long. I thank you," she said, her voice breaking. "Duke Mac Niall was the finest of men. For his name to be sullied for so long ...." She bit her lip and turned her face away. "I am in your debt."

"As I am in yours. You helped me defeat an enemy of the crown." He bowed. "I am hopeful that the events of these last two weeks bode well for a new era of alliance between our peoples, your majesty."

"As am I," she said. "Now we must ensure that you keep your throne."

Braedan turned to Edgar, who shrugged. "I suspected things weren't rosy in Torlach. I asked her to have a look around."

"And what did you discover, your majesty?"

"So far, your uncle maintains an appearance of support for your ascension and reign," she said. "I could find nothing to indicate that you should return to

Torlach immediately. However, I can tell you that your princess does not trust him."

"She didn't trust him when I was there."

"There is one other thing: the Commander of the Royal Guard is missing."

Braedan startled. "Logan Mac Kendrick? How do you know?"

"I heard Princess Igraine discussing his absence with one of her ladies," she said. "I couldn't tell why he was gone, but it seemed that it was a sudden event—possibly under duress."

Braedan twisted his mouth. *Logan would not leave Igraine except under dire circumstances. Something must be amiss.* "Can you go back? Dig a bit more?"

"Not right now. It's a great risk to travel in the manner of the Sidh. There are forces rising that grow stronger each day, and I can't risk my life or the lives of my people to spy for you." She paused. "Instead, I believe I have a better way for you to secure your throne."

"What's that?"

"You must undergo the rituals demanded of the kings of old."

Braedan opened his mouth to respond, but found himself speechless.

Edgar shrugged. "She's right. There's a reason there have been no kings for a thousand years."

"I don't see why ancient rituals would make any difference to Ronan Kerry," Braedan said.

"They won't," Maeve said. "But they will make a difference to the northern dukes, the tribes, and the Sidh."

"How so?"

"If you pass the rites and gain the approval of the wisdomkeeper in the north, the tribes will accept you as an ally and support your ascension," Edgar said. "You will have the swords of every clan and every tribe in the great forest."

"And I can promise you the backing of the Brae Sidh," Maeve said. "I would even come out of hiding for your formal coronation should the wisdomkeeper anoint you."

"Why can't we just make an alliance here and now?"

Maeve threw up her hands. "Humans scoff at tradition and scold those who came before you, then wonder why your worlds and kingdoms do not endure."

Edgar put a hand on her arm. "I cannot speak for the Sidh," he said, "but I can tell you that as far as the tribes are concerned, you would only have the backing of the wolf tribe right now. Traitha Hrogarth is still unconvinced that you are fit to lead Taura. Without Hrogarth, you will not have the nine. You would have four tribes at best, possibly only the wolf tribe."

"And these rites would convince him?"

"If you pass them," Maeve said.

"What would I have to do?" Braedan asked.

Edgar and Maeve exchanged a look. "We don't know," she said. "Again, it's been a thousand years. Many things are lost to time. That's why you must go to the wisdomkeeper."

Braedan hesitated, considering the request. *I am here as much to keep peace and establish a relationship with the Sidh as to deal with Mac Rian.* "All right. Tell me everything."

"When the regency was established a thousand years ago, there were protections—wards, spells—set up around Taura to keep her at peace," Maeve said. "Those same wards and spells have also kept anyone from claiming the throne. Men who have tried have reigned a very short time. They have succumbed to various fates within just months of ascending."

"I've heard." Braedan shuddered. "Are you saying that's what awaits me? Madness, plague, and death?"

Maeve twisted her mouth. "I don't know. That's the troubling part. When you took the throne, we should have seen something—some sign that the wards or the earth were responding to your claim—something that would suggest the magic would subdue or destroy you somehow." She took a deep breath and continued. "We believe that two things happened to give you a chance—the first chance in a thousand years—to claim genuine sovereignty in Taura. First, the wards and spells were weakened by the strife between the Sidh and the tribes."

"There's strife between your people?" Braedan asked.

"Edgar and I are working on that." Her face colored, but she recovered and cleared her throat. "The second thing to happen was that the rightful Taurin heir of Brenna and Aiden's line left Taura. When she left, she ripped the bond of her family to this land. No one else of her exact bloodline exists."

He did not miss the slight emphasis on the word "exact." He held up a hand. "*Exact* bloodline? What does that mean?"

"It is Sidh business."

"It's my business. If there are others who pose a threat to my throne, I need to know."

She tipped her head and frowned. "Brenna and Aiden's heir was a descendant of Cuhail on her father's side. We thought her father had only one child. However, word has reached us that there may have been a son as well—

a child of a second marriage."

"You think there is another heir."

Maeve held up a hand. "We aren't certain. Taurins only trace the father's lineage, but the Sidh—and, in fact, Alshada—trace both lines. If the boy's mother is not of the rightful line, then the boy is not an heir in the eyes of the Sidh or the earth."

"That won't matter to the council."

"This is why an anointing and a proper coronation would serve you well. The heir's absence created a gap—a tear—that can now be filled by you. You can take the throne and rule for as long as you are given—if you do as the earth commands."

"Of course. Whatever is necessary—whatever is best for Taura. I'll do it."

"Then you must go north, to the wisdomkeeper. It's the way the kings and queens used to bind themselves in the old days. The wisdomkeeper is the woman closest to the earth. She can perform the ritual that would bind you to the land and make you king in truth rather than just in word."

Braedan's blood chilled. "Go north? In winter?" *With my dukes rattling sabers and my princess left alone in Torlach? And all of her fears about my uncle—what if they're true?* "Taura is weak—I need time to establish my reign."

"Better to fear the earth," Maeve said. "If the earth destroys your sanity because you never did what was required, then where will the country be? You would leave your throne empty, without an heir, with no kirok and less two dukes for the table. Who would step into your place? Your uncle? Your princess? A foreign woman on the Raven Throne would only lead to more chaos." She shook her head. "Go north, your majesty. Let the wisdomkeeper bind you to the land. You aren't the rightful heir, but you might be a good king until the heir returns. Let the wisdomkeeper decide."

He paced the clearing, thinking of recent correspondence from Torlach. There had been notes from Cormac summarizing the state of the treasury and bringing hope that merchants were returning to the city, but also mentioning tension with strange ships in the southern channel. Affairs of state, various pieces of gossip, marriages and births and deaths he should know about—unimportant court issues filled paper after paper. But he could not dismiss Igraine's fears that Kerry would take advantage of his absence to seize power. *And to risk trapping myself in the far north in winter—it seems too much to ask. Too much could happen in Torlach before spring. But to have the backing of the northern dukes, the nine tribes, and the Sidh ....* He turned back to Maeve. "I will go north, your majesty," he said.

Maeve's mouth curved into a subtle smile, but Braedan thought her body relaxed in relief as well. She straightened and lifted her hands. "If you allow it, I would give you a Sidh blessing for your journey."

"I would be honored, your majesty."

Maeve spread her hands wider. Braedan's skin pricked under his clothes, and the hair on his arms stood up as something unseen wrapped around him with the soft embrace of a lover. The Brae Sidh queen spoke foreign words in a clear, authoritative voice. Her skin glowed, highlighting her beauty so that he couldn't look away from her.

After she'd spoken in the foreign tongue, she spoke Taurin. "May you find sure footing upon the earth; may the air around you be filled with the delights of the seasons; may the waters of many streams bring you refreshment and healing." She lowered her hands.

The sensation of an embrace faded. Braedan put out his hands to regain his balance. "What was that?"

"The elements of air, water, and earth around you," she said. "A Brae Sidh blessing."

"No fire?"

"Fire isn't an element. Why in the name of all the spirits would I surround you with something that could burn you to death?"

"The Sidh don't like fire," Edgar said.

"I tolerate fire because I'm in the world of humans so much," Maeve said. "But it discomforts me." She gestured to the trees. "We hide in a forest, shielded by wood that does not respond to our elemental gifts. Why would I risk fire? It's our greatest vulnerability."

Braedan stepped toward her. She allowed him to take her hand. He bowed. "Tell your son that I look forward to seeing him again. I have apologies to make, and I would do them properly."

Maeve took his hands in hers. "You are already turning into a better ruler than your father," she said. "There is much of your mother in you. The One Hand hold you, Braedan Mac Corin." The air moved again, and Queen Maeve disappeared.

"Gods," Braedan whispered.

"You wanted to know if the Brae Sidh were real. Now you know," Edgar said.

They walked back to the road, and Edgar stopped at the edge of the forest. "This is where we part. I will ensure that Kiern and Fox Hill stay defended and safe. And if Maeve can influence anything in Torlach, I'm sure she will. She isn't shy about meddling."

Braedan turned to him and drew a blade from his boot. "I was prepared this time."

Edgar took the hilt. "Taurin," he said.

"It has no history, no magical properties, no particular beauty. But it was given me by my father."

Edgar examined the blade in the sunlight. "And you do not wish to keep it to remember your father?"

Braedan shook his head. "I have enough memories of my father. He was sometimes cruel and capricious, and I was never a good enough son for him."

Edgar snorted a laugh. "I'm not sure if I'm complimented or insulted."

Braedan pointed at the blade. He'd rehearsed the words. "Redeem that blade, traitha," he said. "Make it an object of use and an instrument of good."

Edgar smiled—a genuine, kind smile that had none of his usual sarcasm about it. He drew a blade from his boot. "And we complete our exchange, as we should have two weeks ago," he said.

Braedan took the blade and put it in his boot. He held out a hand, and Edgar clasped it. "Thank you," he said.

Edgar stepped closer. "A word of advice. You learned from your father that power makes the man, but he had it wrong. It's not power that makes a man or a leader. It's sacrifice."

Braedan's stomach twisted. *Sacrifice.* "I don't understand."

"I can't teach it. You will have to learn it." He put one hand on Braedan's shoulder. "This is your rite. Return to Taura a man and a king."

Braedan nodded. "I will."

CHAPTER THREE

> *The spirits are twinned in the earth's womb:*
> *The life of the Nameless One, and the vengeance of the Morrag.*
> *Between them, the Warrior brings balance.*
> — *Lion tribe lore*

Minerva tucked her hands under her arms and breathed out a long puff of air that rose in the waning light. *This cursed rain. This is what makes everything so cold. Alshada, a few days of dry weather would not be unwelcome.* She shook her head. *I have no right to ask. I am an oathbreaker. Forgive me, Alshada.*

The days of travel with Alfrig had been marked by torrential rains and infrequent, terse conversations. She and Alfrig spoke only briefly over quiet meals and through thick furs wrapped around their faces. Alfrig spoke little even in the best of circumstances; now, in the shadow of a bleak, northern winter with a woman who gave her little reason to speak, she was silent as a stone pillar. Minerva, for her part, didn't mind the silence. She prayed and recited scripture in her mind and tried to think how she might return to the kirok before the earthspirit overtook her.

Alfrig returned to the fire from the trees, jarring Minerva out of her thoughts. She dropped two pheasants at Minerva's feet. "I shot them. You pluck them."

"Yes, traitha."

Alfrig grunted an acknowledgment and turned southward. She rubbed her palm idly. "I must seek the earthspirit tonight," she said.

"Why?"

"There is trouble in the south. I must see if I need to return." She walked back into the trees without waiting for a response.

Minerva let out a long breath. *Trouble in the south. If she goes back to the tribes, where will I go?* She picked up one of the pheasants and laid it down to sever its head. *I can't live like this—with this beast rising inside me. There is no sayada. And even if there were, how could I go back there?*

By the time Alfrig returned, the pheasants were roasting over the campfire. Alfrig sat down across from Minerva, silent and stern, her hands tucked into her furs.

Minerva hesitated a long time before speaking. "Did you find what you needed to know?"

"I am not needed yet." But her voice was strained and tense, and Minerva wondered what she hadn't said.

They ate in silence, as usual, and Minerva wrapped the remainder of the fowl in cloth and leather and tucked it into their packs. "We cross into Taura tomorrow," she said.

Alfrig grunted from her place under a thick fir tree.

Minerva paused, considering her words. "I wondered if you had decided on our course yet."

"North."

I know that much. Minerva sat down near the older woman and drew her knees up to her chin, trying to warm herself as the fire sputtered and hissed under a renewed downpour. "But we must go east sometime. The crossing to the Ragged Isles—"

"What is your question, girl?"

Minerva took a deep breath. "I want to go to Starling's Cross. I want to see if any of the sayas from Torlach still live. Edgar suggested they might have found sanctuary there."

Alfrig said nothing.

The rain pelted the forest, running down tree limbs to coalesce into enormous drops that splatted onto Minerva's head. "If Edgar is correct, Duke Dylan would shelter us, I'm certain. We might be able to replenish our supplies and buy some more furs before we cross to the Ragged Isles."

Alfrig snorted. "I care not about comforts."

Minerva licked her lips. "Neither do I," she said. "But I do care about the sayas."

"Why? The women of the chaste god deny their power and sequester themselves in the name of foolish laws."

"They also serve the poor, the outcast, and the downtrodden." Minerva paused. "Whatever else they are, traitha, they are also my sisters as much as the guardians were once. And as much as you are now."

Alfrig sat silent for a long moment. "We must cross somewhere. Starling's Cross is probably the easiest place for it."

Minerva lowered her face to hide a relieved smile. *Alshada, please let my sisters be alive. Please do not remove your hand yet.*

It took another week to get to Starling's Cross. Most of the week was spent bargaining for rooms in quiet inns and boarding houses, keeping a careful watch on the supply of coins. When the weather was reasonably dry, they camped in the trees.

They came upon Starling's Cross all at once, late one afternoon, just as the sun touched the horizon. Other cities emerged gradually from a loose collection of farms that grew into a town, but not Haldor Dylan's holdings. Starling's Cross sat bordered by hills on the east and west, locking it into a tunnel for any stray winds that blew in off its northern edge. The southern part of the city was protected by a sturdy stone wall, but the northern edge seemed to merely trail off into the seas around the Ragged Isles. There were no houses outside the wall; rather, it seemed Starling's Cross was that rare city whose residents needed the proximity and protection of town life.

They were able to enter Starling's Cross just before the gates closed, and they found Haldor Dylan's manor house approximately at the center of the city. Alfrig reined in at the gates of the duke's estate. "This is where I leave you," she said. "I will return in three days to see what you have decided."

Decided? "What do you mean?"

Alfrig pointed up at the gates. "This is Taurin business. I am tribal. For these days, you are Taurin once more. You must decide: do you wish to remain Taurin, or will you return to the tribes?"

Must it always be so final? So strictly divided? Can't I be both? "Three days, and then we will cross to the Ragged Isles."

Alfrig inclined her head. "I hope you find what you seek, Esma." She turned and rode out of the city.

Minerva approached the gate and reined in. The guards wore the simple insignia of House Dylan—a crest of silver sea waves against a blue background. She steeled herself and asked for the lord of the estate, and when they asked her name, she swallowed hard. "Minerva. I come from the sayada."

They stabled her horse and showed her to the great hall, where a serving girl took her wet cloak and boots and seated her near a roaring hearth. Another girl brought soup and fresh bread, and Minerva ate gratefully, truly warm for the first time in weeks. "Lord Dylan's been told of your arrival, lass," the graying, wrinkled chamberlain told her. "He'll attend ye shortly."

"Tell me news of Taura. Do you hear anything from Torlach?"

"Precious little. Truth, the capitol's a bit far from here to concern ourselves, aye? Takes weeks for news to reach us even in the summer. A king overthrows the regent, issues orders, but by the time we hear them, they could be rescinded. Nae, we concern ourselves with our own business." He laid a blanket across her lap and tucked it around her feet.

"The king made some peace with the northern tribes," she said.

"Did he, now? Well, the mark of a good leader isn't the peace he can make but the peace he can keep."

She smiled and cupped her hands around the warm bowl of soup. "Then let us pray he's a good leader, sir."

The steward retreated with a bow, and Minerva sipped her soup as she surveyed the hall. The estate house had that peculiar forced comfort of the north that refused to acknowledge the inhospitable nature of its surroundings. Stone walls were covered in thick tapestries, and animal skins and furs adorned the furnishings. The hearth dominated the room, a clear central gathering place for servants and family members alike. The floor was covered in straw—not surprising considering the season and the lack of low water to provide rushes—and servants had lined the walls with pallets and down mattresses. Minerva smiled. Dylan clearly took a personal interest in the comforts of his servants; they must use the great hall as a common sleeping area when the worst weather was upon them. *One has to appreciate a lord who cares for the people in his household as his own family.*

Minerva was warm and dry by the time Duke Dylan at last arrived to speak with her. He stomped into the hall, a short man with the red-tinged blond coloring of so many northerners who had Svek ancestors. He had a beaming countenance, a broad smile, and strong shoulders. "Mistress Minerva," he said, his voice echoing off the rafters. He bowed to her and held out a hand. "Haldor Dylan, lass. I understand ye've come from the sayada?"

She stood and curtsied. "I have, my lord. Haldor—a Svek name?"

He waved a hand. "My ancestors came ashore here in little fishing boats when the Svek tried to conquer this island. All that's left now are a few names that refuse to die and some traditional knitting techniques."

Minerva smiled. "I have heard you might be housing some of my sisters?"

"Aye, lass, I am. About a dozen, at last count." He motioned to her. "Come, come. I'll show you where they sleep. Ye'll be wantin' your boots and cloak, though."

She tugged her boots on, and the chamberlain helped her into her cloak. "Don't you fear repercussions from Torlach?"

He scoffed. "Torlach has never cared a whit for what we do up here." He offered her his arm. "Nay, lass—'tis the edge of the world here. The sayas are safe, and when this usurper king comes to his senses or the council decides to grow some balls and restore the regency, the sayas will return to Torlach."

Minerva resisted the unexpected chuckle at her lips. "You do the work of Alshada himself, my lord."

"Bah. I do the humane thing. These women—they wish only to serve their god. 'Tis not for the council or the king to decide they can't."

He led her to a small whitewashed building on the edge of his estate. "Ladies," he called. "Another of your order comes seeking sanctuary."

The heavy wooden door opened, and a woman in white robes gasped. "Minerva!" She pulled Minerva into an embrace. "Sayas, it's Minerva!"

They pulled her into the house, and Minerva was awash in the embraces of a dozen of her former sisters. They peppered her with questions—had she been to the tribes? Did she know what the king was about? Had she brought word of the other sayas who remained behind in Torlach?

She removed her cloak and gestured them to silence. "I will tell you all," she said. "I promise." She tugged off her gloves—

—and regretted it when a dozen gasps filled the room.

"Saya," one of the women said. "Your hand."

Minerva clenched her fist, but the blue light shone through. She hid her hands behind her back. *What was I thinking?* "I—my sisters, I must tell you— Sayana Muriel knew of this, but—"

One of the women, Saya Miriam, hissed and touched her head and heart and folded her hands in the sign of the order. "Witchcraft," she said. "This is—"

"No, I swear, it isn't," Minerva said.

But the din rose to a fever pitch as the women stepped back, clutched each other in fear, and hid their faces. "Take her from us," Miriam told Dylan. "Take her out of here. She sullies the work of our god with this foul power."

Minerva gaped. She felt Dylan take her arm and lead her from the building, but she couldn't speak. *If my sisters reject me, there is truly no place for me. I'm lost.*

Duke Dylan escorted her to a quiet room in the manor house and called for serving women to light the fire in the hearth. He seated her in a chair and produced a skin of oiska from somewhere on his person. "I keep it handy," he explained at her questioning look when he offered it to her. "Never know when ye might need a nip or two to warm the blood."

Warm the blood. "I don't drink. I'm sworn to Alshada."

"So am I, lass." He took a long drink from the skin and offered it again.

Minerva took the skin and drank, still dazed, and grimaced when she handed it back. *I'm not as sworn as I thought.*

"'Tis a tribal mark, that?" he asked, gesturing to her hand.

She buried her hands in her lap, cupping one around the other to hide the glow. "I was tribal before I was a saya. Now ...."

He waited, but when she didn't speak again, he took another long pull off the skin and set it down. "Ye'll listen, now, aye? Blood and oaths, they mean much, but ye'll remember what ye've sworn to, aye? Not the sayas—not women. Not the tribes. Ye've sworn to the gods—to Alshada, to your earthspirit."

Minerva closed her eyes against the sting of tears. "I called the sayada home for ten years. I called the tribes home before that. My blood calls to other places. And yet none of them are safe. None of them are really home." *I have no home.*

He put one thick hand on her shoulder. "Your home isn't here, aye? It's beyond this one."

"May I stay here, just for a few days? I need—I don't know. I suppose I need some rest. My tribal escort will come back in three days."

Duke Dylan pushed the skin of oiska toward her. "Take as long as ye need, lass. Ye're welcome here." He left the room.

Minerva opened her hand and stared down. *If I can't go back to the sayada, if I can't find a home in the kirok, if I can't find a home in the tribes, what is left? The Sidh?* She picked up the skin of oiska. She drank once, twice, and then set it down. She curled up on the bed in her clothes, numb and exhausted and lulled to sleep by the fire and the oiska.

When Minerva left the estate three days later, she found Alfrig sitting on her horse at the gates, just as unyielding and fierce as ever. "You have made your choice, Esma?" the traitha said.

Minerva mounted her horse and fell in next to Alfrig. "The sayas have no room for me," she said, her voice catching.

"Then you are tribal?"

"I am a woman without a people." *Without a home.* Her palm burned.

Alfrig put one hand on her arm in a rare gesture of affection. "It is when the One Hand strips us of worldly alliances that he brings us closer to himself," she said.

I have been stripped to the bone, Alshada. You can take nothing else from me. If you would use me, make yourself known, because I have no more reason to pursue you. Minerva pulled her arm away. "Take me to the wisdomkeeper." *Let her finish this.*

CHAPTER FOUR

> *The prison lies empty;*
> *the raven army rises.*
> — *Second Book of the Wisdomkeepers*

Connor tightened his grip on his sword as a spotted cat padded out of the trees, ears flat on its head. Two more tribal men stepped out, along with an enormous gray wolf with hackles raised and teeth bared. A low growl rumbled in the wolf's chest. "What is this—this bloodbond? Who are you?"

Gareth nodded toward Mairead. "We are hers," he repeated. "We are bloodbonded to her. Traitha, tell your guard to stand down, and we'll show you."

Mairead opened her hand to show Connor the blue glow on her palm. "It started as soon as you swung at him," she said.

He frowned. He'd seen such glows before, but rarely, and only on the palm of an earth guardian with the wisdommark. *Mairead is no guardian, and she doesn't have a brand. How is this possible?* "What is this?"

Gareth sheathed his sword. He pulled the glove off his left hand and held it out to Mairead to show her a glowing blue whorl. "We're here to protect you. The bond led us to you." He gestured to the other men. "Show her."

The other two men also sheathed their swords and took off their gloves to reveal the same glowing blue brand. The cat and wolf remained ready to pounce, both shifting on their back legs while they watched the scene.

"It's the earth magic—the bloodbond." Gareth stepped closer to Mairead and held out his hand.

"Careful," Connor said, tilting his sword toward the young man. *And you have nothing to say about this?* he asked the Morrag. *Is this real? Are these men honest?*

As honest as any man.

Gareth motioned to Mairead. "May I see your hand, traitha?"

She extended her arm.

"It's true," Gareth said. "She is the one—the Deliverer."

"Connor, is this what the tribal magic looks like?" Mairead asked.

"Yes. Sometimes. The traithas and earth guardians can call each other this way, but this—I don't understand this. You're neither traitha nor earth guardian. You aren't even tribal. And this boy—he's not from a Taurin tribe."

"How do you know?"

"His furs are wrong. He's wearing a cat pelt. We don't have many cats on Taura—just a few bobcats. They have ..." He frowned. "Lion pelts." *Gods, is this true? Are they lions?*

Gareth frowned. "You are outland?"

"I am wolf tribe."

Gareth pulled his glove on. "If you are a warrior, why did her mark not call to yours?"

The Morrag cackled, and Connor shivered. *A decision made when I was fourteen, and now I pay for it.* "I have no warriormark. Tell me who you are."

"We are lion tribe. The One Hand set us apart and told us to wait for her."

"Wait for me?" Mairead stepped closer to the men. "What for?"

"You are our traitha—the one foretold from the Breaking," Gareth said.

"There is no lion on the tribal tapestry," Connor said. "How big is your tribe?"

"Thousands. We live beyond the river, north of Galbragh."

"How is it possible you didn't know this?" Mairead asked.

Connor grimaced. "I did know this," he said. "I've heard stories. Rumors. The people of the northern plains have spoken of wild mountain men with braids and tattoos. I always just thought they had met a few of my tribal brothers who were passing through." *This can't be real. But they have marks and the magic.*

"Be careful," said one of the other men, a broad-shouldered warrior with a mass of thick, dark braids. "If he's outland, he can't be trusted. He may hold the girl captive."

"Quiet, Braun." Gareth turned to Mairead. "You're safe with us, traitha. Is this man friend or foe?"

"Friend," Mairead said without hesitation. She stepped closer to Connor. "Friend. He guards me."

"What do you want with her?" Connor asked.

"We came to protect her."

"I protect her. She doesn't need anyone else."

"Then why did she call us?"

"She didn't."

Mairead held up a hand. "Stop." She gestured to the smoldering coals of the campfire. "We can argue warm just as well as we can argue cold."

No one moved for a long moment. Mairead finally knelt next to the fire ring and stirred the coals into flame with small sticks. The man with the cat went next, followed by Gareth. Connor joined Mairead, standing behind her with his sword still drawn, and at last the third tribesman joined them. "I'm Mairead and this is Connor," Mairead said. "Forgive us for being cautious, but we were running from slavers."

Gareth grinned. "I promise you, traitha, we are not slavers." He gestured to the other men. "The solid mass of hair next to me is Braun Lionjaw. The wolf is his companion. The skinny one with the cat is Trypp Goldeneye. I'm Gareth Catspaw."

Mairead leaned back to sit on her heels. "You've caught me at a disadvantage. I'm not sure who you are, how I called you, or if I even did call you."

He held out his hand and showed her the whorl tattoo again. The blue light still glowed. "Our bond has been growing stronger for months, since the night of the half-dark moon. We have all felt it. A few weeks ago, the warriors went into the vision hut, and the three of us were chosen to leave the mountain to find you."

A shiver skittered up Connor's spine. *The night of the half-dark moon. The night I took her from Taura.* "Just the three of you? By yourselves?" Connor asked.

The one called Trypp shrugged, a lazy move that belied the casual tension of his posture. "We are lions."

"It's a relief to see you whole, traitha," Gareth said. "We felt you in danger, and then the bond flared painfully tonight."

She looked up at Connor in surprise. "Tonight—tonight I was—"

"I know." *She must have called them the same time she called me. But how could she be bonded to men she's never met when she's never studied the earth magic?*

Gareth frowned. "This one answers your call, too?"

"He does."

"But how, if he has no warriormark?"

Mairead's brow furrowed. "There is another magic," she said. "Connor and I are connected in another way."

"How?"

"It's not important," Connor said. He crouched next to Mairead and lowered his voice. "I believe them, but even if I didn't, we couldn't go anywhere now, not without a fight. Three tribesmen against one would be hard even for me. Besides, they have animals, and we don't know what that cat or wolf might do. And I don't like the idea of shedding tribal blood unless I must."

"Boy." The burly tribesman called Braun leaned toward Connor and Mairead. "Quit whispering. You have something to say, say it to all of us."

Connor straightened, and Braun stood. "I owe you nothing."

Braun's hand went to his sword, and he turned his head and spat. "You are outland. You are not even worth my instruction, pup."

Mairead stood and put a hand on Connor's arm. "Connor—"

He shrugged her hand away and raised his sword. "You think I need instruction? Instruct me, kitten."

In his head, the Morrag cawed in exultation; her presence swelled in his chest, filling him with ferocious strength. He stepped toward Braun, a low, challenging growl building in his throat. Braun's mouth tightened, and he swung to meet Connor's sword. Connor parried. He drove Braun backward with a series of blows. Braun parried each one, but Connor never allowed him to take an offensive swing.

"Connor!"

Mairead's voice came to Connor only from a great distance. The Morrag was everything, the only thing. *He lies,* she whispered. *He cheats. He has taken what was not his. He has given offense to the One Hand. Destroy him, my raven. He deserves no mercy.*

Braun tripped, fell backward, lifted his sword to block another blow. The wolf stood next to him, teeth bared, a snarl winding up in his throat.

"Connor!"

Mairead's voice at last jolted Connor out of communion with the Morrag. *What did I do?* He stared down at Braun and the wolf, took a stumbling step back, and lowered his sword. "Gods," he whispered.

Mairead was next to him then, one hand on his arm, and the other tribesmen stepped between them and the still-prone Braun. "Stand down," Mairead said to Connor. "He meant offense, but he did not earn death. Stand down, Connor."

He blinked several times. *What was that?* he asked the Morrag.

You are becoming my raven, the Morrag whispered. *You will avenge the wrongs done on this world.*

Connor shuddered. *I thought if I gave in to you, you would keep me from the madness,* he thought. *You promised me Mairead. Did you only promise me what I wanted to make me submit?*

She only cackled.

His stomach lurched. *Don't do this. Please, don't turn me into this creature. I will be yours—I swear I will let you take me—but not now. Not now. I can't leave her—not again. If I leave her again, she might never let me come back.*

Mairead turned to the tribesmen. Gareth and Trypp stood between Connor and Braun with their swords drawn, guarding Braun as he stood and dusted himself off. "Forgive him," she said. "These last few days have both of us on edge. He's not normally so short-tempered."

Braun sheathed his sword. "Does he always have his woman speak for him?"

Connor took a step toward Braun, but Gareth reacted first. "Shut up, Lionjaw," he said, whirling around to stare at Braun. "The traitha trusts this man. That's enough for me."

Braun took a threatening step toward Gareth. "I don't care who your father is, you—"

"This is not about my father." Gareth pointed at Mairead. "This is about her. She's the reason all of us are here. If you can't stand to be with us or with her guard, then she can decide who stays."

Mairead gaped. "Me? But I—"

"Fine." Braun took two steps toward Mairead. Trypp and Gareth fell in on either side of him, poised to fight. Braun stared down at Mairead. "Choose, girl. Who do you want?"

Mairead's body changed in that moment. She straightened her shoulders, lifted her chin, and shifted her weight toward the men in front of her, standing between Connor and the tribesmen. "I would never turn away a willing sword," she said. "There will always be a place at my side for a man who will swear fealty to me."

Fealty. She deserves fealty. She is a queen. Connor knelt and held his sword up to Mairead. "You have the fealty and arms of House Mac Niall of

Taura, your majesty."

She touched his head. "Connor, I'm no—"

"You are," he said, raising his eyes to look at her. "You are Queen of Taura. Whatever else you are to them, you deserve the fealty of your dukes."

Braun spat. "Queen of what? An island kingdom that means nothing to us. What do I care for the outland? I want to know what you intend for this country—for my people, my land."

Connor twitched to stand, ready to defend Mairead, but she didn't need his help. She took a step toward Braun. "I intend peace," she said. "I intend freedom. I intend prosperity."

"Pretty words. How will you accomplish those things?"

She started to answer, but Gareth stopped her. "With her army," he said. He knelt before her, head bowed, sword offered up across his palms. "You have my fealty and my sword, traitha."

Trypp followed in a breath. "You have my fealty and my sword, traitha."

Mairead waited. Braun stared at the kneeling tribesmen. "For this journey," he said as he turned his attention to Mairead. "Until you are safe within the lion tribe—you have my protection. Then ..." He shrugged. "You will have to prove yourself, girl."

"As will you, Braun Lionjaw," Mairead said. She turned to the kneeling warriors. "I accept your fealty and your swords." She put a hand on her stomach. "Fealty and swords do not feed an army, though. Did any of you bring anything to eat?"

"Food." Gareth stood and sheathed his sword. "Forgive me, traitha. You're right. We should have seen to your needs." He stepped into the trees and came back with two horses. He took several furs and a bundle off the back of one of them. "We thought you may need clothing. The women in our tribe offered these things for you."

She opened the bundle and pulled out leather breeches and jerkin, tunics, several small furs, and a pair of soft leather boots lined with fur. "How did you—"

"We came with everything we thought you might need. I brought food and a bow, too."

She wrapped her arms around the bundle and gestured to the trees. "I'm going to change."

Connor started to follow her, but Braun caught his arm. "I know you," he said. He sneered. "The outland tribes are faithless deserters. You will destroy her as you nearly destroyed her line two thousand years ago."

Connor squared his shoulders and faced the burly tribesman eye to eye.

"You listen, kitten. If you ever even think of hurting her, I swear by all the spirits, I will hunt you for the rest of my life and beyond. You will have no rest. There will be no crevasse deep enough, no city big enough, no country distant enough to hide you from me." He walked away before Braun could answer.

Connor paced at the edge of the trees while Mairead changed her clothes. *What you showed me back there—what you told me about Braun—is that what I can expect now? Your whisper in my head about all the ills men have done to each other?* he asked the Morrag.

I see the truth of all men, she said. *I see what they hide from others.*

Connor frowned. *Thoughts?*

At times. Thoughts and deeds and actions. Those things done in secret. Those pieces they thought no one would know.

And what am I supposed to do with this knowledge?

Heed my call. The voice faded.

Connor leaned against a tree and scrubbed his hands over his face. *Please, just give me time with Mairead. You promised me she would be mine if I submitted to you. Just a little time—that's all I wish.* And then he realized the foolishness of the request—*if she gives me time with Mairead, it will only make my leaving that much harder. The wisest thing would be to leave now. But Alshada, how can I leave her again?*

Mairead finally emerged from the trees dressed in fresh clothing. "Everything says you are tribal," Connor said. He flipped her braid back over her shoulder and lifted the bear claw around her neck. "Even this."

"The boots are a bit tight," she said. She took the claw back and tucked it into her tunic, then folded her arms and bit her lip. The silence hung over them for a long moment. She finally uncrossed her arms and took his hand. "Are you well?"

I can't tell her. I'll drive her away. "Yes."

"What happened to you?"

"I think I'm just anxious after last night. Besides, he is rather a jackass."

She frowned. "I can't have you attacking potential allies because they're unpleasant to deal with. Please tell me this won't happen again."

He put his hands on her cheeks and kissed her forehead. "It won't happen again." *Please, don't let it happen again.*

She pulled away and gestured back toward the camp. "What do you make of this? Are they telling the truth?"

He shrugged. "They aren't lying, exactly, but I don't think they're being completely honest."

"In what way?"

In some way that the Morrag can see, but I can't. "I can't explain it. It's just a hunch. I don't think they're going to hurt you, though—at least not if Gareth and Trypp have anything to say about it."

"I fear I can't give them what they want," she said.

"What do you mean?"

She took a deep breath. "They call me 'traitha.' That's the title of a chieftain, isn't it?"

"It is."

"And how can I be a chieftain? I'm not what they're looking for—I can't be. How would that be possible?"

He shrugged. "I don't know."

She stared back toward the camp, arms folded. "They want me to lead their tribe. But they aren't the reason I'm here." She gestured to the forest, the plains, and the countryside. "I'm here for Culidar. I'm here to ensure that no man, woman, or child is ever considered another man's possession. I'm here to make sure that no woman ever endures what I endured." She swiped away tears and folded her arms. "I'm scared," she whispered. "I don't know what to do. About anything."

"I know. Neither do I. But we'll figure it out together."

"Do you mean it?"

He pulled her close and cradled her head against his chest. "I promise." Her body trembled in his arms, and after a moment, he realized that she was crying. He tightened his arms. "Mairead, I am so sorry about all of this—about Allyn's house, about leaving you, about all these demands on you. As much as I am able, I will make amends and help you through this. You need only tell me what you want from me, and as much as it's in my power, I'll provide it."

She drew away and wiped her cheeks. He gave her a kerchief, and she laughed. "How many times will you have to share a kerchief with me?"

He grinned. "With any luck, hundreds."

She took a deep breath, composing herself. "I want to trust you," she said. "I want to believe you. But I've had many days to think about you leaving and get used to you being gone, and now it's hard to think that you've just changed your mind again. How can I believe you, Connor?"

"Do you know what I thought about when I was gone?" He didn't give her a chance to answer. "Dancing with you in Leiden. I thought about how you looked in your dress that night and how you looked in your linen shift when you called me in to see the snake. I wanted you so much that night. I thought about how you fought to save me when the fake kirons attacked us, and how beautiful you were at supper in Henry's palace, and the feel of your hands against my skin when you cleaned the wound on my face after I fought in Galbragh." He took her hand as her tears started to fall again. "But more than anything, I thought about me."

She lifted an eyebrow. "You?"

"It's selfish, I know, but I wondered how I was going to keep from going back to what I was before." He took her other hand and lifted them both to his lips. "You changed me, Mairead. You make me a tolerable man. Maybe someday I'll even be a good man, with your help. You give me purpose."

"Pretty words."

"True words."

She pursed her lips. "Connor, you need to know—if you leave again, I don't know if I can take you back one more time. I want to be with you, I want to build a home with you, but I can't just sit and wait for you all the time. I can't—I won't—be a woman who endures her husband leaving over and over only to be used for his pleasure when he chooses to come home."

The honesty stung. *What if she's right?* "Do you fear another woman?"

"I fear your wandering spirit. And the Morrag. She has a greater hold on you than I do."

His hands tightened around hers. "I promise you that I will do everything I can to stay with you. There will never be another woman. Not even the Morrag." He grinned. "Not even my mother."

She chuckled softly. "You do make me laugh." She pulled away from him and held out the kerchief.

"Keep it."

She smiled and tucked it into a pocket. "We should get back. I'm hungry."

"I'll be along in a moment."

She walked back to the fire.

Connor rubbed his temples. All around him, faint whispers fluttered in the air, just out of reach, like conversation at a banquet that one can only catch piecemeal. *What is this?* he asked the Morrag. *You would drive me to madness with these voices?*

You will see what I see. You will hear what I hear, the Morrag whispered.

Connor grimaced. *The madness encroaches already. Mairead, I hoped I'd have more time with you.* He walked back to the fire, hoping desperately that one of the tribesmen had seen fit to bring oiska.

After a night of fitful dozing—periodically interrupted by the Morrag's voice—Connor finally rose while the sky still bore a hazy gray hue. He dug his fishing line out of his pack, found some grubs and an icy pond, and sunk a line in the water. By the time the sun had fully risen, he had four fat fish hanging on his line.

He straightened to return to camp, but stopped when he heard voices. *Voices? The wind?* He tilted his head and sniffed the air.

—destroy them, utterly and completely—

—conscript the men—

Connor shook his head. The Morrag cackled and cawed. *Destroy them, raven. Rake them. Kill them.*

Destroy who? Connor pressed the bridge of his nose. "Too many voices," he whispered. "Destroy who?"

Her presence swelled in his chest again, but he pushed it back. She asserted herself more, and the collision of wills drove him to the ground, where he curled his knees to his chest as the sensation of a thousand hands tightened around his bones and muscles. His jaw clenched, and he clutched at his heart, gasping for breath, staring at the glassy eye and gaping mouth of one of the fish he had dropped. *Not now,* he begged. *Not now. I need to be back with Mairead. What do you want? I swear, I'll do it—but don't take me from her, not now!*

Heed my call.

He squeezed his eyes shut. Memories tumbled back into his head—things he'd pushed aside, things he'd tried to forget. *Blood on snow . . . fire and smoke . . . the last pulses of a fading heartbeat . . . the stench of burning flesh . . . the screams of a brutalized girl . . . the moans of dying men . . .*

He struggled to his knees. "Not all mine," he whispered. "Not all mine. Not my sins."

Heed my call. Bear the burden.

Connor forced himself to draw a full breath and pushed the pain aside. "Not . . . mine . . . ." He straightened, and the tightness in his chest started to fade. "I won't bear another man's sins."

Heed my call.

Connor leaned against a tree until the pain subsided enough to walk. He stared up at the heavens. "What terror is this?" he whispered. "Would you tear me apart from the inside? Would you destroy me this way—so that she has to watch? What kind of monstrous god would visit such horrors on men?"

There were no answers. Connor picked up the fish and returned to camp.

The other tribesmen and Mairead were awake. A fire crackled under a small kettle bubbling with warm water, and someone had set out a hunk of hard cheese and a loaf of brown bread. Mairead sat on her blanket wrapped tight in a fur and holding a small leather pouch. She gave Connor a hesitant smile and stood. "Trypp's wife sent tea."

"The blessed woman," he said. He held up the string of fat trout. "I found a pond. Fresh fish. I hope you'll suffer fish caught by a wolf," he said to the other men.

"I'd eat fish caught by Namha himself," Trypp said. "I'll help you clean them."

Connor handed him two of the fish. The spotted cat hovered nearby, her stub tail twitching and the tufts of her ears flipping. Connor nodded toward her. "What's her name?"

"Twitch. At least, that's what she lets me call her."

"What about the wolf?"

"Snowbane."

Connor watched as Twitch begged for a piece of fish. Trypp cut off the fish's head and tail and tossed them to the cat. She gave him a small rumble of gratitude as she gulped down the pieces. She licked her mouth and waited. "She's watched you clean fish before," Connor said.

"She has me trained," Trypp said. "She's like a wife."

Connor chuckled. "So you throw fish heads to your wife and she thanks you?"

"I give her what she wants," Trypp said, but there was a fond, wistful tone to his voice. He gestured to Mairead. "The girl—is she your woman?"

"She hasn't decided yet."

Trypp was silent for a moment. "It makes no difference to me what you are to her," he said. He dropped his voice. "But you should know—there are many in the tribe who were hoping to make an alliance with her through marriage."

"Braun?"

"And Gareth. And others. We didn't know who we would find, but there was discussion in the council that if she were a young girl or a guardian, it might be for one of us to wed her."

Connor's stomach twisted. "And yet the earth chose you—a man already wed. Did she expect you to take a second wife?"

"Only if the gods are cruel." He paused. "Gareth is as a brother to me, but Braun .... The Lionjaws and Catspaws have been at odds for centuries. As much as they would like to present themselves as a unified tribe, the lions are anything but."

So she's to be a trophy for the strongest clan leader. But if I wed her, can I keep the madness at bay long enough to give her a life? Connor dropped his voice. "Is she safe? Around Braun?"

"She is. He wouldn't hurt her—not like that. But he and Gareth are both the sons of traithas, and he resents that Gareth was marked to lead."

"That was obvious." Connor paused. "And you?"

"Me?" Trypp grinned. "I'm nothing. Just a tribesman with no name."

"Not even Goldeneye?"

He shrugged. "That was . . . the kindness of an elder tribesman." He tossed the insides of a fish to Twitch and walked back to the fire.

They broke their fast and packed their camp, and Mairead went aside to say morning prayers. "I'm going to join her," Gareth said.

Connor stared at his back. *Is this what you've brought me here for?* he asked the heavens. *To watch another man take her? To destroy me even as she becomes another man's wife?* He grimaced. *You're not making any friends here, Alshada.*

"Wolf."

Connor turned to Braun.

He turned his head and spat. "Is she spoiled?"

"Braun," Trypp said. "You're tribal. When was the last time a tribal woman had to justify herself to a tribesman?"

"I don't want another man's seconds."

Connor tightened his grip on his sword, resisting the urge to draw only with supreme effort. He gritted his teeth and composed himself. "She's purer than all of us together," he finally said.

The Morrag cackled. *He deserves death.*

Trypp stepped in. "Leave it, Braun. She's not chattel. She's a woman grown and capable of deciding for herself."

Tense silence filled the trees. Snowbane approached and nudged Braun's hand, and he scratched the wolf behind the ears. The tribesman relaxed. He stepped away without another word.

Trypp let out a breath and turned to Connor. "Be careful," he said.

When Mairead and Gareth finished their prayers, the group mounted up. Mairead took one of the tribal horses. She fell in between Connor and Gareth, and the other two men brought up the rear. Twitch and Snowbane disappeared into the trees.

It wasn't long before Gareth spoke. "Traitha, may I ask—can I see your palm in the light?"

She held it out to him. "It's just a scar. I fell and cut my hand the night I left Taura. I didn't think anything of it until last night."

"You spilled your blood here."

"Yes. On the shore, on a rock."

He frowned. "We thought you would be different—that you would know the magic. We thought you would already be practiced—an earth guardian, or the wisdomkeeper."

"The wisdomkeeper?" Mairead shook her head. "I'm afraid I know very little about the tribes at all. Only what Connor has taught me."

Braun snorted in distaste. "An outland education. He surely left many things out."

Connor's hands tightened around his horse's reins. "What is it you think I left out, kitten?"

"Does she know about the ravenmarked?"

Connor's stomach lurched. *She knows too much.* "She does."

"Does she know of the prophecy?"

"What prophecy?" Mairead asked.

"The tribal prophets say that one of the ravenmarked will destroy the lion's child," Braun said.

Mairead turned to Connor. "Is this true? Have you heard this?"

Everywhere I look, everything I hear—it only puts her in more danger if I'm around her. He twisted the reins around his hands. "It has nothing to do with us, Mairead."

"Answer me—did you know this?"

The Morrag cackled in his head. "I know that there are thousands of stories, myths, legends, and prophecies about the ravenmarked. And I know that prophecy is just a tradition of half-truths and vagaries that could mean whatever a particular interpreter wants them to mean." He turned away. "I never blindly follow anything, especially prophecy." He spurred his horse forward.

Gareth trotted to catch up. "Wolf," he said.

"My name is Connor."

"Do you have a tribal name?"

The question came on a respectful tone. "It's Ulfrich," Connor said. "My traitha was my father's best friend. I took his last name—Wolfbrother."

"You were not born tribal?"

"My father was a Taurin noble. My mother is ..." He paused. "Not tribal."

"You are earthbonded."

Connor frowned. "I don't understand."

"Adopted."

"A fatherless child is adopted. I was not fatherless."

"In the tribe you were. Your traitha took you in, gave you a father."

"Is that what happened with Trypp?"

Gareth hesitated. "No." He lowered his voice. "Trypp gave up his family and let another father bind him. It was—"

"Compensation." Trypp rode next to Connor. "A son died. His parents had no others. I took his place."

Connor stared for a long moment. "We have no such tradition in the nine," he said. "That was a noble thing."

Trypp shrugged. "It was necessary." He trotted ahead.

"He blames himself," Gareth said. "He was leading the hunt when his friend died."

He lies, the Morrag whispered.

Connor frowned. *Gareth or Trypp?*

She cawed. *They all lie. They deserve death.*

Connor stared at Trypp's back. *If even the men I think I can trust the most deserve death, then is there anyone who doesn't deserve to die?*

They rode most of the morning, emerging from the thin, scattered trees back to the vast plains under a steady snowfall. The snow tapered off gradually, and as the sky cleared and the sun pierced the thin gray clouds, a hawk cried a greeting above them. Gareth whistled and lifted a gloved hand. The hawk drifted down in lazy spirals and landed on his outstretched arm.

Mairead trotted closer. "He's beautiful," she said as the hawk preened and settled on Gareth's arm. "Is he yours?"

Gareth chuckled. "As much as Snowbane and Twitch belong to my tribal brothers," he said. "Traitha, this is Grayfeather." He pointed at the hawk's breast. Amid the brown and red tinged feathers was a single gray one.

"Does he hunt with you?"

"No. He hunts for himself. Sometimes he's gone for days, other times it's only a few hours." The hawk's yellow eyes examined Mairead carefully. Gareth turned to her and smiled. "I think he likes you. He seems calm."

Mairead stretched an arm toward him, then paused. "Can I touch him?"

"That's up to him." He moved Grayfeather closer to Mairead, and the bird took a short hop and landed on her shoulder. She let out a sharp cry. "It's all right. He won't hurt you."

"Do all of your people have animal companions?" Connor asked.

"No, not all, but it's very common." He turned to Connor. "Do none of your people have companions?"

Connor shook his head. "Hunting dogs, livestock—that sort of thing. Nothing like this."

"The other ancients have lost the old ways," Gareth said. "It is said that in the time before the Breaking, the companions fought alongside the people.

Our companions protect us, keep us safe and hidden."

Connor grunted. *With this wretched bird in my head, I don't think I need any more companions.* He frowned and sniffed the air. "I smell smoke," he said.

Mairead took a deep breath. "I don't smell it."

"Neither do I," Braun said. "You're imagining things."

Damn air talent. "Mairead, you know my sense of smell. If I smell smoke, there's a fire somewhere."

She bit her lip. "Connor does have a very acute sense of smell," she told the tribesmen. "Where's it coming from?"

"Southeast."

The voices he'd heard in the morning drifted to him on the breeze. —*conscript them—villages—kidnap—silver in the mountains—*

The Morrag twisted his stomach and tightened his chest. *I need you, raven. I need your sword.*

Shut up! "Mairead—"

She shielded her eyes. "He's right," she said, pointing. "Look—a wisp of smoke."

Gareth sucked in a breath. "I see it." He turned to Mairead. "What would you have us do, traitha?"

Braun put a hand on Mairead's arm. "Girl, this isn't our concern. If you are truly the traitha, you need to stay out of this. These are outland troubles."

Trypp adjusted his sword and reins, preparing to ride hard. "I'll fight. Lead the way, traitha."

"Do not involve yourself, Goldeneye," Braun said. "You risk revealing the tribes. What if a man escapes?"

"Escapes four tribesman and an archer with the best aim I've ever seen?" Connor said. The Morrag tugged at him again. *Go away—I'm not leaving her!* "Mairead, what do you want us to do?"

She bit her lip. "What if it's just a fire—just a house or a tavern?"

"It's not." He nearly spat the words, and his stomach threatened to turn inside out. "It's slavers. It's a village or ranch or homestead under attack. If we don't get there—"

"How do you know?" Braun asked. He pointed. "The girl is right. It could be anything."

"Look, if it's not what I think, we'll turn around and leave without talking to a soul," Connor said. "But if I'm right—"

"If you're right, we fight," Mairead said. She tucked her feet into the stirrups. "Gareth, give me a bow."

"Why?" Gareth handed over the weapon.

"If I'm to help, I need a weapon."

Connor breathed out a long sigh and kicked his horse to a gallop, Mairead close on his heels. Soon, three other sets of hoof beats followed.

Yes, raven. Avenge me.

I don't do this for you—I do this for her.

As they approached the small village, sounds of attack grew louder. Screams, cries, shouts came to Connor on the air, and mixed with the odor of smoke, he detected the smell of burning flesh. Flames engulfed the walls of the village, spreading to animal pens and houses even as he watched.

Mairead pulled up close to Connor and signaled him to rein in. "We need a plan," she said.

He drew his sword. "This is my plan."

"And it's a very good one." Gareth and the others reined in next to her. "But I'd rather ensure that none of us do anything foolhardy."

"What's your plan, girl?" Braun said.

"I can cover you."

"What?" Connor was glad to hear echoes from Trypp and Gareth.

She patted the bow. "I'll cover you."

"You can't shoot from the back of a horse," Connor said.

She grimaced. "No better time to learn." She pulled the bow over her head. "Gareth, you ride in with Connor, right down the middle of the village. Braun, you go around the north side, and Trypp, you go around the south side. Subdue or kill anyone who looks like a slaver."

"Why us?" Braun said.

"Because you two have the animals. Gareth and Connor will cut a swath and send men your way. Circle around and defend these villagers."

"But—"

She cut off his words with a hand gesture. "Connor, Gareth, go."

At last given rein, Connor wheeled his horse around and drove him into the melee that occupied the small cluster of homes and pasture. Dimly aware of Gareth fighting at his right, he could only hear the Morrag driving him forward. Blood pounded in his head, and he jumped off the horse with a vengeful roar, already slashing at the surprised slavers. His steel cut a man nearly in two before the others could even turn around.

Connor's senses narrowed, focused only on the threat. Men in black leathers rushed at him, defending their conquest, but he swung, parried, slashed over and over, the Morrag swelling, growing stronger with every cut, every slash, every death at his hands. The tiny village was a blur of bloody snow as he stabbed and cut.

Yes, raven. Kill them. Avenge me.

Connor had seen battle madness. While he'd always fought to keep his emotions and fury tightly controlled, he'd seen men fall prey to the lust for blood—the need to slash and destroy anything that moved. He'd seen and understood and vowed that he'd never allow the madness to touch him for fear of giving the Morrag too much control.

Now, there was no fighting her—no holding her back. He was only the instrument of wrath, and he could only kill. Blood didn't matter—offal didn't matter. The stench of death, the screams of villagers, the sticky slickness of his hands trying to keep a tight grip on his sword blurred together into one raging, furious shout of vengeance. He tasted blood, sweat, dirt, and Alshada knew what else in his mouth, but he kept shouting, roaring as righteous anger swelled, filling him to overflowing.

And he reveled in it.

It was a relief to finally swing without thinking—to trust that the Morrag would guide his sword to mete out justice. He split the skull of a slaver, and his blade's follow-through killed another. A reflection off steel flickered at the corner of his eye, and he drew a dagger and threw blindly, trusting the Morrag to guide it. He yanked his sword from the man in front of him and whirled to see his dagger planted in the belly of a downed slaver. He stabbed the man through the heart.

It's not enough—rake them, raven. Claw them. Gouge them.

A hand on his back stopped him, and he whirled, his sword slashing up in an arc. A woman shouted. "Connor!"

His sword met another. A braided man stood in front of him. "Stand down, Ulfrich."

"Connor, stop!" the woman shouted. She stepped around the man with the sword. "Stop. It's me. Mairead." She touched his arm.

Connor stopped. The anger drained out of him so quickly that his knees went weak, and he stumbled backward. "Oh gods, Mairead. Did I—are you—"

"I'm all right." She helped him down to the ground, gentle hands on his back and shoulder. "I'm all right. The village is safe."

Ragged breaths tore at his chest. He was vaguely aware of Gareth stepping close enough to kick his sword away. "How many?" he asked. "How many did I kill?"

"Eight. Maybe more," Mairead said.

The Morrag begged for more blood. *Claw them. Kill them. They deserve death.*

He growled, fighting for control of his own body, the struggle to resist her driving pain through every muscle and joint. *No. No more. I won't kill any more of them!* "How many altogether?"

"I can't say yet," she said. "Trypp and Braun aren't back yet. I killed three with my bow. Gareth killed several."

Vengeance is exacted, he told the Morrag. *Are you happy?*

She screamed in his head. *Kill them, raven!*

Spasms wracked his body as he fought the need to stand and pick up his sword again. *No! No more!*

At that moment, Mairead leaned down to press her lips to his forehead. "The village is safe," she whispered.

A shiver passed through him, accompanied by something he could only call a quiet conversation between two entities. The Morrag fluttered, preened, and fell still. She bowed her head. *It is well,* she said. *I will wait a while longer. It is well.*

Connor let out a long, shuddering breath and relaxed against Mairead. *The pain—it hurts so much—please let me go.* "Oh gods, Mairead. Did I hurt you? Did I—"

"I'm all right." She stroked his cheek. "Gareth stopped you from—"

She's all right. "Don't move," he whispered. "Please just stay here."

One hand twitched against his arm. "Why?"

Because you make the beast bearable. "I don't know. Because I feel better when you're here. Because the Morrag doesn't hurt as much when you touch me."

"I don't understand."

"I told you," said a voice above them. "She is the ravenmaster."

CHAPTER FIVE

The lioness devours the false one. The land lives again.
— Tribal prophecy

Mairead looked up into the smooth, round face of the eunuch Phinneas. He dismounted his horse, and she flinched as he approached. "Do not—" she started.

Gareth sucked in his breath. "Ravenmaster—he is—" But as Phinneas approached, Gareth gathered his senses and stepped between Mairead and the eunuch, sword drawn. "Hold!"

The eunuch held up his hands. "My lady, I only wish to help."

"You can help him?" She jutted her chin at Connor, refusing to take her hands from him. "You can help this?"

The eunuch wet his lips. "I do not know," he said. "But I can't say until I examine him."

"Please." Connor's voice sounded far away, a croaking gurgle from the pit of a chasm. Pain creased his forehead. "Please, Mairead."

Alshada—what is this? What have you cursed him with? "Very well."

Gareth let the eunuch pass. The eunuch folded his hands in front of his body, the garish, wildly inappropriate silk robes settling around him in a swirl of color. He was dressed in layers of various hues—red, yellow, orange, brown, green. His white turban was adorned with a large emerald above the center of his forehead, and it trailed a long piece of silk behind it. The man's face was smooth, unlined by age, and he had dark brown eyes, darker even than Connor's. He knelt next to Connor and put two fingers over a spot on Connor's neck. He frowned. "His heart races. It's far too fast for one of the Sidh."

Connor choked a gurgling laugh. "Finally something the Sidh blood is powerless against—the gods-forsaken raven."

"What can we do?" Mairead asked.

Phinneas reached into his silks and pulled out a dark vial. He uncorked it, and a sickly sweet odor filled the air. "Extract of the xioma root," he said. "A painkiller, and it should slow his heart."

"Will that work on him? He said his Sidh blood wouldn't let him get drunk."

Phinneas held up a hand. "This is concentrated and far stronger than even the strongest oiska." He lifted Connor's head. "Open your mouth and lift your tongue. Are you able?" Connor did as he was asked. The eunuch dripped three drops into his mouth. "Let it sit under your tongue."

Mairead watched, anxious, as his breathing slowed and his face started to relax. At last, with a long, shuddering sigh, he opened his eyes all the way. "Thank you."

"I am pleased to help," the eunuch said. "Can you rise?"

Connor sat up. He rubbed his forehead. Mairead reached for him, but he held up a hand. "I'm all right. It's better. Just give me a moment."

She turned to the eunuch. "I thank you as well."

He straightened. "I only wish I had been able to help sooner. Had I been able to accompany you last night, I could have stopped this."

"Stopped this?" Connor asked. "You can control this beast?"

"Only with drugs, my lord," he said. "But yes, I believe I can help you, at least until you learn to control what the Morrag demands of you."

"He can help," Connor whispered. "He can help me."

Mairead thought there might be a tear in his eye, but she couldn't be certain if it was the drug or genuine emotion. *He's like a dying man at last offered hope.* "Yes," Mairead said. "If he speaks true."

He leaned in toward her body again. "I have to trust him," he whispered against her lap. "I have to, Mairead. I can't leave you again. I can't lose you. And if this beast has control of me, she will take me from you, and I—" His words became slurred, and he mumbled into her lap.

Mairead swallowed over a lump in her throat. *He does want to stay. How could I doubt him? How could I mistrust him? It's the Morrag I can't trust.* She wove her fingers into his hair. "Shh," she whispered. "Connor, shh. I'm here."

Phinneas cleared his throat. "My lady." He nodded toward Braun and Snowbane, who approached in the distance. Villagers slowly emerged from hiding places, and a crowd started to form around Mairead and Connor. "Perhaps your men might find something else to do? I can help you and your lord find a place to rest."

"Gareth, take Braun and go find Trypp," Mairead said.

"Traitha—" Gareth began.

"I'll be fine," she said. She held up her hand. "I'll call you if I need you. The village isn't that big."

He looked at the scar on her palm. "The tavern," he said, pointing to a building just a few yards away. "It's still intact. You can find a place to rest there for a time. We'll clean up and take care of the wounded." He walked away to meet Braun.

Phinneas knelt again. "Forgive me, my lady," he said. "But I am certain my lord would not wish the others to see him in this state."

"You are right, of course." She lifted one of Connor's heavy arms around her neck. She swallowed bile at the odor of human remains on his clothes. *Get him out of the public eye—then worry about cleaning him up.* "Connor, can you stand if Phinneas and I help you?"

His head lolled forward as she shifted her weight to stand, but she thought she heard him acquiesce. Phinneas lifted his other arm, and with some encouragement, they were able to help him stand and shuffle toward the tavern.

A haphazardly constructed two-story building, the tavern had little to recommend itself aside from being, apparently, the only one in the village. The exterior whitewash was so chipped that the walls appeared brown with random streaks of white. The interior was not much better. An array of rustic stools, benches, and tables were scattered across a gouged and slanted floor, and the oiled-skin windows were in need of replacement. Mairead didn't expect great things, but despite the worn appearance, the furniture was clean, and the collection of bottles, flasks, cups, and mugs behind the bar was well-organized and tidy. A pot of something hung over the fire, and Mairead suspected pork from the aroma.

A tavern keeper and a few patrons looked up when they entered. The tavern keeper drew a dagger. Mairead held up a hand. "We aren't slavers. We defended your village. May we use your tavern to rest and clean up?"

The man's gaze passed over all three of them, lingering on Phinneas. He finally nodded and sheathed his dagger. "I'll bring water and soap."

Mairead and Phinneas helped Connor to a bench. He slumped over, and Phinneas guided him down to lie on his side. Mairead sat near his head and stroked his hair. He sighed. "Mairead," he murmured. "Don't leave."

"I won't." She looked up at Phinneas. "There is much to discuss, but before we talk about him, I need to know if you are trustworthy."

He folded his hands. "You wish to know why I tried to buy you."

"It's a reasonable question."

"Forgive me. The arrangement was a necessary one." He sat down across from Mairead, arranging the silks as he did. "Let us begin with introductions. I am Phinneas Ja'aster, Chief Eunuch to His Imperial Majesty, the High King of the Eastern Seas, Tal Ja'al the Tenth." He paused. "And you?"

"Mairead."

"And do you have a family name, my lady?"

"I was orphaned. They called all of the orphans 'Brennan.'" *Just a girl with no name and the right blood.*

He gestured to Connor. "And the raven?"

She tightened a hand on Connor's shoulder. "Connor Mac Niall. Of House Mac Niall, the Sidh, and the wolf tribe." *He is so much, and I'm nothing.*

Phinneas pressed the bridge of his nose. "I have been looking for you for decades," he said. "Now, when I had all but given up ...."

"Who is it you think we are?"

"I believe your raven is the one who will defeat the Forbidden," Phinneas said. "And I believe you will begin the reunification of the three lands."

Reunification of the three lands. Could such a thing be possible? "You tried to buy me. Why?"

"Our prophets foretold that a eunuch in the king's service would find you—the ravenmaster—in a slaver's hands. I have purchased every woman I could find who looked even a bit like she could be the one, but had almost given up. I hoped when I found her that I could join her, guide her toward her destiny. I didn't know you were the one until I saw you with your raven."

How many women have you purchased? How many went to your emperor's harem because they weren't me? "Your prophecies would seem to have destroyed many lives. Where did you take the others?"

"We send them back to be trained and educated under our best magicians." A thin, proud smile crossed his lips. "We have produced some of the most talented assassins, artists, healers, and musicians in the known world."

"The Tal'Aster sect," she said. Phinneas inclined his head. "I thought it was a story." *How many things I thought were stories will turn out to be true?*

"No, my lady. The Tal'Aster sect is a group of men and women dedicated to the service of the All-Seeing Lord. They live in the Zhasta Mountains. Those who complete their education go into the world and teach others."

"Missionaries?"

Phinneas gave her a thin smile. "Not as you might think, my lady. They do not found kiroks and sayadas as you might. Rather, they become the hands and feet of the All-Seeing Lord by doing his work in the world."

"And this is how you recruit—by buying people from slavers?"

"You misunderstand, my lady. We rescue men and women—take them away from brutality and give them training and education."

"It's not justification," Mairead said. Her chest tightened in anger. "You took people from their lives, homes, and families for your own ends. That's wrong."

"Forgive me, my lady, but they all had a choice," Phinneas said.

"What kind of choice? Go with you or remain with slavers?"

"No, the choice to go with us or return home. I would have given you the same choice, my lady."

But I had no other home. Mairead pursed her lips, holding her words as the tavern keeper delivered water, cloths, and soap. When he left, she spoke quietly as she started to wash Connor's face, hair, and hands. "How can I be certain? How can I believe anything you say? For all I know, the men Connor just killed were here on your orders. How did you just happen to be here when we were? You told us you were going to Galbragh. Were you here to capture this village and take it to Tal'Amun?"

He stood and bowed. "Very well. As you do not wish my company or my aid, I will go back to Tal'Amun."

"But—" She bit her lip. "He needs you."

"And you?"

"I don't know what I need." She shook her head. "That's not true. I need him, and he needs you."

"Then you wish me to stay?"

"What's your interest in us?"

He spread his hands toward Connor. "I am at your disposal. The Tal'Amuni camp is disbanding as we speak. My colleagues are returning to the east now that we have found you. I alone am left to offer guidance."

"Where do your loyalties lie, Phinneas?"

He folded his hands before him. "I cannot swear fealty to you, my lady. My fealty is already sworn elsewhere. But for now, I am directed to enable your success—and the raven's—in any way I can." He bowed again. "I fear that is the best I can do."

"I need to know one more thing," she said. "What did you intend for me?"

"My lady?"

"In the Tal'Aster sect, in the mountains. What were your plans for me?"

"Until I realized who you were, I had planned to train you in the martial arts. You would have made a brilliant assassin." He paused. "You have already killed several men."

Mairead swallowed hard, remembering the screams of the man whose throat she slit, the grunts and thuds of men she shot, the twitching of Allyn's body when she stabbed him through the eye. "Acts of necessity and survival. I only did what I had to do."

"Such events often reveal the mettle within ourselves," Phinneas said, quiet. "It is as I said. You would have made a brilliant assassin."

She leaned back against the wall. Connor still snored softly. *The lions want me to go into these mountains with them. Connor is needed in Taura and in the Sidh village. There are those who think I should be in Albard, learning how to retake Taura. No one shows any concern for this land, and the killing and kidnapping and raping will continue.* "I'm here to stop this," Mairead said.

"My lady?"

She gestured around the village. "This. Slavery. This maiming of these people. This is why I'm here."

"Forgive me, lady, but how do you know?"

"I don't know how. I just know that's my purpose." She paused. "I will need you to help me."

Phinneas wet his lips. "What would you have me do, my lady? How do you propose to stop slavery? As long as there are people willing to buy, there will be people willing to capture and sell."

"Fight. Damn it, fight!" She stood, anger rising. Connor snorted and adjusted his head and arms, but didn't wake. She twitched to return to his side, but her frustration overpowered her affection. "Prince Henry sits in his gilded palace, watching this go on around him, profiting from the trade while he pretends to be a man of conscience. You desert the plains when you could oppose this trade. The tribe in the mountains refuses to concern itself with outland troubles unless it's dragged into a conflict." She held up a hand when Phinneas started to speak. "I need to walk. Stay here until he wakes, and discuss what you need to discuss. I'll be in the village. Find me when you're done." She left the tavern before he could respond.

Gareth stood right outside the door, hand on sword. "Traitha? Are you well?"

"I'm well, Gareth." She took a deep breath. "I told you to find the others."

"Forgive me. I feared for your safety. I can take you to them, if you wish."

Mairead started walking.

"Traitha? Where are you going?"

She pulled her gloves on and tightened the fur cloak. "I don't know." She stopped and turned to Gareth. "You know about this, don't you? This slave trade?"

He hesitated. "Yes," he finally said. "We do. Years ago, before I was born, there were slavers in the mountains. They tried to take our city and our people."

"And yet you do nothing to help these people who live on the plains?"

"We killed all those who came up the mountain. Why would we reveal ourselves to others by going down to the plains?"

Mairead turned away and walked again until she reached the edge of the village where the horses stood hobbled. She crossed her arms, dimly aware of Gareth standing next to her. "I am here for this. I am here to free this place. I know this." Her palm burned, and she tightened her fist and turned to Gareth. "Phinneas said he believes I am the one to begin the reunification of the three lands—Taura, Culidar, and Sveklant. Even if I never have anything to do with Culidar or Sveklant, I am still connected to Taura by the blood of my ancestors. There is no place more outland for you than Taura. If you would have me lead your tribe, you will have to be part of outland concerns at some point."

Gareth's mouth twisted in conflicted emotion. "We knew this about you," he said at last. "We knew you would be the heir of Cuhail. But I confess to you, the idea that you might have to lead a people other than the lions is ..."

"Overlooked?"

"Underemphasized."

"You call me Deliverer, but do you even know what that means? What I'm expected to do in the tribe?"

Gareth opened his mouth, closed it, and sighed. "The prophecies call you 'Deliverer.' We always assumed that meant you would lead us to our inheritance."

"Inheritance?"

"The plains."

Mairead waved a hand toward the village. "So you can do more of this? Conquer and enslave a people who are already enslaved?"

He frowned. "I confess that now that I've seen these people, it doesn't seem like a place we would wish to conquer."

She bit her lip. "You heard what Phinneas called Connor. You know he's ravenmarked."

Gareth shifted his feet. "I am sorry, traitha. I know you care for him, and he seems devoted to you, but the raven is a beast that will eat him from the inside out. How can you be safe?"

"He is Connor," she said. "He came when I needed him the most, and he has pledged everything to me. I trust him." *Or at least, I am working on trusting him.*

He squinted and stared past her, out toward the distant city. "Riders."

She turned to see a cloud of snow and the faint outline of a large party riding at a full gallop toward the village. "Find the others."

"I don't know what we'll do without your raven—"

She pointed to a barn near the edge of the village. "I'll cover you with my bow."

"Traitha—"

"Go, Gareth!"

He still hesitated. After a moment, he whistled. Grayfeather winged down to him. "Protect her," he said, pointing at Mairead. Grayfeather screeched in response. Gareth ran.

Mairead ran to the barn and used the external corral and water barrel to help her clamber up to the roof. She planted a foot in the thatching and pulled her bow over her shoulder. Grayfeather cawed and circled above. Below her, villagers scattered and hid in their homes. She tightened her jaw and nocked an arrow. *I will not let them take this village.*

But as the riders approached, a standard became clearer, and eventually, she recognized the black hawk on a red background. *Henry!* She climbed down and ran to meet them. "Your highness," she shouted as they reached the edge of the village.

Henry reined in and dismounted in one fluid motion. "Mairead," he called. He put his hands on her shoulders. "Thank the gods," he breathed. He kissed her cheeks. "You're all right. I am so sorry, Mairead—had I known what Melik was, I never would have—"

"It's all right, Henry. I chose to go with him. It wasn't your fault."

He pulled her close. "If you had died—if I had broken my word to Connor—I can't imagine what might have happened."

He worries more about what Connor would do to him than what would have happened to me. She pulled back. "I'm well now. How did you find us?"

"We saw the smoke from a distance. We came to render aid. I had no idea you would be here."

"But Connor's mother said—"

He cleared his throat and turned to his men. "Check the village. Ensure these people are well and safe." He lowered his voice. "May we speak somewhere privately?"

She waved to Gareth, who was running toward her with Trypp, Braun, and their animals in tow. Gareth stopped when he reached her. "Is all well?"

"Everything is fine. This is Prince Henry. He saw the smoke and came to render aid. Help his men, will you? They're preparing to circulate in the village." She turned back to Henry. "We can speak in the tavern. Connor is there."

Henry took her arm. He leaned his head close. "Connor's mother is an unusual creature."

Mairead suppressed a grin. "She would not appreciate the category, my lord."

"I would prefer to maintain at least a semblance of ignorance that such things exist."

"You acknowledge Connor's existence."

"Only half of it, it would appear."

Mairead did smile then. "In truth, I'm glad you met us here. I wanted to speak with you about how to deal with this."

"With what?"

She gestured around the village. "This. The slave trade. How to fight it."

He stopped walking and turned to her. "I'm not sure what you mean. The empires are broken now, thanks to Connor. That creature told me what he did—that Allyn is dead—and we saw the train of Tal'Amuni traveling east. The only one left is Mac Mahon, and he—"

Mairead stared. "You can't be serious."

"Of course I'm serious. He broke the empires, Mairead. It's over."

"He" broke the empires? What did Maeve tell him? "How is it over as long as Mac Mahon is here? You don't expect him to let you fill Allyn's gap, do you?"

"I have a city to run. I have enough troubles. I can't fight a man whose forces and coffers vastly outweigh my own."

Mairead couldn't speak for a long moment. *Connor was right.* "You're a coward."

His jaw tightened. "I—"

"You are. You're afraid of ruining your reputation or spending too much money or losing a battle. You're making all of your decisions based on fear. But if you would fight—if you would rally these people—they would flock to you. They want freedom, Henry."

He put a hand on her shoulder. "Forgive me, Mairead, but they don't. This is what they know. They have lived this way for so long that to give them freedom would be a cruelty beyond words."

An anger so painful that Mairead feared speaking rose in her throat. *Is this what Connor feels when the Morrag rises?* She swallowed the lump and raised her chin. "I killed Allyn. Connor didn't break his empire. I did." She walked away.

"Mairead, wait—"

"Connor is in the tavern," she called back. "He'll want to speak with you."

She walked until she found Gareth talking to the owner of a small home in the center of the village. The man's hands were rough and stained with the work of gardening and tending animals, and his clothes were made of rough, homespun fabric that was patched and resewn in various places. He bowed low when she approached. "My lady. I thank you. My village thanks you."

"Please rise." Mairead gestured around the village. "You have a fair-sized settlement. Why have you not set up more protections for yourself?"

He shrugged. "We work to live, my lady. We are farmers. At the end of the day, if the garden is tended and the animals are fed and penned, we count ourselves successful."

"In the midst of slavers, you do nothing to protect your own property?"

He chewed his lip for a moment. "It has not caused a problem until to-day," he said. "Allyn and others, they take food and allow us to live here as long as we grow what they want and need."

Mairead's blood ran cold. "Then you allow them to victimize you? You allow yourselves to be slaves just as those who are penned and sold?"

He hesitated a long moment before answering. "Better to be slaves here than slaves there, my lady."

They admit defeat before they leave the cradle. This is no life. She took a deep breath. "Why did they attack today, do you think?"

He shrugged. "They did not say, my lady. They seemed more interested in men than women. They started binding the young and able men first. When they had those ones secure, they started burning things and looking for women." He frowned. "I think I heard one say something about Allyn being dead."

Her jaw tightened. "He is dead. I killed him."

"Truly?" He bowed again. "You have done a great service to the plains, my lady."

Not if you only live to be taken by other slavers.

"Mairead."

She turned to see Connor approaching. "Where's the eunuch?" she asked.

"He's treating the villagers' wounds. He has some skill in healing. The tribesmen are helping to put out the last of the fires." He took her hand. "Can we step away for a moment?"

Gareth stopped them with a hand on her arm. "A moment with both of you?"

Mairead looked at Connor, who nodded. They stepped away from the villagers, and Gareth spoke in a low voice. "I would be doing you both a disservice if I did not tell you that Connor will not be welcome in the lion tribe. The ravenmarked are not looked upon favorably."

Connor grimaced. "That much has been clear from our conversations."

"But I don't think you understand," Gareth said. "If they find out what you are, Connor, they will either cast you into exile or kill you."

"Gareth, that's barbaric," Mairead said.

"Perhaps. But we know no other way. The tribe is there to prepare a place for the Deliverer and protect her once she arrives. There are prophecies that predict her destruction by ravens." He paused. "Out of respect for the traitha, I will not reveal your secret. But I would be lying if I said I was not afraid to bring you into the midst of my people."

"Connor wouldn't hurt—" Mairead started.

"He almost killed you today," Gareth said. "He would have if I hadn't stopped him. I have no doubt he would have regretted it and mourned your passing, but that doesn't change what he nearly did in the midst of his madness."

Connor put a hand on Mairead's arm as she started to speak. "He's right," he said. "I am a danger to you and to everyone around me." He took a deep breath. "Did the others see? Braun or Trypp?"

"Braun saw you on the ground with the eunuch, but I told him you just had the wind knocked out of you. Trypp knows nothing."

Connor nodded. He held out a hand to Gareth. "I am grateful for your honesty and your loyalty. Please trust that I am going to do everything in my power to find a way to control this beast so that you never again see what you saw today."

Gareth clasped his arm. "Your admission is the only reason I continue to trust you, Ulfrich." He stepped back. "I'll round up our group and tell them to prepare to leave in the morning." He bowed and walked away.

Mairead turned to Connor. "Are you well?"

He rubbed his head. "I have a headache from the pit of Namha's chasm, but otherwise, I'm all right. The bitch is quiet for the moment. Whatever the eunuch gave me was strong enough to shut her up for a time."

She felt her shoulders relax. *I didn't even realize how tense I was for him until now.* "What did you learn from Phinneas?"

"Not a lot. He keeps many things hidden, but he seems to believe he's supposed to help us." He lowered his voice. "I think he has some kind of magical skill, but I'm not sure what. He doesn't seem to be a threat. He speaks only of helping us."

"Helping us do what? He tried to buy me, Connor. And in this place, everyone is a threat."

He sighed. "I've been to Tal'Amun, Mairead. The eunuchs are very different. Mysterious. But they also lack a capacity for lying. They sometimes keep things hidden, but if he says he wants to travel with us until he finds a way to help us, I believe him. It's just the way they are. They are chosen only when they have passed a series of grueling tests, they give up their manhood willingly, and they spend their lives serving the noble classes. For some reason, even though he is bound to his emperor, he seems to want to serve us."

She gestured around the village. "This place—these people. This is why I'm here. This is my purpose—to stop this."

"I believe you, but I don't know what you want to do about that. Henry won't help you. With the Tal'Amuni leaving and Allyn dead, he'll likely be even more reluctant to act. He'll see this as just himself against Mac Mahon, and he'll form another uneasy truce and wait for the slaving empire to collapse."

"I see that now." She sighed. "It's so hopeless. I'm a pebble in a tempestuous sea."

"We knew this wouldn't be easy."

"It's just all so ugly."

"What is?"

She gestured. "This place. This trade. All of it." She shook her head before he could speak. "We'll stay here tonight. Tomorrow, we ride north."

They stayed in several rooms located on the second floor of the tavern that night. Henry rode away with his men long before sunset, and the villagers set out to clean up and make their village habitable for the night before the real work began the next day. Mairead listened while Connor gave advice on how to reinforce their defenses, and she wondered if anything Connor told the elders made any difference. *They will keep selling to the slavers and enduring this abuse until someone inspires them to live better,* she thought. Her palm burned. When it came time for supper, she found her appetite diminished, and she excused herself early.

She woke in the night to a gentle shaking on her shoulder. "What is it?" She sat up to see Connor kneeling next to her, and she scrubbed her face and stifled a yawn. "Is everything well?"

He put a finger over his lips. "I want to show you something," he whispered.

She pulled on her boots and cloak and took his hand, trusting his Sidh senses to direct them out of the tavern without bumping into anything and waking the other men. "Where are we going?" she whispered when they emerged in the cool, clear night air.

He pointed. "I saddled our horses. We need to ride a bit out of the village."

She didn't question him. Rather, she mounted her horse and followed as he rode north. When they had cleared the village boundary, she dared to raise her voice a bit. "The others will wonder where we've gone."

"They're sound asleep. Except Phinneas, that is, and he'll be sure we aren't followed." He turned to her and smiled. "And yes, I'm well. I promise. The eunuch gave me a few more drops of his drug. She's silent for now."

"Where are we going?"

"The plains north of the village." He would divulge nothing more.

They rode in silence for a time. She reveled in the feel of the winter air on her cheeks, the clear, starry sky overhead, the reflection of the moon on the snow. In the distance, a low line of clouds undulated over the plains, and she thought she heard a quiet rumble of wind somewhere to the northeast. When Connor reached for her hand, she took it and sighed. *It's almost like when we traveled before. Almost.*

As they rode northeast, she gradually realized that what she had thought of as a line of low, undulating clouds on the horizon was actually hundreds of four-legged beasts plodding along the plains in a southward direction. "By the spirits," she whispered. "What are they?"

"Sleigh deer. The people of these plains use them the way others use cattle or horses—beasts of burden, work animals, the like. They sometimes migrate on these kinds of clear nights."

"How did you know about this?"

"I smelled them." He chuckled. "The scent of a migrating herd of sleigh deer is enough to draw any Sidh with a bit of air talent from quite a distance." He reined in.

Mairead stopped next to him. The deer were close enough that she could smell them, hear their snorts and grunts, and see their antlers. "Can we get closer?"

"It isn't wise. They can stampede if they get nervous. Better just to watch them."

She did for some time. At one point, an enormous beast with antlers of at least seven or eight points separated himself from the herd and took several steps toward her and Connor. He snorted, pawed the ground, then lifted his mouth to the sky and bellowed a call of warning. He returned to his place and began directing his herd once more. "He's beautiful," she whispered.

"There is beauty here," Connor said. "On these plains, with these people— there is beauty. There is beauty everywhere, Mairead."

She turned to him. "You brought me here because I said it was all so ugly."

"It is ugly. These last couple of weeks have been ugly. You are coming to realize the truth of this place. It will not be won easily, Mairead." He took her hand and turned to her. "But there is still beauty here, even amid all the ugliness. The ugliness helps us recognize it. You are part of the beauty. If anyone can win Culidar, it will be you."

She bit her lip. "I don't want to win it," she said. "I don't want to be another conqueror. I want to free it. But it all seems so hopeless."

"Not hopeless. Not as long as Alshada is working. Not as long as there is one person in this place who can see something better."

"I didn't think I'd hear you speak of Alshada."

"I've been unduly influenced by a girl I met." She laughed, and he lifted her hand to his mouth and kissed it. "You changed everything for me, Mairead. You will change everything here."

She smiled. "Thank you. For this."

He dismounted and stood next to her leg. "Will you dismount?" She lifted one leg over the horse's neck. He put his hands on her waist, and she slid down into his arms. "I know you are working to trust me," he said. "I know I hurt you, and I am so sorry for everything."

"Connor—"

"I have to say this." He paused. "I have no reason to expect anything from you—to even hope that you might one day consent to be my wife—but I cannot go another moment without telling you that my deepest desire, my strongest wish, is to share my whole life with you. Everything. Morrag or no Morrag, Sidh or no Sidh, I want to marry you, Mairead. I love you."

Her heart raced, and she thought of all the things she could say, but only one thing came out of her mouth. "I love you, too."

He smiled, leaned down, and kissed her full on the lips. In that place, with the sleigh deer migrating in the distance and the waxing moon shining down and the horses lending their heat, she allowed herself to melt into his embrace and fully enjoy the feel of his mouth on hers. Her arms snaked up around his neck, and he pulled her closer, closer, until she thought she never wanted to leave that place—his arms, the plains, that moment.

When he pulled away, he kissed her forehead and drew her close to his chest. "Can we just stay here tonight? Build a shelter and have one night without duty or demands?" she whispered.

He chuckled. "You have no idea how tempting that is," he said. "But this isn't the right night. I'll know when it's right."

"How will you know?"

"You'll bear my last name."

She tipped her head up to stare at him. "And if I never consent?"

He stroked her cheek. "I hope you will. I will wait. I will wait until I know there's no hope."

She wove her fingers into the hair at the base of his skull. "Today, there is hope."

He kissed her again, and again, and a dozen more times, until her lips were sore and her horse snorted in impatience. She pulled away and put her hands on his chest. "We should get back."

He kissed her once more. "I suppose. Promise me we will have these moments now and again?"

"Well, it's a painful duty, but I suppose I can tolerate it."

He chuckled again. They mounted the horses and turned toward the village, and the bellow of the migrating stag followed them.

CHAPTER SIX

There is power in the blood of the unquickened.
— Second Book of the Wisdomkeepers

Emrys hovered between the elements. In front of him, Matthias walked across the Nar Sidhe village with a purposeful stride, confident of his position. Large, blond, and bearded, he'd grown leaner and harder during his weeks away from Taura. He'd taken red tattoos, and he wore a doeskin kaltan and boots and little else. He wore his talisman and his animstone openly, because in this place, such things were symbols of strength. All indications that he had ever been a Taurin guard were gone, and the only thing left was a brutal bully of a leader who couldn't even conjure the same power as the people he led.

Emrys had told Matthias to lead the Nar Sidhe, and he knew they would recognize him for what he was—the one who could mobilize them and prepare them for their glory—but he hadn't anticipated how easily the unquickened Ferimin would rise to power. He watched the warriors run their maneuvers on the practice field. *They are nearly ready,* he thought. *Take them into the mountains, destroy the tribe, and then use the larger army to invade Taura from the north.* He allowed himself a small smile. *It might work.* He slipped into the world and pulled up his hood, hiding his face in shadow.

"Admiring your handiwork?"

Emrys turned, his stomach twisting in recognition. The man next to him wore his patchy black hair in a tangle of braids. Unclothed but for a gauzy kaltan around his midsection, he displayed patchy burns and sores from his face down to his feet. *The pain must be excruciating. He probably loves it.* "How long have you been here?"

The grin he gave Emrys twisted his face into a grotesque mask. "A few weeks. The women have attended my wounds." He gestured down his body. "Quite sad, really. Your little friend over there thought it would be amusing to torture a disobedient man with fire. He didn't anticipate the man would survive and be reborn."

"Disobedient. How?"

"A pissing contest. This man was a powerful warrior. He challenged your pet, and your pet won. He decided that instead of just killing the warrior outright, he'd burn him." He shrugged. "They stopped too soon. They thought the man was dead, but I slipped in. When they saw the body breathing, the healers begged your pet to let them help. He agreed."

Emrys looked back toward the practice field again. "Why didn't he finish you?"

He shrugged. "Wanted to see his handiwork walking around the village. Like you."

Emrys felt his mouth tighten. "Where have you been, Bachi?"

"Around. Where is the whore?"

"Aldora? She was living as a noblewoman on Taura, but the body died in a battle. I don't know where she went afterward."

Bachi grunted. "And now, it falls back to us—the three of us—to bring our master back, give him this world for his kingdom once again."

Emrys couldn't say anything. *We do this again and again—we bow and scrape and serve, and we know it always ends the same—they worship us as gods until truth returns, and then we fall. Why do we do this? Why must the cycle continue?* "Why are you here?"

"The same reason as you. I need an army."

"This is my army. He promised me—he swore I could be the one to invade Taura. This creature is mine—even Aldora—"

Bachi laughed. The raw burns on his face split open and oozed blood and pus. "You believe him? He lies not only to these people, but to us. I take no promises at face value. When will you learn? You have to take what you want. Take this body, for instance. I could have found some other body that would challenge your little creature, but I thought this would help me stay hidden until the time is right. I have things I'm doing back on Taura, and I don't need that creature breathing down my neck."

He's right. Emrys knew it. Those of their kind—the Forbidden, souleaters, immortals, servants of the fallen god—they were all beholden to Namha's wishes. *The price for being what we are—for our immortality, for our strength, we must beg for what we want. What he's promised us.* Emrys' stomach twisted again. "Taura is mine."

"Taura is Namha's. We exist to serve." He paused. "You have something planned."

"I need an army. This is my army."

"Hmm. I need an army, too." Bachi nodded toward the men in the practice field. "We could split up these people. Send your creature to the coast. Have him prepare to invade Taura. I'll make sure I'm along for the trip. You take the rest of the Nar Sidhe and do whatever you planned to do. What was it?"

Emrys mulled over his words. *Taura is mine. I will have it once more—*

I've seen it. But perhaps I should let them think it's theirs. I might still be able to salvage this—if I can build more of an army. He turned to Bachi. "I plan to finish what I started."

"Ah, yes. The girl." He grinned that grotesque smile once again. "She still lives? Your plan to send her to Tal'Amun failed?"

Emrys didn't speak. He didn't need to. Bachi already knew the answer.

"You believe our enemy still has his hand upon her? That he won't allow her to be destroyed yet?"

Emrys' jaw tightened. "I do not know. She is riding toward the lost tribe."

Bachi sucked in a breath. "If she reaches them—"

"You do not need to tell me." *If she grows powerful, she can control the ravens.* "I'd hoped she wouldn't find them, but they found her. Her bond awakened, and she'll soon come into her power."

Bachi grunted. He licked what was left of his lips. "Destroy her or her people—it makes no difference. If you can do one of those things, you may yet find some sympathy from our master."

"Perhaps." *And then I might earn what was mine in the first place.* "What are you doing on Taura?"

"Ensuring our people are protected when they invade. The wards are weakening."

"They've been weakening for years."

"I'm helping them along." Bachi stood silent for some time. "I have to say, it really was one of our mistress' more brilliant ideas to use Duke Mac Niall to sire you. You look just like his son."

Emrys frowned. "He's taller."

"The woman's body—the one Aldora used—she was tribal?"

"Yes. Under a glamour. The duke thought it was his wife." *And all the while, his wife lay bleeding to death in a field. And because she died, he sired the true raven on Maeve. If we had left it alone—if we'd just chosen another body—* But in truth, who could say what might have been. There was only what was.

"You can compensate for the height with evil and mayhem. People are easily swayed. They don't notice things like height. Get some tattoos that match his."

Emrys twisted his mouth. "I hate tattoos."

Bachi clapped Emrys on the shoulder. "I need to get back to my little healers. I wonder when they'll figure out that I'm faking some of my pain just to get them to soothe me more." He shuffled away.

Emrys moved into the light of the village and over to the practice field.

Matthias stood with his arms folded, watching the Nar Sidhe run through physical maneuvers. He noticed Emrys and walked through the men on the field to Emrys' side, a fierce grin fixed on his face. He gestured around. "It's happened—just as you said. They flocked to me."

"You've done well. You're ready."

The hunger in his eyes gave even Emrys pause. "Tell me."

I could steal him now, Emrys thought. *I could take him north with me. He will do anything I ask. But if he stays here ....* "I have a job for you."

CHAPTER SEVEN

The woman promised us joy, but also sadness. She said our hearts would be rent as no parents' since the Breaking. But when my wife saw the child, her heart was already bound.
— Journal of King Cedric Mac Roy

Igraine pushed open Repha Felix's door without waiting for a response to her knock. She dropped the weathered Tal'Amuni book on his desk and pointed. "I've finished it. And I understand. You think I'm Syrafi." She shifted her weight, and the leather strip that held the animstone around her ankle tightened. *Myths and fairy stories. This isn't what he thinks.* "I manage to resist an unknown poison, and I wear a rare stone, and you think that means my blood isn't human?"

"How is your leg?"

"My leg is fine."

"It took you quite some time to read this book," he said.

"I've had duties."

"It's been three weeks. Your leg is long since healed from the arrow wound, and Ronan Kerry has taken many of your duties away and given them to Cormac." He folded his hands in front of him. "What do you fear, your highness?"

The loss of my family, my history. That everything I thought was true isn't. My future as queen, as wife, even as a mother. Losing Braedan. She lifted her chin. "Familiar speech, repha. Are we so close as that, then?"

"I intended no offense, your highness. Forgive me." He gestured to a seat. "Please. I just started a pot of tea. Join me, and we'll discuss the evidence at hand."

Igraine sat. "I don't want tea. I want oiska."

Felix chuckled softly. "The only oiska I have is for medicinal purposes," he said. A kettle boiled over the low fire in his hearth, and he removed it and poured the water into a teapot. "There's a damp chill in the air today. A cup of tea will warm you."

Igraine folded her hands in her lap and stared at the rivers of rain that streamed down the windows of the repha's office. *A damp chill, he says.* "This day has a damp chill the way a court gossip has a few secrets."

He set a cup before her. "You have had a bad morning?"

Igraine shrugged. *A bad month. The morning was only the culmination.* "It would appear one of my ladies has run away with one of Ronan Kerry's guards."

Felix put a hand over his heart. "The impulsiveness of young love, yes?"

"Young love does not braid my hair."

"You have other ladies."

"For the moment." *Until Ronan Kerry decides that I should be sent back to Eirya.*

In the nearly four months she'd been in the castle, Igraine had gone from captive to ambassador to future queen. She'd also suffered three attempts on her life, the loss of a good friend, the absence of her lover and betrothed, the slow erosion of her power, and now, the speculation that she wasn't even human. After Felix had seen the murky gray stone she wore around her ankle, he'd speculated that her mother might have made her wear it to hide her magic blood. He gave her a book of history written by a Tal'Amuni eunuch and told her to read it and discuss it with him.

Igraine had read the book. *Three times. And still, no answers.* She twisted her mouth. *Well, no clear answers. Only speculation.* She leaned forward and opened the book, turning pages until she found the passage that gave her the most pause. "This," she said, resting one finger on the page. "This. 'As the single most powerful fighting force on the side of truth and hope, the Syrafi have yet some role to play in the battle for control of this world. While it may be too much to speculate that the fate of humanity rests on choices made by these creatures, as some who worship these beings are prone to attest, it is possible there is some key role yet to be played by those who bear Syrafi blood.'" She looked up. "You think I may have something to do with this final fate of humanity?"

"You have said you wished to be useful, my lady."

"Useful, yes. I'm not certain I hoped to be a key character in some world-wide cataclysmic event."

Felix poured tea into her cup. "There is no guarantee that you are the one intended to fill this key role."

"But it is what you believe, isn't it?"

He dripped honey into his tea and stirred. When he picked up his cup and leaned back in his chair, he inclined his head. "I do. Yes."

Igraine sighed. "There is really only one way to know. I have to remove the stone and let this power quicken. If it is there at all."

"I would caution against that for now, your highness," Felix said. "That is, if you truly have some affection for the king. You are in a position now where you can do good—help him keep his throne. If you were to allow this power to quicken, who knows where it may lead you?"

She stared down at the tea leaves gradually settling on the bottom of the tea cup. "I must ask, repha. How did you know about the stone?"

The rain pounded the window in the silence that followed. "I am an educated man," Felix finally said.

"I am an educated woman, and I had never heard of it."

"It would not be too much to say that I have some previous experience with animstones."

"Where?"

"Another time. I heard there is a new Eiryan ambassador in Torlach."

Igraine sipped her tea to give herself a moment to respond. "Yes," she finally said. "The letter came this morning."

"You do not sound pleased, highness."

Igraine pursed her lips. *To say the least.* "The new ambassador is an old acquaintance. We have not always had an amicable relationship."

"Ahh." Felix sipped his tea. "Perhaps we both have things to keep to ourselves."

Igraine set her tea down and stood. She pointed at the book. "I want to know more about that. I want to know just where I came from—what you think I am."

Felix spread his hands. "What more can I tell you, highness? Should you not ask your family?"

"My family would have told me something by now."

"Not if they were trying to protect you."

"My father didn't want me to come here. If he had wanted to protect me, why didn't he tell me this news before I left Eirya? Why didn't my mother say something? My family wanted me to stay on Eirya—to wed a noble son and have children for the crown. For my father's legacy. They would have said something."

Felix stood as well. "Forgive me, highness," he said. "But if they knew you were Syrafi, they would also know that you cannot bear children." He paused. "Have you never wondered why they did not fight your decision to serve the kirok?"

Igraine turned away from Felix. "I have to prepare for a banquet. Chancellor Kerry is welcoming the new ambassador." She left the room amid feeble protestations.

In her chambers, Igraine told her ladies to prepare a bath while she retreated to her bedchamber to compose herself. *Rory Nolan. Alshada, you have a cruel humor. I can't let Kerry know about my history with him, but how will I keep myself together around Rory? Perhaps he's grown fat and pox-ridden in our time apart. 'Twould help, to be sure.* She picked up the letter from her father and read it again.

It had taken some time to even open the letter when she first received it. She had expected chastisement, anger, pleas for her return to Maghara and the Citadel—anything but what she read.

> *To His Majesty, King Braedan Mac Corin of Taura,*
> *And Her Highness, Princess Royale of Eirya, Igraine Mac Roy:*
>
> *This letter serves as notice that a new Eiryan Ambassador has arrived in the harbor of Torlach and requests audience with your royal persons at the earliest convenience. Duke Riordan Nolan of Falcon Heights awaits your pleasure aboard the royal transport Red Vengeance IES. He requests heavy guard sent to the harbor at once to escort him to the Eiryan residence in Torlach.*
> *It shall be considered an act of war by Taura should the Duke's person be harmed in any way. Her Highness shall also be aware that she is considered under suspicion of treason for the death of Duke Duncan Guinness.*
>
> *In Eiryan Service,*
>
> *King Cedric Mac Roy*

She sighed. *He sends Rory. Is it punishment or temptation?*

She met Rory when she was sixteen, but at that time, he was a man grown, a merchant who came and went with little more than polite interest in her. When she was eighteen, he returned to attend a royal celebration, and they began their scandalous affair that night in a quiet boarding house not far from the Citadel. He stayed in Maghara for three months, and hardly a night went by that Igraine didn't sneak out to meet him in that boarding house.

When he finally couldn't put off his next voyage any longer, he asked her to marry him when he returned. She consented immediately. A duke's son and the princess royale—it was a good match. She would live in the north and give Rory as many children as he wished, she thought. *I would have played courtier for Rory. I would have been whatever Rory wished.*

But when he returned, he was distant and subdued, and when she confronted him, he confessed that he'd had other lovers on his voyage. He begged her to marry him anyway, but told her he could never promise his faithfulness—not as long as there were willing women in every port.

And likely, he's not changed, not in the slightest. Still, he was Eiryan, and she needed to know he would be her ally should everything in Torlach fall apart. *But I can't be alone with him, and I can't allow him to pursue me. Formality is the key.*

By the time her guard Aiden arrived to escort her to the banquet, Igraine had composed herself in preparation of seeing Rory again. Aiden bowed and offered her his arm. "Your highness," he said. "The Lord High Chancellor requests a word before the banquet."

"Very well."

They found Chancellor Kerry at his desk, dressed in his formal livery and gold and purple sash. He stood upon her entry and bowed stiffly. "My lady. You look ravishing, as always."

"I thank you, my lord."

He gestured to her seat and then sat across from her. "I received word from my nephew."

Her heart skipped, and her fingers tightened on the arms of the chair. "Tell me what's happened."

"His highness was unable to bring the tribes and the Mac Rian house to peace with each other. The tribe and Mac Rian went to battle. Mac Rian and his daughter were killed, and his highness struck a bargain to restore all of the northern holdings to the Mac Niall house—assuming his coronation, of course. He's been trying to get the affairs of both holdings in order for the new duke, Connor Mac Niall."

Igraine allowed herself a relieved sigh. "Thank the gods," she whispered. "Was there no word for me? A message—anything?"

"No, my lady. I'm sorry. Perhaps he's too busy to write." He paused. "The king will be delayed in his return to Torlach. Duke Fingall is rattling his sword—making noise about withdrawing his support for the throne. I sent word suggesting that the king meet with him before returning. My only fear is that he'll be held up in the north for the winter."

"And while he's gone, you'll take more control of his throne, then?"

Kerry leaned back and folded his hands. "You overstep your bounds, my lady."

She felt her jaw tighten. *No—hold your tongue, foolish girl. This is not the moment.* "The banquet, my lord? What will you be expecting of me?"

His mouth twitched as if he'd been robbed of a long-awaited fight. "It's not I who expect you, my lady. It's this new ambassador. It was he who requested your presence. Do you know him?"

She swallowed hard and hoped he didn't notice the pause. "Who was it again?"

"A man by the name of Duke Riordan Nolan. Do you know him?"

Igraine tried to calm the flutter of her belly. "I knew him in my youth," she said. *No sense in lying, but I won't tell him everything. But how discreet will Rory be?* "His father and mine were friends, but the Nolan holdings are in the far north, so I saw him little until he took a merchant ship. Once he came to Maghara Harbor more often, he visited the Citadel and shared news of his travels with my brothers and my father. I think my brother Ian even spent some time patrolling the Galoch Sea for pirates with him." She paused. "I'd not realized the old duke passed on. 'Tis a shame. My father has lost two friends now in so short a time."

Kerry watched her, tapping a rolled up parchment against his chin. "Hmm. Yes." He stood and offered her his arm. "We shouldn't keep him waiting then, should we?"

She suppressed a grimace and took the offered arm, steeling herself for her first sight of Rory as they walked to the main hall. The steward opened the door and announced them, and Igraine's eyes fell on Rory Nolan for the first time in more than six years. *I suppose fat and pox-ridden was too much to hope for.*

Still hale and muscular, even nearing his thirtieth year, Rory towered over most of the other men in the room. His long black hair fell straight and heavy to his shoulders, and his beard couldn't completely hide the dark tan of a man used to spending his days on the deck of a ship. He wore a red wool doublet, black breeches, a ceremonial sword, and a silver ambassador's sash, and the brisk aroma of salt air and freshly mended sails seemed to hover around him.

His deep blue eyes glinted with mischief when he took her hand and bowed, and every bit of resolve she had to be proper and distant faded when he put his lips to her knuckles. "My dearest lady," he said, lifting her hand and cupping his own around it. "'Tis been too long."

Dear spirits, what this man does to me! Though his demeanor and actions were entirely proper, Igraine couldn't stop herself from retreating, just for a moment, into memories, particularly a memory of one passion-filled evening spent on a hillside in Eirya. She took a deep breath, mindful of Kerry's proximity, and forced a calm smile. "My Lord Nolan. I was so sorry to hear of your father's passing."

"Thank you. I was at sea when it happened," Rory said. "Your father's messenger met me at the docks when I last put in at Maghara Harbor." He took a step closer to her and lowered his voice. "There are rumors, my lady," he murmured.

"Rumors?"

"That you have chosen a husband."

She focused on maintaining a studied, cool composure. "I—"

But Chancellor Kerry saved her from responding. "My lord," Kerry said. Rory turned to him, and Kerry gave a slight bow, which Rory returned. "May I offer the condolences of the Taurin Crown on the death of your father? He had a reputation as a fair and honest man. I'm sure he will be missed."

"I thank you, Chancellor Kerry," Rory said. He gestured to the long table where Cormac, Lord Seannan and Aislinn, and other lords and ladies were being seated and served. "May I escort you to the table, your highness?"

Igraine took his arm, and Rory led her to a seat next to him, just to the right of Kerry's head seat. Cormac sat on the other side of Kerry, who remained standing to address the company. "My lords and ladies," he said, raising a goblet. "It is with great joy that I welcome our new ambassador from Eirya, Lord Riordan Nolan, Duke of Falcon Heights. In our king's absence, I raise a toast to the ambassador and pray that his presence here is the first step in healing the broken bonds between our two countries."

A smattering of applause greeted him, and Rory raised his goblet. Igraine noticed the forced smile on his lips. A chill shivered down her spine. *Did my father send him to heal relations or bring word of war?* The truth was that Rory had no training as a diplomat. *What if he's here merely to force me to return to Eirya? Is this an act of war or of peace?*

Kerry sat again, and servants brought out the first course. Igraine drank. "Tell me what news you bring from my father, Lord Nolan."

"I'd hoped to wait for a more private venue, my lady," he said. "But since you ask, I see no reason to demur." He looked at Kerry. "King Cedric demands answers, my lord. He wishes to know why his own daughter and his most trusted nobles have so much trouble on Taura of late. He demands that I speak with the king personally."

Kerry took a bite of pork and let Rory wait while he chewed. "Since the king is traveling right now, I'll be speaking on his behalf as Lord High Chancellor," Kerry said.

Rory leaned back in his chair, the picture of confidence. "Then perhaps you can tell me why our royal lady is first taken prisoner, then nearly killed on the very night that Lord Guinness is killed. Now I hear that another attempt was made on her life after the king left Torlach." He sipped his wine. "If I didn't know better, I'd think that our years of alliance were at risk, chancellor."

Kerry grimaced, but he covered it with a shift of his weight in the chair. "I assure you, ambassador—nothing is further from the truth. The Taurin crown values our alliance with Eirya above all others."

Igraine put down her knife, her appetite waning as tension rose. She placed a hand on Rory's arm. "My lord, these incidents were not the king's doing, nor Chancellor Kerry's."

"Have you discovered who committed these crimes, my lady? Who wishes you dead?"

Her stomach twisted, and she pulled her arm away. "No."

"Your father wants to know why you would marry this usurper and stay in a place where you are clearly unwelcome. I confess—I wonder the same thing. What reason do you have to stay?"

For love—to build something with a man who values me. "I would think my father would be grateful I'd finally found a man to wed."

Rory drank, and a long silence filled the air. "He is," he said at last. "He is just unconvinced that he can support this union."

"Then I will have to convince him," Igraine said, squaring her shoulders.

Kerry laughed. "You have so much confidence in your abilities to influence, my lady. You might hold some sway with your father as yet, but do not underestimate the power of my influence over the king. I am not yet convinced of the advantages of a union between you and my nephew, either."

"He said you approved."

"I did," Kerry said. "But there is an unresolved matter of some indiscretion on your part."

"Indiscretion?" Rory asked.

"Your relationship with the guard, Logan Mac Kendrick," Kerry said.

Rory put down his knife and leaned forward. "What're ye saying, my lord?" he asked.

Kerry turned his cold gaze toward Rory. "I am saying, ambassador, that you and the lady should have a discussion about what constitutes proper behavior for a princess—especially one who wishes to wed my nephew."

Rory sat up straighter and pointed a finger at Kerry. "You'll not be speaking so to the lady, Kerry. The words 'war' and 'insult' have not been bandied lightly in my king's court of late. Ye'll not be giving us another reason to mistrust ye, aye?"

Igraine pushed Rory's arm down. "My lords, there is no need for posturing. Mac Kendrick was never more to me than a guard." She sipped her wine again, forcing it over the lump in her throat at the thought of Logan's escape from a headsman's ax. *Change the subject.* She put her goblet down. "Duke Nolan, have you brought formal word of my father's intent toward Taura?"

"I have, and the documents are within Chancellor Kerry's possession. But I'll be sharing them publicly as well—to be certain all is in the open, of course."

Kerry inclined his head. "Of course."

Rory looked at Igraine. "Your father sends warning that any harm that befalls an Eiryan citizen here in Torlach is to be treated as an act of aggression against the Eiryan crown. He says he'll not be turning down the king's request for your hand yet, but he'll be needing some concessions—assurances, something—to show that the Taurin crown still values its relationship with Eirya."

She steadied her hands on her goblet. "Concessions. Assurances. He'll be treating Taura as a supplicant?"

"He will."

"No one treats Taura as a supplicant," Kerry said. "May I suggest, ambassador, it's foolish of your king to treat our crown this way when we have his royal daughter in our care."

"Threats do not become you, my lord. If Princess Igraine is under threat here, I'll be taking her back to Eirya whether she wishes it or no."

"Rory Nolan, you'd not dare," Igraine said.

He leaned forward, his mouth set in a grim line. "Tempt me, your highness."

Kerry stood. "This meeting is over. Cormac, see that the ambassador is escorted to his house and assigned a heavy guard. The Raven Throne will not be spoken to in this way without consequences."

Rory stood as well. "There's no need for guards, my lord. I'll stay in my house and await your pleasure. But I'll be taking the princess with me." Rory put a hand on her arm.

She shook his hand away and lifted her chin. "No. You've no right to be telling me what to do, Rory Nolan—none. And neither does my father." She stepped away from the table before he could reach for her again.

"I've every right, love." He pulled a piece of parchment from his doublet and dropped it on the table. The king's seal stared up at her. "Your father orders you home, Igraine. It's time to leave Taura."

CHAPTER EIGHT

The Syraf weeps for her children.
— Second Book of the Wisdomkeepers

Igraine stared at the parchment and seal for a moment while she gathered her composure. "I fear I've lost my appetite, my lords and ladies. Good night." She spun and strode out of the audience hall with Aiden and her ladies on her heels.

In the corridor, she heard the door open and close behind her. "Igraine, wait." Rory's voice echoed after her. "Igraine. Let me speak with ye, lady."

"I've no mind to listen to your veiled insults and jealous anger, and I'll not be after obeying any foolish order from my father," she said. "If ye wish to speak with me, ye'll go through formal channels. You can arrange an audience through Lord Rowan. Good night, my lord."

His footsteps followed her, and then there was a clamor of steel and a scuffle of feet. She turned in time to see Rory's arms held tight by two guards as Aiden held his sword tip at Rory's throat. Rory didn't struggle, but he did twitch toward her and flash a charming smile. "My lady," he said. "A moment. Just a moment. For the past."

Her jaw tightened, and she watched him, hesitating. Cormac emerged from the audience hall. "Your highness," he said. "Is there a problem?"

The guards waited. *A moment for the past.* "No," she said. "Ambassador Nolan would like to deliver a few personal messages from my family, if Chancellor Kerry wouldn't mind."

Cormac nodded. "A guard will be waiting to escort you home when you are finished, my lord," he said, then bowed and returned to the hall.

The guards let Rory go, and he rubbed his wrists as he fell in step next to her. The group proceeded to Igraine's study, and Igraine ushered Rory in to have a seat near her desk. "Ye'll stay, Aiden. I'll not be having it bandied about that I've entertained the Eiryan ambassador alone."

Rory grinned again. "Echoes of your father in your words, my lady."

"What do you want?"

He spread his hands. "Only your happiness. You've headed down a fool-hardy course, Igraine. I would spare you the pain of it, if I could. So would your father."

She folded her arms. "And ye'll be after getting between my legs again, aye? Leave it, lad. 'Twill never happen again. Ye lost your chance with me when you dropped your breeches for every whore from Maghara Harbor to Dal'Imur. Ye've likely got a string of by-blows all over the world."

"Your lilt is showing."

She scoffed and tossed her head. "If you've only come to vex me, you can go, Lord Nolan. I'll write my father and you can carry the message back to him: I'll not be leaving Braedan or Taura—orders or no."

He stood and approached her. Aiden twitched. "Dismiss your guard," Rory said. He lowered his voice. "Let me say hello properly, lady."

The timbre of his voice sent a wave of desire through her body. *I worry about Braedan's faithfulness even as this man tempts me back into his bed. What a strumpet I am!* She stepped away from Rory. "Have ye forgotten the last time I saw ye?"

"No, lass. I remember it all too well." He leaned down close to her ear. "I often remember how much fun it was to argue with you—and to make up."

She pointed to the door. "Out, Rory. Now. Get your arse back to Eirya if ye'd like. I'll not be seeing ye again."

"Igraine, wait." He straightened and composed his face into a more serious expression. "Wait, lass. I'm sorry. I'll behave. Just give me a moment."

She sat at her desk and crossed her arms. "Speak, then."

"First, you must know that your father does not expect you to come back to Eirya without force or a good reason." He removed a piece of parchment from his doublet. "'Tis not from your father, love. 'Tis from your mother."

Igraine took the parchment and broke the royal seal.

> *My dearest daughter,*
>
> *It is with the deepest concern and love for you that I share these words. I know that you must care very deeply for this king, for your heart has never been an easy one to win. But there are things I would tell you before you commit to sharing your life with any man—things I*

should have told you many years ago.
Please, my daughter—come home, just for
a time. For a few months. Your king can
wait.
   I would come to you, but your father
fears for my safety, and with good rea-
son. We beg Alshada's protection over
you every day. Your brothers speak of
storming Torlach to bring you back, but
your father holds them at bay. Consider
returning with Rory.
   My head and heart are full of words
for you, but I cannot share them on pa-
per. Please, Igraine. Come home.

Your mother

Igraine folded the parchment and brushed tears from her cheeks. *What if Felix was right?* She turned so that Rory couldn't see her. "And what else?"

"What else?"

"I know my parents wish me back on Eirya, but I knew that before I even saw you. I know that you'll be treating Taura as supplicant. What else must I know?"

Silence hovered around them. "You should know that I'm sorry, lass," he finally said, quiet. He stood and put his hands on her shoulders. "I do recall the last time we saw each other, and I regret it every day. I'm sorry I hurt you, Igraine. I wish it had been different."

She shook his hands away. "Aiden, escort the ambassador out."

"Then that's it, aye?" Rory said.

She turned to face him. "Go back to your house, Rory. If you wish to see me again, you can arrange it through formal channels."

His jaw twitched, but he held his words and bowed deeply, his hair falling down around his jaw. "As you wish, your highness." Aiden opened the door, and the men walked out of the study.

Igraine collapsed in her chair as soon as Rory left the room. She put her hands over her face and sighed. *Rory will not give up so easily. If he wishes me back in his bed, this will not be the end of his pursuit.*

Memories of their last meeting swam in her head. He'd first caught her up in his arms, whispered his desire and love, and taken her to bed. It was only later that he'd slipped and revealed a dalliance off the coast of Espara. "It was the Aldorean Feast, love," he said in his defense. "A man can't be expected to resist when every woman on the island is half undressed and randy as a spring ram."

I could have forgiven one dalliance, she thought. But the more she'd questioned him, the more he'd revealed other moments of revelry and drunken indiscretions, always using the excuse that a man couldn't be expected to go without a woman for the months of a typical sea voyage. She stood and went to her window, staring out over the city and to the hills beyond. *I wasn't enough to keep Rory faithful. How can I expect a man like Braedan to be faithful—a man as handsome as he is, and a king above all? He's probably already found a string of willing whores.*

"My lady?"

Gwyn approached, and Igraine turned. "Yes, Gwyn. What is it?"

"The kitchens found a serving girl to fill in until you appoint another lady. Shall I send her in?"

Igraine sat at her desk again. "Of course, Gwyn. Would you please fetch a small meal from the kitchens? I didn't eat much at supper. And please let the ladies know that I'll be about preparing for bed after I eat."

Gwyn curtsied and opened the door for a young woman with dark blonde hair and green eyes. "Your highness, this is Nimue."

The girl gave Igraine a perfect, graceful curtsy. "A pleasure, your highness."

Igraine tipped her head. "Do I hear a lilt? Are you Eiryan?"

"No, your highness. But I am from the Ragged Isles. 'Tis said my folk sound a bit Eiryan, aye?"

Igraine smiled. "You sound as if you could be my sister, dear. 'Twill be lovely to hear a lilt that's not trying to seduce me."

Nimue gave her a tilted, confused grin. "Beg pardon, my lady?"

Igraine waved her hand. "Leave it. Have you served a noblewoman before?"

"I have, your highness. The Duchess of Starling's Cross—Lady Dylan—I served in her court. My father is one of the duke's vassals."

Duke Dylan never bent his knee to Braedan—not formally. Is this another attempt to monitor me? Igraine smiled. "I look forward to your company, Nimue."

Igraine's sleep was fitful and broken that night, and in the morning, she woke in a temper she was certain would not win her any friends in the castle. After she had eaten and dressed, she settled in to read for a time and was almost immediately interrupted by Nimue. "Pardon, my lady," the girl said when Igraine acknowledged her. "The seneschal requires an audience. May I show him in?"

Igraine heaved a deep sigh. Her alliance with Cormac had been uneasy since the day of Logan's escape. Igraine had no illusions about Cormac's loyalty to her. She knew that the seneschal was loyal only to Braedan, and she suspected that the moment the king returned to Torlach, Cormac would begin a campaign to rid him of her company. *One problem at a time,* she thought. She entered her study and forced a smile when she saw Cormac. "Lord Rowan."

"My lady," he said, greeting her with a bow. "Thank you for seeing me. I apologize for the early hour."

"Of course." She gestured to a chair. "Please, have a seat."

Cormac remained standing, hands clasped behind his back. He wet his lips. "I will stand, your highness."

"Very well. What was it you needed?"

He reached into his doublet and removed a piece of parchment. "This came for me yesterday, my lady. It came with the word from Kiern. I thought you should see it."

Igraine's hand froze on the broken green seal. "The king," she whispered.

"Read it, my lady."

Igraine's hands shook as she opened the parchment. Braedan's unruly scrawl filled the paper with administrative minutiae and random instructions. *He knows nothing of the attack on the castle or the accusations against Logan.* She folded the paper and set it on the desk. "Logan hasn't reached him." she whispered.

"It appears he hasn't."

"There's still time. He may have reached Kiern after Braedan sent this letter."

"The king is already gone. He's left for Salmon Springs."

"Chancellor Kerry told me."

Cormac hesitated for a long moment. "My lady, the king's future is uncertain."

"What are you saying?"

He wet his lips. "I will not serve Ronan Kerry willingly, but if the king does not return, I am prepared to do what I must to keep my position."

She leaned forward. "And what is that, my lord?"

He never flinched, never twitched. He kept his hands tightly clenched. "There are still rumors about you and Mac Kendrick. There are witnesses. And if I need to secure my position with Ronan Kerry, I will not hesitate to reveal what I know about your indiscretions."

Her stomach churned. "There are no indiscretions."

He gave her a thin smile. "The words of a tainted woman rarely hold much weight." He leaned forward. "The king is gone. He may not return. I have resigned myself to serving Ronan Kerry if I must, and Ronan Kerry will not tolerate you remaining on Taura if he becomes king. I intend to secure my position with him."

"What are you asking of me?"

"You have a choice: return to Eirya with Rory Nolan, or endure the humiliation and consequences of having your indiscretions made public."

"And if Braedan comes back? What will you tell him if I'm gone?"

The door to the study opened again, and Nimue entered. She offered a brief curtsy and began to tidy the room. Cormac wet his lips and lowered his voice. "I will tell the king the truth."

"Which truth is that?"

"That you returned to Eirya with your former lover. That your heart was as fickle as your chastity."

Igraine's heart beat faster. "How did you know ...?"

"It was not difficult to surmise based on what I saw last night." He leaned forward and lowered his voice. "There are other noblewomen, my lady. The king will find someone to give him an heir."

Igraine opened her mouth to respond, but Nimue stepped into the gap. "Pardon, my lord," she said to Cormac. "But the lady is looking pale. Perhaps you can continue this conversation anon?"

Gods bless this girl! "I am weary. Please excuse me, Cormac."

Cormac picked up his parchment. "I await your decision, my lady. You have until tomorrow." He left her study.

Igraine let out a long sigh. "I cannot thank you enough for that," she said to Nimue.

"It's the role of a lady-in-waiting to protect the princess, aye?" She folded her hands and tipped her head in consideration. "You could use a restorative, my lady. Tea? With brandy?"

This girl—how does she know me so well? "Yes, Nimue. That will do nicely."

Nimue began heating water over the fire. When she brought Igraine's tea, she curtsied and folded her hands. "Will there be anything else, your highness?"

"Nimue, stay for a time. We should become better acquainted."

"Of course, your highness."

"Fetch a cup for yourself, dear." Nimue moved away to find a teacup. "You handled Cormac as if you were the princess, not I."

"Lady Dylan taught me well."

"Did you enjoy the Dylan estates?"

"I did. The lady was an easy mistress."

"Why did you leave?"

Nimue sat across from Igraine and sipped her tea. "I was needed here, your highness."

Igraine frowned. "What do you mean?"

"I mean, in the city—I have family here. My aunt was ill. I came to help the family, and when she recovered, I looked for a position in the castle." She shrugged. "I was needed here."

Of course. "You remind me of someone," Igraine said.

"Who is that, my lady?"

"My brother's wife. We were close as sisters."

"Do you miss Eirya, your highness?"

Igraine shrugged. "Sometimes. But here, I feel I have a purpose." *If I don't lose my position—or my life.* She leaned forward. "Nimue, I need your help. But I need to know you will not betray my confidence."

"Of course, my lady," Nimue said. "What is it?"

Igraine licked her lips. "I need you to be my eyes and ears in the castle." *I need to take charge of this. If I don't take control of this castle, there will be nothing left for Braedan to return to. And I can't wait for Logan to reach him or send me word—he would have sent something by now if he'd had any kind of success.* "Ronan Kerry is after trying to ally himself with the Seannans. Why else would he keep them here for so long? I need to know the truth of Ronan Kerry's relationship with Aislinn Seannan. And I need to know who still has sympathy for me—besides Aiden and Braedan's few remaining guards."

Nimue nodded. "Very well, my lady, but why me? Why not one of your other ladies?"

Igraine took her hands. "A girl like you? Pretty, witty, competent? You can gain access to any room in the castle, I promise you. Even if you just dress as a serving girl and slip in and out of the kitchens and dining halls, you can discover much news for me. And Gwen and Deirdre would not be trusted by others. They have been with me too long. You, though—you are not well-known in the castle. You still have freedom to move about quite a bit." She squeezed Nimue's hands. "Please—tell me you'll do this for me. Tell me you'll help me keep my king's throne. I promise you, there will be ample reward when he returns to Torlach."

"Of course, your highness. But I feel I should ask—is there anything you haven't told me? Is there anything I should know before you send me off to these duties?"

Igraine thought of the leather strap around her ankle. "No. Nothing."

Nimue gave Igraine a slow nod of acquiescence. "What would you like me to do first?"

CHAPTER NINE

When the tainted soul is cleansed, new waters will flow in the land.
— Svek prophecy

Logan walked through the hound tribe's village with his armload of firewood, ignoring the whispers and speculation of the tribal people. He dumped the wood on the ground outside Hrogarth's hut and started to stack it in a neat pile. The white wool kaltan, too short by inches for a man of his height, skimmed the ground when he crouched to pick up stray pieces of wood. *If they're hoping I'll bend over and give them something to snicker about, they're as foolish as their traitha.*

He'd been stuck in the hound tribe's village for several weeks, ever since he'd escaped Torlach with Cormac and Igraine's help. He'd used the old Brae Sidh tunnels under the castle to travel well outside the walls, whispering the words that would open the door to freedom. The old rush of magic in his blood awoke memories, and he stuffed them away, reminding himself repeatedly that he was not Sidh, that the memories were not his. He walked in the pre-dawn light until he reached a farmhouse, and there he took plain clothes and a sturdy mare and left the farmer a pile of coins worth more than what he'd taken. He stuffed his purse and the letter addressed to Braedan in his tunic and set out at a gallop, listening for sounds of pursuit.

The main road being too well-traveled, he ducked into the great forest at his earliest opportunity. Though he wished to avoid the tribes altogether, he knew they would likely find him. He hoped he could at least convince them he meant no harm and only needed to hide for a few days until he felt safe enough to risk traveling on the main road again. *But I should have known that Alshada has a cruel humor for one like me.*

He reached the edge of the great forest as the sun drifted down to the horizon at the end of the second day of travel from Torlach. In moments, tribesmen surrounded him, and he lifted his hands against the spears and arrows pointed at him. "I come alone and in peace. I mean no harm."

A man wearing a linen tunic and a leather kaltan stepped out of the group. His auburn hair was braided in dozens of strands over his head, and his face was tattooed with the web that indicated he was a chieftain. "Your king promised his Taurin dogs would stay out of our forest," he said.

Logan grimaced. *It had to be him, didn't it?* "I am no Taurin dog. I'm just a man needing shelter. Sanctuary."

"I saw you. In Torlach. You were in the castle. You were one of his men." He gestured, and two tribesmen stepped toward Logan.

Logan dismounted and threw aside his weapons as a show of faith. "Please, listen. The king intends to restore relations with you, Traitha Hrogarth. I am no enemy of the tribes. I swear to you, I need only sanctuary—just for a few days, just long enough to hide from those who pursue me."

"You spy on us—on the tribes."

"No, I swear—I only seek the king. Someone is trying to steal his throne and his woman, and I need to warn him."

"Why should I believe you?"

"Because if you don't, the man who wants to take the crown will destroy you."

Hrogarth snorted a laugh. "Destroy the tribes? It would take a greater man than any weak Taurin noble to destroy a people as ancient as the tribes. He would have to destroy the forest itself."

"What makes you think he wouldn't?"

Hrogarth said nothing. He responded by gesturing to his men to hold Logan's arms while he patted his tunic and breeches down for more weapons. He withdrew the coins and letter from Logan's tunic. "What's in here?" he asked, holding up the letter.

"A warning. The king's uncle wants his throne, and the woman the king wishes to wed is in danger of being forced to leave Taura."

Hrogarth stared at the seal. "Did you read this?"

"Of course not. It's sealed. I would not presume—"

"How do you know it says what you believe it says?"

"Why would the seneschal lie? He doesn't want Kerry on the throne—no one does."

Hrogarth drew his knife and sliced the seal on the parchment. His mouth turned down as he read, and he grunted. "Perhaps you should have read it." He handed the parchment to Logan.

Logan's stomach plummeted as he read.

> *You must return to Torlach immedi-*
> *ately. Your uncle seeks to challenge your*

*throne, and your princess is bedding her
way through your remaining guard. The
bearer of this letter was her favorite. He
has fallen from grace and was nearly beheaded, but I've allowed him to escape to
bring you this warning. Your majesty, all
we fought for is in danger. Take care of
this guard, and then return to Torlach to
reclaim your throne and send the strumpet back to her island. When your throne
is secure once more, we will take care of
the tribes.*

Your servant,
Cormac

Logan couldn't speak. Hrogarth took the letter and tucked it and the coins into his own clothes. "What does this mean, 'take care of the tribes'? Your king will come after us with his full forces? Eh? Where is he now?"

Say nothing. "I will speak only to King Braedan."

Hrogarth's jaw tightened. "I should kill you now. I told your king I would kill any Taurins in the forest. But you are close to him. You may yet prove valuable." He gestured to his men. "Bring him back to the village."

They put him in the white kaltan and linen tunic of an unblooded boy, and Hrogarth set him to work doing chores around the village. Day and night, the tribesmen guarded him, never letting him out of their sight. *Not that they need to,* Logan thought. There was no point in trying to escape. The tribesmen would find him in moments, and Hrogarth had made it clear that even an attempt at escape would mean his instant death. "We'll send your scalp to the king and your balls to the princess," he said. "Appropriate to send your horns to the man you cuckolded, eh?"

"I didn't cuckold him," Logan said. *Not that I wasn't tempted.* "The princess and I are friends, nothing more. I guarded her only."

But his protests held no sway with Hrogarth. Day after day, Logan found himself with endless duties and no weapons. They wouldn't even let him chop wood or use a pitchfork. He was left with children's chores—feeding chickens, stacking wood, washing clothes, milking goats. *My blade's been blooded more times than any of these men in this group, and he treats me as an unblooded boy. And I could destroy all of them if I cared to, if I let myself taste my power again. I'm a wolf hiding among dogs.*

At first, he'd hoped to gain Hrogarth's trust and speak sense to him. But as days and then weeks passed, Logan realized that Hrogarth was a barely contained barrel of pitch—dormant, but ready to explode at the first hint of fire—who would likely never ally himself with a Taurin guard. His wife, Alfrig, kept him in check, but about three weeks into Logan's stay with the hound tribe, Alfrig received word from their oldest daughter that she neared her time to birth another child. "I'll be with my daughters when they birth children," she told Hrogarth over their meal that night. She sat and gave Logan bread and meat. "She may have wed outside the tribe, but she is our daughter still. I'll not let another guardian attend her if I can help it."

Hrogarth stared at Alfrig for a long time. "I am never whole when you are away."

"I know," she said, her tone sympathetic. "I'll speak with Grytha. She can help."

Logan mused on the exchange for some time. It was a sweet sentiment, and one that any married couple might exchange. But Logan sensed something different between Hrogarth and Alfrig—a darkness, or a suggestion of a gap in Hrogarth's sanity in the absence of his wife.

In the days that followed Alfrig's departure, Logan kept his head low and his tone respectful, all the while looking for a way to escape quietly, easily, without risking Hrogarth's wrath. *All those years I wanted to die, and there was no one to take my life. Now I live in death's shadow, and I want to live.*

"Sidh boy."

"Don't call me Sidh." Logan straightened from his crouch and turned to the very pretty earth guardian Grytha. He dusted his hands on his kaltan. "I'm not Sidh."

"You have the blood. And I saw the stone around your ankle."

"My great-great-grandfather was Sidh. My blood never quickened." *Lies upon lies.*

"Then why wear the stone?"

"What do you want?"

Her wide mouth tightened into a frown. "Hrogarth wishes to speak with you."

"Where is he?"

"My hut. Come."

Logan followed her through the village with his day guard, Kyath, close behind him and found Hrogarth pacing in Grytha's hut, fists clenched at his side. An unfamiliar tribesman sat on the floor, hands bound behind him, a bruise rising on his cheek. Hrogarth whirled. "This boy," he said, waving a hand. "This messenger brings word from the wolf tribe. He says your king is in the north, that he's allied himself with the wolves and slaughtered his own noble filth, the Duke of Kiern."

Logan straightened his shoulders. "What of it?"

Hrogarth scowled. "What is his plan now, eh? Now that he has the allegiance of one of my traithas, will he infiltrate the whole forest? Destroy this ancient place? Give land to his favorites—land that doesn't belong to him?"

"I don't know his current plans, but I know he went north to see why your traitha and his noble couldn't keep peace. If he's allied himself with your traitha, it means he believes Duke Mac Rian was in the wrong."

Hrogarth paced again. "The wolf traitha, Edgar—he's always sympathized with Taurin nobles and the Sidh queen. He pictures himself between her legs. It makes him untrustworthy."

"I don't see why your issue with your traitha has anything to do with my king."

Hrogarth stopped pacing and stared at Logan. "He's called a council of the traithas. Edgar Wolfbrother expects me to go north to attend. What will I hear? Words of treason? Words of alliance with this Taurin whelp?" He didn't wait for an answer. "Grytha."

"Yes, traitha?"

"Prepare to go north. I will gather the warriors, and we will confront Edgar and this pretender king. You," he said, pointing at Logan. "You are the most valuable bargaining chip I have. You will come with us."

Thank the gods! "The letter?"

"I will keep the letter. I will let your king know how untrustworthy you are before I give you back to him." He looked at Grytha. "Treat the messenger's wounds, then prepare to leave tomorrow morning." He left the hut with Kyath in tow.

Grytha knelt next to the wounded wolf tribesman and started to clean his cut and bruised face. "I'm sorry for this," she told the young man. "He has not been stable since his wife left."

Logan stepped closer. "Why is he so unstable?"

She stiffened. "Don't you have chores to finish?"

"When someone escorts me back to the woodpile, I'll finish my chores."

She fell silent for several minutes, dabbing at the messenger's cuts with a cool, wet cloth. When she was done, she straightened and turned to Logan. "Come with me."

Outside the hut, Grytha set out at a slow walk next to Logan and spoke very quietly. "I can't decide if you are very brave or very foolish. A Taurin soldier living among tribal people, forced to wear the clothes of an unblooded boy. What are you about, Logan?"

"You're the first to honor me with my name. Even Alfrig wouldn't call me anything but Sidh or boy."

"She keeps peace with Hrogarth even when she disagrees with him," she said.

"You visit Hrogarth every morning. What is it you do for him in Alfrig's absence?"

She fell silent as they passed a warrior. "You picked a poor time to seek sanctuary in the hound tribe," she whispered. "Hrogarth has demons. Our best hope is for Alfrig to return."

Logan frowned. "Why?"

"She keeps his madness in check." She stared straight ahead as they walked, and when they came to the pile of wood he'd been stacking, she turned to him. "The traitha does not trust you, but I see good in you, Taurin. I will protect you as much as I am able." She walked away.

Logan let out a long breath. He didn't know whether to be happy or sad. *I'm going north. Finally. Even if I am a prisoner, at least there's a chance I'll find Braedan.* But his stomach twisted in fear as well. *Does Hrogarth see what I am? There's only one way that's possible, and if he's ravenmarked—* He shook his head. *I can't think about that. Focus on going north. I'll worry about the danger of traveling with one of the ravenmarked later.*

CHAPTER TEN

He brought me to his sanctuary and gave me healing.
— Songs of King Aiden

It took nine days of riding through bitter winds, sleet, snow, and ice for Mairead, Connor, Phinneas, and the lion tribesmen to finally arrive on the border of the lion tribe's territory. Mairead found those days challenging at best. Though Connor had been at peace when he took her out to see the sleigh deer, the Morrag's whispers had returned in full force by the next morning. He traveled in silence much of the time, occasionally riding or walking away from the group. When Mairead questioned him or expressed concern, he only said that sometimes, he just needed to be alone.

Phinneas had his own theory. "He tells me that the raven allows him to hear transgressions, thoughts—things that require justice. I believe he is merely trying to find some quiet away from the whispers and voices."

Whispers and voices. "Tell me true, Phinneas—is he mad?"

"No, my lady—at least, not yet." He paused. "Have you ever awakened with a numb arm or leg?"

"Of course."

"When it starts to feel again, the pain is excruciating. And it gets worse until it eases, and then you can feel normally again. Just so with Duke Mac Niall, my lady. He is feeling again. It will be painful before it eases."

She turned to him. "And what if it doesn't ease?"

He could not answer.

She wet her lips and crossed her arms. "Can your drugs do nothing more?"

"Apparently not, my lady. I cannot tell if it is his Sidh blood that negates their effects, or if it is simply the strength of the Morrag that overcomes them, but I hesitate to give him more. I don't know how much I can give before I hurt him." He paused. "And I am not convinced that I should keep her voice quiet. There is something he is meant to do. He—and you and I—can only postpone it."

She followed Connor at times, despite his request that she ride with the others or stay in the camp. Sometimes, he walked in silence, and she felt she was merely security that he didn't do himself harm. Other times, his steps gradually brightened, and he would take her hand or put an arm around her as they walked. On those walks, the former good humor and camaraderie they had shared while traveling returned, and she found herself beginning to trust that he would not leave again. *If he can help it, that is.*

Gareth treated Connor with respect, but Mairead had the impression that doing so was an act of extreme difficulty. Trypp seemed to warm to Connor the most easily, and Mairead noticed that he often volunteered to help Connor with hunting or various camp tasks. Gareth, for his part, stayed close to Mairead, and she wondered if the two men had decided that they were protecting Mairead in such a fashion. She trusted that Gareth had not revealed Connor's secret, but it wasn't hard to see how close to the edge of madness he walked.

Braun usually watched Connor from a distance, often toying with a blade while he did so. He and the other two tribesmen occasionally spoke with each other away from Mairead and Connor, all three of them casting furtive glances back. "They discuss whether to let me into their city," Connor said to Mairead one night. He picked a stick apart and threw pieces into the fire. "They don't know if they should trust me. Braun would prefer to gut me and leave me here, Trypp speaks for allowing me in, and Gareth can't decide."

Mairead listened to the edgy whispers from the group and tried to make out words, but she couldn't. "How do you know all of that?"

He shrugged. "She tells me."

Mairead shivered. *I share him with a spirit I can't even confront. How can I make a life with him if she's always in his head?* "Has Phinneas been able to help at all?"

"His drugs only helped that first day. There will be no ridding myself of her until ..." He gave a shuddering sigh. "Until she has her way. Until she is finished."

Mairead quickly decided she did not want to know what he meant.

If the days were merely challenging, the nights were almost unbearable. The tribesmen had brought small tents for protection in the worst weather, and they gave Mairead one of her own. Connor insisted on sleeping just outside her tent on the ground, and they often fell asleep close enough to whisper to each other through the hide. His restless sleep became worse each night. He barely slept more than a few hours, and that was broken and fitful. He often rose to walk away from the camp, and Mairead would offer up fervent prayers to Alshada to bring peace and comfort to Connor's spirit.

She followed him one night, a fur-lined cloak wrapped tight around her to ward off the snow and cold, and found him leaning against a tree dressed in only his breeches and boots. She wrapped a blanket around his shoulders. "You'll freeze."

"I don't get cold, remember?"

"But your skin could be damaged, couldn't it?"

"I doubt it." He stared toward the slave camps.

She stared out with him. Her palm warmed inside her clenched fist. She opened her hand and showed him the blue light on her palm. "When I think about the slave camps, the bond flares."

"The Morrag stirs when I look in that direction," he said.

She waited for more, but he said nothing. "She wants us to do something about it. About slavery."

"Yes."

She put a hand on his arm, but he didn't respond. "Connor, if you want me to marry you, you're going to have to share everything with me."

He turned to her and crossed his arms. "Do you know what I used to do for money?"

"Of course. You were a hired sword."

"Do you really understand what that means? What I did to earn my reputation and command high fees?"

Her mouth went dry. She licked her lips. "I'm sure you always acted honorably."

He scoffed. "There was a war in the east several years ago. I had escorted someone to Dal'Imur, and the government there was paying well for swords. They didn't care how long you signed for—they just wanted swords." He shrugged. "I suppose they figured arrow fodder didn't need to commit for long. But when I reported to my first commander, he saw I was better than just arrow fodder, so he made me a captain. They gave me a reconnaissance force. I was supposed to go ahead of them, send my men into villages and strongholds, and report back.

"We started out with our first assignment, and it was just a fortress—easy in, easy out, and the army came behind us and sacked it. The next was more of the same. We infiltrated camps, forts, castles for a few months. It was easy enough, and we didn't have to see all the blood that came behind. But then they told us to go into a village and report on its weaknesses, and ..." He took a deep breath. "There was no challenge—no threat, nothing worth taking. Just a village of poor peasants trying to eke out a living. I went back and told my commander it wasn't worth sacking, but ...." He stopped and stared back at the slave camps.

Mairead's hand tightened on his arm. "You followed orders."

"I followed orders. He told me to kill my conscience. The village was in his way, and he wanted me to destroy it. He said if I didn't, he'd send in my second to do it. I knew I could be easier on the place than my second. I went back and tried to warn the villagers—I tried to give them enough time to run—" His voice broke. He cleared his throat. "They fought back. I killed men who were trying to defend their homes. I watched the men under my command cut down women and children. There was brutality I can't even describe. They burned people alive, flayed men, cut off ...." He brushed a hand over his face. "I left in the middle of it. I never went back. I'm sure I'm marked as a deserter, but after that kind of chaos, I doubt anyone will look for me."

She tried to think of something comforting to say, but couldn't.

He didn't seem to expect anything. "I see those faces at night," he said without pause. "And other faces. Men I killed and people I couldn't save. I think of women I've been with. Can I really say I've never raped a woman?"

Mairead's stomach lurched. "You wouldn't do that."

"Maybe I never threatened a woman or held her at knifepoint or forced myself on her, but how many times did I talk one into my bed just by cajoling her?"

"That's not rape."

"Isn't it? I can be very convincing. A woman says no, I persist, she agrees.

Isn't that rape? Even if it's a game first?"

"I can't—"

"I've certainly not respected women the way I should—the way my father raised me. I can say I protected my clients, but how many times has that involved lying for someone? Covering up a crime? How many things have I chosen not to see because of the promise of coin?"

Her throat swelled with the strain of holding back tears. "It's the past."

"What does the timing matter if there's no forgiveness? I've shamed my family name." He turned away again. "She whispers to me, it's true. And she lets me hear the voices of others—things they've done, things they're planning. I can't resist her forever. I will have to go, eventually, and I'll have to serve her as she wishes, but that isn't what bothers me." He leaned his head against the tree. "What bothers me is that I am no better than the men she will call me to kill."

She stood in front of him and put her hands on his shoulders. "You're a good man. You are."

"There are no good men, Mairead."

The tone of his voice suggested it would be better if she didn't refute him. "What was the war about? The one in the east?"

He barked a laugh. "Just a border dispute. All that brutality over a little water and land. Do you know the worst part?"

She waited.

"The worst part was that the Morrag rose, and I fought her back. I pushed her down until she quit fluttering. I was so afraid of what I would become if I gave in to her that I let all of that happen—all of that brutality, destruction. I could have stopped it, and I didn't."

Stopped it with more destruction. She put her hands on his chest and leaned against him. "I wish I could help you."

He finally put his arms around her and held her tight against him. "You do." But there was pain under the words. "Faltian approaches."

Mairead closed her eyes. "Gareth thinks we might be to the tribe by then. It would be nice to dance the creation cycle with you."

"I don't think I can, Mairead."

She pulled away. "Why?"

"The veil between life and death is thinnest at Faltian. It's thinning even now. I feel it. This is the Morrag's season as much as the earthspirit's, and the Morrag demands blood. She wants balance. I fear what I might do in a city full of people on the night the veil is thinnest."

Mairead slid her arms around his midsection and leaned against his chest.

So much darkness. "I won't let you hurt anyone."

His body relaxed. He rested his cheek against her head and sighed. "Thank you."

As difficult as it was to ease Connor's spirit, Mairead did find solace and friendship with Trypp and Gareth. Braun was most pleasant at night when Snowbane padded in from the cold to curl up next to him. "The wolf soothes him," Trypp said when they spoke quietly one day after Braun and Snowbane ranged ahead. "Twitch does the same for me."

Mairead smiled at him. "You have such an easy way about you, Trypp. Why would you need soothing?"

He shrugged. "The companions know what we need." He trotted ahead to catch up to Braun, Twitch slinking alongside him.

"Trypp has deep wounds," Gareth said.

"From what?"

"The hunt where his friend died. He blames himself. He covers it well, but I have been to his hut when he is in one of his dark places, and it is frightening to behold." He paused. "He thinks he knows why he was asked to be here, traitha. Trypp knows he's not the smartest or strongest among the tribesmen, and he's already wed, so it makes no sense for him to be here as a mate for you. But when we were chosen, the earth gave another prophecy."

"Oh?"

"The guardian who spoke told us that before you took your place among us, one of us would fall. Trypp is certain that he is the one to fall."

Mairead shuddered. "What of the other two?"

"'One to wed, one to fall, and one to betray—these three shall foretell the rise of the Deliverer.' Those were her words. Trypp is wed, and he would sooner die than betray anything he believes in, so he is certain he will fall in battle. He believes he has not yet fully paid the price of his friend's death." He paused. "The wounds on the inside—they take longest to heal." He motioned back to Connor. "Ulfrich knows."

He does, Mairead thought. "I think back to the days in Allyn's house," she said. "I don't remember much of it. I see it all in flashes, and I don't remember killing him."

"Then you understand a bit of what the warrior knows."

"Do you think I'll start remembering things again?"

"When you're ready."

She rubbed her thumb against the scar on her palm through the gloves. *The question is—do I want to remember it?*

They rode six more days after that. Gareth picked along an ancient path that climbed in an easy incline between two mountains at first. After two days, he directed them to a steeper path, one nearly obscured by the scrubby trees of the low mountains. At times, when the snow and ice stopped for a while and the wind was quiet, Mairead heard a river in the distance, and sometimes, wolves howled around them at night. They crested small rises, rode through narrow vales and across fields, and finally arrived at the river. He cut a path to a small lake, and when they rode to the other side, he led them to the final pass.

They reined in. Gareth gestured to the narrow gap between two massive stones. "Cuhail's Eye. The tribe awaits through there, traitha."

She glanced over her shoulder toward Connor. He reined in next to her. "This is it?" he said.

"Yes." She noted the fine lines of tension around his eyes and jaw. "Are you all right?"

He shrugged. "The day is painful." He squeezed her hand. "Being with you helps."

She let out a deep breath. *The day. It's Faltian. Is this the edge of his sanity?* She held Connor's hand tight and turned to Gareth. "What about Connor and Phinneas? Will they be allowed to enter?"

Gareth's hands twisted the reins. "It is for the elders to decide," he said at last. "We do not let outsiders into the city, but for the deliverer, it's possible that an exception might be made. It's not for me to say."

Braun snorted. "You know my feelings," he said. He thumbed in the direction of the forest. "Outsiders have no place in the city."

"Connor is my guard and my friend," Mairead said, squeezing his hand as hard as she could to keep him from speaking. "If you will take me into the city, then you will take him. And Phinneas, too. They will be under my protection."

Braun lifted his reins. "It'll be on your heads," he said, and nodded to the other tribesmen before he and Snowbane trotted away.

"The Lionjaw clan lives to the north," Trypp said. He stared at the pass with a wistful expression. "Well? You can stand out here chewing your tongues, if you wish, but I'm anxious for home." Twitch started toward the village, and Trypp followed her at a trot.

Gareth smiled at his friend's back. "He has a new son at home—their first child. He is an anxious father."

Gareth led them into the narrow cleft between rock walls, and the group fell into a single file line. Mairead held out a hand and touched the wall. *Smooth—as if someone polished it.* The sides of the pass slanted outward just a bit at the top, allowing sunlight to penetrate, but they had the look of a very large rock split right down the middle by an enormous chisel. *Cuhail's Eye, indeed. Not a person's eye—the eye of a needle.*

When they emerged on the other side, Gareth spread his arm in a sweeping gesture. "The lion tribe, traitha."

She gasped. They stood on a ridge overlooking a snow-covered plateau ringed by mountains and divided by a sizeable river. Tribal huts and buildings covered the plateau as far as she could see, intersected by roads and occasionally thinning to allow for pastureland, only to thicken again farther on. Hills and mountains ringed the plateau, and the sparkle of a distant lake caught her eye. There were cattle, horses, sheep, goats—all manner of livestock—penned around the outskirts of the city. The buildings ranged in size from small huts to wide community houses and everything between.

And all around the villages, thick walls formed a haphazard honeycomb.

Connor shuddered next to her. "Walls," he said. "The forest is the only wall the Taurin tribes need. Why do you build walls? This isn't tribal life."

"We exist to protect the traitha," Gareth said. He jutted his chin toward the city. "The walls were deemed necessary."

"What do you call it?" Phinneas asked.

"Isfyrin. It means 'the place where fire meets ice.'"

Mairead startled, and Connor's head jerked toward Gareth. *He was supposed to take me to the place where ice and fire meet. He thought it was Albard—we all thought it was Albard. What if we were all wrong? What if that's not the only thing we got wrong?* "Why do you call it that?" she asked.

He frowned and gestured around the plateau. "There is fire under the ground, and where it meets ice or water, we have warm springs."

Everyone thinks I'm supposed to come from Sveklant. Connor told me he was taking me to Albard—to meet people who would teach me more. She took a deep breath. *I'm here now. I'll figure out the rest later.* "Show us into the city."

Gareth nudged his horse forward again, and Mairead and the others followed him down the small incline to the city gates. Grayfeather circled above him and drifted down to land on his shoulder. The world of the slave camps, the wealth of Galbragh, the turmoil of Taura—it suddenly seemed far away.

They reined in at the gates, and two tribesmen came forward to greet Gareth and Trypp. They spoke in low voices, and the two strangers looked back toward the rest of the party several times. Mairead glanced at Connor, who had a fierce frown planted on his face. "What do they say?" she whispered.

"I can't tell this time. The Morrag seems rather fickle about what she lets me hear and see." He turned to her. "Mairead, I can go somewhere else. I don't want to make trouble for you here. I can take Phinneas and go into the forest outside the walls. I'm sure that if you need me, you can call me through our bond."

"You fear going in the city?" she asked.

"I dread the voices. And being confined in a city like that ...." He shuddered. "I don't think I can stay inside walls for long, especially now that the Morrag is so active."

She started to respond, but Gareth turned back just then. "We can enter. Phinneas and Ulfrich, I will house you until the council meets with you." The gates swung open, and he gestured to the city. "Welcome to Isfyrin, traitha."

Mairead rode behind Trypp, next to Connor. The tribal city had an air of familiarity that she hadn't felt in Galbragh or even Torlach. She had vague memories of estates where she had lived with her father, and the lion tribe's home was much like those small towns and estates from her early life. The people lived in wooden huts of various sizes. Snow-covered paths wound through the houses in random lines with no clear plan or foresight. Children played near the center common area, making statues and throwing snow at each other. Women and men went about their business with the casual air of people who know a place so well that it's inseparable from them. Various animals roamed the city. She smiled. *It feels like a home. I could live here. But could Connor?*

The gate guards started to speak in excited whispers to other men stationed on the wall. One young boy ran ahead into the city, and then the whispers turned into a buzz as word of the traitha's arrival spread.

Sudden fear gripped at Mairead, and she reined in. *What if I'm not what they thought? What if I can't do this? They're waiting for me to do something, and I don't know what—I don't know how to be what they need.* "Gareth," she whispered. "What am I supposed to do?"

And then the air erupted in cheers and welcomes. First three, then nine, then dozens at once came running to meet her. People flooded the street and crowded the horses. Women offered up furs and beaded necklaces; men offered daggers, hilt first. Children brought dried flowers to strew the path her horse walked. "The Deliverer," the people cheered. "She's come—the Deliverer has come! Praise to the One Hand! One Hand be praised!"

Mairead refused the gifts, but her refusal only made the people more ardent. "They cheer because I refuse their offerings?"

Gareth only smiled. "It is as the prophets said it would be."

They made their way through the crowd to a long, sprawling hut in the center of Isfyrin. A tall, bearded man with long braids and a tattooed face stepped forward. "People," he shouted, hands raised. The din died down at the authority in his voice. "It's a day for celebration indeed. The traitha has come to us—to deliver us from our place of hiding into our inheritance." The cheers rose once more, but the man hushed the people. "You have given her a bold and cheerful welcome, and I'm sure she is grateful. But she is also tired and hungry from her journey, for it is written, 'the Deliverer will be of woman born.' Please, let her rest and eat." There were more cheers, but the people did as he asked and started to disperse.

Mairead and the party dismounted, and the man approached them with a wide grin. "I never thought I'd see this," he said. "To be the traitha when our Deliverer would come to us—surely the One Hand has favored me above other men."

Gareth gestured to the man. "Mairead, this is my father, Hedwar Catspaw. Father, this is Mairead, and these are her companions—Ulfrich Wolfbrother, a tribal brother from Taura, and Phinneas Ja'aster, a Tal'Amuni noble."

A frown flickered across his mouth, but he recovered quickly and nodded in greeting. "A strange group of companions indeed. You are all well come to my home."

Gareth gestured to the woman next to his father. "Mairead, my mother, Aerwyth."

Mairead curtsied. "My lady Aerwyth," she said. "It's an honor."

Aerwyth smiled. "Please, traitha—there is no room for that with me. I should be honoring you."

"You honor me simply by your welcome, Aerwyth. Call me Mairead."

Hedwar smiled. "You have the wisdom our prophets foretold." He gestured. "Come in—warm yourselves. We have stew and bread."

"If you'll excuse me," Trypp said with a small bow. "I'll look in tomorrow." He walked away.

Hedwar showed them into the low-ceilinged house, a sprawling building with rooms added in a haphazard manner. "Please, be seated," Aerwyth said, gesturing to a long table bordered by sturdy benches. "I'll bring food and drink." She bustled away.

"My mother and father have taken in many others over the years," Gareth said. "Our house has always been home to a multitude of guests."

"Do you have siblings?"

"I had a sister, but she died of fever when we were very young. My parents had no other children."

Aerwyth and two young women fluttered around the party, setting down bowls of stew, platters of salted meat and cheese, and fresh-baked bread. They filled cups with mead or thick, dark beer or oiska. "Eat," Aerwyth said with an encompassing gesture. "It's Faltian—it's a day for feasting!"

Hedwar sat down with them. A long white and gray weasel ran across the table, up Hedwar's arm, and sat on his shoulder. He gave the weasel a bit of bread. "This is Stripe, Aerwyth's companion. He's much more helpful than he might seem at first, and he's not always such a beggar."

As if the introduction gave him permission to approach Mairead, the weasel ran down Hedwar's arm, across the table, and sat in front of her. She picked a small piece of bread and offered it, and he snatched and ate it. He tipped his head and ran away at Aerwyth's summons.

"It takes some adjustment," Mairead said.

"The animals?" Hedwar asked.

"All of it."

Aerwyth sat down. She smiled. "Your first Faltian with the people. A good way to welcome you."

Mairead hid her frown behind her cup of mead. *And we bring a man who fears the night right into your midst. Alshada, can I control his madness tonight?* "I look forward to it," she said when she lowered her cup.

As they ate, Hedwar told Mairead of the village and named some of the important families and history. "The elders will expect to meet you soon," he said. "We've been watching the skies for days, and when Gareth sent word with Grayfeather, we sent runners to the other clans to bring their elders here. They will wish to hear your story."

Mairead's stomach roiled. She put down her spoon. "Hedwar, I have no story. I am just a girl with no family who was sent from her home under threat of death. I don't know how to be this Deliverer you want."

"The elders will not expect a great plan from you," he said. "They wish only to meet you. The rest? It will happen later."

She took a deep breath. "I hope they are patient."

When the meal was done, Mairead let out a long sigh that turned into a wide yawn. She covered her mouth with one hand. "Forgive me. The journey was very long, and your home is so warm and comfortable. I need to sleep, I think."

Aerwyth frowned. "But the fires—the people will be expecting you."

"Mother, the traitha has had a long journey," Gareth started.

Mairead glanced at Connor. He'd barely eaten, but he had managed several cups of beer. While he'd attempted some polite conversation, it was obvious that the whispers of the Morrag teased the edges of his control. His whole body was ridged and tense. "You should be abed as well," she said to him.

"I couldn't sleep right now."

"Will you go out there? To the fires?"

"Probably."

"Then I will as well. Just let me wash up."

Aerwyth stood and gestured down a long hall. "Come. I'll help you find a Faltian dress."

Gareth stood. "Phinneas, Ulfrich, I'll show you to my hut. You may wash up there." The other men stood and followed him into the city.

Aerwyth showed Mairead to a small room appointed with a thick, soft mat atop a narrow cot, furs, woolen blankets, a small stand with a comb and scented water in a pitcher, and several woven baskets filled with clothes. "The women helped bring all of these things for you, traitha," Aerwyth said. She opened a small chest and pulled out a soft blue linen dress edged with colorful floral embroidery. "This was one of my dresses before I birthed babies. Perhaps you might wear it?"

Mairead smiled. "I'd be honored." She took off her boots and started to unbind her hair.

"Your other tribesman—Ulfrich. Are you joined with him?" Aerwyth asked.

Mairead hesitated. *These people still expect me to marry one of their men. How do I answer that?* "He and I are very close, but we are not wed."

"Hmm." She held out the dress for Mairead. "That's for the best, then."

"Why?"

"An outlander, and from one of the outland tribes, no less?" She shook her head. "Such a man would not suit our Deliverer. A servant would be a better match for you, traitha."

What would you say if you knew of the ravenmark? She smiled. "Thank you for the dress. I'll be out in a few moments."

She found Connor and Phinneas outside the hut with Gareth. The fires in the center of the city leapt higher, dancing over Connor's face and highlighting the darkness there. He seemed to come back to himself when he saw her, though, and he bowed. "You look beautiful, Mairead," he said, lifting her hand to his lips in a courtly gesture.

The dress hugged her bodice and flared just below her knees. The embroidered edges bore the runes and marks of tribal life, and along the sleeves and neckline Aerwyth had sewn small white flowers joined by entwined green vines. Mairead's boots met the dress where it ended, so her legs were still covered, but she had to fight back the old training of the sayada that said she was dressed immodestly. "This is far more comfortable for me than silks and samites," she said. "Braiding my hair and looping it up every day and dressing in all that finery? I couldn't do that for long."

Gareth held out an arm. "Come. Let me introduce you." He hesitated and turned to Connor. "With your permission, of course."

Connor inclined his head, so Mairead took Gareth's arm and followed him to the fires. The dancing to celebrate the creation of the world had started, and young men and women were leaping, twirling, and spinning in pairs and foursomes all around the flames.

Gareth found Trypp, who sat with his arm around a woman with a single long, red braid and freckles. The woman held a babe at her breast. "Traitha," Trypp said. He gestured to the woman. "My wife, Wytha, and our son."

"Alsh—the One Hand's blessings on him," Mairead said.

Wytha cupped her son's head of red-blond curls. "Thank you."

Gareth gestured to more men and women, and the names flew quickly by as Mairead met and bowed and laughed at the good-natured ribbing the men gave Gareth. The unmarried men didn't stay with the group for long. Within moments of meeting Mairead, they scattered to find young maidens to dance with.

Connor fidgeted nearby, his hand twitching on his sword. "I'm going for a walk," he told her.

"Are you all right?"

"I'm fine. I promise." He turned toward the outskirts of the city.

Mairead nudged Phinneas. "Follow him."

"Yes, my lady." The eunuch melted into shadows after Connor.

Mairead turned back to see that Gareth's eyes had fallen on a blonde girl near the fire. She spoke with her friends, all of them laughing and smiling, until one by one the girls paired off with warriors. The girl glanced in Gareth's direction, colored, and turned away. Gareth twisted his cup of oiska in his hands.

Mairead leaned toward him. "You should dance with her."

"You are certain?"

"I'll just enjoy watching for now."

He smiled, tossed back the rest of his oiska, and went to the girl's side. She smiled and took his hand. They fell into one of the circles and started to dance.

The seven parts of the dance would go on for hours, repeating as needed until the couples were tired. The separation of light from dark was the first part, and the women represented the light. Gareth stepped in and pulled his partner tight against him to symbolize the darkness and light as one. She followed Gareth's lead. Their feet moved in time to the slow drumbeat. She kept her eyes fixed on his as he led her around the fire.

Mairead found herself tapping her feet. She'd performed the seven stories before, but only with women at the sayada. They had walked through the stories of creation together, but it was ritual—story, remembrance of when Alshada shaped and molded the earth in his hands.

Now, watching Gareth and the other couples, Mairead understood the dance in a new way. It was sensual and exciting. As the drumbeat became more complex, the steps did as well, and the women stepped farther and farther from the men to symbolize the separation of light and dark. Gareth spun his partner close in to his body, his mouth hovering next to hers for the span of a breath, and then she spun away to another warrior's arms. When she returned to Gareth's arms, he leaned close and whispered to her, and she tilted her head and grinned at him.

Mairead looked away from Gareth and his partner and walked past some of the other fires. One couple paid only cursory attention to the dance forms, reluctant to allow any space between them. Another couple slowed and exited the circle, sliding away from the revelers into the shadows, the young man's hand planted firmly on the girl's backside. Even older couples were retreating to huts. Just watching the couples made Mairead long for Connor.

"Mairead?"

She turned. Gareth and Trypp approached. "Where are your ladies?"

"With the baby," Gareth said. "You are looking for Ulfrich?"

"Yes. Phinneas said he would follow him, but I fear he's very troubled by this night."

"We thought the same," Trypp said. "There's something different about this Faltian—something unsettled."

They walked through the city until they reached the edge, near the wall, and then started to walk the perimeter. Gareth stopped suddenly. He drew his sword. "Traitha, get behind me."

Mairead gasped. "Connor," she whispered.

Connor stood facing the city, sword drawn, with only the eunuch between himself and the entire Catspaw clan. "Mairead," he said, his voice a low croak. "It's time for cleansing."

CHAPTER ELEVEN

When the one with a tainted soul stands clean,
the ravenmarked man will be destroyed.
— Third Book of the Wisdomkeepers

The wolf tribe's huts filled the clearing on the other side of the trees, and Hrogarth stopped his party to gesture to his second, Kyath. "Keep your eyes open," he said. "I don't trust this traitha." Hrogarth pointed at Logan. "I'll not see you sneaking off to the Sidh village, will I?"

Logan buried a flinch. "No, traitha."

Hrogarth grunted. "Then come." He walked into the wolf village.

Kyath prodded Logan with a rough shove, and Logan fell in behind Hrogarth. The proximity to the Sidh village ached like an old wound in bad weather, if such things could still bother him. The animstone felt heavy around his ankle, and the faint glimmer of elemental magic that hovered around the trees and village made him long to weave the stone braids once again. *But it's not for you,* he reminded himself. The flicker of distant memories tempted him. *Not your memories—not your magic.*

The journey had been frustrating, to say the least. Hrogarth kept him bound at night, and during the day one of the hound warriors guarded him even when he went aside to relieve himself. The white tunic and kaltan grew soiled from spending nights on the ground without a blanket or furs. Occasionally, they left him tied outside in the pouring rain, and he rested with his head bowed as the rain ran down his neck and back. Weapons remained out of his reach, and the only consolation was knowing that if he had to—if it came down to a fight—he could defend himself with the one weapon they couldn't take from him. *But I can't open that door. I can't let that beast loose again.*

The weather had turned for the worse during their journey. Though the trees sheltered them to some degree, the air had turned cold, and it had rained almost continuously from the day they left the hound village. Logan knew it couldn't all be due to the journey north. Though he'd lost track of time, he knew winter approached. *And not just from the weather.* Looming, hovering, biding her time, the Morrag watched, waiting for Faltian, for the days when the veil between the worlds was thin, when the earth guardians would make the tribes dance and celebrate life to keep her at bay for another year. He felt her spirit standing just out of reach, and he shuddered. *Your day will come,* he thought, unsure of whether she could hear him or not. *You will have what's left of my soul, or the others will, eventually. But not today. Not yet. I have sins to atone for, and I would do it properly. Then you may wreak your vengeance. Then I will turn myself over to you willingly.*

Faltian arrived two days before they reached the wolf village. Hrogarth was restless all day and night, and Logan sat as still as he possibly could in the hopes of avoiding the traitha's gaze. *If he notices me, I may not survive the night.*

Despite his best efforts, Hrogarth's gaze fell on him as the traitha crouched near the campfire, sharpening a dagger. He stood and walked around the fire to crouch before Logan. He twisted the blade in front of Logan's face, then reached up to straighten a strand of Logan's hair. He sliced it off and showed Logan the tuft, dropped it on the ground, and returned to the fire.

Logan allowed himself to exhale. *If I survive this journey, it will only be because Alshada allows it.*

Two days later, they came to the edge of the wolf village, where dozens of other men in braids and leathers and other tribal attire milled about. Logan shuddered. *One ravenmarked traitha is bad enough. What if there are more among these men? How many ravenmarked men are there now? If someone figures out what I am—*

But he was cut short when a man with the traitha's tattoo and long auburn braids came forward to meet them. He held out a dagger to Hrogarth, hilt first, and took a knee. "It is an honor to see you again, traitha. I, Edgar Wolfbrother, offer you the hospitality of the wolf tribes."

Hrogarth folded his arms and spread his legs shoulder-width apart in a defiant stance. "You've called a formal council. Why?"

Edgar stood and sheathed his dagger. "I thought I explained it in my message. Did you not receive—"

"We received a whelp with words of treason and betrayal," Hrogarth said. He snapped his fingers at Kyath, who brought forward the wolf tribe messenger and shoved him at Edgar's feet.

Edgar tensed. Logan saw the traitha's hand twitch toward the blade in his belt. "You did not—"

"He babbled something about the usurper king and his battle here. He said you wanted audience with me."

"I wanted audience with all the traithas. There are decisions to be made."

"What decisions?" Hrogarth gestured around the village. "The only decisions we should make are the ones that determine when we attack Taura."

Edgar's eyebrows arched. "Attack Taura?"

"Yes," Hrogarth said. "Time to bloody the pretender king into submission before he destroys the tribes." He pointed at the messenger. "See to your boy. We'll camp in the trees." He turned to walk away.

"Traitha Hrogarth, you haven't introduced me to everyone yet," Edgar said.

Hrogarth turned back. He gestured to Kyath. "This is Kyath Bloodscent," he said. "He'll be my second. This is my earth guardian in Alfrig's absence— Grytha Houndspirit. And this one is a Taurin who asked for sanctuary. I forget his name."

Edgar greeted Kyath and Grytha and then stepped over to Logan. "You make him wear the clothes of youth?"

"He hasn't proven himself yet."

Edgar laughed. "This is no unblooded boy, traitha. I can tell by the way he stands. He knows which end of the sword to use. Give him the honor of a man's clothing."

Hrogarth snorted. "You speak of things you can't know," he said, and then spat. "I'll treat him as I wish."

Edgar drew closer to Logan. "What's your name?"

"Logan."

Hrogarth took his arm. "We'll camp outside the village," he said. He forced Logan to turn and led his party back into the trees.

Other tribes were busy setting up camp—traithas with their seconds, their earth guardians, and their guards. The serpent tribe camped to one side, the strange, snaking tattoos on their shaved forearms and their black kaltans and single braids a sharp contrast to the wolf tribe's breeches and tunics. The bear tribe and the wolf tribe were closely allied, and it was hard to tell the difference between the two from a distance. The quiet salmon tribe sat in a circle with their incense and scrolls, the men wearing long, braided beards to indicate their levels of learning. In the trees, the hawks and eagles camped, and the boar and stag representatives had not yet arrived.

Kyath and Hrogarth set up small shelters, and Hrogarth beckoned Grytha into his little tent for several minutes. When she emerged, her face was pale, and she walked with an unsteady gait. She approached Logan. "I must speak with you. After sunset," she whispered.

When the party had eaten, Hrogarth settled into his tent, and Kyath bound Logan's hands and feet for the night. He sat near the fire and watched the other hound tribesmen start a game of dice with some of the men from other tribes.

Grytha noticed. "You can go," she said. "I'll stay with the Taurin and Hrogarth."

Kyath stood. "If I return and he is gone, it will be on your head."

Grytha scoffed. "One bound Taurin is no match for an earth guardian." She waved Kyath away. "Go. Gamble away every fur you own, if you wish."

As soon as Kyath was fully engaged in the game, Grytha moved closer to Logan and untied his ankles. "We won't have much time," she whispered. "Come."

He used a tree to steady himself as he stood, hands still bound behind his back. Grytha led him through the forest until they came to a circle of trees. The echoes of earth magic still hovered around the place, and Logan shuddered. *She's hungry. The Morrag and her sister both. They would not give me quarter.* "A shrine?"

Grytha lifted one eyebrow. "You know something of the earth magic, Taurin?"

"Just a bit."

She gestured at the trees. "We perform sacrifices in these places, but we also use them for handfastings, and women birth babies here sometimes."

"Why did you call me out here?"

"Edgar says you look like you know how to use the right end of your sword."

"What of it?"

"Hrogarth grows more and more unstable," she said in a low voice. "You are not tribal. You could help us."

Logan's belly twisted. "Help you what?"

Her chest heaved with nervous breaths. "I am a guardian. I love Alfrig as a mother, and until Hrogarth became unstable, I would have served him until my dying breath. But I fear ...." She stepped closer to Logan. "If Hrogarth were dead, the earth would choose a new traitha, and the hound tribe could be stable once again."

"You're asking me to murder a man."

She flinched. "I'm asking you to put down a rabid dog."

A rabid dog? "What is he? Why is he so unstable?"

She started to speak, but noise erupted from the direction of the village. Grytha startled and rubbed her palm, but not before Logan noticed the faint blue glow under her brand. "No—Hrogarth."

"What is it?"

She held up her hand. "My traitha is in trouble." She turned toward the village.

I could leave. I could escape right now. No tribesmen in sight. But if I try to run, who might be hiding in the trees? He turned toward the east. *Kiern is over there. Is Braedan still there? Edgar knows where he is.* "Grytha!"

She stopped.

"My hands—I can't run like this." He tried to smile. "Please. I swear I'll not escape."

Conflict twisted her face, and she finally drew her knife, ran back to his side, and sliced the ropes off his wrists. "I'm trusting you, Taurin."

"I won't betray your trust." He fell into a trot next to her.

In the village, Hrogarth straddled a man on the ground, knife at the man's throat, and Edgar and other chieftains stood nearby begging for sanity. "You lie," Hrogarth said to the man. "You *lie*. Where is my wife? My daughter?"

"I swear to you, I have not seen your wife," he said. "Your daughter is safe at home with her babes. She is well and hale, and her youngest babe is nearly three. I don't know why Alfrig lied, but your daughter was not with child."

Grytha knelt next to Hrogarth. "Traitha," she said. "Let him go. This is not his fault. This is Alfrig's lie. You have to let him go."

"He lies," Hrogarth said. There was a dark echo behind it. "He lies. I know he lies."

"Do you truly? Do you?" Grytha's voice soothed. She put a hand on Hrogarth's arm, but he shook it away. "Let me help. Let me still it again."

He focused on the man beneath him. Blood trickled down to the ground in a slow, languid red line. "He lies," he said again, but his resolve had faded. "Grytha, tell me he lies."

"He lies as all men lie. But he may not be lying about this." Grytha put her glowing palm on his bare arm.

Hrogarth's face twisted in a grimace, and he dropped the knife. Another earth guardian stepped out of the crowd. "Let me help," she said to Grytha. They led Hrogarth to the other guardian's hut.

The injured man stood. He wore the soft doeskin typical of the stag tribe and had the swirling blue brand of traitha across his face. "His eyes," he whispered. "Did you see his eyes? By the spirits. There is darkness inside him."

Edgar nodded toward the man's neck. "Go treat your wound and come to the council hut. We'll meet now."

Kyath stepped out of the crowd. "You will not, whelp—not without Hrogarth."

Edgar put one hand on his sword. "You may represent the hound tribe if you wish," he said. He walked away.

"Traitha," Logan called. Edgar turned back. "I ask that you let me attend as well. I have lived with Hrogarth for many weeks. I might be able to help you."

Edgar tilted his head. "You are an outlander—not of the tribes, and not a chieftain. You may attend and give testimony, but you must leave when we make decisions."

Logan followed Edgar to the hut as word spread that the traithas would meet immediately.

It wasn't long before all of the men had arrived and gathered in a circle around a low fire. Edgar motioned them to quiet when the last traitha had entered. He picked up a pouch and threw a handful of herbs on the fire. "One Hand, guide us in wisdom. Earthspirit, let us honor you by bringing balance. So be it."

There was a quiet murmur of "so be its" around the hut.

"You all saw what happened," Edgar said. "You know our stag brother did nothing to bring on Traitha Hrogarth's attack. He went to greet his old friend—the man who is father to his son's wife—and Hrogarth attacked him for a liar." He paused. "This is not the man we have followed all these years. This is an unbalanced man. It may be time to do something we have not had to do since the Breaking."

Tension rose in the hut as the men started to mumble amongst themselves. The salmon traitha made a motion to quiet the group. His gray beard was braided and beaded and made a clacking sound when he spoke, but he commanded respect and quiet from the others. "We need more than one random attack to make such a ruling, brother," he said. "Hrogarth has led the hounds and the nine tribes faithfully and well for nearly thirty years. If he is ill, allowances can be made. If there is more, then ...." He let the words trail off into the wisps of smoke from the fire.

Edgar turned to Kyath. "You are his second. What have you seen from your traitha of late?"

Kyath stood. "He is still Hrogarth," he said. "He leads well."

"Traitha," Logan said. Edgar turned to him. "May I give testimony?"

"You may, and then you will leave."

Logan stood. "I came to Hrogarth several weeks ago requesting sanctuary because I was sought by Taurins for a crime I didn't commit. At first, his treatment of me seemed only petulant, and I tolerated it. But he grew more erratic as time went on. I gave him information about the Taurin crown, and in exchange, he made me dress like an unblooded youth. He guarded me night and day and made me perform the chores of a child. He held me as a hostage so that he would have a way to bargain with my king, and more than once, he threatened to kill me. Even when your messenger brought word of the events in Kiern, he refused to give ear to my words. Tell me—are these the actions of a reasonable man?"

The men shifted in discomfort. Logan continued. "Hrogarth's wife, Alfrig, told us at supper one evening that she wished to visit her daughter to help her birth a babe. She left shortly after. Until then, he'd been tolerable. Once his wife was gone, the young earth guardian, Grytha, visited him every morning, sometimes even more. She never said what she did for him, but it was obvious it was draining her of her strength. She said that our best hope was for Alfrig to return."

The earth guardian who had helped Grytha entered the hut. "Hrogarth lives," she said. "Grytha remains with him, and I will go back in a few moments. But Hrogarth's secret can no longer be kept. The chieftain is raven-marked."

Logan slowed his breathing and feigned an innocent expression. *He can't know what I am.*

A clamor erupted. Edgar shouted for quiet. "You're certain?" he asked the guardian.

"I saw the Morrag when I helped Grytha still her." She shuddered. "The Morrag is driving Hrogarth now. She calls him to join his brethren."

Edgar inhaled sharply. "His brethren—the other ravenmarked."

The earth guardian nodded. "He says she is calling him—that it is time for the ravens to rise. She pulls him east. It started a few weeks ago. It's his attempt to resist her call that tramples on his sanity. He can no longer tell what transgressions are real and what are false. He has no way to control this beast." Logan saw Edgar's mouth tighten. "There may be nothing we can do."

"Thank you, Nedra. Do what you can. I'll see you after the council has decided what to do." She left the hut. Edgar looked at Logan. "You as well, Logan," he said. "I thank you for your testimony."

Logan bowed and walked outside. He found Nedra's hut and heard Grytha crying inside and Nedra trying to soothe her. "You are weak," she said. "You need to regain your strength. No wonder you couldn't still it this morning—he's drawn nearly everything out of you."

Grytha wept harder. "I tried," she whispered. "I'm not weak, I swear it, but every day, it gets darker. Every day she pulled me closer to the edge. She wants justice, vengeance. I can't stop her."

"I know," Nedra said. "I've called for more guardians. They will help me. We'll care for him. You rest."

He heard a rustle and Grytha came out of the hut, her eyes red-rimmed and her face streaked with tears. Her lip trembled. "I have nothing left," she whispered.

She needs the earth. And I need to see Maeve. "Would the shrine help?" She nodded.

He followed her back to her tent, where she picked up two blankets. She gave him one. "Hrogarth was wrong to treat you the way he has. This is not tribal behavior. I will not allow it to continue."

"I thank you." He took the blanket and followed her to the shrine.

She stepped into the center of the trees and folded the blanket across her chest. "This place soothes me," she whispered. "The magic."

Logan flinched. *I could step in there and be done with it. I could let the Morrag and her sister have their way. But I'm just not brave enough to face my transgressions yet. There are things that must be done.* "I have a daughter," he said, quiet.

"A daughter?"

Lies upon lies. Not my life. Not my magic. Not my memories. "She's ten." He paused. "Her mother died. Years ago. I left my daughter with my wife's father. He said he would raise her. I left to join Fergus' army. I couldn't...." He shook his head and cleared his throat. "I was at Kiern when it was attacked. I joined Braedan—his army—because of what happened there."

She waited.

"My daughter doesn't know me," he said. "Not anymore. Her grandfather told her that I'm dead. She is an orphan, and poor, and she has little about her to commend her to a suitor. The Lord High Chancellor promised ...." He wet his lips. "I offered my life in exchange for coin. For her. He assured me that he would provide for her education and dowry."

She finally spoke. "If you sacrificed yourself."

The body is a shell. But it could buy one child a life. "If I would take the blame for the deaths in Torlach and go to the chopping block quietly. I took the blame, but then the princess—Igraine—she talked me into leaving. Escaping to find the king. Now I don't know what Kerry will do—if he will just ignore my daughter or use her as leverage to draw me back to Taura."

She was quiet for a long time. "Why do you tell me these things?"

He shrugged. "So that you understand I'm not just a Taurin. So that you see why I do the things I do. I believe in my king and I love my daughter. Everything I do is for them."

"You may sleep in the shrine if you wish. I would not object to the company."

He spread his blanket on the ground. "I don't sleep much. I'll guard you."

After a long moment, she stepped toward him with her dagger held out hilt first. "I am making no sacrifice. I don't need my weapon."

He took the blade. "You trust me?"

"Will you give me reason not to?"

"Rest. I'll ensure your safety."

When she'd settled in for the night, he sat on his blanket and leaned against a tree. He toyed with the dagger and watched Grytha sleep. *She really is very pretty.* He shook his head. *What am I thinking? I would damn another woman?* He tugged his boot off and untied the animstone from his ankle. He held his hand over the ground, and dark red and orange braids came at his tentative call.

Air braids twined around him, and he stood as they coalesced and then faded to reveal the Sidh queen. He knelt. "Your majesty."

She crossed to him in two steps and put her hand on his shoulder. "You will not kneel to me. The consort of the Sidh queen does not kneel."

Logan stood. "I haven't been the Sidh queen's consort in three lifetimes. More."

"I still see his face." She stepped back and folded her hands before her. "How are you?"

"Well. I'm well."

"The tribes—"

"I heard rumors about you and Edgar."

She had the courtesy to color. "It's not important."

"You would do well to recall that I was your mother's consort, not yours." *And in truth, I was never even that.*

She waved away the comment with one slender hand. "This place is not safe for you. Why are you here?"

"I came into the forest to hide from Ronan Kerry. I only wanted to find the king and warn him of his uncle's treachery, but Hrogarth found me and held me hostage."

"Of all people—" she whispered.

He frowned. "You knew? You know he's ravenmarked?"

She flinched at the word. "I only learned tonight. Edgar left his council long enough to bring word."

"Are there others? Do you know?"

Her jaw twitched. "No."

She lies. "How many are there? Where are they?"

"Logan—"

"How many, Maeve?" His voice rose.

In the shrine, Grytha stirred. Logan took Maeve's arm and steered her farther from the shrine. "If you don't want me to wake her up and hand you over to the tribes, you'll tell me what you know."

"You would not—not if you want to repay your debt."

She's right about that. He leaned closer. "Do not ever forget what I am, Maeve SilverAir. Do not ever forget that your power is nothing compared to mine. Do not forget that you have no hold on me but what I allow."

She tugged her arm, trying to free it from his grip. He tightened his hand. "You have no control over elemental magic," she said, but fear tinged her voice.

The sidhsilk gown shifted under his fingers. *Just a slip—just a few slender threads between my skin and hers. If I tore this gown, if I let it loose ....* He lowered his voice and put his lips next to her ear. "And neither does it have any control over me."

Maeve tugged harder, and he finally let go. She rubbed her elbow. "There is one other that I know of," she said. "He's not on Taura at the moment."

Logan evaluated her scent, posture, and gaze. *She's not lying. At least there's that much.* "Hrogarth tells me nothing. What happened between the king and the tribes?"

"Edgar and Braedan worked with each other to defeat Mac Rian. Braedan used Hrogarth's sacred blade to kill Olwyn Mac Rian." She paused. "She was Forbidden. We think she was Aldora."

"And she wasn't banished."

"No. There were no ravenmarked men around."

Son of a bitch. Logan paced. "Do you know where she went?"

"No. We've seen no sign of her since the battle."

She will not give Braedan quarter. Nor will she give me quarter. Grytha stirred again inside the shrine, and Logan turned back to Maeve. "Go back to your village."

She put a hand on his sleeve. "There have been some successes," she said. "This is not a failure—not yet. The heir is safe because you warned me of Braedan's coup."

First I betray my king, now I try to save him. "Go. I'll contact you if I have any other word."

The braids snaked around her body and carried her away. Logan sat down on his blanket and tied the stone around his ankle. Grytha slept soundly once more, her breath steady and heavy from the center of the shrine. Logan leaned his head back against his tree. *Some rest. What I wouldn't give for sleep. Men*

think only of eating and drinking and whoring, but none realize how much
they would miss sleep if it were taken from them.

When the sun finally rose over the trees, Grytha sat up, stretched, and yawned. She rubbed her eyes with one hand. "Did you sleep well?" she asked.

He shrugged and stood. "You?"

"Yes. Very." She rose and folded her blanket. "We should go back. The other guardians will need me. I need to find out how Hrogarth is."

They gathered the blankets and returned to their camp. When Grytha saw Kyath, she said, "I needed to be in the shrine. I was drained of magic." She entered her tent without waiting for an answer.

Kyath snatched Logan's arm. "Where were you?"

"I guarded your guardian so she could sleep." He shook his arm away from the tribesman. "The better question is, where were you?"

Kyath spat. "Don't think that just because Hrogarth ails that you have some kind of power or sway," he said. "You are still Taurin, still Sidh, and still just a boy."

I've lived a dozen of your lifetimes, if not more. "I'll accept your challenge whenever you offer it."

Kyath's hand twitched. Logan brought one powerful arm up to catch his swing with one gloved hand. He twisted Kyath's arm until he cried out and dropped the dagger in his hand. Logan swept Kyath's feet from under him, picked up the dagger, and straddled Kyath with the blade at his neck. "Attack me again, and I'll risk the punishment of the tribes to see your blood run, whelp," he said.

Kyath's mouth curled into a rictus. "Do it. Finish it. Let the tribes deal with you."

Bloodlust rose in Logan's chest. "Don't think I don't see the corruption in your soul," he said. A growl threatened at the back of his throat. "I hear your words against the Sidh when you think I'm not listening. I know you poison Hrogarth against Edgar and the other traithas." *If I could just show him, just once, how his corruption poisons—*

"Logan." Edgar stood above them, arms crossed. "Come with me. I need to ask you something."

Logan stood. "At once, traitha." He threw Kyath's dagger some distance away. "Fetch, pup." He followed Edgar to the chieftain's hut.

Edgar showed him in and gestured to him to sit. He sat across the small fire pit from Logan. "Tell me: why does a Sidh man who has served as the king's high commander hide with the hound tribe's chieftain?"

Logan's stomach twisted. "I don't know—"

Edgar waved away his objection. "The Sidh queen told me who you are." He tossed a small pile of clothing toward Logan. "This is for you. It's clothing her son left behind the last time he visited her."

"Hrogarth won't be happy."

"Do you want to wear the clothing of an unblooded boy?"

"No."

"Then put those on. You look ridiculous."

Logan stood and changed into the plain linen tunic, leather jerkin, and soft doeskin breeches. He sat to put his boots on. "I thank you. I feel like a man again."

"Grytha didn't take care of that?" He laughed when Logan started to protest. "It was obvious where you came from this morning. You did more than guard her. I'm not a fool."

"Her honor is intact."

Edgar shrugged. "I'm not her father."

I will not damn another woman. "What do you want from me, traitha?"

"To help you." He jutted his chin toward the door. "To help Taura."

"You're tribal."

"Peace in the tribes depends on peace in Taura. It's in my best interests to help the Taurin king." He stood and started to put supplies in a pack. "He's gone to the Fingall holdings. You may be able to catch up with him there."

Logan stood. "And Hrogarth?"

"Hrogarth is the concern of the tribes." He paused in his packing and turned to Logan. "His condition is unchanged. He is no better, nor any worse. We can't know what to do until he is able to speak to us. He must face the earth himself."

"And if he's never able to do that?"

Edgar's mouth tightened. "He has three days. If the Morrag has not let him go in three days, the chieftains will return to the earth and offer ourselves. If she chooses a new chieftain, then that man will have to kill Hrogarth."

There was a knock on the door. "Traitha?"

"Come," Edgar called.

The earth guardian Nedra opened the door. "Hrogarth is awake. Kyath and Grytha are on their way."

"Is he speaking?"

Nedra nodded. "He is lucid. He says he has instructions for the traithas."

"We will be there in a moment." Edgar turned to Logan and held out the pack. "I am offering you a chance to leave. Take these supplies and go—find your king."

Logan reached for the pack. "And you wish nothing in return?"

"Nothing but a stable country to my eastern side."

Logan grunted. "I can't promise that. But I can promise I will try."

"It is enough."

He pulled the drawstring tight. "I wish to say goodbye to Grytha."

"It's risky."

"I know. But I trust her."

They found Kyath and Grytha near a pale Hrogarth inside the earth guardian's hut. Hrogarth frowned. "Where'd you get the clothes?"

"This is no unblooded boy," Edgar said. "He has served in battle many times. He deserves to dress as a man."

Hrogarth sipped something in a cup. "How is this to go? Eh? You'll take my position? Cast me away to the forest?"

"I don't want your position," Edgar said. "I never did. When the earth took us both into the vision hut and gave you the mark instead of me, it was the greatest gift of my life. But I can't allow you to lead if you would kill fellow traithas because of imagined transgressions."

Hrogarth sipped again. "Not imagined. Real. So many of them."

"Traitha," Grytha said. "You must find Alfrig. Do you have any way to know where she went?"

"It's not Alfrig I need. I need to go east. The Morrag, she drives me east."

Grytha knelt next to him. "Then we will go east. I will help you."

"You may find Alfrig in the north," Edgar said. "She took a young Taurin woman north."

Hrogarth's head snapped up. "And you just thought to tell me this?"

"Your wife swore me to secrecy. She is going to the wisdomkeeper."

Hrogarth let out a long breath. "I may never see my wife again once I go east. I will go north first. I must say goodbye."

"Who will lead the tribes when you leave?" Kyath asked.

Hrogarth finished his drink with a long swallow and stood. He faced Edgar. "I am no longer fit to serve as traitha over the nine," he said. He walked out of the hut.

A crowd had gathered as the rumor flew that the traitha was awake. The other seven traithas stood near the hut, waiting. Hrogarth faced them as the crowd fell silent. "People of the nine," he said, the strength of his voice hiding the emotion behind it. "I am no longer fit to serve you as traitha." He drew a blade and lifted it to the base of his skull. Logan drew in a sharp breath, but Hrogarth grinned. "Don't worry. I'm not that crazy yet."

Hrogarth gathered his braids into one hand and sliced through them with his dagger. The result was a mass of braids in his hand and a strange, haphazard array of hair standing up on his head. The gasps that rippled through the crowd turned to whispers that turned to cries of disbelief. "I remove my mark of authority," Hrogarth said. He threw down the braids at the feet of the traithas. "Tonight, you eight and my second, Kyath, will enter the vision hut and seek the earth. I wish you well." He gestured to Grytha, and she fell in behind him as he walked into the trees.

Logan followed. At the camp, Hrogarth turned his knife over to Grytha. "Cut the rest, and then shave it," he said. "I'll have none follow me." He knelt next to her. "We leave for the north as soon as we are packed."

Grytha's hands shook when she took the knife. "And you, Taurin? What have you chosen?"

Logan heard the question under her words: *Will you help me kill Hrogarth if it must be done?*

Hrogarth looked up at Logan. "You are free to go, Taurin. Go find your king."

"Hrogarth, I—"

Hrogarth grunted. "Stay or go. It makes no difference any longer."

Logan turned toward Taura. Edgar's words ran through his head. *He's right. The key to peace is in Taura. But how can I help bring peace to Taura if the ravenmarked are unleashed? If Hrogarth figures out what I am, he'll destroy me. But if he is unleashed on Taura, he is a greater threat to peace than the petty squabbles. Kerry would use one mad tribesman as a reason to destroy the whole forest. I can't let that happen, even if it means my own death.* "I'll come with you."

CHAPTER TWELVE

The blood of kings holds safe the land.
— First Book of the Wisdomkeepers

Braedan shifted in his saddle and pulled his cloak tighter against a northern wind. A heavy, bitterly cold rain had been falling for days, and everything he owned was wet. He pulled his hood farther over his face and tucked his nose inside a thick scarf. No one carried the standard—the weather wouldn't cooperate. It appeared less and less likely that he would make it back to Torlach before the worst winter weather set in. *It's already here.* "Malcolm."

The guard reined in and turned. "Sire?"

"Send someone to range up ahead and find an inn or farm. I'm weary of this."

Malcolm trotted forward to speak to one of the men in the front of the line. The man spurred his horse, and Malcolm returned to Braedan's side. "We shouldn't be far from Fingall's estate, but I sent him to find out for certain."

"I want nothing more than a soft bed and a fire."

Malcolm grunted. "A warm woman would be nice."

Braedan agreed. *I wish I'd never left Torlach. Right now, I could be dining with Igraine in front of a fire. Or wrapped up in a blanket with her.* The very thought made him shudder.

The week of travel from Kiern had been tedious due to heavy rain and wind. They'd opted not to bring wagons, for which Braedan was grateful, but even traveling light, there were constant frustrations with bogged down horses and washed out sections of road. Morale was low; his men found it difficult to build fires and cook, so many meals were cold, and no one had been dry since they left Kiern.

Braedan tried to tell himself that the low morale and wet conditions were the cause of his poor sleep over the last week, but he couldn't deny that his hand drifted to the blade at his side more and more often. Sleep had become a daring act—an exercise in facing fears he didn't even know he had. More often than not, his nights consisted of restless thrashing. He sometimes dozed in the saddle when they rode. *I can't believe a dagger could have such control over me,* he thought. *I'm just anxious to be home, back with Igraine.*

There was no sound to warn them—no whir of an arrow or twang of a bowstring—but suddenly, one of Braedan's guards clutched his neck and fell. The men reined in and sounded a warning. Malcolm reacted, drawing his sword and shielding Braedan with his horse and his body. "Get off the road," he shouted.

Braedan drew his sword. "No—I'll fight."

The world turned to chaos. Horses screamed and reared as they were pelted with misfired arrows, and braided men roared out of the forest in a wave of mayhem that turned the road to blood. *Tribesmen!*

Braedan slashed and stabbed, trying to get free of the attackers. His horse reared with a scream. Braedan leaned forward, but when the horse landed, its forelegs collapsed. Braedan tumbled over the neck and head onto the ground.

Steel flickered next to him, and he rolled away and stood to parry another blow. His feet slipped. The tribesman drove him toward the trees. Pain struck in his right shoulder, and his arm fell useless. He dropped the sword, bent to pick it up, and found himself face down in the mud with a boot on his neck.

He twisted and writhed to gain purchase, breathe, but only got a mouthful of mud for his efforts. His right arm paralyzed with pain, fighting blind from the mud in his face, he twisted his left hand and arm around, grasping for something—anything—to use as a weapon. His hand found the warm hilt of the tribal dagger, and he drew it and stabbed, hoping to connect with some part of the man who held him down.

The blade sank into something soft, and the man above him lifted his boot and cried out. Braedan struggled to his knees and swiped his face clear of mud. He grabbed his sword from the ground. The man had recovered enough to swing again. Braedan blocked and parried, his movements awkward with the sword in his weaker hand. The man swung toward Braedan's neck. Braedan jumped back, and when his opponent's follow-through carried him downward, Braedan stabbed the man through the midsection.

Another tribesman ran toward him, sword at the ready. He swung at the man, his right arm useless, his left arm clumsy and unable to engage with well-placed strikes. The man drove him farther into the melee. One of Braedan's guards stepped in, but the tribesman brought his sword into the young man's chin, slicing his head in half with an upward stroke that splattered brain and blood onto Braedan's cloak.

Braedan roared. He ducked and went behind the man, his sword swiping through the back of his legs and nearly severing them. The man fell screaming. Braedan stabbed through his chest, silencing him.

He stood still, straight, trying to figure out who he should fight. The entire road was a tangle of bloody limbs, torn clothing, and horse entrails. He leapt over a dead Taurin and horse and found a wounded tribesman covered in woad. *Woad. The tribes don't use woad.* The man had soiled himself, and Braedan steeled himself against the smell and knelt. He picked up the man's head to get his attention, and a mass of braids came off in his hand. "What's this?" he said. The entire dark headpiece came off, revealing short blond hair. He used the hair to wipe at the woad on the man's face, and swore when he realized the man was a Taurin soldier—one he'd seen in Kiern. "What is this? Why did you do this—attack the king's men?"

The pain in Braedan's skull brought instant darkness.

He woke on soft bedding. Every twitch sent waves of pain through his head, shoulder, and useless arm. He tried to sit up, gasped, and fell to his side. He groaned.

Cool hands touched bare skin. "You'll be all right," a woman said, her voice low and soothing. "You were lucky."

He rolled to his back, only dimly aware that he was naked except for a thin linen sheet over his midsection. "Head?" he croaked.

"An accident, it appears. Someone struck you from behind during the fight. Your guard, Malcolm, saved you. He defended you until my lord's men arrived."

"Arm?"

"You took an arrow to the shoulder. It will take some time, but it should heal if you do not overtax it."

Braedan swallowed bile over his dry tongue. "Water."

She put a cool cloth next to his mouth. "Just suck on it for now. Your stomach is angry from the herbs I've given you for the pain."

"Damn your herbs. Still hurts." He opened his eyes. The woman above him had a freckled face framed by red hair. "Igraine?"

"No, sire. Cerys. I serve Duke Fingall."

"The duke's estate?"

"Yes. You were close when the attack happened. The men my lord sent to escort you finished off the attackers and brought you and your men back here."

He swallowed again. "My men. How many did we lose?"

"Ten."

Gods. "Need to see your lord."

She put a gentle hand on his forehead. "Soon. I've told him he must stay away until you are stronger." She paused, her hand lingering. "Rest now. I'll brew some broth for when you next wake."

He drifted to sleep again.

When he woke, it was night. His arm throbbed, but the rabid pain had subsided, and he was able to sit up. He groaned.

He heard someone rise and come to his side. "How do you feel?" Cerys asked.

His stomach rumbled in response.

She smiled. "You can eat?"

"Yes." He rubbed his face with his good hand. "How long did I sleep?"

"A full day." She ladled something into a bowl. When she stepped back to his bed, he saw her body outlined in the fire under her thin shift.

He let her spoon the broth into his mouth. "Can I have more?" he asked when he finished.

"Let that settle first."

"I need to see Malcolm."

"In the morning."

He lay back on his bed. "One of them was a Taurin guard," he said. "Why would Taurins—or whoever they were—attack us?" He stopped. *They knew we would be there.* He sat up. "I need to see your lord. Now."

"It's still night, majesty."

"Duke Fingall, Cerys. And Malcolm as well."

"Yes, sire. At once." She stood and left the room.

Braedan's clothes were draped across a chair on the far side of the room, too far away to reach if he needed them. He had no weapons. *I live at the mercy of a man who disputed my claim to the throne. Am I a prisoner or a patient?*

Malcolm entered the room with a short, balding man in nightclothes. Malcolm wore leather breeches and nothing else. A long line of stitches ran across his belly. "Are you well?" Braedan asked.

Malcolm nodded. "It wasn't deep. It's a relief to see you awake, majesty."

"It's a relief to be awake." He turned to the other man. "You're Duke Fingall?"

The man bowed. "I am. May I echo your guard, majesty, and say I am also relieved to see you awake?"

"You'll forgive me if I question your sincerity, my lord," he said.

Fingall blinked. "Majesty—I don't—"

"It wasn't him," Malcolm said. "He came to our rescue."

"How do you know?" Braedan said. "Those men were Taurin."

"They weren't Fingall's men," Malcolm said. "They were the missing Kerry men, your majesty."

Braedan sat up straighter. *Igraine was right.* "You're certain? How?"

"I recognized several of them—they were men Kerry insisted come with us to Kiern. All of them went missing after the battle. They deserted, majesty, and my suspicion is that when they didn't kill you in the forest, they ran and hid to await Kerry's instructions."

"How did they communicate with him so quickly? It's taken weeks for us to get letters from Torlach."

Malcolm shrugged. "One man with urgent news can travel quickly when he's not encumbered by dozens of others."

Fingall stepped forward. "Majesty, I didn't have anything to do with this. In my complaint to the crown, I objected to the appointment of Chancellor Kerry. That he would send you this way is unconscionable."

This is madness. My own uncle would plot against me? He groomed me for this role and helped me win the crown. "Why would you object to my uncle's appointment?"

He shuffled his feet and cleared his throat. "A moment, sire? Without your guard?"

Braedan gestured to the door, and Malcolm left the room.

Fingall sat down. "Did you ever wonder, my lord, why it was so easy for you to take your throne? Why you were able to come to power with such a minimum of fuss?"

Braedan shrugged. "Not really."

Fingall grunted. "That's part of the problem." He took a deep breath. "Your father was regent, it's true, and there has always been someone to hold the Raven Throne, but to have a king in the place of the rightful line is something that's never been considered—until now. When your father was dying, your uncle came to us—to the council—and asked for support for you over your cousin. It was not difficult to agree. Most of us didn't want a copy of your father in control of the Raven Throne, and those who did were assured that you would give them exactly what they wanted."

"Like Mac Rian," Braedan said.

"Mac Rian didn't care who held the throne as long as he continued to get what he wanted," Fingall said.

"Which was what?"

"Money, power, land. I've heard how you handled things in Kiern. Know that if you had acquiesced to Mac Rian's demands, you would have been entwined in his web until the end of your days."

His web or Olwyn's? "So my uncle told you what you all wanted to hear in order to gain support for my ascension."

"Yes, but then you took the throne and surprised us all. You acted like a king. You appointed an ambassador to the kirok and started to make reparations to those your uncle would have seen destroyed. You didn't marry your cousin's widow. Mac Rian didn't get what he wanted." He paused. "You gained my support, sire, and you had it until you appointed the man who would see you destroyed."

Braedan's stomach plummeted. "I gave him the keys to the kingdom."

"You did. And he intends to use them against you." Fingall leaned closer to Braedan. "Your uncle has sent word that you are to be killed or captured for crimes against the dukes." He opened a piece of parchment and showed it to Braedan. "It just came, and he is using Mac Rian's death as an excuse, but now that you've weathered this attack by your own men—"

"They were Kerry's men," Braedan said.

"Yes, sire. And now he makes himself a champion of the dukes even as he steals your throne."

"And you?" Braedan asked. "Your loyalties do not lie with Kerry?"

"No. My theory is that he told you I was challenging your ascension so you would attack me. In the process of defending myself and following his orders, one of us would end up dead. If it were you, he could take the throne without fuss. If it were me, he would be rid of one duke who did not support him and have another charge against you. Either way, he would come out the winner."

Braedan cursed. "The more I discover of my family, the more I believe I am the best the Mac Corins or Kerrys have to offer. That scares the piss out of me." He wet his lips. "We will rest and heal and plan, Duke Fingall, and then we will be away for Torlach."

"You will need men," Fingall said. "You have my support, your majesty. If you want men or arms, you have only to name your request."

"I have men in Kiern. I will send word to them."

"Dylan and Reid will support you, that much I know."

"We can send a messenger to Reid in the south. What about Dylan?"

"Dylan's forces are small, and he doesn't like to come out of the north. His men are a seafaring bunch. I don't know what help they might be."

Braedan brushed his good hand over his face. "We'll speak more of this in the morning. Will you send in the girl? I need more broth."

"Of course, majesty."

There was an exchange of people at the door, and then Cerys was near the fire spooning broth into a bowl. She'd pulled a dress and kirtle over her shift. When she sat next to him on the bed, he noted how tight the dress was. "When can I eat again?"

"In the morning. I'll order you something easy."

"Have you slept in this room all this time?"

"I have a small cot near the fire."

"You can return to your own room now," he said. "I think I'll wake again."

"As you wish." She gestured to the dressing on his shoulder. "Let me look at it once more before you sleep."

Her hands set to work on his shoulder, gentle fingertips passing over the skin around the wound. "It doesn't hurt. Much."

"You lie." She put a poultice on it and rebandaged it. "It's healing well. Get some more sleep."

"I will."

When she left the room, he lay down and stared up at the ceiling, his head spinning with thoughts of Torlach, his uncle, and his princess. *Igraine, forgive me. I'll never ignore your wisdom again.*

THE FIRST few days and nights of Braedan's convalescence blurred together in a haze of medicines and treatments administered by Cerys' hand. When he was well enough to dress, he excused her and sent for one of Fingall's manservants, thanking her for her diligence and care. "I'm sure I would not have recovered so quickly if it weren't for your ministrations," he told her.

"I'm sure a young man as hale as you would have recovered as well with or without my help."

"You flatter, Cerys."

"Does that bother you, sire?"

"No. But I am quite immune to the flattery of young women. I'm much more accustomed to being abused."

She laughed. "Yes, your guard, Malcolm—he's spoken of your princess. He says I look like her."

Braedan hesitated. "There is no question that you are a lovely young woman," he finally said.

A pretty pink flush crept up her freckled cheeks. "Will you be returning to Torlach soon, your majesty?"

"That hasn't been settled yet."

"Hmm." She shrugged one shoulder. "If you need someone to care for your wounds while you travel, I would not object to a journey south."

Braedan cleared his throat. "The steward, please, Cerys. Thank you."

She curtsied and left his room.

When the steward arrived, Malcolm was with him, dressed in his full livery. "Good to see you ready to get up and dress," he said.

Braedan stood, wincing at the stiffness in his arm. "If it hadn't been for the crack on the skull, I likely would have been up and about sooner." He gestured to Malcolm. "What about you and the other guards? Everyone all right to travel?"

"They are. Winter is fully on our doorstep, however. Fingall has given us his leave to remain here until spring if needs be. And Faltian is in three days. We might stay at least that long."

Braedan sighed. "I want to be back in Torlach. I want to deal with my uncle before this whole thing gets worse." He swore as the manservant gestured for him to stretch his arm out to put it through a sleeve. "And I'm worried for Igraine—if my uncle has no qualms about attacking me and my men on the road, what would he do to her? But if I don't go about this carefully, strategically, I could just stumble right into a trap my uncle has set for me." He winced again as the man helped him into a green wool doublet. He turned to the manservant. "Make me a sling. And fetch Duke Fingall."

"As you wish, sire."

"And have them bring me a meal. I'm famished." He put a hand on the man's arm as he started to leave the room. "And wine."

"Yes, sire."

When Fingall arrived in his rooms, Braedan was already on his third slice of beef and halfway through his second cup of wine. He sopped up the drippings of beef with a piece of thick, brown bread and leaned back in his chair to address the duke. "Have a seat," he said.

Duke Fingall bowed and then sat. "I see your appetite is much improved, sire?"

"Much. My father always said there was little that would help a wound heal as fast as a few good meals of meat. Perhaps that was one thing he had the right of." He paused and chewed on his bread. "You offered me men. Do you stand by your offer?"

"I do, sire. Whatever you wish. I would see Kerry out of Torlach and the castle and have you back on your throne."

"What of the other dukes? Do you know their opinions on the matter?"

A servant poured wine for the duke, and he lifted his goblet and sipped. "I can't say for all, majesty. There are many who have still resisted naming you king, I regret to say. The new duke, Mac Niall—your guard tells me he hasn't taken his seat yet."

"No. And he and I were not especially friendly when we were young. I would not expect him to be thrilled that I am trying to claim the Raven Throne."

"Brody Reid will support you, but his house is small and not especially wealthy. If Chancellor Kerry offers him land or money ...."

"Brody Reid would be insulted by an offer of money."

"The father, yes, but the son?" Fingall shrugged. "The younger Brody Reid is a gambler. His father is ailing and no longer runs the estate, and the younger man has gambled much of the family's wealth away." He paused for a sip of wine. "The younger Reid and the younger Mac Niall were close in their youth. Gain the support of one, you may gain the support of both."

Braedan twisted his mouth in thought. *And neither of them like me.* "It's something to consider."

"As for the others, you have likely lost the support of the Seannans."

"Likely."

He ticked off one finger for the Seannans. "You have obvious issues with Kerry." Another finger. "Byrne and Kane have had their eye on the southern tribal lands for decades. If Chancellor Kerry has promised them tribal land, there will be no convincing them to back you for the throne." Two more fingers. "And Farrell—"

"Farrell is my uncle's neighbor on Stone Coast. They have hunted, gambled, and whored together for years. There will be no swaying him from my uncle's side."

Fingall added a thumb and lifted his opposite fist. "Anyone else?"

"Duinn. He'll back Kerry."

Fingall tipped his head. "You say so?"

"He's pragmatic, and he has many interests in Torlach. His lands are right up against the city to the south. He'll not want to risk angering the man who could burn and pillage his estate."

Fingall grunted. "I think you underestimate Duinn's nobility. He loves Taura. He will want what's best for her."

"Then I suppose it depends on what his price is and whether my uncle can pay it."

Fingall tipped his head in agreement. He lifted his index finger. "Then it is six, my lord—six houses against you. Six *strong* houses against you."

Braedan took a long swallow of wine. "And on my side?" He lifted one index finger. "Me—head of a splintered house with few resources left." Another finger. "You." One more finger. "Griffudd."

"Griffudd?"

"He'll be driven by his hatred of my uncle. Unfortunately, he also has a small house. Strong, wealthy, but small. He has few men." He wiggled his three fingers. "Three houses. And we want to take back a fortified city that I only took in the first place by virtue of the men I now fight against."

"Those are not good odds, sire."

"Indeed." Braedan picked up his goblet and swirled his wine. "I wonder, Fingall—would you be willing to travel south?"

"South? I thought you would want me to go to Dylan."

Braedan leaned forward. "No, I want you to go to Reid. There is too much in the past for me to go to Brody Reid. But you—he has no reason to hate you. And I've been thinking about something else as well. As much as I long to see my betrothed again, I'm not ready for my face to be seen in the south. And if Connor Mac Niall comes back to Taura, he's more likely to visit Brody Reid than any other duke. Reid may even know how to reach him." *If his Sidh mother hasn't already visited him.*

"All right. I can visit Reid. And you?"

"I'm going north. I'm going to win Dylan to my side." *And visit this wisdomkeeper, if I can.* He ate and thought for a moment. "How are the roads?"

"Muddy, icy, and rough, but we can traverse them, sire. We can't take wagons, but my men are practiced in rough weather travel. They can take individual provisions. And I confess—a trip to Torlach this time of year would gladden their hearts. The road may be rough, but they would be glad of the amenities of city life for a time." He paused. "But you, heading north—I fear that will not be an easy trip."

"My men can handle it. We're a small force, which will make us nimble and flexible. We can even travel as mercenaries or merchants." He rubbed the few days' growth on his face. "I've been wanting to try a beard, anyway."

"Should you set out now, before you are fully healed—"

"I can travel."

"If your shoulder grows septic, you will be far from any capable help."

"Then I'll bring along your girl," Braedan said. "Cerys. Who is she, anyway? Where did she learn healing arts?"

Fingall shrugged. "To be honest, majesty, I know little about her. She was passing through the village a few weeks ago, and one of my guards had a run-in with a mad dog. Killed it, but not before it nearly tore his arm off. She saw the whole thing and treated his arm and the fever that came after. He said she set him right as a ship on calm seas." He drank again. "She sounds like she might hail from the north, but it's hard to say. Something muddled about her accent. Probably a girl who wanders a bit. She's pretty enough."

"So you've noticed, too?"

Fingall cleared his throat and set down his cup. "My wife is dead and my children grown, but I'm still a man, my lord. It would be hard not to notice a young girl like that."

Braedan grinned. "Very well. Then prepare her to join me. Perhaps she'll be willing to keep one of my men warm on the journey."

Malcolm cleared his throat. "Sire, the blade."

Braedan looked down. He held the tribal blade in his hands, and the stone was glowing as bright a blue as he'd ever seen. "When did I draw this?" he asked.

"When we started speaking of the girl, sire," Malcolm said.

Fingall frowned. "Why is it glowing?"

"It seems to like me," Braedan said. He sheathed the blade and stood. "Forgive me, gentlemen. I grow weary. I should be abed."

That night, as fierce an ice storm as Braedan had ever seen blew in, and the estate was soon covered in ice an inch thick. When Faltian dawned, celebrations were subdued, and Braedan spent most of the night watching the storm from the window of the great hall where he dined with Fingall and his household. They discussed timing and agreed there was no traveling in such weather. "Even my most intrepid horses would be slipping on roads like these," Fingall said. "I'll not lose them to broken legs just to try to get south a week earlier. Take consolation in the fact that Chancellor Kerry can do little this time of year."

Except torment my betrothed and turn the castle and petitioners against me. Braedan drank his fourth cup of wine, frowned, and put it down. "Take this away," he told the steward. "I'll have water."

When he went to his bed that night, Cerys waited in his room. She stood when his guard opened the door for him. "Majesty," she said with a curtsy. "I need to check your dressing."

Braedan pulled his arm out of the sling and started to unbutton his doublet. "It's feeling much better, Cerys. I don't know that we need to keep dressing it."

"You let me decide." She helped him out of the doublet. He started to pull off his tunic, but stopped and hissed at the stiffness still in his shoulder. "Sit, majesty—let me."

He sat. "My thanks."

"They said you'll be going north. They asked if I would accompany you."

Braedan grunted. "Fingall worries that I'm not strong enough to travel yet."

"He is right. You cannot overtax yourself, sire." She paused as her fingers removed the dressing. "But I do wonder why you won't go south and let the duke go north."

He closed his eyes. "That's none of your concern."

"No, certainly. I am merely a common girl. But I thought you would be eager to see Torlach and your princess."

The wine he'd had with dinner had gone to his head. *I am eager,* he thought. *I do miss Igraine. And the city, too.* She started to move away, but he took her hand. "Wait."

She stopped. "Yes, majesty?"

He pulled her closer to him, between his legs, and put his hands on her hips. "My princess is waiting in Torlach." He brushed her hair back from her face with one hand.

She put her hands on his shoulders. "Yes, majesty."

Her voice had a purring timbre that reminded him of some other woman. He couldn't say who. "I promised her I'd be faithful."

"She need never know, sire."

"If you're to join us on this trip, I have to know I can count on your discretion."

She lifted his hand to her mouth to kiss it. "I am always discreet, sire," she whispered.

Igraine wouldn't have to know. At his side, the blade warmed. He pushed her away and stood. *No—not south, to Torlach. North, to Starling's Cross.* "I'm sorry. I shouldn't have—"

"It's well, majesty." She put her arms around his waist and smiled up at him. "I have no allegiance to any man. I would count it an honor to share your bed."

He stepped away. "I'll have a guard present when you dress the wound in the future."

Anger flickered across her face, and he thought she looked at the blade in his belt, but he couldn't be certain. She curtsied. "As you wish, majesty. I'll take my leave." She left the room.

Braedan lay down. He could think only of Igraine. *What a fool. Why do I so easily fall back into drinking and whoring? Cerys is just a serving girl— little more—and I would ruin what I have with Igraine for one night?* Aching need still thrummed through his body, but he fought it back and fell asleep.

Ravens dove again and again at the bodies. Braedan walked among them and found Igraine, her body violated and shredded nearly beyond recognition. He knelt next to her, drew her into his arms, and wept in the courtyard of the castle.

"You could have saved her," whispered Olwyn's voice.

"You would have killed her. You didn't want me to have her," Braedan said.

The woman's low, mocking laugh echoed in the too-quiet air. "I want you to serve me only."

Braedan sat up, sweating, his heart racing. "Igraine, no," he cried out.

The guard at his door entered. "Majesty? Are you well?"

Braedan caught his breath. *Dreams—Edgar said there would be dreams.* "Yes. Bad dream. Too much wine, I think. You're dismissed."

In the morning, Braedan went to Fingall. "I won't wait another day," he said. "Make preparations now."

CHAPTER THIRTEEN

We could not know what would come later. Even with my sight, I could not see the pains and victories the future held. But from the moment I saw him with them, I knew that the raven had found his flock.
— *Journal of Chief Eunuch to the Emperor of the Nine Seas of Tal'Amun, Year of Creation 5993*

They stood before him, the four of them—righteous in their sin, unconcerned with the soil in their souls.

Shut up! Connor tried to resolve the images of the four human beings into shapes he could identify, people he knew. The Morrag whispered, fluttered, constricted his chest. He tried to shake his head to clear her voice, tried to push her away. *Shut up! Stop it! You don't know—you don't know these people!*

He wants the girl, she whispered. *The blond warrior—he thinks of the girl.*

Mairead? Gareth wants Mairead? No, he—

The other one has lied, stolen reputation, stolen a name. The eunuch—

Behind her voice, more whispers. *—conscript the men—capture the women—destroy the people, utterly—bribe them with property—burn the forest—the throne is yours—*

—blood on snow—the faint pulse of a fading heartbeat—the screams of the dying—brutalized women—

Stop it! Stop it! Not my sins—not all mine! "It's time," he said, and in some part of him that still remained human, Connor flinched at the croak of the raven. "Mairead, it's time. This place needs cleansing."

Mairead pushed one of the men aside and stepped closer. "What are you doing?"

"The tribesmen. They've turned this holy night into one of debauchery." He turned his sword, admiring the glimmer of the steel in the moonlight. "This place needs cleansing."

"What do you mean?"

He wants the girl—he thinks of her—imagines her—lust, taking her for himself—

Shut up! Gareth—his name is Gareth—he's just a man who wants a woman, not—

But she cackled in exultant, victorious knowledge. *He lusts, raven. He lusts after her.*

Connor couldn't stop himself. He turned to Gareth. "Many men and women decide not to wait for handfastings during Faltian, eh? The dances around the fire stir the blood." The piece that was still Connor struggled for a toehold in his spirit. *Gareth. His name is Gareth.* "Tsk tsk, boy. Such shameful thoughts about a woman who doesn't belong to you."

Gareth colored from neck to hair. "How do you know—"

"She whispers. The whispers ...." He closed his eyes. *Please let me go. Please stop talking. Please.*

The one called Trypp approached, sword drawn. "It's not your place to judge these people, wolf."

The Morrag exulted. *Vengeance is here. Vengeance is come. The time for cleansing is now.*

Connor croaked a laugh. "Not my place? This is why I was made. This is why I am here. I am vengeance. I am death incarnate."

Gareth's hands tightened on his sword hilt. "Traitha, go back to the fires."

"No." Mairead took another step toward Connor. She held her hand out. "You don't want to do this," she said. "I'm here. Talk to me."

"Talk? The time for talk is done. The raven rises, and she demands blood." Connor tilted his sword point toward Phinneas. *He lies. He deceives. He seeks his own glory. He is not cut.* "You first. I know your secret."

Phinneas stood very still. "What secret is that, my lord?"

"You're no eunuch. You are intact. You've chosen to live as a eunuch because it's easier for you—because you have no interest in women."

"I have not sinned against the One Hand," Phinneas said.

"You lie to me, to yourself, to everyone around you. You say you are cut—that you can't bed a woman—when the truth is you don't want to."

Tiny beads of sweat formed on Phinneas' forehead, glistening in the faint light. "I've been careful," he said. "I've been set apart—from my earliest days, I've been faithful and careful."

"But you still lie." Connor's sword shimmered between them. The point edged closer and closer to Phinneas' chest. The eunuch held his ground. *So easy. So easy to separate bone and flesh. So easy to rid the world of his sin.* "You're close to seven hundred years old. How is it that you have escaped death thus far?"

His face paled. "My lord, the magic, the spells and tricks I know—they keep me alive. Young. Your nursemaid—the one you mentioned—Rhiannon? She will most likely live this long as well."

Connor waved his sword toward the fires. "They've turned a holy night into a night of debauchery," he said, low. "Everyone drinking, dancing, fucking .... They celebrate when they should repent."

"Repent of what?" Mairead asked.

"Everything. All their lies and blasphemy and idol worship. Murder. Theft. All of it."

"We have no idols," Gareth started.

"Don't you?" He turned to Mairead. *If she were gone* .... His sword drifted, drifted, until the point hovered over her breast. "What about her?"

The Morrag laughed and cawed and croaked. *Yes, raven! Yes! Remove their idol. Force their eyes back to the One Hand.*

No one moved. Mairead licked her lips, but she didn't step back. "Is this what you are? Is this really you?"

"You don't know—"

"I do know. I know that Connor Mac Niall would not sully his family name this way. I know Ulfrich Wolfbrother would not shame his tribe by slaughtering innocents."

Connor Mac Niall. I am a Mac Niall. A Mac Niall protects the innocent. I am a wolf. I fight for justice. But the Morrag drowned out the voice of Connor. "I keep telling you—there are no innocents. Not even you." He tipped his head and tilted his sword. "If you were dead, they wouldn't have an idol."

She didn't flinch. "Your time has not yet come." She opened her palm and showed him the blue light of her scar. Mairead pushed his sword away and touched his bare arm. "Connor. Your time has not yet come."

The Morrag quieted in an instant. *I will wait. My sister begs me wait. I will wait.* Tension melted out of Connor. He dropped the sword and stumbled toward Mairead. She caught him and let him wrap his arms around her. "What did you do to me?"

She put her arms around his waist. "I'm here now," she whispered, and only now could he hear the faint tremor of fear in her voice. "We'll get through this together. I'm here. I won't let you kill these people."

"The whispers. She tells me things—tells me what people are doing, what their sins are, what they plan to do to others." His voice cracked. "She lets me hear them all the time. No rest." His arms tightened. "Mairead, I need you, but I can't ask this of you—to bear this beast with me. It's too much."

She bore his weight as he clung to her. "It's not too much," she whispered. "It's not. This is why you were given to me—why I was given to you. I love you."

He tightened his arms around her, and everything else faded. *That she still loves me, that she's not afraid of me, even after I ....* He couldn't finish the thought. *I do not deserve this woman.* "You should leave, now," he said. "You should marry someone else—someone settled and tame, someone who won't hurt you." *Someone like Gareth.*

She pulled back and put her hands on his face, forcing him to look at her. "You listen to me, Connor," she said. "Would you run away the moment I became ill? The moment my duties were too much for you to bear? No, and neither will I leave you when you need me. That's what love is." She kissed him. "And I love you, and I don't want anyone else. Ever."

He pulled her close and kissed her, and she responded, and it seemed they were the only two people in Isfyrin.

"Traitha."

Gareth's voice jarred them apart.

Gareth still held his sword ready to defend her. "He cannot stay, traitha."

"He needs me. He—"

"He's right." Connor pulled away from her and put his hands on her shoulders. "He's right. If I stay, I will hurt someone. I will hurt a lot of people. And I will distract you from your purpose."

She wrapped her arms around him and pressed her head against his chest. "No," she whispered. "No. I won't say goodbye to you again."

His arms tightened, and he buried his head near her neck. "I'll stay close. I'll camp as close as I can without endangering you or anyone else. I'll take the eunuch with me. He can come get you if I need you. And if she quiets, I'll come back." He pulled away again and cupped her face in his hands. "You were right. This is about more than just us. This is about our separate purposes, too. You have things you need to do here. I know that. And I think it's my fate to wrestle with the Morrag. I can't do that here, or a lot of people will die."

"Connor—"

He kissed her. "One day," he said when he drew away. "One day, we will be wed, and I will whisk you away to my house in Espara, and we'll spend a week without all of this—all of these demands and obligations and demons."

She smiled. "Do you promise?"

"I promise." He took the torc from his arm and offered it to her. "Will you be my wife? One day?"

She chewed on her lip, and her fingers closed hesitantly around the torc. "Today," she whispered. "I will be your wife today."

A wild jumble of emotions swelled in Connor's chest—fear, disbelief, joy, excitement, more. "Are you sure? Mairead, are you certain this is what you want?"

She nodded and turned to the others. "How can we marry right now? Is there a guardian or—"

"This is madness," Gareth said. "Traitha, you can't marry this man—not now, not after what you saw."

"I can and I will." She turned to Gareth. "Connor is the one intended for me from the beginning of all things."

"He just tried to kill you," he said, his voice rising. "And this was the second time."

She held up her hand and showed her blue scar. "This protects me," she said. "And it helps him. I can't deny that." She looked at Connor. "You said yourself that I help you. It's my role to bring compassion and care to those around me."

"Don't marry me out of pity."

She put her hands on his cheeks. She smiled, but it seemed forced—as if she were talking herself into her words as they emerged from her mouth. "I am marrying you because I love you. Because there is no other man I want to share my life with."

He put his hands on her waist. "I can't promise you anything more than a night."

"A night, a fortnight, a lifetime—I will take as much as you can give."

This is madness. To draw her into this—to expect this much of her—I can't! But this woman—Alshada, I need this woman. And the Morrag did promise that she would be mine if I submitted to her. I've submitted. Maybe this is my reward. "Are you certain?" he whispered.

"I'm certain," she replied.

He took a deep breath and turned to Phinneas. "Can you do this? Can you perform the ceremony? Do you know enough about Taurin law to make this legitimate?"

"I can ensure that your marriage is recognized in Taura and Culidar, my lord."

"And you will draw up the proper documents to make her my sole heir until we have children?"

"My lord, such a thing is not legal in Taura."

Connor waved away the objection. "It may not be legal, but it is right. Maybe it will take someone defying the law to change it."

Phinneas inclined his head. "As you wish it, my lord."

"Traitha, this is very unwise," Gareth said. "There are prophecies—the scriptures say that you will become a lion. We thought you would be made lion through marriage. Ulfrich is a wolf, not a lion. How can you be a lion if not by blood or marriage? Not to mention the danger in wedding a man who tried to kill you twice."

Mairead rubbed her palm. "It doesn't matter. If it is the One Hand's will that I be made lion, I'm sure he'll provide a way." She took Connor's hand. "But I am also the heir of Taura, and this man is a Taurin duke, and joining my house with his is right and proper for Taura. I cannot forget that I am still bound to the country of my ancestors. This is right—this is necessary."

"But—" Gareth started.

"Gareth," Mairead said. "I've made my choice." She turned back to Connor and took his other hand. "I offer you nothing but a lifetime of fighting for justice and bringing peace to the three lands."

"And a bit of royal blood."

She smiled. "And a bit of royal blood." She kissed him. "You're my first choice, now and always. If there are problems with the lions, I'll face them. We'll face them. If the Morrag tries to take you, she'll have to fight me for you."

This woman. I do not deserve this woman. "I think you might be the only woman who could go up against her and win." He turned to Phinneas. "Please, Phinneas—marry us."

The eunuch inclined his head. "Very well. So be it. We are here to join Mairead Brennan and Connor Mac Niall, Duke of Kiern, together in wedlock."

Connor held up the torc. "Let you all witness," he said. "This bears my family crest. By this token, I swear to those present that I am giving my family name, Mac Niall, to this woman, Mairead." He put the torc on her arm. "I, Connor Mac Niall, Duke of Kiern and member of the Table of Councilors, also known as Ulfrich Wolfbrother, hereby take you, Mairead Brennan, heir to the Taurin crown, as my wife. I promise to respect, honor, and love you all of my days. I will never forsake you for another." *My mother will flay me alive, but I don't care—I will have this woman for my wife, Sidh blood or no.*

Mairead's hands shook when she took his. "I have nothing to give you."

"You need nothing. You are enough."

She smiled, and her eyes glistened with tears. "I, Mairead Brennan, hereby take you, Connor Mac Niall, for my husband. I promise to respect, honor, and love you all of my days. I will never forsake you for another."

He squeezed her hands. "Is that enough, Phinneas? Can I call her my wife?"

Phinneas inclined his head. "I believe that's enough. In my eyes, you are wed."

Connor cupped Mairead's face in his hands and kissed her. "I love you,

Mairead Mac Niall," he whispered.

She put her hands on his waist. "Mac Niall. I'm a Mac Niall."

"You're a duchess, my lady." He kissed her again. "I think the first thing we need is a very quiet place without an audience."

He could see her face color even in the darkness. "Connor," she whispered, but there was excitement under her breath that stirred his own desire. "Where would we go? The city is—"

"You will use my hut tonight," Gareth said. "I will stay with Trypp and Wytha. But I have one request of you, Ulfrich: tomorrow, you will leave the city and remain outside the walls."

Mairead whirled. "But we are just married. Can't we have some time together—can't we have a few days?"

"We'll have time," Connor said. "I'll stay as close as I can without endangering you or the tribe. I'll visit you often. This isn't like before—I'm not leaving forever. I'm just keeping you and the tribe safe."

Her voice was husky with unshed tears. "I will work to change it. I will."

"I expect nothing less."

Trypp returned to his own home, and Phinneas excused himself to Aerwyth and Hedwar's house, promising that he would draw up the necessary documents during the night. Connor stopped him before he walked away. "What I said," he whispered. "Phinneas, I am sorry."

Phinneas inclined his head. "The truth of my nature has been revealed in more brutal ways than this," he said. "It is forgiven." He melted into the shadows of the city.

Gareth showed Connor and Mairead to his hut. Connor opened the door and ushered Mairead in, then turned to Gareth. He held out a hand. "I thank you for your hospitality."

Gareth clasped his arm. "I would wish the same kindness if it were my beloved," he said. He paused for a moment. "Ulfrich, it is not that I dislike you. I have a duty to protect her. I am sorry that you must leave. I can see how much it hurts her."

"Let us pray it's only temporary."

Gareth inclined his head. "May the One Hand bless your marriage, Ulfrich Wolfbrother."

Connor entered the hut and let the door shut behind him. Mairead stood with her back to him, fidgeting. She gestured to his sleeping mat. His pack sat next to the mat. "This is your bed?"

"Yes." He put his hands on her shoulders and leaned down to kiss her neck. *The Morrag said she would be mine, and here she is. But what if I ruin her? What if I do exactly what I fear—what if my mother is right? I do not deserve this woman.* "Do you want a fire?"

She shook her head. "I'm nervous."

"So am I, oddly. I've been a lover, but I've never been a husband."

She turned to him. "Is it so different?"

"With you, I know there's no going back."

"Do you already regret it?"

"No. Gods, no." He cupped her face and kissed her. He put his hands on her shoulders in an attempt to slow himself down. *Don't go too fast. Don't scare her.* But the dress Aerwyth had loaned her hugged her curves in an irresistible way, and he traced the neckline down to where the laces met at the top of her breasts.

She put one hand over his. "Please," she whispered, her breath coming in short, quick bursts. "Go slow."

"I will. We'll take the whole night, if needs be." He untied the laces on her dress. The faint light of the village flickered off her pale skin, and he leaned down to bury his face against her. The scent of her surrounded him, drew him in, more intoxicating than the strongest oiska. *This woman. That she would trust me this way, that she would give herself to me—I am blessed beyond all men.* "I don't know what this is," he whispered.

"What?"

"This thing you do. The way you quiet the Morrag." He sank his hands into her hair, pulled the dress off her shoulder, kissed her bare skin. "But I know that the more of you I touch, the quieter she gets."

Her body trembled in his arms, and she put a hand on his hip. Her fingers tightened. "I don't know what to do."

"You don't need to know anything."

"But I don't want to disappoint you. I—"

He silenced her with the gentlest kiss he could give. It was a soft flutter, barely skimming her mouth with his. She pursed her lips, closed her eyes, and stretched up to kiss him again. "You can't disappoint me, Lady Mac Niall," he said.

"But you've been with so many women, and I—"

He kissed her again. "Not as many as you think. Besides, I married you. I have never wanted a woman more than I want you right now. With you, I'm safe. Home. Exactly where I want to be."

Her eyes brimmed with tears, but she smiled and put her arms around his neck. "I love you, Connor."

"I love you, Mairead."

She untied the jerkin and pushed it off his shoulders. Her hands snaked up into his tunic, and he helped her pull it over his head. Her hands shook on his chest. He pulled her dress open to reveal the shift underneath, and she closed her eyes. Her lips parted. He leaned down to kiss her again. She opened her eyes and looked up when he drew away. "I'm not afraid," she whispered.

He wrapped her in his arms, kissed her, and carried her to his bed, and every fear and worry faded in Mairead's arms.

And for a moment, the Morrag was silent.

CHAPTER FOURTEEN

Remember the work of the One Hand. His creation is in the dance of our fathers.
— Tribal wisdom

Mairead was awake long before sunrise. She lay nestled in the crook of Connor's arm, listening to his heavy breath as he slept. *One night was not enough.*

Her first night in Connor's bed was all she had longed for, and at the same time, not enough to sate her. His every touch, every kiss was considered and deliberate. He waited with her every hesitation, whispering words of love and desire and reassurance.

But there were moments, even in the midst of their passion, when he disappeared. She couldn't think of any other way to describe it. It seemed that, for a moment, something else held his attention—something dark—and his eyes would grow distant. When she spoke his name, he would shake his head and return to her. But Mairead couldn't forget the hint of pain on his face. *And it seems he doesn't even notice it—as if he's so accustomed to it that he doesn't even know what real peace is like.*

They lay awake long into the night, and he did finally build a small fire. When he returned to bed, she traced his tattoos in the firelight, asking the meaning and story behind each one. When she reached the ravenmark on his thigh, he gasped and chuckled. "Be careful," he said in a low voice. He put his mouth next to her neck. "There's more in that area than just a tattoo."

Mairead felt the heat creep up her cheeks. "The ravenmark isn't as faded as the others."

"It's not ink. It's her mark—however she makes her mark."

She will always be between us. Have I made a terrible mistake? What if this really is the only night we ever have? "Connor, I don't want to lose you."

"You won't lose me."

That's a promise you can't make. But she merely pulled him close to her and kissed him and tried to forget the specter of the Morrag between them.

Even when Connor slept that night, Mairead didn't. She lay pressed up against him, awake, worrying and praying. When he finally woke just before sunrise, it was with a satisfied sigh and groan. His arm tightened around her shoulders. "Good morning."

She propped her chin on his chest. "Good morning. How are you?"

"Content."

At least there is that. "We need to get you out of here before someone in the city sees that we've been together."

"If they're really tribal, they won't care," he said, but he sat up anyway. They both washed and dressed, and Connor finished packing his things moments before the sun peeked over the horizon.

Phinneas knocked on the door just as Connor was belting on his sword. He bowed and held out several pieces of parchment when Connor opened the door. "The documents, my lord. Gareth says he has ink and quill in his hut."

They stood at Gareth's small table and reviewed the documents. Connor read everything first, then gave it all to Mairead as he finished. "You are hereby my only heir," he said, pointing to a clause in one of the documents.

Mairead read it. "Are you certain you want to challenge Taurin law this way?" she asked. "You just got your title and name back. Is this really wise?"

He shrugged. "I was a bastard with no name for twenty-seven years. I don't mind being one again."

She put down the parchment, hands shaking. "But what about me? Or our children?"

"If you are ever in trouble and I can't help, seek the Sidh. My mother will help you. I'll see to that."

"Oh gods," she said, looking up at him. "I didn't even think of her. She's—"

"Going to learn to love you," he said.

Mairead let out a long breath. "Connor ...."

He tightened a hand around hers and lifted it to his mouth. "I love you, Mairead Mac Niall."

It was enough. Mairead's hand shook every time she signed "Mairead Mac Niall," but she also couldn't help smiling at Connor's confident scrawl next to hers. *Married. Alshada, I would not have thought—could not have guessed— this man would be my husband.*

They met Gareth outside the hut, and he nodded a greeting and escorted them to the edge of the city. The guards were just opening the gates for the day.

Gareth drew a dagger and offered it to Connor, hilt first. "I know how much you value her. I will protect her as I would my own sister. I swear this to you."

Connor pulled one of his own blades out of his boot. "I thank you." They exchanged daggers and clasped arms, and then Connor turned to Mairead and took her hands. "This isn't forever," he promised again. "This is just for now."

She blinked back tears. "You will call for me if you need me, won't you?"

"I promise." He kissed her forehead and pulled her into an embrace. He let go of her, mounted his horse, and followed Phinneas into the forest outside Isfyrin.

Mairead watched Connor and Phinneas until they finally disappeared into the distant trees. *I will not cry,* she willed herself. *I will not.*

"You are well this morning?" Gareth asked quietly.

"Yes." She turned to Gareth. "I know you don't trust him, but you have only seen him since this darkness came upon him. I traveled with him for three months, and I only saw nobility. This is no different from an illness, Gareth. We will learn to manage it."

Gareth frowned. "The ravenmarked warriors of the past never learned such. What makes him different?"

Mairead didn't have a satisfactory answer to that.

Most of Isfyrin had not yet awakened, and as they walked back to Hedwar and Aerwyth's home, Gareth assured Mairead that no one would even notice if she disappeared to sleep for a few hours on the morning after the Faltian fires. He left her at the door of his parents' home, and Mairead crept in quietly to avoid waking anyone. In her room, she undressed and lay down, blinking back tears as she curled herself tight under the blankets. She held the torc up to the faint light in the room and rotated it to look at the Mac Niall family crest. *Strength. Valor. Truth.* She bit her lip. *I hope I can be worthy of such a motto.*

She woke near midday to the aroma of fresh bread and frying meat. She dressed, braided her hair, and put Connor's torc around her ankle, inside her boot. The bulk of the silver felt oddly comforting, and she smiled. *Like a secret engagement from some old romance.*

Gareth sat at his parents' table across from his father. Aerwyth was busy setting food on the table, and Stripe darted around her feet as she walked to and from the kitchen area. Gareth stood when he saw Mairead. "Good day, traitha."

"Good day." She took a deep breath. "Aerwyth, something smells wonderful."

"The last of the pears for the year, I fear," Aerwyth said. She gestured to a pile of pastries in the center of the table. "Enjoy, traitha."

Mairead sat and took a pastry, and she nibbled as Gareth spoke. "My parents asked about Connor and Phinneas," he said. "I told them of the change in plans."

"It's for the best," Aerwyth said. "Outsiders have never been looked upon favorably, and no one trusts those of the outland tribes."

What if you knew he is ravenmarked? "Connor is a good man," Mairead began, but stopped when Gareth shook his head.

"I am certain he is," Hedwar said. "But you will have an easier time with our elders if your ties to the outland aren't so obvious."

"Then this is politics."

Hedwar offered her a thin smile. "Everything is politics."

After their meal, Gareth volunteered to give her a more thorough tour of the city. "You can use the distraction," he said. "My father will send Stripe to find us if someone needs us."

"I would enjoy seeing the city."

They walked toward the center of Isfyrin, and Gareth pointed out homes and families he knew and introduced her to friends and acquaintances. People greeted her with everything from mild curiosity to interest to near-worship. "I wish they wouldn't act so enthralled," she said after enduring another man kneeling and asking her blessing.

"Why?"

"I'm not worthy of it. I'm not a god, and I've never even done anything particularly important." She stopped walking and turned to Gareth. "My whole life, everything I am or supposed to be—it all hinges on blood, prophecy, and magic. There are so many people who could do these things better."

He twisted his mouth in a thoughtful expression. "Perhaps there are some with more experience," he said. "But I don't think I've ever met anyone who cares more about doing what's right."

A slender woman with dark braids approached. "So. You are the Deliverer, eh? I pictured someone stronger." The woman stepped close to Mairead, toe to toe. Mairead noted that the woman was a head shorter, but she didn't think the woman would have any trouble besting her in a fight. "These people greeted you with cheers and gifts," the woman said. "And you will deliver them in blood."

Gareth put a hand on Mairead's shoulder. "Letha, perhaps formal introductions first? Mairead, this is our clan's chief earth guardian, Letha Catspaw.

Letha, this is Mairead, the Deliverer we have waited for."

"Letha," she said. "I'm pleased—"

The guardian interrupted with a grunt and folded her arms. The snaking tattoos across her face twisted into wrinkles and knots as she evaluated Mairead. "You are no guardian," she said.

Mairead shook her head. "I am not tribal."

"She means she is not of the nine," Gareth said.

Letha scoffed. "I know what she means, Gareth." She reached for Mairead's hand and pulled it close to her, running two fingers across the scarred palm. "You have no mark. Only this scar. No mark, no tattoos, no tribal training. The One Hand does have a sense of humor."

"What do you mean?"

"I mean that the prophecies rarely seem to turn out the way we expect," she said.

"Letha is the guardian who sent us out to find you," Gareth said.

Her visions were the ones that drove their search. Maybe she has answers. "What did you mean about delivering this tribe in blood?"

"Prophecy, girl. It's prophecy." She paused. "'The lion awakens. The mountain bleeds.' This deliverance is not what the people think. Rebirth is accomplished in blood."

Mairead wet her lips. "May we speak privately?"

Letha dropped her hand and nodded. "Come."

Letha led Mairead and Gareth to her hut, a small structure clearly designed for only one person. A circle with a cross through it was painted on the door. She opened the door and gestured. "Come in."

Gareth hesitated. "I'm going to see if any of the other traithas have arrived. I want to see if the council has set a time to meet you yet."

"I will find you when we are finished," Mairead said.

Gareth walked away, and Letha gestured to Mairead to sit down near a small pit that glowed with the remains of a fire. "What do you wish to discuss?"

Everything. Mairead sat cross-legged. "What do you mean that this deliverance won't be what people expect?"

Letha grinned. "You do not waste time with pleasantries. How refreshing." She held up a hand as Mairead started to apologize. "I do not waste time with such, either. We are, perhaps, more alike than we realize." She took a deep breath. "For centuries, this tribe has waited in the mountains for a Deliverer to take them down to the plains. They have always been convinced that their inheritance is on the plains. They expect to be led down there to conquer.

They do not realize how much tribal blood will be shed in the process."

"And I am to preside over this bloodletting?"

"Apparently."

Gods. "Can I speak in confidence?"

"Of course."

"There were two others who traveled with us."

"Yes, I saw them. One of the cut men of the east and a warrior."

"Connor—the warrior—he is ravenmarked, and—"

"A raven? You traveled with one of the ravenmarked? And he was here in Isfyrin?"

Mairead swallowed over a lump in her throat. "He is—was—my guard."

"And now?"

"Last night, during the celebrations, Connor became very agitated. He said the Morrag wanted blood. I touched him, and he said when I touched his skin, the Morrag retreated."

"How did you know to touch him?"

"I did it once before, just by accident. He was in the grip of the Morrag, and I touched him, and he just ...." She clenched her fist. "I don't understand it, but he relaxed. Everything just stopped, like a freak spring storm that just lasts for a few moments and ends as suddenly as it began."

Letha held out a hand. "Let me see the scar again."

Mairead opened her hand. "It's not much, really, or it wasn't until two weeks ago. I cut myself when I first came to Culidar. I bled on the rocks on the shore. I didn't think anything more of it until Gareth and the others found us."

"What happened then?"

"My hand reacted to them. To their marks, the marks on their palms. When they came into the clearing, my hand blazed with blue light, and then again when Gareth held his hand near mine."

Letha held out her own palm. Mairead took note of the mark. Instead of a whorl, Letha's palm was marked with the same circled cross Mairead had seen on her door. "When young men return from their vision quests, they are given the mark of the warrior—the whorl you saw on Gareth's palm. When the guardians pass their initiation, they are given this—the wisdommark. The marks connect us to the warriors. When they need us or we need them, these marks allow us to call each other. The wisdommark is also the way we communicate with the earthspirit. She allows us to call her through this mark, and we use the connection with her to speak to the warriors, the tribe, even the earth itself. It is how we keep the balance of life and death in our tribe."

"I don't understand how a scar I received from an injury would give me such a power," Mairead said.

"It wouldn't," Letha said. "There are other things you must know, other rituals you must do. You have no training in the tribal rites or knowledge."

"Then why would this scar give me any power or ability?"

Letha frowned. "I do not know," she admitted. "Has it reacted any other time? Besides the night you met the lions and the times you connected to the Morrag?"

"When we were traveling, if I looked toward the slave camps, my palm would grow warm."

Letha pursed her lips. She closed her eyes and whispered words that Mairead couldn't understand. Somewhere in the midst of Letha's words, Mairead heard her own name, and a moment later, her palm warmed so quickly and fiercely that she cried out and jumped.

Letha opened her eyes. "It called you."

Mairead nodded and showed Letha the glowing mark. "What did you do?"

"I called you as I would call a warrior." She crossed her arms. "It would appear you are connected to both the earthspirit and the warrior."

"Is that rare?"

"It has never happened before, to my knowledge. It could be that the Morrag senses your connection to the earthspirit, and that's what quiets her—that connection to her sister."

Mairead sighed. "This isn't what the sayas prepared me for," she whispered.

"Sayas?"

"Servants of Alshada."

"Ah, yes. Women of the chaste god."

Mairead clenched her fist again. "Whatever this power, wherever it comes from, I know two things: it must be subject to Alshada—the One Hand—and he must have some purpose for giving it to me."

"This is the beginning of wisdom."

"Do you believe I am this Deliverer your prophets foretold?"

Letha pursed her lips. "I do not know," she finally said. "I don't know what to call you. I do not believe you are a guardian, but I do not believe I should call you a warrior."

"Why not?"

"You are a woman," Letha said gently. "It is true that all of our women fight, but none of them are marked and branded warriors. That is for the men."

Mairead let out a long breath and stood. "I need to walk. I need to clear my head."

Mairead wandered toward the edge of the city, avoiding the nods and bows that the people offered. She found the city gate, tempted to leave and try to find Connor, but she couldn't bring herself to approach the guards. *I think this is for me to sort out on my own.* She tightened her fist and found a shadowy corner, where she sat down in the dirt and pulled her knees up to her chin. She buried her head against her knees. *Alshada,* she began, and then her face flared. *I'm a wife now—wedded and bedded, as they say. But you are still there, aren't you? You listen to the prayers of the wife as well as those of the saya, don't you?* She sighed. "I want to be what you want, Alshada, but I don't know if I can. I don't know what you want most of the time, and when I think I have it learned, you change things."

She thought back over the last several months. First there was the sayada and the knowledge that one day, the sayas would turn her over to a husband to bear children for the rightful line. *But no indication that I would have to be queen—no reason to think I would be anything more than a wife and a mother.* And then Braedan's coup and her journey with Connor changed everything. *I ran, learned to fight and survive in the wilds, was kidnapped and almost raped, killed several men, and became a warrior. And I fell in love—with Connor and with Culidar. And you still had more—you had this tribe and its expectations, and you had new titles for me—Deliverer, wife, traitha. What else is there?*

She opened her hand and stared at the scar. Knowing now that her amorphous scar connected her to both the warrior and the earthspirit, she could see the pieces fall into place. *The ease with which I learned to fight and shoot—it's because of the warriormark. The ache I feel for the poor—that's the earth.* Letha had said deliverance would be accomplished in blood. *I have no desire to conquer Culidar. I don't want to damage the people any more than they are already damaged. But what if these lions could liberate the land and live on the plains? There's plenty of room. Would they do it? Would they follow me to the plains to liberate a people they don't care for?* "Only one way to know for certain," she whispered. *But what would that mean for Taura? For my position there?* She put her head against her knees again and let her prayers pour out through whispered supplication.

Gareth found her after she'd been sitting for an hour or so. She looked up as he crouched before her. "The council is assembled."

"I thought they would be."

"Are you questioning your path?"

"Among other things."

He was silent for a moment. "What did you expect, Mairead?"

She took a deep breath. "I knew I was the Taurin heir—I remember being anointed, and the sayas talked about it often. My teacher, Sayana Muriel, told me I'd marry and have children and carry on the line. I expected them to marry me off and send me away with a husband somewhere safe. I expected—" She bit her lip. "I expected a normal life."

He gestured toward the city. "This is a normal life."

"Not for me."

"What did you think normal would be?"

She shrugged. "A little house in a town somewhere. Serving the kirok, raising babies and chickens, being a mother. Having a husband to provide material things. Something settled—staid. Not magic or blood or slavery. Not a husband with a wandering spirit. Not everything I've already been through, or this deliverance I'm supposed to bring."

"You have the strength of your ancestors," Gareth said. "You will find your path and your purpose."

I think I have. The question is, will your people follow? She stood. "Take me to the council."

The elders mumbled in a low simmer when Mairead entered the meeting hut. At least twenty men sat around a long, low table. Hedwar stood. "Traitha. We've been waiting."

The murmurs stopped. Mairead's stomach churned. She stepped to the head of the table, next to Hedwar. "Forgive me. I needed to clear my head."

Hedwar stepped away, leaving her at the head of the table with all of those men staring at her. *No, not just men.* Letha and several other women were there as well—earth guardians who shared the table with the men. Her throat went dry. She wiped her hands on her breeches and swallowed, trying to think of something to say. *Don't let them see your nerves.* "I am Mairead Mac—I am Mairead," she said. "I th-thank you for welcoming me. I know little of your ways, but—"

One man snorted and stood. His graying braids were tied back, and a scar ran the length of his neck and disappeared under the furs over his shoulders. "We have waited two thousand years for this? A girl who can barely speak without a stammer?"

"She is new to the tribe, Wulf," Hedwar said. "She has much to learn, but be assured—this is the one we've waited for. She has already fulfilled several prophecies. She refused the gifts first given her. She came at Faltian. And she has the mark and the magic."

The man folded his arms. "Prove it."

"Call her," Letha said. "Warriors, call her as you would a guardian."

Mairead heard the whisper of spells around the room, and her hand warmed. She lifted it for the men to see. There were murmurs of acknowledgement.

"Now, guardians," Letha said. "Call her as you would a warrior."

Again, the whispers began. Mairead's hand warmed again. She held it up.

Hedwar frowned. "I don't understand."

"She is not a guardian," Letha said. "But she is connected to the earthspirit. She is also connected to the warriorspirit. Her scar reacts as a warriormark. She is bound to both wisdom and war."

"And what does that mean?" Wulf said. "How will she bring deliverance?"

Mairead straightened. "I will lead you to the plains," she said. "We will liberate the people, and you will settle among them."

Wulf stood. Gareth twitched behind Mairead, and she heard his sword loosen in its scabbard. "What do we care for outland troubles?" he asked. "And what do the plains offer us that the mountains don't?" He sneered. "Follow you to the plains? You're nothing. You have a little cub to protect you, and you're a girl who's never blooded a blade."

Never blooded a blade? A swell of anger rose in Mairead's chest. She jumped onto the table and crossed to Wulf in three steps. She leapt and kicked. Her foot met his chest, and he fell. She jumped to the floor, knelt, and put the point of her dagger under his jaw. She spoke, low and fast. "I've blooded my blade. I've killed men who would harm me and my companions. I've fought a dozen men and brought down six of them before they took me. And I watched the bastard who tried to rape me bleed out on the floor of his own house. Never blooded a blade? You have fought and hunted, Wulf, but I have blooded my blade with human blood more times than you in your safe city can imagine."

He regained his breath and glared from under gray eyebrows. "You would cut me into following you?"

She stood. "No. You choose, Wulf. You follow me, or you walk away."

Wulf stood and spat. "You're nothing. You're not one of us. You can never be one of us."

She turned to Hedwar. "What do I need to do? How can I be one of you?"

"A marriage," Hedwar said.

"What else?"

He shrugged. "You could go through an initiation, like one of our unblooded boys."

Mairead sheathed her dagger. "Arrange it."

"What are you trying to prove?" Wulf shouted. "Just what is it you think you are to us?"

Mairead turned to him. "Perhaps you should check your prophecies. I'm your traitha, kitten." She walked out of the hut.

Gareth and Trypp joined her. "I don't think old Wulf has ever been knocked down by a girl before," Trypp said. "Can't have been good for his pride."

Gareth snickered.

Mairead turned to both of them. "Do you think this is a joke? Do you think I enjoyed that? A wise man told me once that sometimes you have to bloody a few jaws to avoid chopping off heads. From what I've read, armies work best with their heads attached."

"You're right, traitha. It's not a joke," Gareth said. "And if you don't lead the Lionjaws, you don't lead the tribe."

"The Lionjaws and Catspaws are the most powerful clans," Trypp agreed. "I think the Catspaws will follow you as long as Hedwar believes, but Wulf will be a hard one to win. You need to become a lion, and that means more than just surviving the mountain through an initiation. That's part of it, but I'm not sure even that will satisfy Wulf and those who follow him."

"You have a mighty task before you." Letha joined them. "I heard what you said. I can teach you our ways and educate you in our history. That will help."

She nodded. "Gareth, can you get me a sword?"

He blinked. "Yes, of course, if you wish. But why? Are your daggers not enough?"

"My daggers are fine for some things, but if I'm to be a chieftain, I need to improve my swordplay. I need one of you to train me."

"Gareth's a better sword than I am," Trypp said. "But I can tell you about the mountain. I'll train you to survive up here, but they won't expect you to do it until spring. We don't turn out our boys on the mountain until we're sure the winter storms are done."

It's as good as I'm going to get. She took a deep breath. *My first council,* she thought. *These three—they're my first council of advisors.* She took a deep breath. "We shouldn't waste a moment. When summer comes, I want to take the lions back to the plains."

"To do what?" Gareth asked.

She lifted her chin. "We will free Culidar from slavery, and I will set up my kingdom with the lions at my side."

CHAPTER FIFTEEN

And the cries of the Morrag ranged the earth
until the rivers ran red with blood.
— First Book of the Wisdomkeepers, Cuhail's War, Lion Tribe Translation

Connor and Phinneas rode in silence until the city was no longer visible. Connor finally spoke. "Last night, you saw a glimpse of something most men don't even imagine exists. Had it not been for Mairead, I would have done very violent things in that city."

"Yes, my lord."

"I can't let that happen ever again. If you see the Morrag rise like that again, and if you can't fetch Mairead, I need your word—I need to know that you'll do what you must."

"My lord?"

Connor gestured over the eunuch's body. "I don't think those silks are just for looks. You must have a dozen or more little instruments concealed in there. Maybe near all of your drugs."

Phinneas' face could have been carved from marble. "My lord listens to too many rumors about the Tal'Aster sect."

"But I've also been to Tal'Amun enough to know that I'm right."

Phinneas merely blinked.

"If the Morrag rises again, and you can't find Mairead, you will do what you must, yes?"

"My lord—"

"Just make it quick. And no poison."

Phinneas tipped his chin down at last. "As my lord wishes. But let us pray that it never comes to such an end."

"I have a wife now. I intend to go back to her. But I don't want to go back only to kill her." Connor chose a direction and nudged his horse to a walk. "You spent a good bit of time wandering on your own yesterday. What did you learn?"

"You flatter me, my lord. Yes, I did manage to discover a few items of interest. For instance, the tribe is not unfamiliar with ravens."

"I suspected as much. What do they know of the ravens?"

"They have an unusually high occurrence of the ravenmark," he said. "One of their earth guardians was rather loose of lip once the fires leapt higher. She seemed enamored of my silks. When boys come back marked by the raven, the tribe sends them away."

"Away. Exile?"

Phinneas' head dipped once, quickly.

"Where are they?"

"She did not know exactly. The official belief is that they are left to die on the mountain or find a home down on the plains somewhere. Some may do that, but I have reason to believe they have a settlement somewhere." He pulled a small piece of parchment from a pocket and offered it to Connor. "Here. A map."

Connor took it. "Your earth guardian didn't give you this."

"I procured this from an unwilling contributor."

Thief. Liar. He deserves death.

Connor shook her voice away. "You stole it."

"I borrowed it for a good cause. I will return it when my lord is finished." He pointed as Connor opened the map. "There."

Connor frowned. "The cave?"

"It would make sense, yes? This whole mountain range is full of caves, tunnels, geological formations that defy explanation. How else could a tribe thousands strong remain hidden up here for millennia? How easy would it be for a small number of them to simply tuck themselves away, waiting for someone to give them a path—a purpose?"

They've been preparing for Mairead at the expense of their tribal brothers. Connor folded the map. "Northeast, it looks like."

"Over rough terrain, most likely."

His voice carried no hint of trepidation, fear, or dismay. In fact, if Connor had to put a tone to it, he would say the eunuch sounded excited about the possibility of mountain trails. "You don't mind?"

"I spent most of my life in the mountains, my lord. I welcome this challenge."

Connor grinned. "We'll get along better than I thought. Let's see what this mountain has to offer."

They rode northeast, and as the city grew ever more distant, the evidence of the tribes faded. *They hardly ever come out of their city,* Connor thought. *Do they ever hunt? They've become farmers and settlers. I don't understand this tribe.*

At midday, they took shelter in the trees and slept for a short time, then continued through the thick forest until they came to another crossing on the river Gareth had led them over once before. The water wasn't as wide or deep in this place, and the horses plodded across easily. When they climbed the incline on the other side of the water and emerged from the trees, Connor pointed at a steep ridge ahead. "I think that's on the map. The cave must be up there."

"Yes, my lord. But it's a long climb. Might I suggest we camp here for tonight?"

Connor agreed and dismounted. The men made camp in a small clearing, but Connor couldn't shake the feeling of eyes on his back. He frowned. "I think we're closer than we thought. They're watching us. Or someone is."

Phinneas closed his eyes. His face went slack. "I sense no one," he said finally. "Are you certain?"

Connor shrugged. "I'm going to explore a bit." He held up a hand at the protest brewing on Phinneas' face. "She's quiet right now, and I can take care of myself."

He walked farther into the deep forest and opened his senses the way his mother had taught him. *The elements. Separate the elements.* He summoned water braids and let them wind around his body, let the water inside of him merge with the water in the air, felt himself break apart into millions of miniscule pieces until he became one with the water. He hovered in the forest until the water drew him upward, into the sky. He poured thought and spirit into the water braids, and they pulled him back down, into the ground, until he joined with a dark pool. He looked at the pinprick of light above him. A shadow covered him, then a splash, and he pulled his elements together to avoid being hauled up by the bucket. *A well. In Isfyrin?*

He sank back into the earth. It was easier than before, and he poured intention into the braids until he emerged in the air once more. Another presence touched him through the braids, and he recognized it immediately. He sank into the ground again and returned to the forest, shedding the water braids as the other presence did the same. "Mother."

"How long have you been able to do that?"

"That was the first time I did it without the Morrag's help. How did you know I—" He stopped. "Mother, did you put the bond back on me?"

She clenched her fists. "Do not make me—"

"Did you put the bond back on me?"

Her lips tightened into a thin line. "No," she finally said. "You would have known."

"Then how did you know—"

"I traced your aura. I always do."

Connor didn't know whether to laugh or curse. "Of course you do. The gods forbid I should have a chance to live my own life."

"I am the Sidh queen, and you are the most powerful male Sidh ever born. It's my duty to know where you are and what you're doing."

I hope you weren't paying attention last night. "Ah, duty—the refuge of controlling mothers throughout history."

She squared her shoulders. "You have a duty to the Sidh. You must return to the village and fulfill it."

He swore and turned away. "I know what you want. The answer is no. Go home."

"When will you start thinking of your duty? Your name?"

"I am thinking of my duty *and* my name," he shouted, whirling back to face her. "I have a duty to Mairead, and I've sworn my fealty and my heart to her. I will not betray her—not now, not ever."

"She's not your wife."

"Yes. She is."

A tense silence fell in the clearing as Maeve evaluated his words. Her face turned to chiseled, stony anger, and Connor thought the wilderness around them had quieted in the way it does when a predator approaches. "You've wed without my consent?" she finally said.

"I don't need your consent. I'm a duke of Taura. I have wealth and a name of my own that does not depend on you." He took a step closer to her. "I have wed Mairead, Mother. Your only choice is whether you will accept her as your daughter or not."

Maeve let forth a long string of very impolite Sidh words. Connor reflected that if he could make his mother swear—and make her swear in Sidh—he had accomplished something akin to moving the foundations of the earth. She paced the clearing, hands on hips, muttering curses and epithets that he barely understood. Braids in every color stirred around them, and a light breeze rose as a few rocks started to tremble.

At last, she took a deep breath and straightened her shoulders. The elements quieted, and the braids faded. She turned back to Connor. "How do you propose," she asked, her voice entirely too quiet for his comfort, "that I ensure the survival of our people without an heir?"

"Mother, I don't know how to solve the problem of your heir, but I do know the solution does not lie in me siring a child on some Sidh woman."

"And were both of you simply driven by your loins, or did at least one of you think about the difficulties of you marrying each other?" She held up a hand again. "Not just political and legal problems. What about your blood and hers? What about outliving her?"

"She knows the implications. So do I. It doesn't matter. We are wed, and, spirits willing, she will bear children to continue the Mac Niall line and her own line. We will worry about the rest later."

She opened her mouth to respond, but they were both halted by the crunch of snow in the trees. Connor motioned for silence. He stood very still and sniffed the air. *Three men. More in the trees.* His hand slipped toward his sword. He motioned to Maeve to leave, and she wove the elements around herself and disappeared into the ground.

Connor drew his sword. "Whoever you are, you may as well get it over with."

Stay your blade, raven.

The Morrag's voice cracked with command in his head. His sword faltered. *You command me? I've never heard you—*

The biggest man Connor had ever seen stepped out of the trees, his hands up before him in a gesture of peace. Two more men followed, their swords still sheathed, their hands held up in front of them. "I've been waiting for you," the big man said. "We all have."

The man is a siege engine. A chill shuddered down Connor's back. "Are you a raven?"

He was massive—taller even than Connor, heavy-built, with arms that could likely crush three pureblood Sidh in one careless embrace. He had brown hair and ruddy skin, and his braids and beard were long and matted. He wore simple leathers and an old sword, and when he offered one massive hand, Connor thought he might not be able to put his own around the man's forearm. "I'm Wyll," he said.

"You're ravenmarked?"

Wyll spread his hands and bowed. "Ravenmarked and outcast, in the finest tradition of the lion tribe."

"All of you?" Connor said. "You're all marked by the Morrag? Outcast?"

"Yes. And there are more of us."

"How many?"

"About a hundred or so. We've been waiting for you—for both of you." Connor frowned. "Both of us?"

"You and the girl. We know she's with you—we've sensed her presence at least three times. Where is she?"

Connor realized he was still holding his sword in an attack posture, ready to fight. He tightened his grip. "She's in Isfyrin. She's safe."

"As safe as anyone is in Isfyrin," one of the men behind Wyll said.

"When did you sense her presence?" Connor asked.

"Several months ago, there was a half-dark moon. All of us sensed the earthspirit move, but the Morrag was still. We assumed it was the arrival of the Deliverer."

Connor jutted his chin toward Wyll's hand. "Didn't your warriormark flare?"

Wyll turned his hand toward Connor to reveal an unbranded palm. "They don't let us take the mark. As soon as they see the Morrag's brand, they make us leave."

"Then how did you feel the earthspirit?"

He gestured to the other men. "We dreamed of her—of the girl, not the earthspirit. We saw her with the Morrag."

Connor shivered. *So you have your talons in Mairead, too?* "What were the other two times?"

"They were more recent. A couple of weeks ago, the Morrag fell silent for all of us. She just rested," Wyll said. "Then last night, she rose again, and all of us were restless and fighting her, and then she fell silent. Rested again."

Connor finally lowered his sword. *Mairead turned her away. She listens to Mairead. How is this possible?*

She is the ravenmaster. She bids me wait.

He sighed. *Why am I here?*

You will be my first. My raven.

Connor sheathed his sword and stepped forward to offer his arm. "Connor Mac Niall," he said. "Apparently, I'm supposed to lead you."

One of the younger men behind Wyll snorted in derision.

"What's his problem?" Connor asked.

"Aelfred is from the Lionjaw clan originally. They are the least understanding of the Morrag's demands."

Aelfred snorted. "Least understanding? You have a gift for understatement. I've seen them kill a raven just for trying to visit his woman in the city."

"It was Faltian," Wyll said. "The Morrag was rising, demanding blood, and someone mistook something he did for an attack. It didn't end well."

"When was this?" Connor asked.

"Twenty years ago. More."

"And ever since then you hide in the forest?"

Aelfred folded his arms. "We've been in the forest much longer than that. Generations of men have lived and died in hiding, sneaking into Isfyrin at night to see their women and children, desperate to be accepted as tribesmen but banished for something they had no control over."

Wyll put his hand on his shoulder. "Easy, friend," he said in a low rumble.

"The lions determined centuries ago that ravens could not be trusted. When a boy comes back from his initiation with the mark, he's given food, clothing, supplies to start a life, and sent back into the forest, never to live with the tribe again."

Centuries? Generations? "And you stay here on the mountain where they could find you?"

"This is home," Wyll said, his voice a knot of pain. "The mountain belongs to us, too. We are lions as much as they are. But we are also ravens."

Phinneas padded into the clearing. "My lord, is all well?"

"Yes. Pack up. We're going to the raven village."

Wyll, Aelfred, and several men with them led Connor and Phinneas along a canopied path into a deep thicket of trees at the bottom of a shallow ravine. A wide clearing had been cut, the wood used for a smattering of rough shelters around the perimeter. In the center of the clearing was a common fire pit, and a dozen men sat around it for heat. *They live as outcasts,* Connor thought. *Only the vestiges of pride remain.*

Wyll stepped forward and raised his hands. "Men of the raven," he called. "I bring you the one we've waited for since the Breaking. Our leader—Connor Mac Niall, the First Raven chosen by the one who marked us."

No cheers greeted him—no gifts, no bows. Rather, the men in the rude village stared with distrust, fear, and apprehension.

"Where's the girl?" one man called. He jutted a chin in Connor's direction. "You said he'd be with a girl, Wyll. Where is she?"

Connor stepped over to the man. "You need a woman that much, go to Galbragh. I can give you the names of a few brothels."

Men snickered, and the man in front of Connor spat a wad of leaves to the side and gave him a tilted grin. "You're supposed to lead us, eh?"

Wyll gestured. "Connor, this is Osgar. Our traitha, of a sort."

"What are you?" Connor asked.

Wyll tilted his head. "Consider me the resident earth guardian."

"He can tend toward the feminine," Osgar said.

"I'd hate to meet a woman with arms like that," Connor said.

Osgar spat again. "Wyll claims you come to lead us. He claims you were going to bring a girl to reunite us with our tribe, but unless he mistook your magician there for a girl, I don't see anyone here who fits the description of our Deliverer. How can we be sure you're who he says you are?"

"You can't." Connor turned to Phinneas. "I suppose if we aren't wanted here, we can go back to our campsite."

Wyll flinched. "Wait. Just wait, please. Meet the men and learn more about us. Not all of us are as hesitant as Osgar and Aelfred."

Connor skimmed the eager faces around him. *Is this what you want me to do? Is this why I'm here?* he asked the Morrag.

She preened. *You will be my first, raven.*

"Show me the village," he said to Wyll.

The burly tribesman led Connor and Phinneas around the village, introducing them to the men and few women who lived there. Connor saw old craggy faces under heads of silver hair and young, round faces that couldn't have seen a razor more than three or four times. *At least I had Edgar,* he thought. *And Nedra and the wolves. The only person who seemed to have a problem with the mark was my mother. I was lucky.* "How long have you been here, in this clearing?" he asked after some time.

Osgar tipped his head to one side. "We've only been here a short time. Wyll had a visit from the Morrag. She told us to camp here and wait for the girl."

"So your old village was better fortified?"

Wyll and Osgar exchanged a look. "We were in a cave," Wyll said. "We didn't need to fortify."

Connor frowned. "Did you lose all of your tribal training when she marked you? I would think you'd still know how to protect yourselves."

Osgar spat the rest of his leaves. "Why protect ourselves? The tribe lives safe and sound behind walls. They don't care what happens to us. They cast us out years ago."

"But what about people from the plains? Slavers?"

"We're too hard to get. The mountain protects us." He jutted his chin toward a hut. "Such a discussion requires oiska. Come."

So you manage to have oiska, but minimal bows and swords? How have you survived? Connor followed Wyll into one of the huts where a woman sat cooking over a fire. She set out oiska and cups for the group.

"My wife, of a sort," Osgar said. "She lets me call her Edda."

The woman inclined her head toward them all. She had fine blonde hair with faint streaks of white in it. As thin as Osgar, there was still an air of strength about her—a wiry, hardy strength born of a hard life. Scars marred what had once been a wholesome beauty. She didn't speak, but she poured oiska into their cups and gestured to them to sit.

"Edda is mute," Osgar said. "She came from the slave camps years ago."

Connor sat. "I didn't see any children in your village."

"A raven village is no place for a child," Osgar said. He held out his cup.

Connor toasted them and they all drank. "Where do you send the children?"

Wyll and Osgar exchanged a look. "We can't risk that a child would give us away," Wyll said. "Our women bear our children inside the city. Some stay and raise their children in the tradition of the lions. Others leave their children with parents or friends and come back here to be with their men."

"It's not ideal," Osgar said. "It's painful to tell a woman she cannot keep a child. Most of our women try not to conceive if they want to stay. No woman wants to choose between a child and a husband."

Connor shuddered, but he hid it behind another shot of oiska. *What if Mairead had to choose?* "How do you supply yourselves? Food and wood I understand—the forest provides—but where do you get steel?"

"The mountain provides," Osgar said with a grin.

"There's silver up here," Wyll said. "We take some to Galbragh every few months and stock up on what we can't get here. We don't like to go, though. We don't want to risk revealing ourselves or the other lions."

Silver—Declan said he was getting silver up here. "You have alliances with traders on the plains."

"We do as we must," Wyll said. "We survive. We protect the lions, and we wait for the girl."

Osgar put down his cup. "Enough of this. Where is the girl?"

Edda came forward and poured more oiska for Connor. He drank, and she refilled his cup. He drank again, but his stomach twisted in objection when Edda offered more. He held up a hand, and she sat near Osgar. "She's with the tribe," he said. "Inside Isfyrin. They tell her she's bloodbonded to the lion tribe. She has a scar on her palm. It glows like a guardian's mark."

Wyll let out a long breath. "It is her."

Osgar barked a laugh. "Did you doubt?"

"I did. It's hard to keep faith."

"It is," Connor said. He leaned forward. "Mairead believes that she is meant to lead here—to bring rule to the plains and to Culidar. But right now, all she has is faith, desire, and a little money. She needs an army. Are you the start of that army?"

"I don't know," Osgar said. "What does she want us to do?"

I don't know. "That's for her to tell you."

Osgar and Wyll exchanged another look. "She can't come here," Osgar said. "The lions won't let her out of their sight that long. She'll lead them right to us, and they'll slaughter us."

Connor laughed. "You shouldn't be living in fear. You're ravens."

"Weak ravens," Wyll said. "We can't defend ourselves against even one clan, much less the entire lion tribe. We're one hundred men and a few women who can shoot a bow well enough to eat—that's it. We are no army."

The Morrag stirred inside Connor. "So you live like mice in your cubby-holes? No. There is no shame in being a raven."

"You don't understand," Osgar started.

Connor stood. "I do understand. And I won't have this."

He walked outside and found the village waiting to hear from him. They all stepped back, and he raised his voice to be heard. "Men of the raven," he said. "Too long have you lived in fear and shame of your mark. The tribe may have driven you away, but I say a lion cannot harm a raven as long as a raven can fly."

"What will you have us do?" someone called.

I can see the Morrag in every face here, Connor thought. *That pain—that tightness that comes with holding her back. The same pain I see when I look at my own reflection.*

These are yours, raven, the Morrag whispered. *Lead them.*

He lifted his voice again. "We will rise," he said. "We will go before the lion and bring justice to the plains. We will be the elite—the best—because we're ravens. No more hiding, no more cowering. We start training tomorrow."

He turned back to Osgar and Wyll. "I want a hut of my own and one for Phinneas."

"For the eunuch?" Wyll asked.

"He's a Tal'Amuni magician. He knows how to train assassins."

Osgar snorted. "Assassins? You plan to make us all into murderers?"

"No, assassins. There's a difference. Every army has an elite force. If I'm going to help Mairead bring a government to this place, I need to train you all to be the elite. It's not enough of an army, but it's a start."

Wyll knelt. "I am yours to command."

The Morrag fluttered and resettled her wings inside Connor's chest. *You are my first,* she said. *My raven.*

Osgar frowned. "Do you expect us to kneel, outlander? You expect fealty?" Several murmurs of agreement rippled through the crowd.

Above him, the trees rustled. Ravens alit in the branches around the little village. Connor pointed at them. "Ask her. Ask the Morrag. Let her tell you what to do."

The men cast glances at each other. No one spoke.

"The lions took your names from you," Connor said. "I know what it is to have no name. No longer will you be nameless men. No longer will you find shame in being ravens." He paused. "You are lions, but you also belong to the Morrag. You will take her name. From this day forward, we are Morragmen."

The afternoon was filled with a flurry of activity as Connor directed the ravens to begin building defenses around their clearing. Rather than succumb to the temptation of walls, they designated a perimeter and began drawing plans to reinforce it with spikes and traps. Connor met the men and evaluated their skills with the blade and bow, and he began to design squads and a guard rotation. By the end of the day, progress had been made, and he sat a distance away from the campfire and watched the Morragmen talk about what they had done.

Wyll approached him, swaying slightly on his feet and holding a skin of oiska. Connor wondered idly how much a man that size must drink to sway on his feet. Wyll sat on the ground next to him and offered the skin. Connor took a drink and handed it back. Wyll swallowed and let out a long sigh. "I thank you," he said.

"I haven't done anything yet."

"You have. You've shown them hope. They haven't had that in .... They've never had that."

Connor leaned forward, elbows on knees. *I should tell Mairead. But if I tell her, she might be tempted to tell the tribe. Or they might find out—what if she slips? These men aren't ready for her to know about them yet.* "What do you expect from the girl who will lead you?"

Wyll shrugged. "Doesn't matter. Just a purpose. That's all." He stood, stepped back, steadied himself, and recovered his footing. "I'm off to bed."

"You have first watch."

Wyll waved his skin in response.

"They will need time to adjust," Phinneas said. He approached from the darkness of the surrounding trees and stood next to Connor.

Connor stood. "Watch them for me, will you? I need to visit Mairead." He summoned the air and whispered back to Isfyrin.

It took a bit of time, but he finally found Mairead asleep in her bed in Hedwar's home. He watched from inside the braids for a moment, hesitating, wondering if he should let her sleep. One braid snaked out and touched her, and she smiled in her sleep. He shook off the elements and sat next to her on the bed. He touched her cheek with his hand. "Mairead."

She inhaled deeply and stretched, rolling onto her back. She smiled at him and sat up, then frowned. "How did you get in here?"

"Air talent," he said. "I wanted to see you, but I didn't want anyone to know. How was your day?"

She covered his hand with hers and shrugged the opposite shoulder. "Surprising. Yours?"

"About the same."

"Anything you care to share?"

"Not yet. You?"

She shook her head. "Are you all right?"

"She's quiet. For now."

Mairead let out a long breath, and her shoulders sagged a bit. Once again, he regretted bringing her into the Morrag's circle. *But then, I didn't do it. Alshada or the fates or some other force did.*

"Can you stay tonight?" she asked, and he noted the tiny quiver in her voice.

"I shouldn't. You don't want Gareth's parents to know about me." He inched closer on the little cot. "Besides, I don't think this cot is sturdy enough for what I have planned."

She laughed a nervous laugh. "There is a floor."

He grinned and kissed her, and her arms went willingly around his neck as she responded to his kisses. He pulled her closer with one hand at the back of her head, the other hand tight on her ribcage. She groaned against his mouth.

And in the back of his mind, the Morrag cackled.

—blood on the snow—the cries of a dying girl—not my sins—conscript the men—the throne is yours—

He jerked away from Mairead and stood, desire gone. She sat on her cot panting heavily, one hand near her mouth. "Connor, what—"

"I can't," he said.

"Can't? I don't understand."

I can't tell her about this—your voice! First my mother, now the Morrag—will I ever have a will of my own? He turned to Mairead. *She's so pretty—so eager—and neither my mind nor body will cooperate.* "I don't want to risk it."

The Morrag cawed in his head. *Thief! Liar!*

Mairead stood, and the fact that her shift only fell halfway down her thighs made Connor's resolve waver. He turned away. She touched his arm. "Connor, look at me. Please turn around."

"I can't, Mairead. I have to go. I will find you later." Before she could respond, he wove the braids and returned to the raven clearing.

Phinneas sat cross-legged on the ground where Connor had left him. He stood. "I trust the lady is well?"

"She's fine."

Phinneas frowned and leaned closer. "The raven—she troubles you."

"I'm going to check the perimeter. Get some sleep."

"As it please you, my lord."

Connor checked the raven perimeter as promised, then found a spot in the trees where he couldn't be seen. He knelt in the dirt. *I don't know what you want from me,* he told the Morrag.

Justice. Cleansing.

Besides that. Can I not even have a woman without you in my head?

She cawed again, and he realized it was her angry voice—the one she saved for sinners. *Thief! Liar! You deserve death!*

He bowed his head. "You said I could have her if I submitted," he whispered.

You will cleanse my earth for me. You will cleanse it of sin before you find release.

Connor's blood ran cold. "And if I sire a child? If Mairead becomes pregnant?"

The Morrag laughed in exultation. *All of them—children of men—all of them—cleanse the earth of all of them.*

He closed his eyes and took a deep breath. *You will not rest until we have all given you cleansing and then killed ourselves, will you? And you will leave me the last man standing.*

CHAPTER SIXTEEN

Ruin? Destruction? Mere opinion.
The greatest wealth and peace the world ever knew was under Ohmin and Aldora.
— Esparan Scholar

Astounding how rapidly these villages can burn even in the middle of winter, Emrys thought. He rode through the place and stopped to watch two of Alasdair Mac Mahon's men separate captives into three groups able-bodied men, women and girls, and children and the elderly. One boy on the cusp of manhood resisted, kicking and fighting to stay with his sister. The girl screamed from the arms of a man who carried her away.

"Stop." Emrys dismounted, and everything came to a halt. Two men held the boy between them, while the man carrying his sister turned back. Emrys gestured. "This one would not comply?"

"We are free men and women," the boy shouted, and Emrys reflected that his voice still hadn't dropped. "We live in peace. We will not be conscripted and fight alongside slavers."

"Perhaps they didn't tell you what awaits, boy," Emrys said. He pointed north. "Gems, silver, forests with everything you need to live. All you have to do is join."

The boy fought those who held him. "No, I won't—I won't be part of this!"

Emrys motioned to the man carrying the girl. He crossed to Emrys slowly, looking carefully at his cohorts, obviously wondering if it would be frowned upon to disobey Mac Mahon's orders in such a manner. When he finally reached Emrys' side, he handed over the girl. Emrys held her against his torso and put a hand around her neck. She and her brother gasped; the girl stood still, but the boy twitched toward her. "There is work to be done. It's not a place for girls. You may stay here, if you wish, but you will do so to bury your sister. Go do the work necessary in the mountains, and she might live to see you again."

A choking cry escaped the boy's throat. Emrys held the girl tight against him, but it was not hard to do. She was a frail thing, small, perhaps six years old, and not even worth the effort of drawing her soul into him. *As eating a locust might be to one of these soldiers.* But she was valuable as a lesson, and he watched the boy contemplate his choices. "Serra," he said. "Be good."

She started to cry then. "No, Colm, don't leave—don't go—"

Emrys removed his hand from her neck. The Mac Mahon soldier took the girl away as she screamed and reached for her brother. The boy stood with tears streaming down his face as he watched her go. Emrys put one gloved hand on his shoulder. "You made the right choice, Colm. You let your sister live. Now, go earn the chance to see her again."

The boy swallowed hard and turned to join the conscripts.

Emrys mounted again and kept riding. Bodies of those who'd resisted littered the ground. Alasdair's men had gathered those they did not need or want in a large barn. Mac Mahon himself sat mounted outside the barn, watching with a sneer of distaste. He turned to Emrys. "This is not in my purview," he said. "For you to demand my presence here is—"

"We needed to meet."

Mac Mahon frowned. "And you could not come to my estate?"

"And leave these men without a leader? With all these conscripts who might revolt?"

Mac Mahon grunted. He pulled his cloak around himself more tightly.

"Why here? Why not in one of their homes?"

"The village is burning. Go inside one of those homes and you may not live."

The slaver's face showed the first hint of anything besides contempt as he glanced at the flames licking at a small house nearby. "Get on with it, then."

"You have nearly three thousand now, including the Nar Sidhe men I brought, but the snows are settling in on the mountain. It's not a good time to head north. We need a place to winter."

Mac Mahon sighed. "You did not think of this before you came to me with this plan?"

"I did, in fact, think of this. I have a proposal." He paused and waited for Mac Mahon to turn to him. "Take Galbragh."

Mac Mahon snorted a laugh and turned away. "Take the richest—the *only* real—city on the northern plains with only three thousand men who aren't even fully trained? Impossible."

"Not impossible with the Nar Sidhe men. Not impossible if someone lets you in the gates."

Mac Mahon turned to him and arched an eyebrow. "You have someone inside?"

"I do. A few concessions, and she will gladly help you into the city."

"Concessions. What concessions?"

"Title and money. Give her a position of authority in your kingdom, and you will have her loyalty for a lifetime."

"Done. And you will arrange it?"

"I will return to you once it is arranged." He paused. "There is one other thing."

"Yes?"

"I need some of your best men—just a dozen. I need them to range up the mountain. There are things we can do to prepare the way for spring."

"Of course. Take who you wish."

Emrys gave a small bow from the back of his horse. "Stay with the men. I will return tomorrow with more instructions."

Mac Mahon gestured around the village. "Stay here? How? You've burned the place to the ground."

"They have tents. They will set up something to ensure you are out of the elements."

He scoffed. "Sleeping on the ground. Vulgar."

Emrys gestured to the barn. "There are dozens of young girls in there. You might find a new favorite."

Mac Mahon rode closer to the barn and surveyed the cowering women and girls. He pointed. "The blonde, there. And the redhead. Bring them to my tent." The girls wept and cried out, but Mac Mahon's personal guards dragged them away from the barn and toward the main body of Mac Mahon's army.

Mac Mahon watched them go, then turned to Emrys. "This will be worth it in the end, yes?"

Emrys bowed once more. Mac Mahon said nothing. He rode away, the remainder of his guards trotting behind him.

When Mac Mahon was out of sight, Emrys turned back to the barn. "Burn it. Make sure a few escape. Let them carry word of whose work this was."

One of Mac Mahon's men drew an arrow soaked in naphtha and lit it on a torch. He fired it onto the thatched roof where it smoldered for a moment before catching on the drier straw under the wet top layer. He shot another arrow into the loft, another into the haystack near the animals. Soon, the barn blazed.

Emrys walked away with the screams of the dying ringing in his ears. In the midst of the cries was the small, frail voice of a girl who would never see her brother again.

Her cries were sweeter than her sins would have been.

CHAPTER SEVENTEEN

The heart of the Syrafi is rent.
The earth cries out.
— Scrolls of Prophecy in the Syrafi Keep

Igraine lifted her face to the sun. It was a rare break in the midst of weeks of rain, ice, and wet snow. She pulled her cloak tight around herself, but smiled at the warmth on her face. *I've been inside too long.*

She had bought herself some time from Cormac's threat by promising him she would return to Eirya with Rory as soon as Rory was ready to leave. She requested, though, that she be allowed to remain in the castle until that time to avoid the appearance that she had returned to her lover. "I swear to you I will keep out of castle business, aye?" she told him. "Unless Chancellor Kerry requests my presence or my aid, I will remain merely a pretty royal lady tucked away with her embroidery."

Reluctantly, he had agreed, but the time since had not been easy. Castle eyes studied her every move. She had only been able to leave when accompanied by a contingent of Ronan Kerry's guards, and she was no longer able to send letters or messages without one of Kerry's scribes reviewing them. *I am tempted to stay with Rory just to have my freedom back*, she thought. *But I'd only be exchanging one cage for another—a very tempting, very seductive cage that I do not want to enter again.*

For his part, Rory had asked her to return to Eirya with him at her earliest convenience. It had taken some cajoling, but she had convinced him Eirya had a compelling state interest in the future ruler of Taura. "If ye stay here, lad, ye may yet have some influence over the throne," she told him. "There is trade to consider, and alliances, and other things my father will ask you about. I am not the only task ye have here."

He had grinned at that. "No, but ye're by far the most challenging—and the most entertaining." But he agreed to stay, and Igraine breathed a sigh of relief.

Igraine looked out toward Macha Tor. Horseback riding would be a welcome distraction. *But how fun would it be with a half dozen Kerry men following me? And in the mud and muck? This cage is worse than a prison. At least in a prison I would not be taunted with my freedom.*

"Forgive me, my lady."

Igraine turned. "Yes?"

Nimue curtsied. The girl had quickly become a favorite of Igraine's with her grace, sharp wit, and easy manner. "A messenger, your highness—Eiryan. He requests audience."

"Send him away."

"Pardon, my lady, but he says Duke Nolan has news you will be interested in."

Igraine scoffed. "He labors under the mistaken impression that I am interested in the contents of his breeches."

Nimue laughed and immediately covered her mouth. "Forgive me, your highness."

It's not the first time she's laughed at something bawdy. This girl is a kindred spirit. "Does this messenger refuse to leave until I see him?"

"He does, your highness."

Igraine sighed. *Best be done with it.* "Very well. Send him out."

Nimue left the garden and returned a moment later with a thin man dressed in Eiryan livery. "Your highness. I bring a message from Duke Nolan." He held out the parchment.

She broke the green wax and read. "He wishes me to dine with him tonight?"

"He does, your highness. He requests you come alone."

"Does he not realize how hard it is for me to get away on my own, then? Or how it would appear if I went to his house unescorted?" She folded the parchment and thought. Nimue stood nearby, hands folded demurely before her. *She would do well in Rory's house. Gwyn and Deirdre—they're serving girls. This girl is born to nobility whether her blood acknowledges it or no.* "Very well. I will attend—if I can get away—but tell him my lady Nimue will be in attendance as well. I'll not have it said I dined with the ambassador alone."

The man bowed and retreated.

Igraine beckoned Nimue to her and gestured to her clothing. "Do you have anything more formal? Something suitable for dinner with the ambassador?"

Nimue's hand flew up to her dark blonde hair in its coif. "No, my lady, I'm sorry to say I don't. I have never had a need—"

"The king's mother was a slender woman. I have some of her old gowns. We'll find something from her wardrobe for you." Igraine took her arm to lead her into the castle.

"My lady," Nimue said. "Forgive me, but a serving girl in noble clothes would be—"

"Long overdue."

"I'm a bit apprehensive about spending an evening with nobility."

"You were born for this, Nimue," Igraine said. She stopped and turned to Nimue. "Rory is easy. Laugh at his jokes and flirt with him a bit, and he'll be following you around as a lost lamb by evening's end."

"And what then, your highness? You suggested he was a bit ..." Her mouth tilted in a grin. "Lecherous?"

"He is. But we'll keep each other from being shattered by his blue eyes, aye?"

Igraine turned Nimue over to Gwyn and Deirdre and the other servants. "Nimue will be my personal attendant at a supper tonight," she told them. "She needs to look every inch a noble young woman. You may use some of Lady Alison's old clothing; her wardrobe is in my former chambers. Gwyn and Deirdre, you will also accompany me, so you will need to dress in your best attire." The ladies curtsied, and Igraine left her bedchamber to find Aiden in the hall. "Take me to see Chancellor Kerry."

Kerry's guards greeted Igraine with reluctant bows when she arrived at his study. Beyond the doors, Igraine heard raised male voices. "Your highness," one of the guards said. "The chancellor is not available right now."

"I will wait for him."

"Pardon, my lady, but perhaps you might wait in your chambers."

It wasn't a request. Igraine hesitated as long as she could, attempting to make out the details of the argument. She recognized Kerry's voice, but the other was unfamiliar. *I would have expected Duke Seannan or Cormac. If someone else is unhappy with Kerry, this may be good news.* "Have you any idea how long he may be?"

The guards exchanged a quick look. The unfamiliar voice shouted something incoherent, and there was a pounding of fists on a desk or table. "We will tell him you came by, your highness. He can summon you when he's ready to see you."

At that moment the door opened, and a slender man with gray hair and beard stormed out of the room, followed by Kerry. "Jamie, wait," Kerry said.

The first man turned. "No, Ronan. We are through. Find another lackey." He walked away, nearly bumping Igraine aside before he corrected his course, muttered an apology, and stormed out.

Igraine quickly skimmed a list of Taurin lords in her head. *Jamie Farrell,* she remembered. *One of Kerry's oldest friends. This is interesting news indeed.*

Kerry stood with hands on hips, grimacing. He took a deep breath and turned to Igraine. "Your highness. What can I do for you?"

She gave him a small curtsy. "I've been invited to sup with Ambassador Nolan," she said. "I'll not be attending supper with the usual party tonight."

"I trust all is well?" he asked.

"'Tis well," she said. "I suspect he wants only to discuss home and family. You'll excuse me from dining with you tonight?"

"Of course. I will send the usual guards."

"If you wish." She laced her fingers together, hoping to hide her rising tension. *Make it clear you're not seeing Rory alone.* "My serving girls will attend with me."

"An unusual decision. Are you treating servants as ladies-in-waiting now? I was led to believe you only wanted to have serving girls. If you are considering ladies-in-waiting, there is always Lady Aislinn."

Of course. Put the girl you're bedding in my chambers. How lovely that would be. "I have refused ladies-in-waiting because I did not want to be seen as favoring certain families. Besides, it's a foolish practice. Women choosing ladies for political expedience? 'Tis hardly better than wedding our children to each other."

"How enlightened." He waved a hand. "Please—by all means, attend the ambassador."

That was too simple. Igraine curtsied. "Good day, chancellor."

The anticipation of seeing Rory again tempted Igraine toward a foul mood, but watching Nimue turn from pretty serving girl to a beautiful young noblewoman eased her irritation. "I fear you will outshine me," she said.

Nimue curtsied. "My lady, you flatter." She gestured to the pale blue silk and simple pearl jewels. "I do confess, though, that I rather enjoy wearing such finery," she whispered.

By the time Aiden arrived to escort them to the waiting carriage, Igraine and all three maids were prepared to grace the ambassador's house. Igraine arranged her silk wrap around her bare shoulders and took Aiden's arm. "Let's be about this. The sooner we're off, the sooner I can be abed tonight."

"Yes, your highness."

The carriage left the castle grounds and rattled through the ancient streets of Torlach. Igraine offered distracted waves to city people who waved to her. At one corner, a hooded man gave her a chilling grin. His face was burned nearly beyond recognition of a human face, and the grin turned his mouth into a grisly, feral snarl. She nodded in his direction, but didn't relax until he passed from view. When the carriage halted at the door to the Eiryan ambassador's house, Igraine took a deep breath.

Aiden opened the door and held out a hand. "Are you well, my lady? You look pale."

"I'm well. There was a man back there—a burned man. Did you see him?"

"I did." Aiden frowned. "There was something frightening about him. I didn't like the way he watched your carriage, my lady. And there are the stories ...."

"Stories?"

"Rumors about a burned man who's murdering children."

"Where?"

"Throughout Taura, my lady. Haven't you heard?"

She tightened her mouth. *Blast that chancellor!* "No, I hadn't heard. But there are many burned men. We can't go rounding them up on suspicion."

"No, my lady, I only meant—the way he looked at your carriage. It reminded me to be vigilant with your safety."

She patted his arm. "I thank you, Aiden. I do feel safer knowing you protect me."

Rory met them at the door. He held out his hand and bowed. "Your highness," he said. "I dismissed my steward. I wanted to greet you myself."

She curtsied and took his hand. "Duke Nolan."

He held up a hand to the Taurin guards who followed Igraine. "The lady will be fine. You can wait outside the gates."

"We have orders to remain with the lady at all times."

"Aye, but she is on Eiryan land now. And Eiryans don't give a rodent's arse about Taurin orders, lad." He waved them away. "Outside the gate."

"If you will permit, my lord," Igraine said, one hand on Rory's arm. "My personal guard Aiden may stay."

"As the lady wishes." He opened the door for her and her ladies and Aiden, but didn't close it until the castle guards had retreated beyond the gates.

Once inside the house, Rory took her hands and surveyed her appearance. "Igraine, I believe ye only get lovelier each passing year."

Does he have to be so charming? "I also get more difficult."

He chuckled. "I miss your difficult nature." He turned his attention to her ladies. He bowed, every bit as gallant and dashing as he'd been the first night Igraine had shared his bed. "Ladies, you are as a garland of sweet bluebells round her highness' neck. Be welcome, ladies."

"Tell me your news, my lord."

"Your curiosity would not let you rest, aye?" He laughed at her irritated expression and put her hand on his arm, and she fell in step next to him. "I recall at our last meeting that you mentioned the king was going to visit a . . . Duke Fingall, wasn't it?"

"It was."

"So I thought." He paused, and a servant opened the door to his dining hall. A short, balding man in nondescript woolens stood and approached. "Princess Igraine Mac Roy, I present to you Duke Cameron Fingall."

Igraine gaped. The duke stepped forward and bowed. "My lady Igraine," he said. "It is a true honor. The king has spoken of your beauty. I find he did not exaggerate."

"Why are you here?" she whispered. "Where is Braedan—why have you not gone to the castle?"

He straightened and held out a piece of parchment. "This will explain some," he said. "I will explain the remainder when you have read this."

She took the parchment and broke the seal. *Braedan's seal.* Irritation faded to relief and then dismay as she read.

My dearest Igraine,

I wanted to be back in Torlach by now, but I fear I must travel to the far north. Duke Fingall and I are working together to secure my claim to the throne. Follow his instructions, and trust him to protect you from my uncle.

*My love, forgive me—I should have
believed you. I was a fool. But as soon as I
return to Torlach, I will take back my
throne, and you and I will wed.*

Braedan

Igraine covered her mouth with one hand. "Where did you get this?" she whispered. "This isn't—where did this come from?"

"From my estates, my lady," Fingall said.

Rory gestured to the table. "Please, your highness. Be seated. Duke Fingall has much to share with you, but he realized the danger in going to the castle. He came to me in the hopes that the promise of a meal with me might lure you here."

Dazed, Igraine let him lead her to a chair. Nimue fanned her as Gwyn poured wine. "I doubt he realized what a gamble that was," Igraine said.

Rory and Fingall both laughed. "My lady," Fingall said, seating himself. "You must know—the king spoke of nothing but returning to you. He wanted to return once his wound was healed, but—"

"Wound? Is he—"

Fingall held up a hand. "He is well, my lady. But I should start at the beginning."

As dishes were served, Fingall recounted the events that had brought Braedan to his estates and the discussions he'd had with the king. "The king wanted to keep Kerry in the dark over his health. Neither of us have sent word to anyone over what transpired. We want to see what Kerry will do if he suspects that both of us are still alive, that we haven't come to blows."

Igraine sipped her wine. "At least he's well—or was when you last saw him."

"As you say, my lady," Fingall said. "And I do apologize for my own delay in visiting you. I traveled along the eastern road, and it always takes longer, especially in winter. Then when I arrived here, I spent some time considering how best to contact you without the chancellor discovering my presence."

"But he'll know now," she said.

Rory shook his head. "As soon as the duke announced his identity to me, I dismissed all of my servants—sent them home for a few days. Fingall's men have been the only servants and guards here, save for my personal Eiryan guards. I sent most of the Eiryans to the ship."

She leaned back in her chair. "I don't know what to say—what to do, how to instruct you, Duke Fingall."

"There is little you need to say or do, your highness," the duke said. "The king already instructed me to discover all I can of his uncle's plans and to try to win House Reid to his cause."

"How will you do that?"

"I need some time, first," Duke Fingall said. "I am investigating the chancellor's activities right now. If needs be—if I am summoned to court—I will appear in a timely manner, of course." He paused. "My lady, I may have to appear to betray the king. Please, be assured—I have no allegiance to Ronan Kerry. I am a king's man, through and through."

She smiled and reached for his hand. "Thank you, my lord. There are some small things I can tell you about some of the other dukes. I have little detail right now, but I do know that Jamie Farrell stormed out of Kerry's office today in high dudgeon." She relayed what had happened when she went to speak with Kerry.

Fingall listened and arched his eyebrows. "The king and I assumed that Farrell would be Kerry's man until the bitter end. I wonder what's happened."

Igraine shrugged. "I can't say. But we will try to find out more, aye, ladies?" The ladies agreed. Igraine was certain Nimue seemed excited for the adventure.

When Rory walked Igraine to the door at the end of the evening, he bowed to the ladies and turned to Igraine. "A moment in private?"

She nodded. "A moment." Her guards and ladies withdrew.

Rory took her hands. "Am I forgiven now?"

"I will have to think about that." She stretched up to kiss his cheek. "Thank you, Rory."

"Those are not common words from your lips."

"Perhaps they should be more common."

"Perhaps if I could convince you to give me another chance, they would be."

"Rory, we've discussed this. And one act of contrition on your part is not enough for me to leave my betrothed for you."

"I didn't ask you to leave him, lass."

She clenched her fists. "Ye've likely no need for companionship, my lord."

He chuckled. "I've not been a eunuch since I arrived here, that's certain." He held up a hand to her rising indignation. "Save it, lass. Just listen. You would do well to recall that in dangerous times, things happen. I'll not be making threats on the king's person. If something should happen to your king, if you should need to return to Eirya, I would take you to wife."

"And talk some serving girl into your bed the moment you're bored or I refuse you for a night. No, Rory. I won't fall for it again."

"Igraine—"

"I saw the way you looked at my lady Nimue tonight. I'm not a fool."

"Well, she is a very pretty girl."

She resisted the urge to respond to that. "I'm weary. I need to go home."

He let out a long breath. "And that's it, isn't it? Eirya isn't your home anymore. Taura is."

She considered that. "I believe so."

The carriage rattled to a stop outside. He passed her arm to Aiden. "Thank you for the lovely supper, your highness."

"You'll keep me informed of Fingall's efforts, aye?"

"Of course. Your lady Nimue—I'll send word through her."

Igraine bristled and leaned closer to Rory. "You'll be keeping your hands off her, aye? She's a lovely young girl who could make a good match with some merchant son or minor lord. If I ever think you've even hinted to her—"

He laughed. "I do know how to rile you, love."

That he does. She let out a breath. "On second thought, 'twould be best for you to send word through her." *'Twould be best for me to avoid you completely.*

She returned to her carriage with her ladies in tow, and the vehicle clattered back through the streets. Gwyn and Deirdre fell into quiet conversations punctuated with giggles. Nimue sat next to Igraine, her mouth curved into a secretive smile. "Duke Fingall's men made quite an impression on your maids, my lady," she whispered.

Igraine smiled. "And you?"

Nimue shrugged one shoulder. "I am that rare woman who has little interest in men. There are far more important and interesting things to occupy my time, and none of them cause as many entanglements as men do."

"It is a rare woman who can resist Rory's charms." *Or Braedan's.*

"He is a very handsome man, to be sure. But one can admire a rose without being pricked by its thorns."

"Indeed," Igraine said. *But Rory likes the thorns. So does Braedan. Gods forgive me, I've fallen for a man exactly like the one I left.*

CHAPTER EIGHTEEN

The path of service is one of sacrifice and reward.
— Tribal wisdom

Ice pelted Minerva's back, and she pulled her cloak and furs tighter. *For all the good it will do. Alshada, this cursed place will be my death.* The Ragged Isles were easily the most inhospitable place Minerva had ever been. *Well, except the house of the sayas at Starling's Cross.*

Minerva and Alfrig had fallen into their silent travel once again upon leaving the Dylan holdings. It took two days to get to the ferry crossing, and when they finally reached it, Alfrig had to bargain for passage with her few remaining furs while Minerva waited in silence with the horses. "Thought he wouldn't rest until he had me undressed," the older woman muttered when she finally joined Minerva.

"I have a small bit of money left," Minerva said. "I should have offered."

Alfrig grunted. "Keep it. It's easier for me to come by furs than you to come by coin."

Minerva stared out toward the endless blue of the northern sea to where it met the equally endless gray of the winter sky. Her stomach roiled when the rough water slapped the side of the ferry, and she gripped the rail and steadied herself.

"Landers are not meant for this," Alfrig said.

Minerva turned to her. "Have you been asea before?"

Alfrig gestured. "Just this ferry—just to see the wisdomkeeper, many years ago, for my training." She took a deep breath. "Hrogarth says the pirates and merchants travel on ships that look like big floating houses. He says they stay under the deck much of the time. I can't imagine feeling the sea rock my floor without breathing fresh air."

"I came to Taura on a ship," Minerva said. "I don't remember it. I was small—just a child. My sister was still a babe in arms."

"I recall the day you came to us," Alfrig said. "You were barely a woman—barely old enough to make such a choice."

Minerva smiled at the memories. "That time with the guardians—living with the other girls—it was sweet, even when you and the others expected much of us. I miss it."

"Were the sayas not the same?"

"No. There were other blessings in the sayada, though." *Until they decided I was a witch.* "What happened to all of the others?"

"They have all found their places in the tribes." Alfrig stared down the wind, her face a mask of proud ferocity.

Minerva steadied herself against another wave. She swallowed hard, unsure if her stomach's unrest was a result of the waves or the conversation. "I have missed it. Sometimes. I miss the way the earth felt when we would dance. I miss the shrines and the feel of the loam in my hands and the way—" She stopped.

"The magic has not let you go. The earthspirit holds you."

Minerva tucked her hand under her arm, trying to fight down the magic in her palm. "Did you truly want me for your heir? To be earth guardian over the nine?"

"Yes."

"I am sorry. Who will it be now?"

Alfrig shrugged. "It is not for me to say. It is for the earth. But I have considered several possibilities. Grytha, my second, is strong in magic, but I do not see great things in her future. Nedra, the wolf guardian, is stronger in the magic than I, but she does not check Edgar enough."

"What do you see in me?"

The guardian turned to her. She took Minerva's hand and pulled her glove off. The brand on Minerva's palm glowed blue, and Alfrig put it against her own. "I see strength," she said. "And devotion, and wisdom."

"My heart is inconstant—I—"

"Your heart is unsettled. It is not inconstant. It has only ever wanted one thing—to serve the One Hand."

Alshada, is it true? Is this all I've wanted—to serve you? But where? The kirok and tribes are closed to me, and the Sidh are not—I could not serve you in that life. "What have you wanted?"

"In my life? I have wanted to serve the One Hand by serving the earth. I did that by wedding Hrogarth and bringing balance to his spirit. I gave the earth six children—three earth guardians and three strong warriors. I've spoken to the earthspirit more times than I can count. I've held life in my womb and in my hands, and I've watched it slip away to the endless circle."

"Do you love him? Hrogarth?"

"More than my own life." A sad smile crossed Alfrig's weathered face. "I hoped to be with him even into death, but perhaps that isn't to be." She turned back to the sea before Minerva could ask what she meant, and it was clear from her posture that their conversation was over.

They came ashore on one of the Ragged Isles and unloaded their horses, and Alfrig led her horse northward without saying anything. Minerva followed. Alfrig stopped walking near a jagged cleft in a rock.

"Do you want me to find shelter?" Minerva asked.

"No. Our shelter is beyond that entrance." She walked to the narrow passage and knelt.

The wind howled around Minerva while she watched. Alfrig didn't move. Minerva couldn't tell what she was doing, but she sensed it was not her place to interfere. Her feet started to grow numb in her boots, but her hand was warm in her glove, the brand tingling with the magic that flowed through her. *It's been so long. Surely it wouldn't be sinful, would it? If Alshada did not wish me to have this power, would he not take it from me?* "Forgive me," she whispered. "Forgive me, Alshada." But the thrum of the magic still passed through her body, vibrating to the core of her spirit and soul.

At last, Alfrig returned to her side. "Leave the horse. Take what you can and unbridle it. There are wild horses around this isle. They survive. These will as well, or they will return to the earth. And if we need them again, we can find them. The isle isn't that large."

Minerva took what she could carry from the horse's back and freed it from the reins. She followed Alfrig, watching the ground to make sure her numb feet stepped where the traitha's did. *How many toes will I lose for this adventure?*

Alfrig led her into the narrow cleft, and the wind instantly halted. Minerva's head spun with the silence. Her ears couldn't find anything to fill the void left by the wind. The little opening in the rocks was not precisely warm, but it was at least dry and free of snow and ice.

Alfrig motioned her farther into the darkness of the cave, and Minerva followed the sound of Alfrig's feet when she could no longer see the traitha's back. "How can you see?" she finally whispered.

"There is no need to see. I know the way."

"Where are we?"

"At the entrance to the sacred mountain."

Minerva swallowed hard. Her palm burned. *This place—the magic is raw here. Unbridled. Alshada, keep me pure—help me remember I am yours.*

She followed Alfrig until a pinprick of light showed through another crack ahead. Alfrig stopped. "Great Mother, your daughter seeks counsel and wisdom," she called. "By your leave only will I tread on the sacred ground." She removed the glove from her branded hand and held it up.

An old woman stepped out of the dim light into the space in the rocks.

"Daughters of the earthspirit," she said. Her voice rasped with disuse and age. She rapped a staff on the ground. "You are granted entrance. Come."

The old woman turned to walk through the faint light of a cavern. Alfrig followed, and Minerva fell in step. She couldn't see where the light came from—only that it had no apparent source. There were no torches or candles anywhere, and the scent of stale air indicated there was likely no source of sunlight. The old woman's steps never faltered. She led them on, down and down until the pungent odor of sulfur pierced the air. Minerva coughed and held a kerchief over her nose and mouth.

The old woman cackled. "You'll grow used to it, daughter," she said. "We're almost home. The odor is not so strong there."

They finally came to level ground and a wide cavern away from the odor. The old woman ushered them in and gestured. "There are candles somewhere. Light them if you wish."

Alfrig removed her furs and sat near a low fire. "There is no need. The fire is enough." She gestured to Minerva. "Sit, Esma."

Minerva moved into the cavern and sat on the floor near Alfrig. The old woman sat across from them, and Minerva gasped at her first clear view of the wisdomkeeper. "You're blind," she said.

The old woman laughed and turned rheumy eyes to Minerva. "There is little need for sight here. I have no use for vision. My duties require only devotion, wisdom, and service."

Minerva pulled her furs tighter. "You speak as a woman of the sayada."

"They speak as I do."

Minerva swallowed hard. "Thank you for allowing me to see you."

"She is called Great Mother," Alfrig said, quiet.

"There is no need for formality, daughter," the wisdomkeeper said. "Have you at last come to take your place and relieve me of my duties?"

Alfrig's mouth tightened. "I made my choice. It has not wavered."

"The raven you chose still lives."

"He does. He is more than raven. He is traitha and father and lover. If you have an issue with my choice, take it up with the earthspirit."

The old woman's mouth twisted. "I have. She is silent."

Alfrig was quiet for some time. "You still believe Hrogarth was a mistake?"

"I have not yet seen any evidence to the contrary."

"He is my husband. He has been good to me. I will not believe his creation or his mark or the earthspirit's choice of him for traitha a mistake." She waved a hand. "I have not come for this. I have come to bring this woman to you. She seeks guidance."

"Guidance? Or absolution?"

Minerva cleared her throat. "I need to be shed of the earth magic."

The woman grunted. "There is no shedding. You have lived with it too long. It's taken root inside you."

"Then teach me to use it," Minerva said.

"Do you plan to return to the tribes?"

Minerva's mouth went dry. "I-I can't—I am an oathbreaker."

"Then I cannot teach you to use it. The secrets are guarded for the tribes. To share them with outsiders—with an oathbreaker—would violate my oath."

Then this is what it comes to—I must give up my life. "Then make it quick," she whispered.

"There may be another way," Alfrig said. Both women turned to her. "Let her take my place."

Silence fell around them. "I don't understand," Minerva said.

But the wisdomkeeper's mouth was twisted in a thoughtful expression. "A substitution. A sacrifice. She would need to be bound to the earth."

"There are few tribes who would give her quarter if they discovered she took vows to Alshada over her vow to the tribe. But here—no one would know. She would become only the Great Mother."

Minerva started to understand. She leaned forward. "You mean to give me over to the magic? To make me into that—into her?"

Alfrig frowned. "There is no shame in it. Would you prefer to die an oathbreaker? Or would you be doomed to force your magic back day after day, never able to still it, until it drives you mad?" She paused. "Choose, Esma: fight the magic and risk the spirit of the earth consuming you, or accept what you've been given—a chance to serve the One Hand and keep the magic of the tribes sacred and safe."

Minerva's stomach twisted. The brand flared and pulsed with blue light. *Alshada, I wanted only to serve you. How could this be serving you?* "I can't," she whispered.

"She has chosen," the wisdomkeeper said. She picked up a dagger. "Come, girl. Let's do it quickly before you lose your nerve."

Minerva stood on shaking legs.

Alfrig stood next to her. "Esma," she whispered, and her voice broke once. "Reconsider. There is reward in service to the One Hand."

But Minerva ignored her and followed the wisdomkeeper deeper into the cavern. She fought for every step, refusing to let her tears fall. She clenched her fist tight. *If only he'd lived, if only I hadn't been prideful, arrogant. One Hand—Alshada—forgive me. Forgive me for being such a fool. Give me peace.*

The wisdomkeeper stopped and turned to Minerva. "Remove your clothes."

Minerva took off everything and crossed her arms over her breasts. She sensed Alfrig's presence behind her. "What do I do?"

The wisdomkeeper gestured to the ground near her. "Kneel." She pointed down.

Minerva knelt on a whorl carved into the stone. *The mark of banishing.* She lowered her head. "Make it quick."

The wisdomkeeper started to chant in the ancient language of the tribes. The whorl glowed with rising blue light under Minerva's knees. *Alshada, forgive me.* Her palm burned under the brand. The world dissolved into the old woman's chants and Alfrig's quiet, tense breathing behind her. Minerva's heart beat faster. She forced herself to remain upright. *Make me brave—don't let me flinch—don't let me—*

The point of the blade went to the base of her skull—

"Wait," Minerva gasped. "Wait."

The wisdomkeeper stepped back. "You have reconsidered?"

Alshada, forgive me. "I . . . have reconsidered."

The old woman knelt. "You face a choice, daughter," she said. "Return to the tribes, or let it consume you. What do you choose?"

"I need time," Minerva said. "I need to think. And pray. May I have time here?"

The crone nodded. "You may."

Minerva's shoulders slumped, and tears stung her eyes. She was only faintly aware of Alfrig putting a covering over her. *I cannot do this, Alshada— I cannot break your law this way, by letting her kill me just to free me of this pain. But I cannot forsake my vows, either. If you are still there—if you still hear me—tell me where to go. Show me the path you have for me.*

Minerva sat next to a fire in the wisdomkeeper's little cave deep inside the sacred mountain. The faint odor of sulfur stung her nose, but despite the staleness of the air, she had seen vents to the outer world. Enough fresh air entered the caverns for breathing and small fires. A distant pool bubbled up from under the stone, warming the inside of the mountain. In ages long forgotten by men, Brae Sidh stone talents had carved the intricate passages and rooms of the mountain, and in the process, they'd also carved a heating system that kept generations of wisdomkeepers and their students warm. The hot water and steam that rose from the pool was channeled into the rocks, and nowhere in the mountain was Minerva ever cold.

Still, she huddled at the fire and shivered. It was a shiver of apprehension, of fear, of tension. Her palm burned inside her gloved, clenched fist. *Alshada forgive me, I can't figure out how else to face this.*

After days of tears and prayers and supplication, she'd requested audience with the wisdomkeeper once again. It had been two weeks, at least, but the time revealed nothing more. Minerva waited. She worked around the wisdomkeeper's home, sewing, weaving, cooking, and doing whatever else was asked of her. She read the scrolls and books Alfrig and the wisdomkeeper gave her, but they revealed nothing she didn't know. They contained ancient tribal wisdom that sounded much like kirok teaching, which only confused her more. She fell asleep often with tears streaming down her cheeks from the effort of keeping her magic at bay while the mark on her palm flared and burned with the need to touch the earthspirit.

And that—the whole idea of the earthspirit—was wisdom she had put aside for more than a decade. *I serve Alshada,* she reminded herself. *My vows to him bind me—I am his, I do not serve the earthspirit, I will remain pure and unsullied by the magic.* But the more she read and the more she spoke with the other women, the more the magic tugged at her. And the more it tugged at her, the more she thought about the earthspirit again and remembered how the lifespirit of the earth had thrummed through her when she was with her husband, when he hunted for her, when she danced with him after the hunt and then let him take her to their hut and lost herself to his arms and legs and passion.

But there are the dreams. The dreams haunted her with growing insistence—the dreams that suggested the wisdomkeeper's time drew to a close, that the time of earth magic was fading and a new era was dawning.

As frightening as it all was, there was connection and warmth in being with Alfrig again. The older woman had been so much like a mother to her once, and to be in her presence, in this place where Alfrig was also a student—it gave her peace. *Except when she suggests that I might be wisdomkeeper in her stead.* The thought had come up several times, and although Minerva still refused, the wisdomkeeper's resolve faltered. "It may be," she said after staring for a long time at Minerva. "It may be."

Minerva flinched at the gaze and put down her kerchief full of food next to the fire. "I don't want it. I can't—"

Alfrig put a hand on Minerva's arm, and for the first time, Minerva saw a pain there she couldn't identify. "Little sister," she said. "Denying your path will only bring sorrow. I denied mine once, and only when I found it was I whole once more."

"With Hrogarth?"

"Yes. I came to this path—I came here prepared to take the place of the Great Mother. But Hrogarth haunted my dreams, and only when I returned to his side did I feel complete."

"But what if this isn't my path?" She twisted her hands in her lap. "I thought my path was with my husband. Then I thought it was with the sayada. I don't know—"

"The One Hand's will is woven as a blanket," the wisdomkeeper said. "He can use all of your choices for his weaving. You are not so important or so powerful that one wrong choice will destroy the blanket he weaves."

Minerva stood and excused herself. "I must pray," she said.

On her little pallet in the wisdomkeeper's cave, she prayed for guidance and wisdom as she'd never prayed before. She recited verses, songs, and prayers. She begged Alshada for answers and implored him to give her a dream, vision, or *something* that would finally tell her where she should spend her life.

No clear answers came, and Minerva straightened after hours. *If you cannot tell me what I should do or where I should be, then I will choose for myself,* she finally said.

She went to the wisdomkeeper's room and found her puttering around her fire. Without a word, the crone invited Minerva in and gestured for her to sit down. She put a kettle over the little fire and spooned tea into two clay cups.

"You have so many niceties of civilization here," Minerva said. The wisdomkeeper's silence often unnerved her.

The old woman grunted. "I have friends. They bring me things."

"What friends?"

"The guardians, for one. Most bring offerings, sacrifices, supplies from the tribes. I never lack for the things I need, and I often have small comforts as well."

"Who else brings you things?"

The wisdomkeeper's mouth broke into a rare grin. Minerva was surprised to see the woman still had most of her teeth. "Ah, the secrets of the keepers." She chuckled. "The One Hand provides, daughter."

Minerva rubbed her palm. "I've made a decision."

"Yes."

It wasn't a question. Minerva wondered if the wisdomkeeper already knew her choice. "I have no place among the sayas. They brand me a witch and believe I will lead the Forbidden and other dark forces to them. I have no place in the tribes. I am an oathbreaker. I could stay with the Sidh, but I would be surrounded by tribesmen. Besides, I have no desire for a life of ease. I am meant for work."

"Then you will wander the world without purpose, eh? Find some little village where you can live as a Taurin, always hiding your palm and waiting for the day the Morrag and the earthspirit finally claim you?"

"I could no more live in a Taurin village than in the sayada. Someone would see my hand at some time, and I would be branded a witch again."

"You would get what you want, though. The villagers would stone you, burn you. You would find yourself meeting the One Hand just as you wish."

"I no longer wish it," Minerva whispered. She blinked back tears. "I wish to live."

The old woman was silent for a long moment, but there was a relieved quality to the silence, as if she had been waiting for those very words. Her voice was gentle when she spoke again. "Then what have you decided?"

Minerva took a deep breath. "I will stay here. I will be your eyes and your hands. I will help you with the young women who come—I will serve them as a silent sister, never speaking, never giving advice, never teaching."

"I have no need of a servant," the wisdomkeeper said. "And the women who come are able to care for themselves."

"Forgive me, but you do have need of a servant," Minerva said. "Sometimes your feet falter in the passageways. Sometimes you try to recall the words in the scrolls, but you forget. I have eyes and hands and feet. Let me use them for you until you find a replacement."

"You still will not be my heir?"

Minerva bit her lip. "Alfrig still wishes it. You and I—we are not as certain as she is."

The fire popped, punctuating the quiet that fell. "No," the old woman said. "We are not."

"But I will stay. I will learn. Perhaps Alsh—the One Hand will make his will known through our time together. Or the earthspirit may tell you or me what my duty is if we just give her enough time to speak."

The old woman gave her a slow nod. "It may be," she finally said.

"Then you will let me stay?"

"I will let you stay. You will be my eyes and hands and feet."

Minerva let out a long breath. *She knows this is for me, not for her. She knows this is my way of hiding, my way of buying time. She sees that the earth comforts me, holds me here. Yet she says nothing. I could not be like this woman. I could not hold this much wisdom.* "You will not be sorry," she said.

"No. I suspect I will not."

Footsteps outside the small alcove caused Minerva to turn her head. Alfrig stood in the entrance, her face pained and grim. "You have reached some decisions, daughter?" she asked Minerva.

"I have. I will stay here for a time. The Great Mother will allow me to serve her as she teaches me."

Alfrig grunted. "Then do I have your leave to return to my tribe, Great Mother?"

The wisdomkeeper frowned. "What haste is this, daughter?"

Alfrig opened her hand and showed them the faint blue glow on her palm. "My husband," she said, her voice strained. "Something is wrong. He needs me. I must go."

Minerva stood. "Where is he?"

"I can't say. Close. His brand calls me." She closed her hand. "I would depart with the low tide," she said. "Do you have a coracle? At low tide without horses, I can get across the sea on my own, without the ferry, even in this weather."

The wisdomkeeper stood. "Near the entrance to the mountain. Come. I will show you."

They started to walk away, but Minerva put a hand on Alfrig's arm. "Do you—would you like me to help you across the sea?"

"I have no need of help," she said. "But if you would like to come so that you may return the wisdomkeeper's boat to her, I would not turn down your company."

"I will dress more appropriately and meet you at the entrance."

She returned to her little room and dressed in breeches, tunic, and furs, and she loaded her pack with a few necessities in case she should be trapped outside come nightfall. *I'm tribal,* she thought, looking down at herself. *I was hiding under white robes all those years when my true nature was tribal.* She shook her head. *I don't know what to think.*

At the entrance to the sacred mountain, Alfrig and the wisdomkeeper stood next to each other, heads bowed together, speaking in low tones. Minerva cleared her throat. "Traitha?"

"You know how to manage a coracle?" Alfrig asked.

"Passably."

"The seas can be rough," the wisdomkeeper said.

"If I must, I'll stay the night on the mainland and return tomorrow at low tide."

"Very well. Safe journey to you both. The One Hand keep you." The wisdomkeeper put a hand on the stone entrance and shuffled into the shadows.

Minerva pulled her furs closer around her. The biting wind and stinging cold of the ice and snow was painful after the warmth of the mountain, but she gritted her teeth against it and stepped closer to the coracle. "We should carry it together."

Alfrig positioned herself at the front of the boat. Together, they picked it up, flipped it over, and settled it onto their backs. The musty scent threatened to choke Minerva at first, but she grew used to it as they walked.

It didn't take long to arrive at the edge of the water, but low tide was still some time off. They set the coracle against a little pile of rocks and huddled under it together, keeping each other as warm as possible. "Foolish man," Alfrig mumbled through her furs. "He couldn't wait until the storm cleared to find trouble?"

Minerva smiled. "Do you have any sense of what's wrong?"

Alfrig rubbed her palm. She sat silent for a very long time. "Hrogarth should not have been," she said, quiet.

Minerva couldn't respond. She waited, knowing that to push Alfrig at that moment would drive her away.

"I have loved Hrogarth since I was a little girl," she said. "I loved him when I was ten and he was fourteen. I loved him when he returned from his rite with the mark of the raven. I loved him when he brought a freshly killed buck and laid it at my feet the day I went before the earth, and I loved him when he offered me his name and his hut and gave me sons and daughters." Her voice cracked. "I love him still. But he should not have been traitha. I know this, and the Great Mother knows this, and Hrogarth knows this. We cannot say why he was named traitha, but we know it should not have been."

She fell silent, and Minerva waited again. "And now?" she whispered after a long moment.

Alfrig sighed. "His balance has always tread a thin line. I fear ...."

Minerva understood. "You fear that without you, he may be losing his grip on sanity. And there is no one to check him, so—"

"So the Morrag may claim him. Yes. Or he may decide it is his time to cleanse the earth. This is also a fear. But do you know what I fear the most?"

Minerva waited.

"I fear that he will not die. I fear that he will merely go mad, be doomed to live a life without me, without his children or his tribe, where the only voice he hears is the Morrag telling him to cleanse the earth. And if that happens, I fear he will be unleashed on Taura and cause more strife between our people and hers."

Minerva wet her lips. "Then you fear that you may have to keep that from happening."

Alfrig leaned her head back against the coracle. "It is too much to ask," she whispered. "For a woman who is an oathbreaker, for a woman who has no reason to help me, I should not ask. But—"

"Yes," Minerva whispered, though her stomach twisted and her chest ached to say it. "Yes, traitha. If you deem it necessary, I will kill your husband for you."

CHAPTER NINETEEN

Peace comes to the bloodied land on lion's paws.
— Second Book of the Wisdomkeepers

It's not much to look at, Braedan thought as he stared out at the small hamlet of Starling's Cross. *A hundred little stone hovels and corrals, rocks, and ice. I miss Torlach.* He pulled furs up around his face as a shield against the wind. *It's hard to believe this is still my kingdom.* He frowned. *Or at least, I think it is. Unless my uncle has made his move.*

It had taken two weeks to get to the northernmost outpost of the Taurin government, and with the Ragged Isles now in sight, a massive winter gale had brought ice and snow like Braedan had never seen down from the north. Braedan and his party approached the heavy oak gates of the Dylan estates, and Malcolm rode forward to speak with the guards. The guard bowed and stepped into the gatehouse, and in a moment the gate creaked and groaned open.

Braedan's eye caught a glimpse of red hair next to him, and his stomach twisted. Cerys reined in and regarded the gate with a sly smile. *Probably wondering how many men she can corrupt,* he thought. Cerys had not been shy with her affections on the journey, and he was certain she had never shivered for lack of warmth at night as he had. She offered herself to him most nights, and it was becoming increasingly difficult to turn her down. But when he found himself tempted, he twisted the length of Igraine's blue silk around his hand and held it to his nose and mouth. *Gods, spirits, if any of you be true, take me back to her,* he begged each night.

If the days of the two-week journey had been tough, the nights were growing unbearable. Edgar's predictions were proving true, though Braedan didn't want to admit it. Every night, his dreams were more terrifying, more haunting. He envisioned Igraine's violent death, the destruction of Torlach, the earth opening up to unleash fire and molten rock, demons from the sky, and other horrors he could not name. Even worse, he saw himself presiding over the horrors, along with an unfamiliar woman. The nights he awakened merely sweating were a relief; some nights, he woke screaming. When he did, the guards and Cerys would come running, and Cerys would always offer him tinctures or draughts to help him sleep. More and more often, and against his better judgment, he accepted.

He stared at Dylan's manor house and found himself hesitant to enter the estate. *This place is not right. There is something here for me.* The blade warmed against his hip. It did that often these days, more and more, it seemed, and his hand went to it.

"Something amiss, your majesty?" Cerys' purring cadence broke into his thoughts.

He shifted his body to look at her, his hand remaining on the blade. Again, he noted the anger that scampered across her face when her eyes landed on his hand and the blade. *Why does she hate this blade? What is it to her?* "Just cold," he said. "Ready for a warm bed."

She gave him a tilted, seductive grin. "Perhaps I can be of assistance, your majesty."

"I'm sure Duke Dylan can provide furs and a fire."

She frowned. "You should not trust this duke, sire."

"Why not?"

Her eyes fixed on his face. "There are forces here that would see you cast down," she said in a low voice. "I sense them."

Braedan's stomach twisted. *Much to fear. Dylan never bent his knee. What might he do when I am a guest in his home?* He shook his head. *No, don't listen to her. She sows dissension in every other way—why would she not sow dissension here, between me and my duke?* He realized his hand gripped the hilt of the sacred blade still. He let go of the blade and rubbed the ache out of his fingers. *Gods, what is happening to me? Is this the madness Edgar warned of?*

The guard at the gate pulled down the furs over his face enough to talk with them. "Sire," he said. "I've informed the duke of your arrival. He advised me to give you and your men every comfort. When you've refreshed yourselves, he will be honored to meet with you."

"My men and I thank you."

The guard led them into the courtyard, where young men in layers of heavy furs took their horses and directed them to the main hall. Braedan allowed a serving girl to take his cloak and boots as another stoked the fire in the hearth. "My lord bids you wait here while he finishes his other duties, sire." She offered him a cup of warm mulled wine.

The last thing I need is more drugs to dull my senses. "Just water."

"My lord, you need something warm."

"Then bring tea."

The servants brought food and drink for everyone, and the men took turns crowding around the massive stone hearth to hold numb hands and feet before the fire. More than one man bore cracked or blistered skin from riding in the ice, and Braedan wondered if his own toes would survive the warming process. He scratched at his new beard. *It helps, but it's not enough. I should have been growing it longer.*

By the time Duke Dylan arrived, half of the men had stretched out on the straw to nap, and the other half had fallen into half-dozes before the fire. Braedan himself struggled to keep his eyes open, but when Haldor Dylan burst through the door, he was awake in an instant.

Dylan stomped across the hall to offer Braedan a perfunctory bow. "Haldor Dylan, Duke of Starling's Cross." He straightened. "So it's to be conquest then, aye?"

Braedan considered the duke for a long moment before he answered. "Does it need to be, my lord?"

Dylan grunted and crossed his arms. "We are a distant estate, aye, but I hear news from the south. I heard about Kiern. It does make me question your intentions."

"Mac Rian violated our most ancient treaty. He wanted tribal territory."

"He thought he'd have an ally in you, aye?"

"He was wrong."

Dylan spat. "Death was too good for Mac Rian. To my mind, Taura owes ye a debt of gratitude. But ye canna deny that a man like me may be wondering what your plans are."

"I have no intention of conquering your estate, Lord Dylan," Braedan said. "I came to request your aid. I need you to help restore rule of law to Taura."

Dylan snorted. "Rule of law? Says the man who took the throne outside the law."

Braedan flinched. "You are not the first to point that out," he said. "Please, my lord—may we speak privately? I would explain myself."

"My study." Dylan turned and led the way out of the hall. Braedan cast a glance at Malcolm, and they both followed Dylan.

Dylan sat behind a massive oak desk, meaty hands folded on the surface and his blue eyes narrowed into fierce slits under the red-blond hair. "Out with it."

Fingall wasn't my biggest supporter at first, but at least he showed some respect. Then again, I haven't done much to earn Dylan's respect. Braedan took a deep breath. "I've come to beg your fealty."

"Aye, well—"

Braedan held up a hand. "*Beg* your fealty, my lord. Not demand it. I'm in no position to demand anything. My kingdom is under attack from within, and I need every man I can get. My uncle moves against me in Torlach. My throne is at the mercy of men who would overthrow my rule. I need good men to fight with me, and I want you to be one of those men. If you haven't given me fealty yet, there must be a good reason. I only hope you tell me what it is so that I may address it and rectify it if needs be."

"Hmm."

"My lord Dylan, I realize that the way I claimed the throne was not ideal, but it's my hope that by fostering cooperation and goodwill between the crown and the twelve ducal seats, I can restore Taura to its old glory. What must I do to win your fealty?"

Dylan pursed his lips. "What are your plans with the kirok?"

Braedan frowned. *The kirok? Why does he care?* "Princess Igraine is my ambassador to the kirok. She's written to open talks between the crown and Aliom, and she's hoping to bring the kirok back to the island to rebuild the sayada and the other buildings."

"The ones you ordered destroyed."

Braedan suppressed a flinch. "I noticed yours was still standing, my lord."

Dylan grinned and scratched his jaw. "Sometimes messages go missing up this far north, aye? Let's say we never got the orders here."

Of course not. "The kirok will be welcome back to the island once her highness negotiates a treaty we can both live with."

"Negotiations and treaties." Dylan scoffed. "Ye're dealing with affairs of other worlds, lad. Ye don't negotiate with Alshada. He goes where he wishes."

"I have no desire to negotiate with gods," Braedan said. "But if the kirok wishes to have a place here, it will have to give me some assurances that my government will be left alone." He crossed his arms. "Your fealty, my lord. What do you need?"

Dylan straightened and poured a shot of oiska. "I need you to be a king, aye? Not a spoiled royal brat who should have been turned over his father's knee two decades ago. Not a man who finds more pleasure in deflowering sayas and drinking himself stupid than in learning to govern."

"I won't argue with you over the sins of my past," Braedan said. "I was a foolish child. But I would beg you allow that years of exile can change a man." He stepped closer to Dylan. "My throne is in danger. I need to go back to Torlach, but I need men—strong men, men who will swear fealty to me over my uncle. I need to know that you will be one of those men."

Dylan opened the door to the study and called for his guard. "Ye'll not be going anywhere for a while—not with this storm brewing." He turned to the guard. "Show the king to a bedchamber and find a place to house his men."

"How long do you think the storm will last?" Braedan asked.

"Hard to say. Sometimes they blow themselves out in a day, sometimes a week. Ye'll not be going anywhere at least till the wind breaks." He put a hand on Braedan's shoulder. "I see the boy I met in Torlach years ago, but I hear the humble strength of a man I could follow. I'll not bend my knee yet, but I'll allow for it quivering a bit."

Braedan chuckled. "As long as it doesn't collapse for Ronan Kerry, I can live with that." *For now.*

The guards showed him to a simple room on the north side of the manor house, and he asked Malcolm to fetch two guards to stand outside his room. When they arrived, they brought Cerys. "No, the girl will sleep in the kitchens with the maids," Braedan ordered.

Malcolm frowned. "Majesty, she said—that is, I understood that you requested her company."

"She lied." He turned away.

"Sire, allow me to examine your shoulder," Cerys said.

She just wants to make sure I'm well. He shook his head. *No, she wants more.* "She'll sleep with the kitchen maids. Send her away and take your position outside my door."

"As you wish, sire."

Braedan undressed and climbed into the bed. The wind howled through cracks in the walls, and he shivered under the furs, even though the servants had built up the fire. *If I ever get back to Torlach, Igraine and I will not leave our bed for a week,* he thought, yawning. Despite the cold, the comfort of a real bed overtook him, and he was asleep in moments.

Screams . . . shouting . . . feet racing past the door . . . Braedan sat up to sounds of chaos. *More dreams?* But the sounds were outside his head. He jumped out of bed and dressed, lacing his breeches closed just as Malcolm threw open the door to his room. "Sire, quickly," the guard said. "The kitchens—"

Cerys. He threw a tunic over his head. "What is it?"

"They need you. A girl is dead."

"Cerys?"

"No, sire, I don't believe so," Malcolm said. "But Lord Dylan insisted you attend him there."

Braedan followed Malcolm to the kitchens and found the burly duke kneeling near a body before the cookfire. He straightened and pointed at Braedan. "You. Your people did this."

"My people?" Braedan frowned. *There's no blood.* The girl's body was limp and pale, but Braedan saw no wounds, no blood, no bruises. *White robes. Who wears white robes in the kitchens?* "I'm sorry you've lost one of your people, my lord, but I don't see how I could have had anything to do with it."

Dylan's face twisted in anger. "Where's your girl? The whore?"

"You don't think she did this, do you?"

"Who else?" Dylan gestured around the room. "My estates are a safe place, sire, or they were before you and your witch came."

"Witch? Cerys is a healer. She may be free with her favors, but she's not a witch."

"Ye're blinded to what is right before you, lad. The kitchen maids tell me she wears a talisman of dark magic and asks for herbs that no healer would ever need. And now a girl is dead—a girl under my protection."

Protection. "She's a saya, isn't she?"

Dylan's mouth formed a tight line. "She was."

The commotion had awakened men and women all over the estate house, and more of the Taurin guards appeared even as Dylan's men filled the room. "My lord, I trust the men I travel with, and Cerys has been invaluable in caring for an arrow wound I sustained weeks ago. I can't believe anyone in my party had anything to do with this," Braedan said.

Dylan stormed around the room, his heavy footsteps pounding over the quiet sobs of kitchen maids and the howl of the wind outside. "We're not a big holding, aye? Ye'll be seeing us as nothing but rocks and ice. It's a hard life here, but it's a good life. I'll not be risking it to house a spoiled royal brat and his witch."

Braedan stepped toward him. "My lord—"

"Forgive me, sire, but I'll be asking you to leave now."

Superstition and fear—powerful motivators, indeed. "Where's Cerys?"

"Can't say." He jerked his head toward the door. "If you're lucky, lad, she's out there freezing to death."

"Find her," Braedan whispered to Malcolm. The guard saluted and walked into the storm. Two of the Taurin guards stepped closer to Braedan, hands on swords as they watched the Dylan men. "What are your plans, Duke Dylan?"

The duke turned back to him. "Toward the throne?"

"Yes."

"I plan to stay here in my holdings until I have a reason to go south, sire. And right now, I have no reason to go south."

"My uncle will give you reason."

He scoffed. "I defy Ronan Kerry to attempt to force himself on this holding. He can't even manage to stay in Stone Coast. He'll not be wanting to journey up to this frozen finger of the world."

Braedan stepped closer and lowered his voice. "Ronan Kerry rarely resorts to arms, my lord," he said. "He has other ways to demand your allegiance, and he'll use them."

"He'll not be enforcing anything, aye?" Dylan shrugged. "Not unless he shows up here. And as I said, sire—things have a way of going missing up here. That goes for pretender kings as well as messages."

"Pretender kings—like me?"

Dylan's voice had the low, hot rumble of a distant fire. "These are my holdings, sire. Mine. And unless ye'll be seizing my property and putting my head on a spike, I'll be protecting 'em as I see fit."

Malcolm returned to the kitchens then, one hand on Cerys' elbow. She smiled at Braedan.

Something dark in Cerys' eyes tickled the edges of Braedan's memory. He rubbed his temples. *Seize this place. Arrest him. Have him beheaded. Force his fealty. You've done it before. He refuses to bend his knee. He deserves to be punished.* "Malcolm," he said. "Take the duke into custody."

Malcolm hesitated. "Sire, I—"

"Arrest him!" Braedan shouted, pointing at the duke. "Or you'll get the lashes he deserves."

Malcolm saluted, fist over heart, and seized Duke Dylan's arm. The duke swung around and brought his fist up toward Malcolm's face, but the guard blocked the blow with his other hand. He twisted Dylan's arm back until he forced the duke to his knees. Dylan grunted, but he didn't cry out.

Braedan's men formed a circle around him, swords drawn against the estate guards who reacted. "Make a move against me and your lord dies," Braedan shouted. Everyone fell silent. Malcolm held a dagger at Dylan's throat. Braedan stepped closer to the duke. "You're on your knees now, my lord. Anything you'd like to say while you're there?"

Dylan smiled. "Fuck you, sire."

Braedan waved Malcolm away. "Take him to his room. Bind him and guard him. No one goes in or out."

"Yes, sire."

Braedan retreated to stand in the doorway with Cerys. "If you have any love for your duke," he called to the kitchen staff and the guards around the room. "You will stand down. I swear to you that no harm will befall him as long as I remain unharmed. But if you touch me or one of my men or this woman, your duke will die. Do you understand?"

There were small nods of acquiescence, and Braedan stormed away back toward his room, only dimly aware of the men and Cerys behind him. She followed him into his room and dismissed his men, and he paced. "I gave him a chance—I told him to bend his knee," he said.

"You were more than fair, sire," she said.

He stopped pacing and took her shoulders in his hands. "What did you have to do with that girl's death?"

"Nothing, your majesty." But the edge of her mouth tilted up in a half-smile. "Sire, allow me to look at your shoulder?"

Braedan stepped back. He touched his shoulder and drew his hand away. *Wet.* He brushed his thumb across the balls of his fingers. "Bleeding—"

"You've stressed yourself," she said. She put her fingers on his face. "Come, sire, sit down. Let me check it."

She directed him to a chair in front of the fire and pulled his nightshirt off. "Your touch is soft, but you know what you're doing," he mumbled. *Like Igraine.*

Her fingers skimmed his neck, shoulders, back, chest. She leaned down from behind to whisper into his ear. "I also know what I want." She put her lips against his neck.

You promised Igraine. You promised. He tipped his head, and Cerys' lips traveled down to his shoulder. She moved around to kneel before him and reached for his breeches. "Don't—"

Her hands skimmed up his belly and chest to his shoulder. "Don't do what, sire? Dress your shoulder?" She raised up on her knees and nudged herself between his legs. She unbuckled his belt and let it drop on the floor next to him.

She looks like Igraine from this angle. So close. It would be so easy. Igraine wouldn't have to know. Her eyes met his, and he saw something in them that sent a shiver of horror down his spine. *Victory.*

He pushed her away and leapt out of the chair, desire gone as fear replaced it. "What are you? Who are you?"

She stood. "No one, sire." She beckoned to the chair again. "Let me dress your shoulder, your majesty."

"I'm faithful to Igraine."

"Of course you are, sire."

He sat down. Her fingers brushed over the wound, and she dabbed at it with a wet cloth. The memory of her kneeling before him seemed hazy, and he wondered if he'd only imagined it. "What did you do to me?" he whispered.

"I've cleaned your wound," she said. She lifted his arm to begin winding a bandage around a wad of linen over the wound.

"You were tempting me—"

Her warm breath washed over his skin when she laughed, raising goose-flesh and stirring memories of Igraine next to him, beneath him, around him. "Sire," Cerys whispered. "I know that you adore your princess. She is a lucky woman to have caught your eye. But you've been away from her for so long now. Surely a young man like you must be growing weary of sleeping alone."

He shook his head. "I promised." *But it's getting harder and harder to keep that promise.*

She tied off the bandage and straightened in front of him. "It might interest you to know that Duke Dylan has been keeping something from you, sire."

"Oh?"

She laced her fingers before her, a picture of demure patience. "If you trust me, I'll show you."

He stood and rubbed his shoulder. "Where is this thing he's hiding?"

"Outside, across the estate." She picked up his tunic and offered it. "You'll need to dress, sire."

He pulled on his tunic. "Go get your cloak."

She left his chambers, and Braedan ordered his guards to fetch their cloaks as well. He dressed himself in several layers of wool and fur while he waited for them to return and then fell to pacing across the room. When Cerys and his guards returned to his chamber, he pulled on gloves and gestured to her to lead the way. He fell in step behind her, unable to look away from the straight, proud posture or the firm backside under her clothes. He stepped up to her side. "You tempt me still."

"I'm merely walking, sire."

He took her arm roughly and lowered his voice. "If this is nothing, if you lead me here for nothing, I will cast you out into the ice and wind, woman."

She stopped walking and turned to him. "You would not, my lord," she said. She put a hand on his chest. "You. Would. Not."

I would not cast her out. I need her. I need her healing talents. And she knows things—sees things, understands things. I need her advice, her wisdom. He shook his head, but his thoughts seemed foggy and unfocused. *Cerys will help me figure it all out. I can't cast her out.* "Show us this secret."

She led them through the manor house and out to the grounds. He flinched when he saw his own guards outside the barracks where Dylan's men slept. He started to go in that direction, but Cerys put a hand on his arm. "This way."

He followed.

She stopped at the door of a dark, cold outbuilding on the very edge of Dylan's estate and knocked on the door. "Who's there?" called a woman in a frightened voice.

Braedan's guard pushed forward. "Your king demands entrance," he answered, shouting over the wind. "Open the door or stand aside for it to be opened."

The wind howled through the long pause that followed. Braedan waited, frowning. "You led us out here for a woman?" he whispered in Cerys' ear.

"Not a woman, sire," she answered. The door creaked open before her, and the guards pushed through. "A dozen women."

The guards stood aside for Braedan. "No one here but women," one of them said. "This is Dylan's secret?"

Braedan's eyes adjusted to the faint light of a very low fire in the hearth. A dozen women wrapped in blankets and cloaks sat huddled near the fire, fighting the chill of the night air. "What is this?" he asked Cerys.

"These women are sayas," she said. "Dylan disobeyed your orders to destroy the kirok and seize the property. He sheltered women who escaped Torlach when you attacked. These women should have been taken prisoner months ago, but they weren't." She stepped forward and gestured around. "This is why he was so reluctant to swear fealty, sire. He protects the women you ordered out of Taura."

Braedan's stomach twisted. "Is this true?" he asked.

One of them—a petite blonde of no more than twenty—stepped forward. "She tells the truth, my lord," she said. She tipped her head, and her fine straight hair fell forward off her shoulders. "We came from Torlach when you took your throne. We feared for our lives and safety. Duke Dylan provided sanctuary."

Braedan turned to Cerys. "How did you discover this?"

"I saw one of the women in the kitchen. She fetched food, and I followed when she carried it all back here to the house. I asked a kitchen woman who they were. She told me."

"She betrayed their confidence?"

Cerys gave him a tilted smile. "I was very convincing, sire."

Braedan paced toward the door, thinking. "The girl who died was one of these as well."

Cerys did not answer.

"Someone build up the fire," he said. "And light some candles. I want to see who I'm facing."

There was a flurry of activity behind him, and when the lights grew bright at last, he turned around again and approached the blonde saya. "Did you know why I took the sayada?"

"Yes, my lord. You sought the Taurin heir."

"And she escaped. You and your sisters helped her escape."

"Yes."

"Why?"

"We assumed you wanted to do her harm, my lord."

He folded his arms. "What if I told you I wanted to wed her? What if I had planned to make an alliance with her?"

"Did you?"

The dark man told me to kill her. I couldn't. "Do you know where she went?"

The girl bit her lip, the first sign of weakness or hesitation he'd seen on her face. "Yes," she said at last.

"Sire." Cerys hovered close to his shoulder. "The duke defied you. He kept these women here against your orders. He housed and sheltered them when you wanted them off the island."

Braedan folded his arms. "He's a traitor."

"He's a traitor. And so are these."

"You didn't leave. Why didn't you leave? You had time—you could have left Taura. Why did you stay?"

"Because we had a duty to serve Taura," the girl said. "We had reason to believe you wanted to kill the Taurin heir. But the Taurin heir should never leave Taura, so I stayed. And these women—" she gestured behind her "—these women stayed with me. We stayed to protect her, to pray for Taura."

"Sire." Malcolm stepped through the door.

Braedan held up a hand to silence him. "You stayed. When you could have saved yourselves, you all stayed."

"It was our duty."

"And what do you do here? Holed up in this place, surrounded by ice and snow and wind? What could you possibly hope to accomplish?"

She spread her hands. "We pray. We ask for Alshada to change your heart—to intercede on our behalf. We remain devoted to the vows of the sayas, and we seek wisdom, devotion, and service."

Cerys drew in a sharp hiss next to Braedan. "The woman lies," she whispered.

"What does she lie about?"

"I cannot tell. But she lies, and she will destroy you with her lies."

"What would you suggest I do, then?" he asked, turning to look at her.

"You must kill them," she said. "They are traitorous bitches who seek your downfall. Destroy them, utterly. Leave nothing of their poison in your kingdom."

The gasps of a dozen women echoed through the little building at that, but the young blonde girl only flinched, and even that seemed subdued. "Sire," she said. "Sire, before you give such an order, I must beg for the lives of my sisters."

"Sire," Malcolm said, his voice increasing in urgency. "Your majesty, may we speak?"

Braedan finally turned. "What is so important that you—"

Malcolm had drawn his sword, and he now swung it up to point at Cerys. "This bitch is the liar," he said. "These women only want to live in peace. This woman wants them dead for reasons of her own. *She's* the poison."

"He lies," Cerys whispered. Braedan turned to her. The only expression on her face was a chilling smile of triumph. "He lies, your majesty. You know he does. These women want one of their number on the throne. They want to control the country by putting some untried girl on the throne. They seek to replace the regency with a church government."

Braedan turned to the blonde girl. "Who are you?"

She took a deep breath. "I am Mairead Brennan. I am the Taurin heir."

CHAPTER TWENTY

Not of lion born, the Deliverer finds sanctuary.
— Lion tribe prophecy

Two days after Faltian, it started snowing.

This was not the soft, romantic snow of the plains—the snow Mairead recalled drifting down onto Henry's castle and coating it with a sugary sparkle. It was not the wet, cold, half-rain snow that she and Connor had fought their way through the night they saved Kenna. It was not even the more serious snow that piled up on the boughs and branches of the scrubby evergreens, but left the space under them dry and warm.

Mairead had never seen such snow before. It started with a sky of slate gray clouds on the horizon. The lions rushed around the city to put livestock in barns and shelters. Homes were inspected for previously unseen damage—loose thatching or panes, boards that would not withstand a storm. Children brought in piles of firewood, and young men butchered extra chickens and rabbits.

Aerwyth and Hedwar were no exception. Mairead helped them stock the larder, stack firewood, care for livestock, and anything else they asked for. Gareth helped as well. "Do you mind if I stay here during the storm?" he asked his mother.

"Of course not, but you don't need to. We'll manage."

"I know, but I'd prefer to not be stuck in my own hut alone for a week or more."

Mairead startled at that. "A *week?* We could be inside for a week?"

"If we're lucky," Hedwar said. "These blizzards have been known to keep us housebound for two weeks or more."

Mairead bit her lip to avoid revealing more, but Gareth understood. He put a hand on her shoulder and leaned down. "I'm sure he'll be fine."

When the storm hit, it did not start with a few scattered flakes. The air turned eerily quiet first, and then the wind and snow hit with blinding force all at once. The snow fell in white sheets of huge flakes for hours without rest, and the wind howled around the city, teasing at even the smallest cracks and crevices of Hedwar's well-built home. Gareth built the fire up in the hearth, and Aerwyth warmed wine, but Mairead could not find it in herself to relax. She curled up in a pile of furs and sipped her wine and tried to make polite conversation, but her thoughts remained with Connor and Phinneas. *One Hand, please care for them.*

The blizzard lasted three days. Mairead slept only fitfully the entire time. When the wind broke and Gareth suggested they could venture out of the house for a short time, she very nearly ran to find her boots and cloak. She had to shield her eyes and squint when he opened the door. "The sun is always blinding when it first comes out after a snowstorm," he said. He held out a hand to help her over the drifts that had piled just beyond the covered entry. "But Isfyrin is beautiful after a storm."

Mairead blinked several times, but once her vision cleared, she sucked in a breath. "Gareth, it's breathtaking," she whispered.

The white covering on the city was less a blanket and more of a lumpy down mattress, but the soft curves and bumps and valleys of the snow provided an oddly smoothing effect on the landscape. All around them, other families emerged with caution. Adults examined the skies, houses, and livestock pens, while children dove into snow banks and pelted each other with snowballs. The distant hills stood against the blue sky like diamonds, and the crisp sun gave the city a sparkle that Mairead couldn't compare to anything she'd ever seen.

Gareth turned to her. "Will you help me check the animals?"

"Of course. Can we walk out of the city today?"

He understood the question she didn't ask. "It's not wise. This is the time of year when we need to stay vigilant—another storm can arrive at any moment. These breaks are the times when we make sure we're ready for the next one." He paused. "I'm sure he's fine, Mairead."

She couldn't find any solace in his assurances. "He hates the cold."

Gareth smiled. "Then it is a testament to his affection for you that he stays on the mountain rather than return to the plains."

She forced a smile in return. By the time they had finished checking the animals, she found her spirits revived, and she even managed to participate in a small snowball fight with a few of the village children before they returned to Hedwar and Aerwyth's home.

Connor came to Mairead on the air that night, after she had bedded down. She jumped up and threw her arms around his neck, and he chuckled. "That's the kind of greeting I could get used to."

She drew back, kissed him, and then swatted his shoulder. "I was worried about you. That was a good storm."

He shrugged. "I've seen worse."

"You are well, then? You have shelter?"

"I do. I can't visit during those storms, though. It's not safe to travel in the air or water—the elements are too unpredictable, and I don't want to end up losing anything important." He grinned. "There are certain parts of me you might miss."

She let out a long, relieved breath as she blushed at the implication. "I miss them right now."

"Temptress," he teased. He put his hands on her cheeks. "The cold air agrees with you. You look pretty tonight. You're practically glowing."

She fidgeted with the laces on his jerkin. "You could stay, you know."

"I wish I could. I don't want to risk anyone finding out about us."

She put her arms around his waist and rested her head on his chest. "I hope you weren't disappointed."

"Disappointed? In what?"

"In me. In our wedding night."

"Mairead, I could never be disappointed in you."

"But I'm not experienced or—"

"It's not about experience. It's just that I don't want to betray you to the tribe. There is too much distrust of the ravens for them to find out you've wed one."

He's hiding something. "Is that all?"

He hesitated. "Yes."

"Connor—"

"When the Morrag is in my head, it's . . . difficult to concentrate."

She took a deep breath. "When can we have a life like a normal married couple?"

"Never."

She laughed. "Probably not."

He grinned. "I have to go, but I will return whenever I can. Whenever I'm safe and it's safe here." He kissed her goodbye and wound the braids around himself.

It was only a few days later when the next blizzard struck, and this one challenged even Gareth's patience. After five days of howling wind and driving snow, he started to pace and fidget, checking the weather frequently. "Do you fear for Grayfeather?" Mairead asked.

He shook his head. "He knows where to bed down and wait these things out. But our animals—they need fresh water and food. I don't want to find dead livestock when this is over."

The harshest weather of the winter settled in on the mountain, and Mairead found herself with what she thought must be a general malaise from being stuck inside so much. Gareth stayed with his parents during the storms. He seemed to try to keep Mairead's dark frame of mind in check, but even his geniality and Hedwar and Aerwyth's hospitality couldn't jog her out of her mood. She sat near the fire for hours, her stomach churning, her spirit longing for sun and warmth.

Connor visited rarely and only stayed long enough to reassure her that he hadn't yet succumbed to the Morrag's madness. Between his visits, Mairead's emotions could not decide where to reside. At night, she would lie on her cot and wish for his presence, tempted to call him through their bond but not wishing to worry him or make him travel if it was unsafe. But during the day, there were times when she would watch Aerwyth and Hedwar and realize that their comfortable domesticity was likely impossible with Connor. *He could never settle down and tend livestock, serve on a council, and live inside city walls, even if he didn't have the Morrag inside him. He's not a man for this kind of life, and yet this is the kind of life I wanted. What if marrying him was a terrible mistake?*

There were a few days when Gareth said it was safe enough to venture outside the city, and Mairead used the opportunity to learn to walk on snowshoes. Sometimes Connor met them. One late afternoon, during a rare warm break in the weather, they found him waiting near their path with a skin of oiska. "Where did you find that?" Gareth asked.

Connor grinned. "Been saving it." He offered the tribesman a drink, and Gareth took it and gave the skin back. Connor offered it to Mairead.

She put a hand on her stomach. Bile rose in her throat. "Not tonight."

"Are you well?"

"Yes. My appetite is just a little off." She smiled. "Tell me what you've been doing."

"There's nothing to tell. Just waiting out the winter."

In the distance, a sharp scream pierced the waning light. "Lion," Gareth told them. "Probably a female trying to find food in this snow." He stood. "We should get back into the city, traitha. She could be miles away, but we don't want to risk it. She's probably hungry."

She stood. "Will you come into the city tonight?" she asked Connor. "Just for the safety of the walls?"

"I'll be safe enough." He bent and kissed her cheek. "Good night."

He hides things from me. But before she could confront him, he'd wrapped the braids around himself and disappeared again.

A week later, Mairead and Gareth found him leaning against a tree when they walked out of the city. She gave him a smile, and they exchanged a quick kiss. "How did you know we'd be here?"

"Lucky guess," he said. When she frowned, he chuckled. "All right, I was listening when you walked through Isfyrin earlier. You don't always see me when I'm in the braids." He held out an arm to Gareth. "You look troubled, lion."

Gareth clasped his arm and shrugged. "It's not important."

But Mairead knew the truth. In her weeks with the tribe, Gareth had grown as close as a brother, and Aerwyth and Hedwar had begun to treat Mairead as a long-lost daughter. Unfortunately, the amount of time Gareth and Mairead spent with each other and the closeness she shared with their family lent credence to rumors that Gareth and Mairead would soon be betrothed. Mairead overheard girls mourn the loss of the most eligible bachelor in the village, but she knew Gareth only had eyes for Elsbet. "Elsbet believes that Gareth and I are betrothed—or will be soon," Mairead told Connor.

His face turned into a tight, non-committal mask. "Why does she believe that?" he asked in a strained tone.

Mairead's grip on his hand tightened. "Because I live in Gareth's parents' house, and they seem happy to believe I might wed their son. And I can't tell anyone that I'm already married."

"I tell Elsbet it's not true, but she doesn't believe me," Gareth said.

"Mairead," Connor said. "Perhaps it's time to find somewhere else to live."

His voice had grown tighter, more strained. "Gareth is my friend—nothing more."

He lowered his voice. "Can we speak privately?"

She nodded, and he took her hand to lead her away from the clearing. "What's going on between you and Gareth?"

"Nothing—nothing more than what you've seen or heard."

His eyes went distant for a moment, and he let out a long sigh. "You're telling me the truth."

She crossed her arms. "You have to ask her? Don't you trust me?"

He pressed the bridge of his nose. "I don't know. She showed me once—I thought he wanted—"

"Me? You thought he wanted me?" She shook her head. "Even if he did, why do you think I'd want him?"

He scoffed and gestured to himself. "Why wouldn't you want him? He's exactly the kind of man you need—not me, not someone with all this madness." He waved a hand when she started to talk. "Leave it. I'll return when I get this thing under control."

And before she could respond, he'd wrapped the braids around himself and disappeared into the earth.

Gareth put a hand on her arm. "Mairead?"

He rarely called her by her name, and the kindness deflated her anger. Her stomach roiled, and her head spun. "I'm not feeling much like walking now. Can we return to the city?"

She ate little that day and went to bed early. She awakened in the darkness to the gooseflesh of Sidh magic. "Connor," she whispered as she sat up.

But the braids dissipated to reveal Maeve. She frowned. "Where is my son?"

Mairead stood. "He's not here."

"But I saw—" Maeve stopped. "Oh, gods. Oh *gods*."

There were equal amounts of fear, joy, and anxiety in her voice. "What is it?" The magic pricked her skin again, and Mairead gasped as the braids wound around and through her. This time, though, Maeve did not bind her or restrict her movements. The magic teased and cajoled as it flowed in and out of Mairead's body. The gentleness of it reminded her of the Sidh healing. "What are you doing?" she asked.

Maeve withdrew the magic and put her hands on her hips. "You are with child. My grandchild. My heir."

Mairead's hand flew to her belly. "I'm—*what?*"

"Pregnant. You carry Connor's daughter. She has all three talents and the *codagha*." She laughed a laugh of genuine relief. "I've been such a fool! It's not the woman—it's him! He's the one who matters."

Mairead frowned. "Perhaps it's both."

"I'm sorry, dear, but no. You have only the slightest hint of Sidh blood. You could never pass it on, not even in the smallest form. No, for your child to carry the *codagha* and the three talents, it must have been passed on by Connor."

Mairead rubbed her belly. *Pregnant. I'm pregnant. With his child. And now he's gone.* "You're certain?"

"She is already strong. I sensed her from Taura. It was she who brought me here. I thought Connor wanted to see me, but I think it was your child. Her heart beats. Her mind is forming. Already she practices weaving the braids." She tilted her head. "It's very early. You've missed your monthly bleeding, yes?"

Mairead thought for a moment. She sat down on her cot. "I suppose I have. I didn't even …." She crossed her arms in front of her. "A child. How is this possible?"

"If you don't know that, child, the kirok failed you."

"I don't mean that. I mean, we only had one night."

"That's all it takes."

They were interrupted by a knock on the door. "Mairead?" Aerwyth called. "Is all well? I heard voices."

Mairead cringed. "All is well," she replied. "I was just talking to myself."

"May I come in?"

Maeve startled. "No," Mairead said. "No. I am fine. I'm just thinking aloud."

There was a long pause. "Very well," Aerwyth finally said.

Mairead motioned Maeve closer and dropped her voice. "They don't know," she whispered.

"A moment." Maeve's eyes took on a distant expression, and Mairead saw violet air braids twist around the two of them and drift up and out of the room. "We may speak now," the Sidh queen said at last. "The braids will take our words away."

Mairead let out a long breath. She rubbed her belly again. "I am with child."

"Yes."

"And you say this child is a girl? And your heir?"

"Yes. I only hope her power does not overwhelm you—that a human can carry such a powerful child."

Mairead bristled. "You carried Connor."

"And it nearly killed me." She took a deep breath. "I do not intend to demean you, child, but we are different. We may be able to have children together, but that does not always mean it is a good idea."

"And yet this bad idea has given you your heir, apparently."

Maeve raised an eyebrow. "Your will has not dimmed, I see. If anything, it's stronger than the first time I had to remind you of my power."

Mairead sat up straighter. "You make many assumptions, your majesty. Why do you believe I will allow my daughter to become your heir? She may be called to other great things. Perhaps she'll be *my* heir."

"You can have another child. Have as many sons as you wish with Connor. You've taken him from his people—why not—"

"Because I can't be sure he'll be here for any of them," Mairead snapped.

Maeve stopped short, and her mouth tightened into a grim line. "So. You see what I warned you of all those weeks ago."

"You told me. You said he would ruin me and leave me." She told Maeve about the events of their last encounter. "I can never tell if he'll return," she said. "And even if he does, I don't know how many times I can take him back. I don't know if there's room for me in his life." She sighed. "I can't share him with the Morrag."

Maeve sat next to Mairead. She laced her fingers in her lap. "I know what it is to share a man."

"I thought Connor's father was a widower."

"He was, but I fell in love with him before his wife died. He was honorable, but my heart betrayed me. And then, after Culain's wife died and I finally had his heart, I realized I could never really share his life. I always shared him with a woman I could never compete with—Taura." She gave a rueful laugh. "In some ways, I would have preferred to only share him with his wife. Taura was a demanding mistress."

"I think the Morrag is more demanding." Mairead took a deep breath. "This child is also the new Taurin heir," she said. "She might be the future Sidh queen, but she is also my only child, and therefore she'll have to carry the Taurin line. And it is a noble line. It has Mac Niall blood, too."

"Perhaps she won't have to carry both," Maeve said.

"What do you mean?"

"You may not wish to think of this now, but it may be that the only reason for your union with Connor was to produce this child. If he leaves or dies—if the Morrag intends to use him up and discard him—" Her voice caught on emotion, and she paused to compose herself. "He is one man. There are others. You are young. You may yet find another man—another Taurin man, or a tribesman from this place—to give you sons to carry your line."

"And this is all I am? Some vessel with the right blood, destined just to carry children of the proper line?"

Maeve put a hand on her arm. "I do not think my son would have wed you if that's all you were."

"How can I feel so divided?" Mairead whispered. "How can I be so angry with him and so hurt by him and still love him?"

"Because your anger and hurt are fueled by your love," Maeve said without hesitation. "If you did not love him so deeply, it would not hurt so much or cause so much anger."

"Perhaps." She took a deep breath. "Whatever you think of me, your majesty, I do love your son. I fear what he will become, but I love him. I will always love him."

"I know." Maeve reached for Mairead's hand. "We are different women, you and I, but we share two things: my son and your child. Whether you wish it or no, the child has my blood, too. I will ensure that you and she are always cared for, even if no one else does."

The words brought relief Mairead didn't expect. *No one else. It's possible I'll be shunned for this—that people will think I conceived out of wedlock. It's possible a tribesman will use this to claim me as a wife.* She took a deep breath. "He ensured I would be cared for. He made me his wife on paper and made me his sole heir. But I fear ...."

"I know." Maeve squeezed Mairead's hand. "He deserves to know that he is a father. He deserves to hear the news from you."

Tears spilled over, but Mairead kept them from her voice. She nodded. "I will ride out to find him as soon as it's safe. Your majesty," she started.

"Maeve." It came out of the queen's mouth with a certain tightness.

"Your majesty?"

The queen offered a tight smile. "Call me Maeve. Or 'Mother,' if you prefer."

Mairead tried to picture herself addressing the tiny queen as "Mother." "Maeve," she said. "That will—"

"—Take some adjustment, yes."

Mairead smiled. "Thank you, Maeve," she said.

Maeve patted their clasped hands. "You are welcome, Mairead."

CHAPTER TWENTY-ONE

The spirits of creation wait for the command of their Creator.
– Tribal wisdom

Mairead had every intention of riding out to find Connor the next day, but the night brought another blizzard—the worst one yet. Gareth managed to make his way through the weather to his parents' house, but he wouldn't even consider her request. "We may have seen our last days of good weather till spring," he said. "We could be inside the city for a month or more."

"Will we have to be in the houses that long?" Mairead asked, envisioning endless weeks without fresh air.

Gareth laughed at the dismayed tone of her voice. "No, probably not. We can get out a bit during the breaks. At least within the city there are ways to see where we are, and there's always a house close by where we can take shelter if necessary. It's only the fields or pastures or beyond the walls where things get dangerous."

Mairead wasn't happy, but she assured him that she understood. She prayed for Connor to return, but even when the weather broke for a time, she didn't see him. She tried calling him through their bond, but he didn't respond, and she didn't know if it was because he feared traveling in the winter weather or because he'd finally succumbed to the Morrag. She buried her fears and anxiety in books provided by Letha and Aerwyth, and eventually, the sting of his absence faded into a dull ache.

Settling into the tribal life brought both comfort and confusion. There was a growing closeness with Aerwyth, Hedwar, and Gareth, and she developed friendships with Letha and Wytha and the other women. During the short breaks in the weather, she was able to walk inside the city and visit Trypp's family or the earth guardians, and she began to learn more of tribal ways. *This place is becoming more of a home than the sayada ever was,* she thought often.

But under the façade of hospitality, warmth, and friendship was a dark thread of fear and distrust of outlanders and the ravens. The novelty of having the Deliverer in their midst was wearing off, it seemed, especially outside of the Catspaw clan. While the Catspaws and their allies seemed willing to accept her as the prophesied deliverer, other clans were less enthusiastic. Even among those who claimed to believe she was the Deliverer, Mairead found herself entering into conversations with caution. No one believed the plains had anything good to offer, and if Mairead discussed the slave trade or poverty or the lack of order on the plains, the lions seemed satisfied to believe that the people of the outland had exactly what they deserved.

"How can they cheer me as a Deliverer?" she asked Gareth and Trypp. "Your own prophecies acknowledge that you are to go from the mountains to the plains, and yet they seem to have no desire to go."

"I think the idea has always been to just wait it out," Trypp said.

"What do you mean?"

"Just let the plains burn," he said. "When the place is burned out, weak, and empty, we can go down and take what we want."

Mairead's stomach twisted. "There are people dying right now," she said. "They are human—they are as human as we are. Do they not have the right to live?"

"Some lions believe they are more human than others," Trypp said.

"Your words have echoes of empire, too," Gareth said. "There are those among the lions who believe that empires bring nothing but sorrow and tyranny."

"I have no desire to promote tyranny."

"I know that, but what of your descendants? Say you build this empire and reunify the three lands. When you die, how can you promise your descendants will rule as you have?"

Mairead fought the urge to put a hand over her belly. "I don't know," she confessed. "All I know is that right now, the plains need order, and the lions are strong enough to provide it. I can't promise anything beyond that."

Mairead noticed other concerns in the city. There were not as many children as she would have expected. When she asked Gareth, he frowned. "I don't know why we don't have bigger families. We celebrate every child. Are you saying the other tribes have more children?"

"I don't know about the Taurin tribes, but in the cities of Taura and Culidar, families with four, five, six or more children are uncommon."

He blinked, surprised. "So many—I don't know how we would accommodate so many children."

"Perhaps this is what happens after centuries of remaining isolated."

He shrugged. "Perhaps it's the One Hand's way of helping us survive. The mountain has much, but this is a hard life. We have known many seasons of want. Better to have fewer children to conserve our resources."

But the previous season had been one of plenty, Mairead noted. Feasts were commonplace in Isfyrin, and Aerwyth hosted many of them. She could find any excuse to surround her table with friends and neighbors, and Mairead thought that Aerwyth hated the harsh winter weather only because it prevented people from visiting her home. It was not unusual to find her table filled with roasted pig, several chickens, dark molasses bread, baked roots, pickled vegetables, preserved fruits, and all manner of sweetcakes and puddings. Beer and oiska flowed freely in Hedwar's home, and Mairead usually found herself caught up in the spirit of the occasion, singing tribal songs along with the others. There was always someone to watch the weather and ensure that everyone could get home.

Gradually, slowly, the blizzards faded, the weather grew warmer, and the days of clear skies started to gain on the days of snow. There was even a day with rain, finally, and Aerwyth declared winter on the wane. She invited most of the clan to her home, and the feasting went on long into the night.

As Aerwyth started to graciously shoo all of the guests away, Elsbet approached Mairead. "Traitha," she said. Her cheeks were bright with the heat and the evening's festivities, but her posture was tense and angry. "May we speak?"

Mairead put down the dishes in her hands. "Yes, we should speak."

Elsbet's words tumbled out in a semi-incoherent rush. "The girls in the village—they say that you and Gareth—and I know that his mother loves—but I've cared for him since—and he's all I've ever—"

Mairead put her hand on Elsbet's arm and led her away from the crowd to a quiet corner. "Gareth is in love with you," she said, cutting off the girl's attempts to speak further.

Elsbet's sigh of relief relaxed her entire body. "He is?"

Mairead smiled. "He speaks of little else but courting you, but he struggles with the expectations that are on him. He fears disappointing his family if he doesn't wed me." She saw the look of tension return and put her hand on Elsbet's arm again. "It has nothing to do with you, Elsbet. His family has never said anything against you. I have every reason to believe they would welcome you into their family."

Elsbet fidgeted and glanced toward Aerwyth. "I should go help Aerwyth clean up."

"I think that's a very good idea."

Elsbet walked away and spoke quietly to Aerwyth, who gestured to several bowls and cups that needed to be cleared. Elsbet returned to the table, and in a moment, Gareth joined her. Mairead smiled. *He was born to be a husband.* She thought of Connor, and her stomach twisted. *Will I ever get to have a real husband? One who's here? I told him if he left, I didn't know if I could take him back, but now that he's gone, all I want is his return.* She let out a deep breath. *I need some air.*

She found her cloak and ducked out of the house when Aerwyth was distracted. She found a bench in the center of the city and sat down to enjoy the relative quiet after the noise of a feasting house. The cool evening air felt good against her warm face, and the sky overhead was clear and full of stars.

"Mairead."

She turned to the deep voice. *Not Connor. I still expect to see him everywhere.* "Braun. Good evening."

He stepped closer. "I have heard rumors. They say you are learning our ways, becoming a tribal woman."

She stood. "I am trying. What are you doing here, in this part of Isfyrin?"

He turned in a slow circle, gesturing around the city with the skin of oiska in his hand. "Surveying my inheritance," he said over a thick tongue. "That's what my father would have me believe, anyway. 'Isfyrin needs a strong hand,' he always says. 'The Lionjaws—that's the only clan with the strength to lead.'"

Mairead swallowed hard. *Be careful.* "And he thinks you're the one who should rule the city?"

Braun snorted. "Rule the city—listen to you. You speak as an outlander. Tribesmen don't have rulers." He took a long pull from his oiska. "Kings and queens and princes—tribesmen are too noble for such titles. We serve the earthspirit, and she gives us traithas."

"Your prophecies say I am a traitha."

He wiped his mouth with the back of one hand and grunted. "Some call you such. But the prophecy says 'Deliverer,' not traitha. My father has been very clear about that—Deliverer."

"Why does that matter?"

"If you are not a traitha, you will need to wed a traitha. And who better than a Lionjaw?"

Mairead's stomach lurched. *Is that what all of this is about—this idea of making me into a lion? I can't be traitha, so they would use me as a figure-*

head? A symbol for some traitha to use for his own ends? She clenched her fists. "Go tell your father that I have no intention of wedding a Lionjaw. I will lead you as traitha, or I will not lead you at all."

He stared, swaying on his feet, and she wondered if he would even remember everything she had said. He finally took another long drink. "I have sons," he said. "Two. Strong little boys, learning to use a knife already. Their mother is a Lionjaw. She's beautiful. But I didn't marry her because my father told me not to. He said it might still be for us to give the Lionjaw blood to the Deliverer. He puts his faith in me."

Mairead stepped back as Braun stumbled forward. He went to one knee. *He's as much a pawn as I am.* "Go home," she said, gentling her voice. She bent and lifted his arm. "Go home, Braun. See your woman and your sons."

From the shadows came a low whine, and Snowbane trotted out. He nudged Mairead's hand, and she scratched his ears before she let him go to Braun. The tribesman stood on shaking legs, and the wolf slunk in to brace his weight near his knee. Braun turned his head. "I want to believe in you."

The words came over a thick tongue, and Mairead couldn't be sure he meant them. *But perhaps men are most honest when they are drunk.* "I will give you reason to trust me," she said. "Go home."

He stumbled away with the wolf at his side.

Mairead returned to Aerwyth and Hedwar's house and lay thinking for hours. *It may have been a mistake to wed Connor, but I can't imagine wedding one of these men. They can't believe that I am only to be some figurehead, can they? Just some Deliverer in name who serves only as a rallying point?*

She put her hands behind her head and stared up at the ceiling, remembering ancient stories and legends. *Queen Emyr, Queen Brenna, the Sidh queens—they were warriors. I am a warrior. I will not bend the knee to outdated ideas and false presumptions about who and what I am. But I need proof—I need something to convince them—something that even the Lionjaws can't refute.* She rubbed the scar on her palm. *It's time to seek the earthspirit.*

CHAPTER TWENTY-TWO

It is an oft-forgotten footnote in tribal history, existing mainly in whispers, but there was a time when the tribal chieftains led their own warriors to kill the ravenmarked among them. The chieftains justified the act with a "greater good" argument—that is, they claimed to save countless lives by killing men who were determined to cleanse the earth by wiping it clean of human taint.
—*A Brief History of the Three Lands*

Connor stood outside his hut in the raven village with his head tipped toward the sky. He sniffed the air and smiled. Despite the thick, heavy clouds overhead, he sensed a burgeoning warmth. *Spring,* he thought. "Thank the good spirits."

"Pardon, my lord?"

He turned to Phinneas. "It feels like winter is finally waning."

The eunuch offered a thin smile and a slight head inclination. "A welcome change."

All through the worst of the winter weather, the eunuch had never once given any indication of cold. He wore the same silk robes every day. Connor had suspected they were sidhsilk—something that held the heat of the season in which it was woven—but he didn't see any telltale elemental residue around the robes. He wondered if the Tal'Aster Sect had some kind of weaving method that gave a similar result. *How else could he remain warm? This is the closest I've ever been to being cold, and he's just managed to glide through this weather without blinking.* "I think it's time to start training again. Gather them up in the center of the village."

Phinneas bowed. "Of course, my lord."

Connor started to pull on his bracers as he watched the ravens emerge from their huts. The weeks since his last encounter with Mairead had not been easy. Between the weather, the self-recriminations, and the grumbling of the ravens, Connor had found it difficult to even stay on the mountain at times. He'd been tempted—especially during the worst of the weather—to simply gather the braids around him and disappear to a warmer clime. *Gods-forsaken weather,* he thought almost every day. *What I wouldn't give for a warm dive in the Aldorean Seas right now.*

The weather had almost done in his resolve dozens of times. The days leading up to the worst of the blizzards were filled with preparations—

stringing a line around the village that would connect all of the huts and livestock pens for use as a guide, fetching provisions from the cave the men had used before he joined them, and fortifying the buildings. When the storms hit, the men were mostly ready. They stayed inside during the worst of the weather and only emerged during lulls.

Training exercises were at a standstill since no one could even grip a sword or bow in the middle of a raging blizzard. The location of the village was fairly sheltered, which protected the huts and buildings from the worst of the wind, but it was still a constant struggle to keep doors and gates clear, animals watered and fed, and firewood stocked in huts. In between rounds, he stayed inside and tried not to think about Mairead.

Without training exercises or work to keep him busy, the long, brutal storms were painful reminders of the last time he'd spoken with her. He regretted his hasty words and wished he could take them back. Logic told him it was not in Mairead's nature to be unfaithful to him, that it wasn't even really in Gareth's nature to pursue a woman who belonged to another man. Reason suggested that the Morrag's lack of specific accusations where Gareth and Mairead were concerned meant she really *didn't* have anything to accuse them of, so he shouldn't have been jealous. Rational thought evaluated the situation and proclaimed Mairead and Gareth's innocence.

But at night, when the village was dark and the wind howled and the Morrag's whispers were the loudest, he doubled over in agony and fought the temptation to believe the worst of Mairead, Gareth, and all of the lions. "Not true," he whispered over and over. "Not true. Mairead is pure. She married me. She shared my bed. You lie—you lie!"

The raven cackled. *—blood on snow—conscript the men—sell the women— burn the village—*

The pain of the words and images tightened every muscle and joint in his body, and it took all of his control and resistance to push the Morrag away. *Not my sins. Not all mine. I won't attack innocents in your name. I won't kill indiscriminately for you.*

There are no innocents, she would reply.

He could only force her back through physical effort that often left him weak, shaky, and sore the following morning. Phinneas had long since declared his drugs no longer helpful, and Connor had to agree. "She pushes right through the fog," he told Phinneas one day. "And when the fog of the drugs is there, it only makes it harder to resist her. I'm safer without the drugs. I can actually resist her when there's no fog in my head."

During the brief breaks between storms, he'd taken to the elements to visit Isfyrin, trying to catch a glimpse of Mairead. He knew she hadn't seen him—he'd figured out how to hide even the braids from her—but there were moments when just watching her had stirred such longing that he'd been tempted to shake off the elements and beg her forgiveness. He watched her in the city with Gareth once, and he wondered if the Morrag was right about their relationship, but then they met up with Trypp and a woman who appeared to be an earth guardian. *There's nothing there,* he thought. *She sees him as a friend and advisor, nothing more. He doesn't walk with her as a man who is courting a woman. He defers to her as a man defers to a leader.*

There were risks in traveling in the elements, though. Aside from the possibility of encountering a sudden storm that might pull his own elements apart, the Ferimin were growing more active every night. During one of his evening sojourns in the water braids, he heard one of the Ferimin screech in the distance, then screech closer to him. There was a sudden rush of air over his water braids, and he quickly retreated into a snowbank to hide. The Ferimin circled his location several times before landing. It ducked its head and turned an eye toward Connor. He pulled his elements in as close as possible. *I'm practically a snowball,* he thought. After several long moments, the creature screeched again and rose into the air. Connor waited until he thought it safe, then returned to the raven village.

After that encounter, he no longer traveled in the air or water braids. He did try the earth braids once, but there was something unsettling about the mountain. He couldn't put a finger on it, but there was a kind of instability in the earth elements around Isfyrin and the raven village, as if the ground could shift at any moment. *It's almost as bad as traveling in the wind and snow,* he thought. *And since I don't want to leave a leg or arm trapped in a rock somewhere, maybe it's just better to stay in the raven village for right now.*

While separation from Mairead, the winter weather, and the constant whispers of the Morrag were all stressors, often the most pressing issue that arose was the persistent rumbling of dissent among the ravens. The village included many jaded, bitter men who didn't want to return to the lions and resented the idea of serving a woman, if she even existed. Some of the ravens left in the early days of Connor's leadership, saying they would be better off in Galbragh or the forest. Connor didn't try to stop them.

Wyll frequently tried to talk the ravens out of leaving the village. "They give themselves up to the mountain just because they can't be patient," he said to Connor one day after two of the older ravens left.

Connor shrugged. "That's their problem. If they want to wrestle with the Morrag on their own, let them. Those who stay here will have the benefit of

Mairead's presence."

Wyll ran a hand through his braids. He chewed a lip and thought for a long moment before leaning down close to Connor's ear. "Tell me true—is she really here? Can she truly help us? Lead us?"

I don't know. Connor put a hand on Wyll's meaty forearm and met his eyes. "She's here. I promise you. I will bring her here as soon as the weather allows, and you will see that she is worth serving."

Wyll nodded and let out a long breath. "I have faith," he said. "But I can't have enough faith for every man here."

"I don't expect you to."

Osgar stubbornly refused to do anything except drink, sulk, and grumble. Edda, his wife, took care of the home and its surroundings while he watched the other men train and prepare for winter weather, all the while sipping from a skin of oiska. Connor fully expected that when spring arrived, Edda would leave for the plains. *A woman can only take so much,* he thought. *Once she's been pushed too far, there will be no reconciliation with him.* He winced as he wondered how far Mairead could be pushed and whether he would be the one to push her to that point.

As Phinneas made his way around the village, waking men and informing them of the practice session, Connor watched them emerge one or two at a time from the little huts. Wyll approached, tugging on his bracers. "Warm enough to practice, but the ground is going to turn to mud as soon as we start dancing around."

Connor shrugged. "Good preparation for a battlefield. What do you think it's like to fight with blood and offal spilling all around you?"

Wyll grunted. He gestured to Osgar. "He's going to give you fits today, I can tell. He's already drinking."

Connor nodded. The older raven walked in a crooked line to the edge of the common area and collapsed on the ground with a skin of oiska in hand. "Ignore him. If he wants to waste away, let him."

The men partnered up with sparring swords—some wooden, some old blades with dulled edges—and prepared to fight. Connor paired himself with one of the younger ravens. "Warm up," he told them all. "Easy swings, loosen your muscles, get the feel of the blades again. You've been inside several weeks. I don't want anyone getting hurt today." He grinned. "There's plenty of time for that." A few of them chuckled, and they began to swing at each other.

"Good luck, Catspaw," Osgar shouted at the young man Connor sparred with. "I've never yet met a Catspaw who knows how to use his sword." He followed it up with a vulgar gesture.

The young man, Tyr, kept twitching to look back at Osgar with each insult. His face was tight with frustration and anger.

"Ignore him," Connor said. "You have to ignore worse than that on a battlefield."

Tyr nodded, but as he and Connor started a new round of swings, Osgar shouted again. "Little man with a little stick!"

Tyr couldn't help himself. He whirled to face Osgar, and Connor's sparring sword connected with his shoulder. Tyr yelped in pain and danced away.

Connor discarded the sparring sword and crossed to Osgar in three long strides. He bent and grabbed Osgar's tunic and hauled him to his feet. "You don't want to train? Fine. Don't train. But I will not tolerate your insolence or your interference. If you can't shut up or participate, go somewhere else. Leave the village, for all I care."

Osgar snorted a laugh, and Connor's head reeled at the scent of oiska. "You speak as though this is your command," he said, slurring his words. "They aren't yours, wolf. You're an outland tribesman. You have no authority here. And this woman you claim to know—this ravenmaster—we don't even know if she exists." He stumbled and caught himself.

Connor drew his sword. "You want to command them? You had a chance, and you couldn't manage it. If you want to best me for the opportunity, please try. But we'll be using battle swords, not sparring swords."

Osgar's jaw tightened. His hand fumbled for his sword, but he lost his balance and fell backward.

Connor nodded. "As I thought. I won't turn you out to the mountain right now, but I don't ever want to see you out here in the practice yard again until you're ready to be a Morragman. If you won't submit to my authority, you will leave, Osgar Lionjaw."

"You can't tell me—"

"If you wanted to command this group, you could have done it long before I arrived," Connor said. "Go back to your hut, Lionjaw."

Connor turned back to the sparring circle. Every man had lowered his sword to watch the exchange. "That goes for all of you," Connor shouted. "If you don't like the way I'm leading you, challenge and best me or leave. I would rather have a force of twenty loyal, well-trained men than a force of hundreds of whining, insolent jackasses."

They stared, several of them gaping. "Where would we go?" one of them, an Elkbane, finally said. "There isn't anywhere else for a raven tribesman. My woman is in Isfyrin. My only hope of making a life with her is to stay here, with you, and pray that one day, we can be together without fear or shame."

Connor nodded. "How do the rest of you feel?"

"My parents are in Isfyrin," Tyr said. His voice still hadn't dropped completely, and Connor suspected that a year of solid training would make the young man into a force to be reckoned with. "My sister and brother, too. I didn't choose the mountain. But you've given me the most hope I've had in two years."

Other men echoed the words. Connor finally turned back to Osgar. "Sounds like they've made their choice," he said.

Osgar looked up from the ground. He lurched to his feet again and spat. "You will never command me, wolf."

Inside Connor's head, the Morrag cackled. *Faithless—liar—oathbreaker.*

Connor covered a flinch by crossing his arms. "Then leave," he said to Osgar. "We don't need you."

Osgar shook his head. "I'm waiting for this woman you promised. Surely I have the right to wait for that, don't I?"

Silence hovered in the sparring circle. Inside Connor's head, the Morrag fluttered. The weight of her agitation pressed on his chest. *He plots . . . he dreams of murder . . .*

Connor tried to shake her away. *He's only waiting to see if she really exists. Then he'll be gone. If I can bring her here soon, maybe I can get rid of him. He'll never be led, but maybe I can just convince him to leave on his own.* He finally nodded to Osgar.

Osgar took another drink. "Then I'll wait in my hut."

Thief! Liar! He deserves death! the Morrag crowed inside Connor's head.

Connor pressed the bridge of his nose. *Just one day of gods-forsaken peace,* he thought. *Why can't I have just one day?*

The men practiced all morning, and the Morrag whispered at Connor the entire time. She accused every raven in the village of every crime he could imagine. *Thief! Liar! He lusts. He boasts. He seeks glory for himself. He seeks power. He despises the One Hand. He has murdered. He cheats. He raped a woman. He hurt a child.* No amount of physical activity would quiet her, and Connor finally dismissed the men at midday and retreated to his hut.

Phinneas followed. "A bad day, my lord?"

Connor nodded. "Just give me a few hours. I'll be all right." *If I just don't look at them—if she's not looking at them through my eyes—maybe I can turn off her voice.*

But the whispers and pain got progressively worse as the day wore on. Connor paced inside his hut, rubbing his temples and pushing back against her whispers. "Not mine," he said. "Not all my sins."

Thieves! Liars! Kill them, raven—take justice to the city and the plains!

"No," he groaned. "No, I won't kill innocents."

No innocents—none—conscript the men—burn the villages—blood on snow—the last pulse—sell the women, children—burn the sayada—

The whispers continued in a jumble, past and present and future all merged into a long litany of transgressions committed anywhere humans congregated. *The screams of a brutalized girl . . . the agony of men on the battlefield . . . forests destroyed, fields burned . . . lust, greed, murder . . . .*

Connor finally walked out of the hut, only to see several men staring at him, including Wyll and Phinneas. *Seven hundred years old . . . he lies . . . he's not cut . . .*

"I need to walk," he told Phinneas. "Follow me."

Wyll stepped closer. "What is it?"

The Morrag cackled. *Lust, greed—he's taken what isn't his . . . he's abused the earth . . . he's sought his own glory . . . idolator, thief . . .*

He does not deserve death! "She's on a rampage," he said, and cringed at his quavering voice. "You're not safe with me here." He stumbled out of the village.

Phinneas and Wyll followed. Connor noticed through the fog of the Morrag's touch that dusk had fallen. *Gods—the whole night ahead of me. I don't think I can do this.* He stripped down to his waist and removed his sword and daggers. He picked up the sword and stabbed it down into the ground, then knelt in the snow and stretched his arms out at his sides. "Do it," he said through gritted teeth. "Gods, Phinneas. Do it now. I can't stand this anymore. Finish it."

Phinneas' approach was nothing more than the whisper of silk on snow. "My lord, you are needed."

"I'm not. There are a hundred other men who can do this. I can't—I can't hold her back."

The Morrag cackled inside his head. *Cleanse the earth, my raven. Take up your sword and cleanse the earth.*

Images of blood-soaked earth and hacked off limbs and burned bodies filled his head. "I can't even close my eyes. I can't get away from it."

A cool hand touched his neck. "My lord, your time has not yet come."

Avenge me, the Morrag whispered. *Avenge my sister. Avenge the earth-spirit.*

Connor's hand twitched toward his sword. "I . . . won't . . ."

"Your time has not yet come," the eunuch said again.

Avenge us.

Wyll held a skin in front of him. "Drink."

"Oiska won't help."

"It will. Drink."

"Sidh blood .... Can't get drunk ...."

"No, but you can take the edge off." He nudged the oiska toward Connor's nose. "Drink. Drink the whole skin if you must."

Connor drank three long swallows. It wasn't enough. "Go," he whispered. "Please, Wyll—go, before I hurt you."

"Ulfrich, I'm your friend." Wyll put a hand on Connor's shoulder.

Lust for power—he longs to touch the earthspirit—he disobeys, refuses to heed me—

Connor lifted his head slowly, slowly, a growl building in his throat. "You are as bad as the rest," he said. He stood on shaking legs, one at a time, as Wyll let go of him and took a step back. "You seek power that isn't yours. You wish to control the earthspirit, the Morrag—you think you know better than she does."

Wyll shook his head. "Ulfrich, no, I—"

Connor pulled his sword out of the ground. "You want my command, Wyll? You want it? Take it from me. Best me now. You want to control the Morrag? I am the Morrag. I am death incarnate." He swung his sword in an overhand arc toward Wyll.

But Wyll was ready. He'd drawn his sword, and he met Connor's blow with a solid parry. Their swords scraped off each other, a brief shower of sparks lighting the snow beneath their feet. Wyll lifted his sword again. "You are not this beast, Connor," he said. "You are not the Morrag. You are a man. Do not let her take you."

Connor twisted his sword back and forth as he advanced toward Wyll. "I am death. I am justice." He swung again.

Wyll parried once more, and they danced around the clearing as Wyll continued to try to speak sense to Connor. "You are not the Morrag! Resist her!"

But Connor could only channel rage. Phinneas darted around the two men, his swirling silks a blur. —*seven hundred years old—he is not cut—he lies, he cheats death—* Connor focused on Wyll. *He longs for power—he lusts for women who aren't his—he disobeys—*

Wyll finally parried and twisted his sword up in a fierce arc with an angry shout that merged with the rising wind around them. He brought his sword down in a blow that would have killed a less skilled swordsman. Instead, Connor's sword met Wyll's with a clang right over Connor's head. Wyll twisted his blade and drove all of his strength into flinging Connor's sword away to land in the snow.

Connor fell to his knees again. He looked up at the sweaty, panting tribesman. *My friend. This man is my friend. And I almost killed him, as I almost killed Phinneas. As I almost killed Mairead.* "Gods, Wyll. I can't . . . I can't do this anymore." He sat back on his heels. *All right, you bitch. You win. You've bested me.* "Let Phinneas finish me."

"My lord—"

"*That's an order!*" Connor shouted. "You swore you would do it—you swore you would serve me this way. Gods, please—finish it before I hurt someone."

The clearing fell silent, and Connor heard Phinneas let out a long breath. There was the sound of steel against leather. "Very well," he said. "As my lord commands."

CHAPTER TWENTY-THREE

The foundations of the earth were shattered in that moment.
Alshada splintered the ground, and even as the chasm came to be,
the earth folded on itself and formed the vast northern mountains.
— First Book of the Wisdomkeepers

The sun climbed behind a thick gray sky as Logan returned to the camp he shared with Grytha and Hrogarth. *Not that we can see it. This northern land is cursed, I swear it.* An early morning hunting trip had yielded two rabbits, and he'd found some roots along the bank of the stream. *A life like that—a normal life where I could just fish and hunt and cook—it's too much to ask. Enjoy it while it lasts.*

It had taken three weeks of weaving through forest, towns, and wastes to get to this small grove of trees on the outskirts of Starling's Cross. Hrogarth brooded, but he quit calling Logan "boy." When they reached little inns and public houses, Hrogarth sat in the common room drinking until even the innkeepers made him go to his room.

Now, camping in Taura's frozen wilderness, the wind blowing down from the northern icecaps and the very air freezing to the stubble on his cheeks, Logan found Hrogarth sitting on the ground and Grytha kneeling behind him with a knife. "What's this?" he asked as he skewered the skinned rabbits and propped them over the fire.

"She's shaving it again," Hrogarth said. "I won't have anyone think I'm fit to lead."

Grytha didn't look up. She drew her knife across the week's stubble on Hrogarth's scalp. She nicked Hrogarth. "Forgive me," she said.

He shrugged. "It is well." When she'd finished, Hrogarth stood and rubbed a hand over his head. "My thanks." He walked away into the trees.

Grytha let out a breath and sat next to Logan. "He prays," she said. "I've never known Hrogarth to pray."

"How is he?"

"On the edge of madness."

Logan focused on cleaning his knife. "I'm sorry."

"Tell me more about your daughter."

He shrugged. "I don't even know her. I haven't seen her in years."

"Why not?"

He set down his knife and turned the rabbits. "I saw her last when she was four. Or three. She probably doesn't remember me. I was called to duty in Kiern, and then I deserted to follow Braedan. I spent his exile with him in Culidar. When we returned, there was no time to find my daughter. I thought I would, eventually, but everything—" He bit off the words and stood. "I have things to do."

"Logan."

He turned back.

"Go to your child. We can carry your message to Braedan. Go make sure your daughter is well."

"I have a duty to my king." *Besides, it's not that simple.*

Hrogarth returned, his face twisted in anguish. "Her call grows stronger."

"Whose call?" Logan asked.

"The Morrag." His voice was strained. "She wants us to join her."

Logan swallowed hard. "Us?" *Not me—please, not me. Not yet.*

"Her warriors. The ones she's marked. She has her first, now. She wants us to join him." He took a long breath. "I want to see Alfrig. I will go to the Morrag, but I need to say goodbye to my wife. I worry for her. She's in danger."

"But you thought she went to see the crone," Grytha said. "It's the one place in Taura that should be safe for a guardian."

"Not for Alfrig." Hrogarth clenched his fist. "I need to get to her."

Logan frowned. "Why isn't the sacred mountain safe for Alfrig?"

Hrogarth and Grytha both spun to face him. "How do you know of the mountain?" Grytha asked.

What a stupid slip! "I heard an earth guardian speak of it," he said. *Lies upon lies.* "What is it?"

"The wisdomkeeper lives there. She's the chief earth guardian in the tribes. She speaks for the earthspirit." Grytha paused. "Alfrig reports to her. She should be safe there."

Hrogarth grunted. "The crone expects much of Alfrig." He ran a hand over his newly shaved head. "I need to get to her. I need to see her." He choked off the words. "I need to tell her that she can take her place now. I need to say goodbye."

"There's no way we can make it across to the islands right now," Logan said. "The weather is too rough. We can wait out the ice storm in the city."

They reached the city gates of Starling's Cross at midday, and Logan frowned and reined in when the guards came into view. "Wait," he said. "Those are Taurin guards. I recognize them."

"We've found your king?" Grytha asked.

"I don't know." *Something isn't right.* He rubbed his chin. *Not enough stubble to obscure my identity.* He pulled the furs up tighter around his nose and mouth. "Speak for us," he mumbled to Grytha. "Find out what's happening here."

She rode to the front of the group. One of the men held up a hand at the gate. "State your business in Starling's Cross."

"We're just passing through," she said. "I need to cross to the Ragged Isles. We'd hoped to wait out the storm in the city."

The man jutted a chin toward Hrogarth and Logan. "And these?"

"My guards."

"You're tribal?"

Hrogarth tensed and put a hand on his sword. *Steady, traitha,* Logan thought. *Don't panic. This man's only doing his job. We don't need a fight.*

"I'm a guardian," Grytha said. "These men guard me."

"Guardians usually come through alone, or with other women," said another man—a peasant or servant, if his clothing was any indication. "This is not normal."

"These are not normal times," Grytha said. She pulled off her glove and showed them her brand. "Do you wish me to call up the earthspirit herself to prove what I am?"

The man in Taurin livery gestured them through the gates. "Go on. Wait out the storm."

"The last time I came through here, Duke Dylan was still in charge," Grytha said. "Has something happened to the duke?"

The guard grunted. "The duke was well when last I saw him."

"Then why are men in Taurin livery guarding the gates?"

"A lot of questions for a tribal woman. Keep asking them and you might end up getting answers you don't like."

Hrogarth twitched again, and Logan put a hand on his arm. "Keep still," he muttered.

The Taurin guard frowned. "Do I know you?" he asked Logan.

Logan shook his head.

"Your voice—it has a familiar ring to it."

"It's the wind," Grytha said. "It plays tricks on the ears."

The man stared at Logan a bit longer, and then a gust of wind made him shudder and step back. "Go on—find a place to wait it out. Keep your heads down, too. Stay out of business that don't concern you."

Grytha pulled her glove back on. "I thank you," she said and spurred her horse through the gates.

The village was quiet, and Logan had the sense that it wasn't only due to the storm. *Northerners are used to storms. They don't let a storm keep them from duties and company.* All around, houses and shops sat dark and still, the only signs of life the faint tendrils of smoke that wafted up from the chimneys. Streets were empty and barren, and the villagers they did see hurried from one building to another as hunched over mounds of fur and wool. All of them avoided the eyes of the Taurin guards who milled around with hands on swords and spears.

Grytha reined in near a small public house and dismounted. Logan and Hrogarth joined her. "It wasn't this quiet when I was here before," she said in a low voice. "I feel as if I should whisper."

Hrogarth grunted. "These men—these Taurins—they have darkness around them. There's something wrong."

"I've seen this before," Logan said.

Grytha frowned. "Where? When?"

In the time of myth and legend. "I can't say now. Let's get inside and see what else we can figure out."

Hrogarth found a stableboy to take their horses, and they stomped icicles and mud from their boots and entered the dark common room. "Oiska," Hrogarth called.

Logan sat at a table in the darkest corner of the room and surveyed the people. Only a few tables were occupied at all, and those with men who brooded in their ale, mumbled to companions, and eyed strangers with apprehension. "I don't like this," Logan muttered.

Hrogarth grunted and pulled furs off his face and shoulders. "Your king spreads more goodwill, I see."

"This isn't Braedan," Logan said. He lowered his voice. "He's done his share of immature things, but he doesn't spread fear and ill will."

"Except in Torlach, when he's after a throne that isn't his."

Logan twisted his mouth. "Taking the throne—that wasn't all his idea."

"No?"

Logan shook his head and fell silent as the serving girl put down cups and a jar of oiska. Grytha poured for Logan and Hrogarth, and all three of them drank. *What I wouldn't give to feel the burn of oiska once again,* Logan thought. He put down his cup and leaned forward. "Braedan wanted the throne, it's true, but the way he took it—that was mostly his uncle, Ronan Kerry. He's the one who convinced Braedan to kill his cousin, Daron."

"And who convinced your king to destroy the sayada? Eh?" Hrogarth said. "Was it you? You still hide things from me. You have transgressions that I—"

"I didn't want Braedan to do anything to the sayada," Logan said, trying to control the irritation in his voice. "I swear I didn't. It's because of me that the sayas lived." He stood. "I'm going out. I want to find out what's going on."

Hrogarth stood. "I'll come with you. I don't trust you alone."

"Traitha." Grytha put her hand on Hrogarth's arm. "Let him go. He knows these men."

"That's what I fear. What if he returns to his king and then sends the Taurin pigs after us?"

"You don't trust me? Fine. Come with me. I don't care." Logan pulled his furs back up around his mouth. "But if you come along, you leave her unguarded. Your choice."

Hrogarth glanced back at Grytha. "She can take care of herself."

"Suit yourself." Logan walked out into the ice and wind, the traitha close on his heels.

They found the estate gate unguarded, and Logan assumed the guards had retreated to warmer quarters. Logan pounded on the closed gate until he finally got someone to open a peephole. "We need to speak with Duke Dylan," he shouted over the wind.

"He's not available," the man shouted back. "Gates are closed until the storm passes. Come back then."

"How long do these things normally last?" Logan asked.

"Hard to say—could blow itself out tonight, could last two weeks. When you see the gates open, come back." He closed the peephole, shutting off possibility of further conversation.

"No use in trying further," Hrogarth said. "Let's get back to the public house."

When they arrived back in the common room, Grytha was already finished eating. She gestured to the food on the table. "Eat before it gets any
colder," she said.

Logan turned away. "Not hungry. I'll get us a room."

"It's taken care of." Grytha pushed a key toward Logan. "Down the hall—
first door on the right. Our things are already there."

Logan found the room and unlocked the door, but something raised the
hair on the back of his neck when he stepped inside. He spun around, fist
connecting with something solid. A muffled "oof" responded to the punch,
followed by a gloved hand over Logan's mouth. "Wait," the man said. "Commander—wait. It's me. Malcolm."

Logan jerked away from him. "Malcolm? What are you—"

The other guard stepped into the dim light of the room. His clothing was
disheveled and dirty, and he had several days of beard on his chin. "The king
is here. He's been here for two weeks. I've been shut out of the estate, though."

"Why?"

The guard shrugged. "I didn't please his little whore."

Logan frowned. *His whore? Has he betrayed Igraine?* An odd mixture of
dismay and hope rose in Logan's chest. He shook his head. *No. I won't damn
another woman.* "How did you find me?"

"I came in for a meal while you were gone. I saw you come back with the
tribesman and recognized you." He paused. "Why are you here and not back
in Torlach?"

Grytha and Hrogarth appeared in the door, both of them holding blades.
"We heard a scuffle," Grytha said. "You are well?"

Logan nodded. "This is Malcolm, one of my men from Taura. He says the
king is here." He closed the door and lit a lantern. "Malcolm, this is Hrogarth,
former traitha of the nine tribes, and one of his guardians, Grytha." He
gestured around the room and sat down, unwrapping furs from his face and
neck. "I think the four of us have some things to talk about."

Malcolm sat. "You were about to tell me how you came to be here."

"It's a long story," he said. He recounted his arrest and escape, the weeks
he'd stayed with the tribes, and the journey north to find Braedan. Hrogarth
grunted in disagreement once or twice at Logan's retelling, but to his credit,
he didn't interrupt. "Ronan Kerry is after Braedan's throne," he said. "He
thought if he got me out of the way, he could control the army." He stopped
short. *Don't say anything about Cormac—not yet. Best to tell Braedan that
part.* "Why are you here? The king—he's well?"

Malcolm's jaw tightened. "Physically, he's fine. He sustained an arrow wound outside of Salmon Springs, but it's healing."

"You were attacked?"

"Kerry set up an ambush. He made it appear that Fingall wanted Braedan off the throne. But Braedan survived, and he sent Fingall to Torlach with messages for Igraine." He paused. "Braedan can't go back right now. I fear he's falling into madness. He has a woman with him—a little healer named Cerys—who seems to have some kind of hold over him. I didn't think she did at first, but she's gained his trust, and now he seeks her counsel on nearly everything."

"Has he bedded her?"

"I don't know. She's bedded her way through the rest of the guards, though. Never asks for money—she just does it for the enjoyment." He cleared his throat. "I even had a taste of her, but . . . there's something about her, commander. She makes you see things—think things—" He shuddered.

Hrogarth let out a long breath. "That's it," he whispered. "That's what I sense. That's why this place is so dark. It's the woman."

Logan nodded. *It's Aldora. No wonder the city is so quiet. She's got the whole place in a grip of fear.* "So how has Braedan managed to avoid being seduced by her?"

"At first, by sheer willpower, I think. He swore he'd remain faithful to Igraine. I think he came close about the time he arrested Dylan. That's when she whispered to him that he didn't need me, that I wasn't loyal to him, and he sent me away. But there's something holding him back from her, and I'm not sure what it is."

"He arrested Dylan?" Grytha asked. "Why?"

"Dylan wanted us to leave. A girl died, and he seemed to think Cerys had something to do with it. Dylan and Braedan argued, and Braedan arrested him and seized his property. Then Cerys showed him one of Dylan's outbuildings. Turns out Dylan has been sheltering former sayas for months. One of them claims to be the Taurin heir."

Son of a bitch. Logan let out a long breath. "Is it her? Is it truly her?"

Malcolm shrugged. "Don't know. We were told to look for a young blonde girl, right? She's a young blonde girl. But we also think the sayas sent decoys to distract us. Braedan doesn't seem to know what to do. I'm not sure what Cerys is whispering to him, but I think Braedan is torn. He seems . . . stuck. Like he's waiting for something to break—Cerys, the sayas, or the blade."

"The blade," Hrogarth mumbled. "Yes, now it makes sense." He looked up at Logan. "I had a vision—the earthspirit told me to give him that blade, but I didn't know why. It's protecting him from her."

"Why does he need protection from a woman?" Malcolm asked.

"Because she is no woman," Logan said. He looked at Hrogarth. "You know what she is, don't you? Your mark tells you."

Hrogarth's face had turned to stone, but his eyes were wide with fear. He nodded once.

"What is she?" Malcolm asked.

"One of the Forbidden," Logan said. He turned to Malcolm. "She is a souleater. She eats the souls of those who are not protected by the One Hand. She delights in sin and chaos and devotes herself to creating more. Where there is chaos, there is depravity, and every terrible act one human commits against another only strengthens her."

Malcolm paled. "Gods. It's her—Olwyn Mac Rian. He killed her at Kiern, and now—"

Logan nodded. "Now she wants her revenge." He paused and turned to Hrogarth. "I suppose it's fortuitous that we have you with us."

Malcolm looked at Hrogarth. "Why? What is he?"

"I am ravenmarked," Hrogarth said. "Only the ravenmarked can banish one of the Forbidden to the chasm. But if you think I'm going to risk going up against that creature, you are mistaken."

Grytha startled. "But—traitha, why? You can defeat her."

"I can't!" he shouted. "Gods, Grytha—I can't. I've seen it. If she is loosed on Taura, she will destroy this land."

"Then destroy her before she can," Grytha said.

He shook his head. "I can't promise I can defeat her. My dreams show her destroying me, my wife, the tribes, everything I hold dear." He buried his face in his hands. "I'm not strong enough. If I try and fail, she will become too powerful, and I can't risk that."

No one spoke for some time. Eventually, Logan nodded. "He's right."

Grytha turned to him. "What?"

"He's right. It's happened before, during the war of the Breaking. One of the Forbidden used the transgressions borne by the ravenmarked warriors to become more powerful. The ravenmarked almost failed. They only defeated her because they joined together. We only have one ravenmarked man. We can't risk it."

"How do you know this?"

I was there. I saw it. "I am well-educated in the history of Taura. We will do what we can without Hrogarth." He turned to Malcolm. "Are you still loyal to your king?"

"I'm loyal to the king I followed into Torlach, and I'm loyal to the king I knew before Salmon Springs. This king—no."

"You want your king back?"

"I do."

"Then I think we need a plan."

CHAPTER TWENTY-FOUR

The Crone, the Warrior, the Raven—
So shall they meet on the bloodied hill.
— Second Book of the Wisdomkeepers

Mairead didn't really sleep after Braun returned to his home. Rather, she spent most of the night tossing and turning, dozing briefly, and waking to more fears. It was long before dawn when she finally gave up on sleep entirely. She pulled on her boots and furs, rebraided her hair, and slipped out of the house as quietly as possible to avoid waking anyone. She walked toward Letha's hut and saw a thin curl of smoke rising from the chimney. She raised her hand to knock.

The door opened. Letha grinned. "You need to work on your footfalls, traitha. You will never sneak up on an enemy the way you walk."

Mairead gave her a shaky smile. "Connor tried to teach me to walk quietly, but I'm too used to being Taurin, perhaps. You're awake early."

"I usually wake at this hour. I enjoy this time of day."

Mairead nodded. "May we speak?"

Letha held the door open and directed Mairead into her hut. She sat down before her fire cross-legged and picked up a steaming cup of tea. "What can I do for you?"

Mairead sat across from her and held out her hand, revealing the scar. "I am struggling with this," she said. "Trying to figure out what this is, what it's about, who it's for. I've never even touched the magic—not really. Everything I've done has been on accident. And I need to know about Connor."

"Connor?"

Mairead shook her head. "Ulfrich. I need to know ..." She took a deep breath. "I need to know if I should be with him."

"What do you wish from me?"

"Your warriors can ask you to seek the earthspirit, can't they? That's what I wish. I need you to seek the earthspirit for me."

"You are also bound to the earthspirit. You can seek her yourself."

Mairead nodded. "Can you show me how?"

Letha put her cup down. "You are a woman of the kirok."

Mairead tried to form words to express what she felt. *I was never a woman of the kirok. I was always meant for other things. But Alshada, I want to serve you. And yet you put magic in my path, and now I must face it—this thing I was taught was a myth, was not of you, was sinful and evil. Why would you bind me this way? Why would you give me this path?* "I am a woman of the One Hand."

Letha stood and gathered a few items. When she returned to the fire, she took both of Mairead's hands in her own. "Before we start, I must tell you something. The first day you came here, do you know what I saw? Not pain, sadness, or fear. Not the earth. I saw zeal—but not for power or wealth. I saw zeal for truth." She turned Mairead's hand over to reveal her scar. "Do you know why you won't go astray? Because your zeal keeps your eyes on truth."

"There is one other thing."

Letha waited.

Mairead took a deep breath. "I am with child."

Letha laughed over a long breath. "You finally admit it," she said. "I have been waiting for weeks for you to say something."

"You knew? How?"

"I am a midwife, Mairead. I can see the signs."

Mairead rubbed her belly. "I fear I can't hide it any longer. Even now, I can't lace up my breeches as tight as before."

"This is the raven's child?"

"We wed on Faltian. We only had that one night together."

Letha laughed. "A Faltian child is thrice blessed, they say," she said. "So an autumn baby. It's a good time. You feel well?"

Mairead shrugged. "I am sick sometimes, but not enough for anyone to notice. I have little aches and pains. And I'm so tired."

"All normal. The tiredness will ease now for a while. These next few months will be pleasant. You should feel the child quicken soon."

Mairead blinked back tears. "I am afraid, Letha."

"But you are courageous." She squeezed Mairead's hands again. "You are a warrior, Mairead." She stood. "Come. We will go to the vision hut."

The city hadn't fully awakened yet, and they passed only a few men and women moving around as they crossed to the vision hut. Those they passed nodded greetings. Mairead reflected that everyone she saw had the same relieved expression, and she wondered if they were just pleased to have survived the harshest weather of the winter.

In the vision hut, two other guardians moved about, tending the fire and preparing herbs. Letha placed her belongings near the small fire in the center of the hut and turned to Mairead. "Remove all your weapons, belt, boots. Unbind your hair."

Mairead did as requested. Letha did the same and instructed Mairead to sit cross-legged on the mat near the fire. Letha spoke quietly with one of the other guardians and returned to Mairead with a cup of steaming liquid. Mairead took the cup. The odor was strong and bitter. "What is it?"

"It will cleanse your head of outside thoughts."

"No. If I do this, if the One Hand or the warrior or the earth wants to speak to me, I do this on my own."

Letha frowned. "This is the way the rite is done," she said. "Without this, we cannot see the earthspirit."

"No. If the spirit is strong enough, if she is real, she can speak without the herbs."

Letha took the cup and gave it back to the other guardian. "It is as the prophecy said: the Deliverer refuses the vision path." She turned back to Mairead. "Are you ready?"

"Yes."

Letha put her hand next to Mairead's. "One Hand, guide your servants," she whispered.

Mairead's scar began to glow. She didn't fight it. Her senses opened. The magic beckoned. Her heart thumped, frantically resisting her attempt to let the magic wash over her. She forced her fear back.

A still, quiet voice from outside of her whispered peace. *I'm here.*

She smiled. *One Hand.*

Her heartbeat and breathing slowed, and the earth magic reached out to her with tentative tendrils. She lifted her hand away from Letha's and put it in front of her. Her spirit merged with the earth's in a sudden jolt.

"What is it?" Letha asked.

"N-n-nothing—" she said. "It's so ...."

Letha was quiet. "Tell me what you see."

Mairead couldn't describe it. "Everything," she whispered. "The spirit of the earth. She's a creation. She knows the One Hand. She worships him, too, but she groans." A stabbing pain pierced Mairead. She clutched her left side and bent over. "What people have done—the transgressions, the way they've abused the sacred places—there is so much pain." *Is this what Connor sees? No wonder he's on the edge of madness! How can he live with it?*

Letha was very close. "This is our purpose. To bring balance—to serve her, to make sure she does not become too wounded."

Mairead let her spirit step further into the pain. It was black, full of lifeless rot. There wasn't even mold—*mold would be alive.* Mairead touched the spirit of the earth. "This was not the One Hand's plan. She withers, and this side of her takes on the mask of the Morrag."

Letha drew in a breath. "You see her—the Morrag?"

"I do."

Tense silence filled the vision hut. "The guardians never see her," Letha said. "We know of her, but she hides from us. We see only the earthspirit."

"But I am bound to the warrior," Mairead said. *The warrior. Are you the warrior, too?*

The woman stood at the edge of a chasm. Black mist swirled around her feet, over her head, into the endless dark sky above. *I am part of the warrior, but not all.*

And me? What am I?

You are justice.

Mairead frowned. *And Connor is not justice?*

My First Raven. Her voice very nearly purred, and Mairead felt oddly jealous. *He is vengeance. He is cleansing.*

Mairead's spirit shuddered. "Show me your sister," she whispered in that place.

The woman pushed back the black hood she wore, and then Mairead saw that despite her age, she was a fierce, dark, perfect beauty. Terrible, but perfect. *All will see me,* she said. *All must face me.*

"No." Mairead backed away. "This can't be all. The earthspirit can't be only death and pain. Where is the life?"

The spirit turned around, and everything changed. Life bloomed everywhere, the chasm was gone, and another woman stood before her, this time dressed in white.

Mairead faced her. "The earthspirit?"

The woman lowered her white hood. No perfect beauty, this—the woman was a crone as old as any Mairead could imagine. Her skin had the faint green of moss, and sticks and dirt clung to her ragged clothing in odd places. Her eyes had the piercing blue cast of a deep snowdrift. *Lead, child. You are stronger than you believe. You are more prepared than you know.* A long pause. *Seek the ravens.*

"Ravens? You mean Connor?"

The ravens on the mountain. Find them. You will lead them, though one will betray you.

Mairead paused. "I don't know if you can answer this—I don't know if I should even ask—but Connor—"

You wonder if you will have a life with him.

"I fear I've made a mistake," Mairead said. "I fear I should not have wed him."

The earthspirit's face brightened with amusement. *Do you think the One Hand is so weak that he depends on the whim of a child? Do you think that this world is so fragile that it depends on you choosing a particular man to marry?*

Shame flooded Mairead's face. "When you say it that way, it sounds so foolish."

The One Hand's will is not a line of events that can be shaken by a single misstep. It's a blanket woven of thousands of threads in many layers. You have chosen the raven. Your life with him will not be a life of ease, but it will be a life of purpose. The One Hand will use you, Mairead.

Mairead noticed then that rot encroached on the edges of her robes. "You are weary."

My time grows short.

A chill seized Mairead's heart. "Short? How do you mean? How can you—"

I am not eternal. I fade. Alshada brings his will. It is as it will be. The woman held out a gnarled hand. *There is work for you to do, Mairead. You have the blessing of the One Hand.*

Mairead's spirit swelled as joy infused her entire being. She gasped. *One Hand, make me worthy of doing your work here.* She stepped back into herself, in the hut next to Letha.

Letha sat next to her. "Are you well?"

"I'm well." She stood. "I need to seek the ravens."

"Ravens?" Letha blinked.

"She said there are ravens on the mountain." Mairead held up her hand when Letha started to speak. "I must do this, Letha. I need to find Connor."

"Traitha, they are ravens. They must be left to the mountain. The prophecies—"

"Prophecy be damned." She stood. "I'm going to seek them out. You and Gareth and Trypp can come with me or not, but I have to go."

Letha followed Mairead to Gareth's hut. Grayfeather screeched from his perch outside. Mairead lifted her finger to the bird, and he nipped it. She stroked his chest. He resettled his feathers with a contented chirp.

Gareth opened his door. "Mairead." He glanced at Letha. "Guardian."

"I need your help," she said. "And Trypp's. Can you two find provisions for a short journey? A week at most." *I hope.*

He frowned. "Of course. But—"

"I need to seek the ravens," Mairead said. "They're on the mountain somewhere, but I don't know where. I want to be prepared to camp if needs be."

Gareth and Letha exchanged a look. "This is not wise, traitha," Gareth said.

"Come or don't come—I'm going onto the mountain with or without you."

Gareth let out a long breath, then nodded. "I'll get Trypp right now."

"Meet us near the eastern gate," Letha said.

"I will."

Mairead returned to her room for her weapons and warmer clothing. Hedwar was not in the house, and Aerwyth busied herself in the kitchen. "Aerwyth?"

Aerwyth looked up and smiled. Stripe sat on a shelf over the stove, watching, his head cocked to one side. "Mairead. You're up early."

She nodded. *One Hand, forgive my lie.* "Gareth, Trypp, and I are going into the woods. They're going to teach me some hunting skills and help me learn more of the mountain. And Letha said she'd help us as well."

Aerwyth nodded. She wrapped some bread, meat, and cheese in a towel and gave it to Mairead. "I'm sure Gareth will be prepared, but allow me to help," she said. "How long will you be gone?"

"A few days, perhaps. They say it's a good time right now."

Aerwyth sighed. "Well, take care to watch the weather. There's always the possibility of a spring storm."

"We will." She hugged Aerwyth and left the house.

When she met the others at the edge of the village, Letha had at least four daggers and a bow and quiver. "I'll be armed before these men," she said.

"I think Connor knows where they are," Mairead said. She mounted her horse. "Let's start by ranging around just outside the city. I think they're closer than we realize."

"I don't like this," Letha said.

"If they wanted to harm the tribe, they would have done it long ago," Trypp said. He mounted as well. "You two can stay here if you wish. I'm going with the traitha."

Gareth mounted, and Letha sighed and mounted her horse finally. "I'm keeping my bow close," she muttered.

They rode away from the city until Gareth and Trypp decided they were well outside the area where the lion tribe would hunt. For hours, they ranged out in small circles, Trypp and Gareth dismounting occasionally to look for signs of men in the underbrush. As the day wore on, the sky darkened and the winds rose, tugging at cloaks and furs. Mairead pulled her clothes up tighter around her mouth and nose, but the wind still pierced through to her chest. *If we find Connor, I won't know whether to scold him or beg for warmth.* "Are we still safe?" she called to Gareth.

He looked at the sky and shrugged. "The wind is cold, but I don't think those clouds bring snow. We might be in for rain, though."

Near sunset, Mairead reined in and sighed. "We won't find them today, and we're too far from the city to go back tonight. Let's set up camp."

Grayfeather swooped in over their heads and rose again. "He wants to show us something," Gareth said.

Twitch gave a low rumble in her chest and stopped walking. Her ears flicked back and forth, and her stubby tail almost seemed to wag. She gave another low growl, then set out ahead of them at a slow trot. She stopped, looked back, then disappeared into the trees ahead.

"She senses something," Trypp said.

"We learn nothing by sitting here freezing," Mairead said. "At least it won't be as windy in the trees." She followed Twitch's tracks.

In the trees ahead of them, Twitch sat poised to pounce. The air around them stilled but for the faint rustle of the wind high in the firs. Mairead lowered her hood and motioned for silence. Nothing moved but Twitch's ears. Mairead set her horse at a slow walk. Twitch led the way, and the others fell in behind them.

The darkness of the forest grew deeper with each step until Mairead had to rely almost entirely on Twitch for direction. "This is discomforting," Gareth said, quiet.

"Stop being such a timid kitten," Trypp said.

"You only say that because I have a sense of trepidation about things that can kill me."

"The things that can kill you are the most fun."

Mairead motioned again. "Someone is up ahead."

"You hear the wind, traitha," Letha said. "The forest can play tricks on the ears and mind."

"It's not the wind. There's something—" Her palm flared, and she yelped and rubbed at her hand through the glove. "Connor—he's—" She dismounted and followed Twitch into the brush, and she sucked in her breath at the sight before her.

Connor knelt in the snow, stripped to the waist, his sword some distance away. Phinneas and another man stood behind him. Phinneas turned to her, and she saw something in his hand. "Phinneas, no!" she shouted.

"My lady." Phinneas' voice was breathy with shock. "What are you—"

"Mairead," Connor said. "Go. I'm not safe. Go. Now."

She stood paralyzed for a moment. *Phinneas had a knife—I know he did. And Connor—by the spirits, what's happened? How did it get this bad?* Gareth and Trypp tried to pull her back to her horse, but she twisted her arm away from them and knelt before Connor in the snow. *I should have been here. I should have been with him. I could have kept this from happening.* "No. I'm not going." The moment she said it, the moment it was decided. Tears welled up in her eyes. "I made you a promise, Connor. I promised you I would be your wife for good or for ill. I will not break my promise. I love you."

"Mairead—"

She put her hand on his head. "Connor. I'm. Not. Going."

He flinched away from her. "That won't work this time," he said. He stood. "Your little trick of turning away the Morrag—it doesn't work anymore. She knows you too well. She knows your transgressions. You're not enough to turn her away."

Mairead gritted her teeth and pulled her glove off. "She will listen. She has no choice." She put her scar against his bare arm. He started to pull away, but conflict crossed his face, and he stood still. *Show yourself, Morrag.*

A cold, lifeless darkness covered her mind, and she saw the same creature she'd seen in her vision—a woman of terrible, chilling beauty standing at the edge of a chasm. The woman held up a hand to her. *Sister—*

Mairead resisted the urge to flinch away. *His time has not yet come.*

He must cleanse the earth. He must lead these men.

Mairead heard men shouting, a woman talking, another man telling them to step back—all of them miles and leagues and continents away. There was only the Morrag and the earthspirit. *Our time is not yet come,* Mairead heard the earthspirit say. *A little longer, sister. A little longer, and then we will be one again.*

The Morrag stepped back and bowed her head. *I will wait.*

The breath went out of Connor, and the brand on Mairead's hand cooled. "Oh, gods," he said, his voice cracking. "Oh, Mairead."

And then his arms were around her, and she sank into his kiss, and there was no one else but Connor.

CHAPTER TWENTY-FIVE

The northern dukes do not come by their reputation without cause.
They are, indeed, the blood of hounds.
— Ronan Kerry

Pulling away from Mairead was the hardest thing Connor had ever done. "It's been too long," he whispered. He kissed her again and again. "Mairead. I'm so sorry for the things I said, for not trusting you."

"I'm sorry, too. I am." She held his face in her hands and kissed him. "There's nothing between me and Gareth or anyone else. There's only you. I love you."

She loves me. How can she? "I love you, too." He wrapped her tight in his arms. "I thought she would take me this time—I thought this was it, that I would be lost to her. I was waiting for Wyll or Phinneas to—" *You can't tell her that.* He tightened his arms around her. "I don't know how long this will last—this thing you do to tell her to leave."

"I don't know either." She gave a shaky sigh against his chest. "But for now—for right now—"

He buried his face against her neck. *For now, we have peace.* He put one hand on the back of her head. "Don't leave," he whispered. "Please, Mairead—don't leave."

Her arms tightened. "I won't. I promise." Her soft hand rested on the small of his back, her brand pulsing through him, restoring life and sanity and peace. The relief was more than he could express, but even as he held her, he knew the truth: he could never guarantee her safety, not with the Morrag threatening madness. *And yet, Mairead seems the only one able to help. How can I burden her with this? How can I expect her to deal with this? I need this woman.*

Phinneas cleared his throat. "My lord?" he said. "There are introductions to be made."

Connor straightened with extreme reluctance. He kept his arm around Mairead's shoulders. "We should go back to the camp—get out of the wind. Then I'll make all of the appropriate introductions. How did you find us?"

"Twitch and Grayfeather found you," she said. "Or they hinted at where you were. You live here?"

"We live a bit deeper in the forest. I'll show you." He took her horse's reins and started to lead her toward the small raven village, his arm never leaving her shoulders.

The others came behind. Connor's path wove and meandered through the dark until he came to the cluster of huts. He swept an arm across the men and their belongings. "Your Morragmen, traitha."

She blinked and gasped. "By the spirits," she whispered. She stepped forward. "This village—it's been here this whole time?"

"No. It's only been here for a short time—just before we came to the tribe. Our resident earth guardian had a visit from the Morrag. On his word, they moved here." He gestured around the village. "I've helped them fortify this place and hone their skills. These men are the best, the most faithful, the most elite warriors you will have, Mairead. They are prepared to serve you, even unto death."

The tribal woman—an earth guardian, if the swirls on her face were a proper indication—stared around the village. "I had no idea," she whispered.

"Neither did I," Gareth said.

Connor turned to them. "You've all been so worried about a vague prophecy that you've outcast your own people—your own men—because they are subject to a force beyond their control." He gestured around them. "This is what your foolishness has wrought."

"The prophecy—" the woman began.

"Prophecy be damned," Connor started.

"Stop," Mairead said. "You're both missing the point. They cast out the ravens because of distant history and vague prophecy. You trained the ravens out of fealty to me." She gestured as well. "What began as a misunderstanding turned into the One Hand's will. Don't you see? Their practice did protect me. It gave me this team of men." She frowned. "The One Hand weaves his will."

The lion woman turned to Connor. "I would meet the man who calls himself an earth guardian."

"Connor, this is Letha Catspaw," Mairead said. "She is the chief guardian in the clan. Letha, this is Connor. Ulfrich, as Gareth and Trypp call him."

Connor gestured Wyll forward. The big raven looked like he might burst from the tension of holding in his emotions if Connor didn't introduce him soon. "Thank you for waiting, my friend."

But Wyll had no interest in anyone but Mairead. He stepped forward and went to his knees. "It's you," he whispered. He drew his sword, put it across his hands, and bowed his head. "It's you—the one we've waited for, the Deliverer. Please, accept my fealty. Accept me, traitha, and I will serve you till death."

Mairead reached out, slow, and touched Wyll's head. "You're accepted. Rise."

The Morrag fluttered in satisfaction in Connor's chest, and he felt a swell of pride. *She knows what they need even when she doesn't know how it all fits.* He stepped closer to her. "Mairead, Wyll Elkbane, one of your Morragmen. Wyll, your traitha, Mairead."

He raised his head. Tears streamed down his face. "I've waited . . . I've waited so long. I didn't know—I thought maybe it was all wrong, that I missed something or—I don't know. And here you are."

Mairead took the sword from him. "I accept your fealty, Wyll. I accept your sword and your life. I will strive to be worthy of your trust all my days." She kissed the blade and gave it back to him. "Please, rise."

He stood and turned to the men streaming out of huts around the village. "Men of the Morrag! Our Deliverer is come!"

Connor stood guard over her as men came, one by one, and offered swords, daggers, bows—whatever they had—in fealty to her. She kissed every blade and bow and returned it with the same promise. She sat with the men and learned their names and stories. They told of sweethearts left behind, of fathers, brothers, and friends watched from a distance during the annual hunt, of Faltian nights spent around a cold fire pit because they had no women to dance with. They told darker tales, too—days of angry desperation in Galbragh when they did nothing but drink and whore, longing for purpose. Some told quickening stories similar to Connor's—of nights when the Morrag rose with such powerful need that only blood and death would sate her.

Connor watched Osgar and his band of dissenters hover to one side of the village, all of them watching and talking quietly. "Osgar," Connor called. "You said you were waiting for her. Here she is."

Osgar walked forward and spat. Gareth and Trypp closed around Mairead. "She asks for fealty?" he said. "I offer fealty to no one. The Morrag took my fealty when she claimed me." He lifted a skin and drank. "If you want my fealty, claim it back from her."

Connor started to speak, but Mairead put a hand on his arm. "I will take no vows of fealty that do not come from a sincere heart," she said. "I would rather know who my enemies are than fear that they lurk behind an oath."

Osgar grunted. "On that we can agree, girl." He held out his skin. "They offer to fight for you, but I offer to drink with you."

Connor frowned. "Osgar—"

"No," Mairead said. She took the skin and drank a small swallow. "I pray that one day we will fight together."

Osgar leaned close to Connor. "You're a lucky bastard," he said. He walked back to the group of men.

Connor gestured to them. "What of the rest of you? Do you yet withhold your fealty as well?"

Aelfred stepped out of the group. "We are not so gullible as these others," he said with a sweeping gesture. "We would see what she has to offer us before we swear. We want proof that she is this promised one before we follow."

Mairead held out her hand to show them the glowing scar. "I share the bloodbond with the lions," she said. "I did not ask for this. In that, I am like you. I am an outsider, branded by the earthspirit, shunned by some, unsure why I was given this path and this burden. But I have sworn to follow this path and do what's right for the lions and for Culidar." She paused. "I want to do what's right for the Morragmen, too. If you cannot swear fealty to me now, I will wait. I will prove to you my worth."

Thick silence surrounded them. Aelfred stepped closer to Mairead. "I will wait," he said. "But until we know more of you, I will withhold my fealty."

Connor started to say something, but Mairead put a hand on his arm. "This is right, Connor. I would rather have a dozen loyal men than a thousand who serve me out of grudging obligation."

Wyll chuckled behind them. He jutted his chin toward Connor when Mairead looked at him. "He said almost the same thing earlier today. Well, with saltier language."

"Of course." She forced a smile. "Forgive me," she said, raising her voice. "It's been a long day, and I find my strength waning. I would hear more of your stories tomorrow."

Connor put an arm around her again and led her to his small hut. When the door closed behind them, she turned to him. Her face was pale, and she fidgeted with her hands and shuffled her feet. "This is where you've been all this time? With these men?"

There's something different. Mairead's normally lithe and trim body was curvier, more rounded. He found it tremendously appealing. *Probably being held inside during all this bad weather—she's probably grown a bit soft. Not that I mind ....* "I wanted to tell you, but they fear discovery." He paused. *So many things to say.* "I've missed you."

"I've missed you, too." She stepped toward him and crossed her arms. "What I saw in the forest—how often has that happened?"

He took a deep breath. "That was a bad one, but I can't lie to you. I have dark days," he said. *Understatement.* "I remember things I thought I'd forgotten." *I'm haunted by visions of my past.* "I think about the way I used to be, and I'm ashamed." *Wracked with guilt.* "But being here—there's something comfortable about it. I have a purpose here. And I understand these men." The silence lingered. He cupped her head in his hand and pulled her closer. *She's more beautiful than ever. She practically glows.* "How are things in the tribe?" he asked, wincing at the obvious strain in his voice.

She put one hand on his chest. "All right. Some trust me. Others ...." She shrugged. "It takes time. They don't know me well, and I'm learning, too." She paused. "They say no one has a mark like this. They say I'm connected to the earth and the warrior."

He pressed his forehead against hers. "I know no woman with more of a warrior's heart than you."

"I am no warrior, Connor."

"You are." Desire grew with every word she spoke. "How long will you stay?"

"We planned for a week in the forest." Her voice had grown tight, strained. Her breath quickened. "A week. If you'll have us."

"I will." He tipped her chin up. "Do you—I mean, where were you planning to sleep?" *Are you coming back to my bed?*

She bit her lip. "There's something I have to tell you." She took his hand in hers and kissed it. She moved his hand down to her belly.

She didn't need to say anything. He felt the small rise of flesh that had not been there before, the indication that their one night together had resulted in much more than sealing a marriage. *A child. That's why she looks different.* "Gods," he whispered.

"Your mother knows."

"How?"

"She felt the baby weaving braids. It's a girl. And she has all three talents and the *codagha*."

He couldn't speak. His knees faltered with the weight of her words, and he knelt before her. He pulled up her tunic to expose the soft swell beneath it. *—the last pulse of a fading heartbeat—* He shook the thought away. Mairead's belly was perfect and round above her breeches. *Alive and round and perfect.* "A daughter."

"A daughter. Letha says it will be an autumn baby."

He put his lips on Mairead's belly. *Is this redemption or retribution?* He closed his eyes, fighting memories and demons and guilt. *Alshada, please—do not punish her for my sins.* "Mairead, I swear to you—this child will lack for nothing."

She turned his face up toward her. "Even a father?"

It stung. He covered her belly with his hand. It was nothing, and it was everything. It was small enough to hide under layers of furs, small enough to cover with one hand, but large enough to feel, large enough to capture his heart and hold it tight. *I want to give you everything—give this child everything. Mairead, please don't hate me if I can't be the right man—the man you need, the man this baby needs.* He stood and took her hands in his. "I will do all I can to give our baby a father." *It's all I can promise.*

She smiled. "I will stay here if you will have me."

"For good?"

"For as long as I can. A week, for now."

"It's a start." He tightened his hands on her hips and kissed her. "Half a year ago, I was in Espara with a woman who expected nothing from me but a sword during the day and pleasure at night. I had no desires but to amass money and seek women. And then I met you, and now ..." He took a deep breath. "Now I want only you. And this baby. I want to give you a home, a life. I want to be a better man for you and for her."

She stretched her arms up around his neck. "Can you concentrate tonight?"

He grinned. "I think I'm already concentrating."

She laughed and pulled his head down to hers, and for a while, there was no Morrag—there was only Mairead.

Later that night, while Mairead slept, Connor sat up and wrapped his arms around his knees. He bowed his head. *—the last pulse of a fading heartbeat—Alshada, how long must I remember it?*

The only answer was the croak of the Morrag.

He kissed Mairead's cheek and dressed. Outside the hut, several Morragmen still sat around the fire, drinking and commiserating. He sat next to Osgar, who passed him a skin of oiska. "A peace offering. Can we declare a truce?"

"For now." Connor took the skin and drank. "She's with child," Connor said.

He thought Osgar's face paled a bit. "A raven's child. Twice cursed."

"Why twice?"

"Cursed with exile. Cursed with no father."

Is that all my wife and child have to look forward to? A life of exile? A life without me? He drank another long swallow. "Then at least I have something to fight for," he said, returning the skin to Osgar.

Osgar snorted a laugh. "Fight for? Returning to the tribe—to those who shun us? At least you have your outland tribes. What do we have? A lifetime in this forest—a lifetime away from hearth and home."

"You could make this your home," Connor said. "You have a woman, you have a hut, you have a sword. What more does a tribesman need?"

Osgar stood and faced him. "A people." He walked away, drinking as he went.

"Don't mind him," Wyll said quietly. "He bears much anger for the way he's been treated, but he's mostly piss and vinegar."

Connor wondered if Wyll had the right of it. "He's a man without purpose and people," he said. "There is none more dangerous than a man who would do anything to have what has been denied him."

Wyll grunted. He nudged Connor's arm. "A child, eh? Congratulations." He held out his skin.

Connor took the skin and drank once. "Is it reason to celebrate for one such as I, Wyll?"

"A new life in the world is always reason to celebrate."

Connor nodded, but doubts lingered. *A new life, and one already cursed with magic and a father who can't promise anything.*

And in his head, the Morrag cackled.

CHAPTER TWENTY-SIX

It is said that the other side of mercy is ruthlessness.
I saw that in her the moment I met her.
— Journal of Chief Eunuch to the Emperor of the Nine Seas of Tal'Amun

Mairead woke in the night to sounds outside and inside the hut. "Connor?"

"I'm here."

She turned toward the fire. He crouched next to it, feeding small sticks into the smoldering coals. "What are you doing?"

"Building up the fire. The temperature dropped. It feels like a blizzard." He glanced over at her. "You fell asleep quickly."

"Growing a person is tiring work." She watched the flames dance off his dark skin, unable to erase the terrifying thought that she had wed a madman. "Come back to bed."

"In a few moments."

She listened to the wind. Something hard splattered off the sides of the hut. "Ice?"

"Possibly. More likely snow. The wind is just blowing it around."

"Aerwyth thought the big storms were over for the year. Gareth thought this one would just be a rainstorm."

"It is a bit late, but mountain weather is tricky. It probably won't be as bad as some of the others." A strong gust came up, and he flinched.

Mairead frowned. "Are you all right?"

He put another stick on the fire. "I'm well." But his voice suggested otherwise. Another gust shook the hut, and Connor flinched again. "It's getting stronger."

"Are you worried?"

He sat silently for several moments, his face fixed on the firelight.

"Connor."

He jerked out of his reverie. "Yes?"

She gestured to his sleeping mat.

He grinned, but it was hollow. "Go back to sleep. I'll be there soon."

Mairead rolled over, but she didn't sleep until he returned to bed some time later. He pulled her into his arms.

She smiled next to his neck. "Don't you find me unappealing right now?"

"You are the most beautiful I've ever seen you right now."

She surrendered to his hands without another word.

In the morning, she woke to bitter cold and wind outside the hut. She burrowed closer to Connor, but he jerked awake and sat up. "What—oh, Mairead." He let out a long breath and scrubbed a hand through his hair. He lay back down and pulled her close to kiss her. "I'm sorry. I was dreaming."

"About what?"

He said nothing for a long moment. "A battle I was once in."

She waited, but when he said nothing more, she spoke. "In Tal'Amun, like what you told me before?"

"In Dal'Imur. Across the border, in the Zh'asta Mountains." He sighed. "Maybe this weather is dredging up memories."

They lay silent for a long time. He finally rolled to his back. "You won't be going anywhere for a while from the sounds of this storm."

"Who says I want to go anywhere?"

He chuckled. "They'll be expecting you in Isfyrin."

"Isfyrin can wait." She rested her chin on his chest. "Where do you go when we're . . . when we're in bed?"

"What do you mean?"

She bit her lip and thought about how to explain what she meant. *I don't want to hurt him. I fear what he might say—how he might react. But he needs me—I know he does.* "You are so far away."

"Far away." He turned his head toward the wall of the hut.

Mairead waited, but he said nothing more. "It seems like she's here with us sometimes—the Morrag. As if you are with her, not with me."

"I'm sorry. I'll try to pay more attention."

That's not quite what I mean. She cleared her throat and lay back down with her head in the crook of his shoulder. "How long do you think this storm will last?"

"It's always hard to say, but spring draws nearer, so this one probably won't be as bad as some of the others. You need to get back to Isfyrin, though. Your work is there. My work is here." He sighed. "I need to deal with the Morrag."

The blizzard lasted for five days. In their little village, the trees kept the Morragmen sheltered from the worst of the storm, but there were still drifts and frigid temperatures to contend with. Animals were brought inside huts, snow was melted over fires, and the men and few women present huddled together for warmth and companionship. When the snow and wind finally stopped, Mairead looked at the piles of snow around the clearing in a mixture of dismay and relief. There would be no returning to Isfyrin until the snows melted.

Her nights with Connor were not what she thought they would be. She'd hoped that his dreams and restlessness would be better with her near. If anything, he suffered more than she'd ever seen before. He assured her that she helped, and she wondered how bad the terrors and dark memories had been before she came. He sometimes mumbled in his sleep—words she couldn't understand, anxious words, orders, frustrated commands. Several times he suffered nightmares and night terrors, and he would wake screaming after several moments of fitful, anxious sleep that Mairead couldn't wake him from.

The days were nearly as bad. When he was lucid, he was solicitous and kind. He cooked for her, fed her, and wrapped her in Sidh braids to keep her warm. But his moods would shift without notice, and he would retreat into his own head, muttering dark, broody thoughts that Mairead couldn't make out. If she touched him in those moments, he flinched or startled and seemed shocked to see her.

There were moments she treasured, though—moments she hoped would become more frequent. They reminded her of the easy friendship they had formed when they'd traveled together. *That was the marriage I wanted—one of banter and playfulness, not this razor-thin thread we have now.*

One night, they lay in a pile of furs near the low fire, and she shivered. He kissed her forehead. "I'll build the fire up."

She pulled him back down to her side. "No. Use your magic."

He chuckled and wove stone braids around them. He lifted his hand and summoned the braids to himself, and she watched them swirl around his skin, obscuring it and twisting in and out of his arm. She raised her hand to join his. "How does it work?"

He laced their fingers together, and the braids swirled around her arm as well. "The elements are made of very tiny pieces—smaller than any human can see. The Sidh have those same elements in our blood. So do humans, in fact. But our blood has more of them." His other arm pulled her closer against his chest. "Do you know how magnets work?"

"Yes, after a fashion."

"It's the same with our blood, in a way. The elements in our blood attract the elements of stone, water, and air. Because we're so closely connected to the elements, we can merge with them. Our blood braids the elements together."

"So when I see you inside the braids—"

"I've actually merged with the elements. The braids are partly me, partly elemental."

She pulled her hand away from his and rolled over. "Where do your clothes go?"

He chuckled. "It's sort of strange. The braids keep the shape and hide the clothes and other things I'm carrying, and when I let them go, I just sort of fall back into them." He shrugged. "The first time I traveled on the air and stone braids, it was the Morrag controlling everything, so I didn't question it. The second time, here in the mountains, I came out of the braids with my breeches on backward."

She laughed. "You did not."

"No. But it made you laugh." He kissed her. "I did have to concentrate, though. It's harder than it seems." He wove more braids around her.

Mairead gasped and put her hand on her belly. "She moved."

He stopped weaving the braids. "The baby?"

Mairead held his hand on her belly. "Here. She was here a moment ago." They waited, but she didn't move. "Weave the braids again."

Connor did. In a moment, wispy thin orange braids appeared to join his. Inside Mairead's belly, the baby turned and tumbled and rolled. Connor grinned and laughed. "She knows me."

"She knows you." Mairead laughed, too, and watched as her husband and child shared the tendrils of earth braids. *One Hand, why can't we have more of these days?* "I see a picture of my future—a future of always being on the outside of this magic you will share with her."

He grinned. "Maybe they won't all have the magic."

She smiled. "All? You think there will be more?" *Oh, please be here to have more children. Please stay with me. Please, One Hand, restore his sanity and let him stay with me.*

He shrugged. "I hope so." The wispy tendrils faded, and the baby's movements quieted into small quivers inside Mairead's belly. Connor sighed and lay down next to Mairead, his hand still on the baby. "We should think of a name for her."

Mairead pulled him close to her. "I'm sure your mother will have some input on that topic."

"Probably."

She kissed him. "I like knowing how powerful you are."

"Powerful." The one word shifted his mood, and he turned dark without warning.

And in a breath, I've lost him again. She sat up to look down at him. "It's a good power, Connor. And it's part of you."

"I don't have to like it." He rolled away from her.

When he opened up, though, he shared more about his life than he ever had before. When they'd traveled, most nights were filled with small talk or her own rambling stories of childhood and his amused grins and chuckles in response. Connor had always been guarded with his own history, telling her an occasional short anecdote that he deemed harmless or deflecting her questions with humor or duty or simple reticence.

Now, he seemed to make up for lost time. He told her about growing up in Kiern, about his sisters and nieces and nephews, about how he never felt at home there or in the Sidh village, and that the tribe was the only place he ever knew he had a purpose. He told her about his first freelance job—how he'd stumbled upon a female merchant whose party was being attacked by thieves, and how, in her gratitude, she'd hired him to guard the party the rest of the way north. From there, he'd met Declan Clennon and others who hired him. He told her about tavern brawls and battles, about old friends and warriors he'd known and lost, even about Helene. "She's noble and haughty, but she's a brilliant woman," he told Mairead. "She keeps her word, and she has a lot of power in Espara."

"Do you wish you'd stayed with her?"

He hesitated. "I did when I first met you. But looking back, I think by the time we got to Leiden, I was falling in love with you. I don't remember even thinking of Helene or any other woman after that."

"Did you love her?" As soon as she asked it, she regretted it. *Please don't go to your dark place. Please don't leave me again because of a stupid question.*

The silence cocooned them. "Yes," he finally said, quiet but steady and without a hint of the darkness. "I think I did, after a fashion. Perhaps I loved Aine, too. And there was another girl in Kiern—a pretty village girl I wooed when I was young, before there was any other woman. I could have loved her. I thought I would marry her, but my parents wanted me to wed someone highborn."

"And what about now? Do you still love any of those women?"

He shrugged. "What does it mean to love someone? I have affection for them—fond memories and the like. I would help them, defend them. But bed them? No, I wouldn't do that." He paused, thinking. "After Kiern, I never thought I'd marry. You changed that. You changed me. There have been other women, but none I wanted to spend every night with—none I wanted to build something with. Not till now."

The raw honesty stamped out any possibility of jealousy. She stroked his cheek, faint stubble rough against her fingertips. *And yet still, you disappear and make love to me from a chasm I can't see into. Where do you go, Connor?* "I think sometimes you feel more deeply than I do."

"You're the one who weeps at poverty."

"But I think you have been wounded so many times that you just developed more scar tissue over your heart." She put her hand against his chest.

"And now? You think the scar tissue is tearing?"

"I think the key to the Morrag lies in the depth of emotion you and the ravens have."

"It seems wrong. Backward. She doesn't allow emotion from us—only hers. She only wants death—punishment, cleansing. Her only emotion is anger. Vengeance."

The darkness encroached, and Mairead put her hand on his head. "Connor. It's not time. Your time hasn't come. Her time hasn't come."

He let out a long breath. "But it will. And when it does, I fear what I will become."

Eventually, the sun came out, though the air remained frigid for several more days. The paths on the mountain were impossible to traverse. Mairead worried to Gareth and Trypp that the lions might start looking for them, but Trypp only shrugged. "They may worry, but they won't risk their own safety on icy paths like this. We're fine here as long as the paths are unsafe."

Gareth agreed. "They will wonder, but they know Trypp and I can take care of ourselves. And no one will worry about Letha. The earth guardians answer to the earth."

Within a few more days, the weather warmed considerably, and melting ice turned the paths to mud and slush. "It's inconvenient, but on horses, it's not a problem," Gareth said. "We probably should go back."

Mairead reluctantly agreed. When she ate with Phinneas and Connor that night, she suggested to both of them that it might be time for the lions to return to Isfyrin.

Connor shrugged. "I think you should do as you wish." He put down his bread. "I'm going out for a bit. I'm restless." He left the hut.

"The Morrag demands much of him," Phinneas said.

Mairead shuddered. She put her food down. "He said you're seven hundred years old."

Phinneas inclined his head and folded his hands.

"How is that possible?"

"I know how to hide between the elements. It preserves life. The spells and enchantments—they allow me to see the gaps where elements don't touch."

She frowned. "Is it like the Sidh power?"

"No, my lady. The Sidh power is in the blood, and they embrace the elements. When they hide, they break apart—merge with the elements. Their longevity comes from the blood itself."

"You already see my question, don't you?"

A thin smile flickered across his face. "It was not hard to surmise."

She let out a long breath, and her thoughts tumbled out over it. "He'll outlive me. I never wanted to live forever—I still don't—but the thought of him living tortured like this, without me, for decades—it frightens me. If I could just live as long as Connor—share his life, balance him—"

"My lady." Phinneas' voice was low and gentle. He reached one hand over to take hers. "There is a great price to pay for the knowledge of how to exist in those gaps. It is a price I don't think you would be willing to pay."

She blinked back tears. "You said Rhiannon had this knowledge, too. Did she pay this price?"

"She must have, or at least, she knows what the price is and she has shunned it." He paused. "When I was very young, men recognized my gifted mind. They took me to the Zh'asta Temple. I was set apart for a very specific purpose—to meet you and your raven and help you defeat those who would control the world." He shrugged. "When you have no more need of me, I may be released from my vow. But I will know that the price I paid was worth it."

Mairead's stomach twisted. She gestured around. "Worth this?"

The thin smile returned. "Worth seeing you and your raven. You are my life's work."

It's too much to expect of one person—two people. "I'm not hungry, either," she said, standing. "I'm going to speak with Gareth and Trypp."

By the time Connor returned that night, she was already undressed and nearly asleep. He crawled under the furs with her, pulled her close, and nuzzled her neck.

She rolled over toward him. "Are you better now?"

"For the moment."

"Will you be all right if I leave?"

"I don't like it, but I'll live. I'll visit when I can."

"So will I." She bit her lip. "We'll start out tomorrow."

"If you must."

"I need to get back to the city. And the lions need to go back, too." She kissed him. "But I'm here tonight."

"I don't want to go another season without you in my bed."

"You won't. We'll find a way."

He kissed her. "I love you, Mairead. I promise you that I do. I don't know what kind of husband I can be, but I know that I will give this marriage everything I can. Everything I'm capable of."

She smiled and pulled him into her arms, and it seemed like he finally emerged from the darkness.

She woke to his screams in the night. She sat up and shook his arm. "Connor—Connor, wake up!"

He sat up, shaking, and buried his face in his hands. "No—not my memories, not my sins. Please—I didn't—I swear I didn't—" He curled up and rocked back and forth, a low growl emerging from his throat. "Gods, no. No no no no no no."

Mairead's throat tightened. "Connor, wake up!"

"No no no no no no no—"

Mairead pulled her clothes and boots on as quickly as possible and ran through the slush and mud to Phinneas' hut. She hammered on the door with a fist. "Phinneas!" Others stirred, some coming to the doors of their huts. "Phinneas, help! Connor needs you!"

Phinneas appeared at the door already dressed. "My lady—"

"The Morrag has a grip on him. I can't wake him or soothe him. Please, can you help?"

Phinneas started to run toward Connor's hut, but he wore a grim expression. "I don't know, my lady. I have given him every drug I can think of. I had hoped your presence might ease the pain he feels."

I'm not enough. "I don't think anything is enough," she said, opening the door to Connor's hut. "He's—"

But Connor had found the wherewithal to rise from his sleeping mat and dress. He stood before Mairead in full leathers, sword drawn. "You will let me pass."

His voice. There was nothing of Connor left—only the croaking rasp of a raven. Mairead stepped into the hut. "Connor, it's me. Your wife. Mairead. Please let me help you."

He lowered his sword to her neck. "My sister begs me wait, but I will wait no longer. The time for cleansing has come."

Mairead swallowed hard and refused to move. "Connor—"

And in a crash of feet and clash of swords meeting, Gareth was there, standing between Mairead and Connor, his sword holding Connor back. Mairead stumbled backward and fell. "You will not, raven," Gareth said. "You will not touch her."

Connor's hand barely flinched. "As it shall be. We will start with the lion."

"No!" Mairead pushed Gareth away and addressed Connor. "No, M-Morrag. You will not harm this man. And you will not harm me. Your time has not yet come."

Confusion flickered across his face. "Mairead—"

Connor's voice, not the raven. She took a step toward him. "Your time has not yet come, Morrag."

Connor flinched. "Not my sins," he whispered. "Not all mine." He shuddered. "The earth weeps. My sister weeps. I will exact vengeance." In the dim gray of early dawn, Mairead saw only the black eyes of a raven. "I will exact vengeance, my sister. I will avenge you."

Mairead reached for him, but his sword flew in an arc toward her neck. A breath of air, a flash, and she stood outside the hut. Phinneas stood next to her. Inside the hut, she heard shouting and the clash of swords. "Phinneas, what—"

"I had to, my lady," he said. "Stay here." He opened the door to the hut, and the fight spilled out onto the ground. A dark pool formed in the snow, but it wasn't from Connor. Trypp's left arm hung limp at his side, but he and Gareth continued to attack Connor from both sides. Connor would not be defeated, though. He whirled, slashed, parried, and it was all the lions could do to protect themselves.

The other ravens had emerged from huts and tents in the commotion, and Wyll ran forward with his sword drawn to join the fray. "Stop!" Mairead screamed. Phinneas joined them, his hands moving at lightning speed as he twirled, ducked, and dived in and out of the jumble of swords, hands, and bodies. She couldn't tell what Phinneas did, but the small flashes of light around him and Connor suggested that he was trying to use whatever magic he owned to stop the horror before them. Still, they were no match for Connor—*no, for the Morrag.* Mairead stood paralyzed, unable to decide whether to risk her life to approach Connor or remain outside of the melee. *No weapon—where's my bow? If I could just get his attention—shoot his arm or something!* But she knew it was foolhardy even as she thought it. Connor's body moved with such speed that she could see only a blur of limbs and weapons.

It was a pinprick at first—a tiny flash of violet, then orange, then green. The Sidh braids wrapped around Connor from every direction—air, water, earth all in a jumble of color. They coalesced, merging into a thick black cloud that covered Connor's entire body. The cloud began to spin, and everyone fell back. As it spun faster, Mairead saw small bits of debris—*leaves? Sticks? What is that?* She blinked. *Gods—feathers. It's the Morrag.* The cloud spun faster and faster, and feathers became more and more distinguishable. Mairead held out a hand, afraid to step closer but afraid to stand still. "Connor, no," she whispered.

The cloud slowed and resolved into a massive raven—at least as large as the Ferimin Mairead had seen, if not larger. The bird rose above them, its wings blocking any light that might filter through the trees. It lifted its beak and cawed. The lions and Wyll and Phinneas fell back, staring in awe at the figure hovering above them. "One Hand, save us," Wyll whispered.

The figure—she couldn't call it Connor any longer—hovered for a moment, swooped toward her, and stopped. She stood her ground, unable to speak around the tightness of her throat. Tears streamed down her cheeks. She forced the words to the surface. "I love you," she said. "Please, Connor—don't do this. Don't give in to her."

The only reply was the croak of a raven.

And the Morrag rose on dark wings and flew north.

CHAPTER TWENTY-SEVEN

In the depths of the sacred place, my soul cries out. I thirst for freedom.
— Songs of King Aiden

This castle was not built for defense, Igraine thought as she padded down the stairs toward a quiet nook she'd discovered several weeks before. Her hand trailed along the stone wall. The Citadel, her childhood home on Eirya, was in every way a coastal fortress, set high on a hill and surrounded by impenetrable stone walls. *But this place? Anyone could sneak in or out. It has holes for humans like some buildings have holes for rats—and just when we find one and plug it, another appears.*

It hadn't been her first impression of the castle. From the outside, the walls and gates appeared just as impenetrable as those of the Citadel. But as Kerry tightened his grip on Igraine's freedom, she'd been forced to look for hidden nooks and passageways—places where she could speak with those who remained loyal to her without fear of discovery. Her rooms—*Braedan's rooms,* she reminded herself—were watched, she was certain. As she'd discovered more and more hidden doors and passages in the castle, she had become convinced that Kerry had spies everywhere, including her study and her bedchamber. *This place is a testament to haphazard construction,* she thought. *It was not built for governing. It was built for politics.*

The stairs curved around a pillar, and she found the narrow door she'd used in the past already standing ajar. She pushed the door open and found Nimue in the room, waiting in a chair, a book open on her lap. The girl stood and put down her book. "Your highness," she said with a curtsy. "Thank you for coming."

"Of course." Igraine closed the door. "You were not followed?"

"No. The lady Aislinn is thoroughly convinced that you and I had such a severe falling out that you cannot stand me to be in your presence. She has come to trust me implicitly. Her trust convinces Chancellor Kerry." Her brow furrowed. "Although, Kerry would be more convinced of my loyalty if I spread my legs for him."

Igraine adjusted her skirts and sat. "Kerry is a simpleton. He thinks that a woman's permission ensures her loyalty. He has a very limited understanding of women."

"He is unwise if he doesn't watch the lady Aislinn closely," Nimue said.

"The lady is very cunning. She has her own end in mind with her seduction of Chancellor Kerry." She sat down again.

Not a big surprise. "She wants a crown, aye?"

"She does, my lady." Nimue crossed her ankles and tucked them under her skirts. "But there are far more troubling things going on than just Lady Aislinn's machinations."

Igraine grimaced. While Cormac and Kerry kept most relevant news from her, Aiden and Nimue had managed to share what they could of the troubling events throughout Taura. Throughout the countryside, children disappeared with increasing frequency, their bodies found hanging from trees and drained of all blood in some kind of ritual sacrifice. "More deaths?"

"In the city now—a young girl who worked in a brothel. They said a burned man visited the brothel before she disappeared. She was only eleven or twelve, my lady. She wasn't even a prostitute—just a serving girl."

"What is Kerry doing about these deaths?"

"Lord Rowan claims to be looking into them, and Chancellor Kerry has said publicly that he is deeply troubled and will punish the offender to the fullest extent he's able once the man is found." Nimue shrugged. "But the chancellor has other concerns as well."

"Seizing more power away from Braedan, no doubt."

"No, my lady—well, at least not publicly." She wet her lips and dropped her voice. "An army amasses across the channel. Chancellor Kerry fears an invasion. He's sent some of his men across to investigate, but none have returned. My lady, I fear ...." She bit her lip. "A foreign army is a bigger threat to Taura than one selfish, ambitious lord, my lady. While we squabble here in the capitol, the army across the channel will invade and squash us."

Igraine frowned. *What if it's Braedan? He came from Culidar before— what if he went back there on Logan's advice and put out a call to arms?* "What do you know of this army?"

Nimue bit her lip again. She reached into the pocket of her kirtle and pulled out a leather lashing with a bone depending from it. "The army is Nar Sidhe, my lady," she whispered. "Their fires burn brighter every night, and ships coming into Torlach report that they are harried by longboats manned by men with red tattoos."

Igraine scoffed and stood. "Superstitions and myths," she said, turning away from Nimue. "The idea of Nar Sidhe hordes waiting to invade Taura is a bedtime story to frighten children."

"My lady, forgive me, but the Nar Sidhe are real," Nimue said. "I have spoken with men who have seen them. Some freelances build entire careers out of escorting merchants through their territory." She paused, and Igraine turned back to her. "Until recently, they remained confined to their woodlands and the land south of the Wilds. For some reason, they are now moving north in a massive group once again."

"Why have they waited so long, then?" Igraine asked.

"They waited for the right time, the right leader, the weakness of the Taurin throne—it could be any number of reasons." She held out the trinket in her palm. "But this—this is the biggest change. They wear these amulets for protection."

Igraine snorted in derision. "Superstition," she repeated.

"No, my lady—magic." Nimue wet her lips. "The Nar Sidhe have the same blood as Brae Sidh, but they are not connected to the Brae Sidh queen through the *codagha*. If they came onto Taura without some kind of protection, the Brae Sidh wards would tear them to ribbons."

"And these bone trinkets protect them?" Igraine studied the talisman. "You would do well to recall I do not put faith in Brae Sidh legends, either."

Nimue frowned. "My lady, the Sidh are real."

"Human-like creatures who can bend and control elements to their will? You believe such things?" Igraine shook her head. "Legends and myths for another time."

Nimue pointed. "Then how do you explain these trinkets?"

"Red paint applied to animal bones—nothing more."

"Blood on Brae Sidh bone," Nimue said. Her voice was tight with pain. "This is why children are dying, I believe. Somewhere, someone who knows how to make these is finding children or young adults with unquickened Sidh blood and murdering them. They drain the blood and conjure the old earth magic around an old Sidh bone, and the magic writes the runes in blood." She shuddered. "These things—the *amasidh*—they are an abomination."

Igraine's blood chilled. *A child died for some ridiculous superstition?* She shuddered. "What if that's nothing more than a bird's wing and a bit of pig's blood, eh?"

"It's not." Nimue frowned. "My lady, children are dying to make these for an army that wants to take Taura. Whether you believe the magic is real or no, the threat remains the same."

Igraine let out a long breath. "You are right," she said. "What is Chancellor Kerry doing about this threat?"

"It's hard to say, highness. He has sent some patrol boats into the harbor. They bring reports of more longboats, more tents, more fires on the shore. We have only estimates of what we're facing, but Chancellor Kerry believes there may be three or four of their men for every one of ours."

Igraine shivered. "And the tribes? What of them?"

"He sent word to Traitha Hrogarth, but the traitha disappeared some weeks ago, apparently. There is another man—Edgar, I believe—from a northern tribe. He tells Chancellor Kerry he will only treat with Braedan."

Igraine let out a long breath. *That's some good news.* "I have been too long away from court," she whispered.

"This is true, my lady."

"Lady Aislinn has told you much."

Nimue shrugged one shoulder. "Not really. I just listen. She wheedles and coerces the chancellor into sharing things with her, or she sits back with her embroidery and her tea and listens while he discusses things with Cormac. People quickly forget that I'm in the room."

You belong anywhere, Igraine thought. *You have a unique ability to hide in a crowd of three as easily as in a crowd of thousands.* "Tell me where you got this amulet."

"An Eiryan trader docked at the harbor two days ago. The captain and a few of his officers met with Duke Nolan. He sent for me, and I snuck out to meet them. They had some trouble with the longboats when they came into the channel, and after a bit of a protracted fight, the Eiryans managed to board the longboat and kill most of its crew. Several of them wore those trinkets. One of the trader's officers asked me to take that one to you."

"And who was this officer? Do I know him?"

"He said you would. He didn't give me his name, but he said you would recognize his title." She frowned. "It was just a nickname, though. I'm sure of it. He said to call him Prince Thinbeard."

Igraine blinked in surprise and started to laugh. "Oh, lass," she said, tears of relief and hope welling up in her eyes. She swiped at them, smiling. "Oh lass, ye've not met an obscure Eiryan sea officer."

"I haven't?"

Don't say who he is here—just in case someone is listening. "I need to get to Rory's house, but the way I'm watched, I don't know how I can manage it. Do you have any ideas?"

"I do, your highness." She stood. "Tell Chancellor Kerry that you're not feeling well and that you wish to spend the evening in your chambers. Dismiss everyone and check all the corners for ears. Aiden and I will come see you later. We'll get you out of the castle and over to Rory's house after dark. Will that do?"

Igraine's heart leapt. "It will, love."

Nimue curtsied. "Then I'll see you near suppertime, my lady."

Igraine waited until Nimue had time to climb the stairs and then returned to her chambers. She scribbled a note to Kerry and asked Gwyn to carry it to him. Gwyn returned saying that the chancellor excused her. *It's not surprising,* she thought. Kerry rarely cared what she did as long as she remained out of court and inside the castle. *I'm effectively a prisoner. But at least I'm alive, and as long as I'm here, I might be able to help Braedan.*

Aiden came to her chambers later, accompanied by a serving woman she didn't recognize. "What's this, then?" she asked.

The woman smiled. "Don't you recognize me, my lady?"

"Nimue? How did you—"

"Uncanny, isn't it?" Aiden said.

Igraine couldn't reconcile the face before her with the voice. The woman's hair was redder, and her face was older, thinner, graced with fine lines near the eyes and mouth—not the round nubile face of her lady-in-waiting. There was an imperceptible plumpness to her body as well—just a fuller appearance, slightly wider hips, rounded shoulders worn down with serving highborn people for years. *And is she shorter? I don't understand how this is possible— it's her, I can see it, but there's something different.* She reached out a hand and touched the hair draped over Nimue's shoulder. "You dyed your hair."

"Just a bit. A henna wash." She stepped into Igraine's chambers. "I'll cover it with a wimple until it washes out."

"I just—I can't believe it's you," Igraine said. "You look older, wearier. How?"

Nimue chuckled. "Tricks of the theater, your highness. I knew some performers in my youth. I learned to alter my appearance through subtle means."

In your youth? "So you altered your appearance to look like me?"

Nimue passed her hands over herself. "To a degree. You can exchange clothes with me. I'll stay in your bed in case someone comes to check on you."

Igraine took a deep breath and put her hands on her hips. "Well, then, let's be about it."

Aiden waited in the study while Igraine dressed in Nimue's serving clothes. "Stoop slightly," Nimue advised. "And frown—it will give you lines and wrinkles on your face. Look down and keep your hands folded. If you squint just a bit, you can look older around the eyes as well."

Igraine copied the younger woman. "Better?"

"Yes." Dressed in Igraine's shift and dressing gown, her hair a dark red and her shoulders once again straight and thrown back, Nimue would easily pass for Igraine. She smiled. "Much better, your highness."

Has she always had freckles and I just didn't notice? "Thank you for doing this," she said.

"Of course, your highness. You will tell me who this Prince Thinbeard is, won't you?" She held out a common woman's cloak for Igraine.

Igraine let her drape it over her shoulders and fasten it. "When the time is right."

Igraine joined Aiden in the study. "How are we to go about this, then?"

He had dressed in simple wool breeches and linen tunic, and he wore a nondescript cloak. "We can get out through the kitchen if we hurry. There are many servants who go home at night. They'll be leaving soon."

He led her to the kitchens and out the back of the castle. The rain fell in torrents, and Igraine held her hood close around her head as Aiden directed her through the mud and around puddles in the courtyard with a hand on her back. They ducked through the gate amid the other servants trying to hurry through the rain. The guards didn't stop anyone.

They wound their way through the streets and down the hill toward the ambassador residences. Igraine started to walk through the front gates, but Aiden stopped her. "You're a servant, remember? You'll go through the back."

"Of course—thank you."

They walked around to the servant's entrance and knocked. One of Duke Fingall's men answered the door. "Who is it?"

"Duke Nolan's woman is here."

Igraine tensed. *Duke Nolan's woman? He has a woman?*

The man frowned. "I wasn't told anything—"

Aiden leaned closer. "She's here to see Prince Thinbeard."

"Of course." He opened the door all the way and ushered them in. He bowed as Aiden took Igraine's cloak. "Your highness. Forgive my hesitation. We've been told to be cautious."

She waved her hand dismissively. "Where is he?"

"I'll take you to him."

She followed the man through the Eiryan ambassador's house with Aiden close behind her, and Fingall's man stopped finally and knocked on a heavy oak door. "My lords? A lady here to see Prince Thinbeard."

Footsteps approached the door, and Igraine's stomach turned with excitement. When the door opened to reveal a dark-haired, bearded young sailor, she flung herself against him with a little gasp of delight. "Ian," she whispered against his chest. "Oh, Ian, you can't know—you can't have any idea—it's so good—" And then she dissolved into relieved, happy tears.

He wrapped his long arms around her and laughed against her hair. "It's good to see you too, sister."

Igraine allowed herself to remain against her brother's chest for a long moment. *He smells like the sea, like oiska, like home.* "I have missed you. I have worried about you so much. After you sent Ursula to the Citadel, we heard so little. And then I left, and—"

"You worried for me?" He laughed again. "Dear sister, I have done nothing but worry for you since I heard about this coup. It took all of the persuasive powers in my possession to convince Captain Dougal to come here now, at this time of year. And then to encounter those beasts in the channel—by the spirits, I'm just happy to see you alive and well."

She pulled away from him and put her hands on his cheeks. "In two years, this is the most your beard has filled in?"

He shrugged. "Perhaps I don't have Father's hirsute tendencies."

Rory and Cameron Fingall both bowed to Igraine. "Your highness," Rory said, reaching for her hand. He brushed his lips across her knuckles. "It's been too many weeks. How are you?"

"Is that genuine concern I hear, Rory? Or just the obligatory greeting of one of my father's nobles?"

Rory straightened, a grin planted on his lips. "Genuine, I assure you, love. You look well."

She sat down and arranged her skirts. "Do our parents know you're here, Ian?"

He poured a cup of wine and offered it to her. "If they don't, they will soon. I sent word with a ship sailing to Eirya when we left Espara."

They should feel better knowing someone is here to watch me. She sipped her wine. "Then you aren't here to bring me home at their request?"

Ian laughed. "No, of course not. I know how foolish it would be to try to talk you into something you don't want to do."

"How long will you stay?"

He sat. "Captain Dougal has already left for Eirya. He is taking word of the trouble in the channel to our parents. I'm here until Rory leaves." He sipped from his own cup. "Which means I'm here until you agree to come home on your own or I'm convinced you're safe enough to stay here."

"And what will it take to convince you of that?"

He hesitated. "Rory, Cameron—would you mind giving me a few moments alone with my sister?" The other men stood, and Igraine dismissed Aiden. When they were alone, Ian crossed the room to sit next to Igraine and picked up her hand. "Igraine. I'm not here for Father or Mother or our brothers or anyone else. I have nothing in mind but to make sure you are well and whole. I don't care if you come back to Eirya or disguise yourself as a boy and become the first mate of a ship. I'm here because you're my sister and I love you."

"What is your point?"

"Tell me why you are doing this." He made a sweeping gesture around the room. "All of this—staying here on Taura, marrying this usurper—"

She stood and crossed her arms. "I don't owe you anything, aye? You're not my father. You're not a god or a priest. You're just a third son of a royal couple with no prospects but what our father chooses to give you."

Ian only chuckled. "I know exactly what I am. If you're thinking to wound me, sister, you'll have to try harder." His voice gentled. "Igraine, it's me. Ian."

She turned back to him, and for a moment, she didn't see the tanned, muscular sailor she'd seen at first. Instead, she only saw the little boy she'd climbed trees and ridden horses and shot a bow with. Only a bit more than a year separated them, and most of Igraine's fondest memories involved Ian. The effort of keeping herself composed, of trying to play politics with Cormac and Kerry, of missing Braedan's presence—it all crashed in on her. "Oh, Ian," she whispered.

His arms were around her then, and the words tumbled out against his chest as she told him all about the fall of the sayada, her original agreement with Braedan, the way the handsome, charismatic king had won her heart and convinced her to marry him, and the way Kerry and Cormac continued to move pieces into place to take the throne for Kerry.

"Why didn't you come back to Eirya?" he asked.

"D'ye have to ask, lad?" She pointed at the door. "How long d'ye think our father would have waited before he married me off to that man?"

Ian picked up her hand. "Dear sister, I know that Rory is not the man for you. I know that he hurt you, deeply, and that your heart is more tender than you are willing to admit. And I know that you would not be so loyal to this king of yours without good reason. But I also know that you are in danger here, and that whatever your feelings for Braedan, if you don't leave, you will die. It's not a question of if—it's a question of when."

"And what would you have me do, then? Run away when my king needs me? Flee my duties, my promises, just because fulfilling them is difficult?"

Ian chuckled. "I'd sooner ask a southern breeze to blow in winter. I am not asking you to desert your king. I am asking you to stay safe enough to return to him when the time is right. Igraine, this is not yet your throne. This is Braedan's throne, and if he's meant to have it, he will find a way to rid the castle of Ronan Kerry. But your hold here is tenuous, at best, and you will be no good to Braedan should your head be impaled on a spike."

Igraine tried to hide her shudder by stepping away from Ian, but she suspected he saw the response. She crossed her arms. "And you suggest I go to Eirya?"

"Just for now," he said. "Just until Braedan returns. But if I cannot convince you to go back, then I will stay here and hope I can find some way to keep you from ending up on the wrong end of Kerry's anger."

"You will not convince me to go back, Ian. Not now."

He nodded. "I thought as much. Then I will stay here."

She let out a long, relieved breath and took his hand again. "I thank you. Just knowing you're here—it does help."

He squeezed her hand. "Shall we let the others back in now?"

"Wait." She hesitated. "What if . . . what if you could go find Braedan?"

He frowned. "Igraine . . . ."

"Please, Ian. You would draw no attention. No one knows you're here except the few of us in this room. You could ferret him out—warn him, remind him of what he should be doing here, bring him back safely, if necessary."

"But how would I find him?"

"I don't know. You could start north of Fingall's estates. Take some of his men. Ride like merchants or tradesmen." She took his other hand. "I'm sure you've heard of the guard I sent—Logan Mac Kendrick. I don't know if he ever found him. I just need to know that someone has taken word to him."

Ian's mouth drew down into his beard. "You're serious?"

"Rory is here—he can watch over me." *As much as I let him.* She cleared her throat when he raised an eyebrow. "I can take care of myself, aye? I am not without resources still. I have a very clever lady-in-waiting."

"Is her swordplay any good?"

Igraine twisted her mouth. "I have more means of defense at my disposal than just blades."

He grinned. "I'm sure you do." He paused. "You're certain you wish me to do this?"

"What good can you do here? You'd be stuck in Rory's house, sending messages to me through Nimue, but there's nothing you can do to keep me safe unless I come here to Rory's house—and that's something I have no intention of doing."

"You'd be safer here."

She snorted a laugh. "With Rory trying to get into my skirts? Please. He'd be after seducing my ladies first, and then I'd wake and find him in my bed and—"

Ian's face had turned the color of a stormy sunrise. He grimaced. "All right, all right. No need to go on." He sighed. "Very well. I'll do as you ask—I'll head north and try to find your king. Shall we let the others back in? We have some arrangements to make."

When Cameron and Rory entered and returned to their seats, Rory cast Igraine a brief look. "And ye'll be staying here for a bit, then?" he asked.

"I will remain on Taura for a bit longer," she said, turning to Cameron Fingall. "My lord, I have a great favor to ask of you."

He bowed. "Of course, my lady. Name it."

The evening passed making plans for Ian to leave at first light, before word had a chance to leak out that he was in Taura. He planned to start at the first village north of Salmon Springs and follow the king's trail from there. "Use Fingall's men, use tribesmen, use whoever you can find—just bring him back armed and ready to reclaim his throne," Igraine begged when she finally said goodbye to Ian at Rory's door that night.

He pinned her cloak closed over her shoulders. "I will. Grainy," he said, paused, and sighed. "I know it's been two years since I saw her, and I know that you came here a year ago, but do you know how Ursula is? Have you heard anything from her?"

Igraine put a hand on Ian's arm. "When last I saw her, she was serving as a lady-in-waiting in the Citadel and tending her trees in the royal orchard and pining for my wandering brother."

He chuckled. "I haven't stopped thinking of her in two years. It's foolish to long so for a woman I only spent three days with, but Igraine—there's something about her."

She tightened her hand. "After you find Braedan, go back to Eirya and marry that girl."

"If only it were so simple. A princess from a distant, isolated country that fears foreigners and shuns outsiders wedding a seafaring prince who thinks the world is his own personal plaything, designed just for him to explore?" He shrugged. "I don't see it happening."

"Our grandfather did not believe he would see his daughter wed a common merchant, but now that merchant rules the kingdom." She took his hands in hers and smiled. "Love is not considerate about where it blossoms, brother. It travels with the wind and takes root where it lands. Our choice is whether to water it or pull it out by the roots."

"And you've chosen to water yours."

"I have." She squeezed his hands and kissed his cheek. "And when you meet my king, I'm sure you'll understand why."

Aiden led her back through the alleys and narrow streets of Torlach, but when they reached the castle gates, he stopped and put a hand in front of her.

"What is it?"

"We thought one of Logan's men would be at the rear gate tonight," he whispered. "But that's one of Kerry's men."

Igraine's stomach lurched. "You don't think he knows I'm gone, do you?"

"No way to tell." He fell silent, thinking. "There might be another way in."

"Where?"

He nodded toward the ruins of the sayada. "If we can get in there, can you find your way through the catacombs and into the castle?"

"I don't know what you think of me, lad, but I was never one for skulking through the bowels of the sayada."

"Of course not, your highness," he said. "But it would be very useful right now if you could pretend to be the kind of young woman who would."

She sighed. "I might know one way down into the catacombs, but from there, we'll have to guess."

"It's a risk we have to take. Unless you wish to return to Duke Nolan's house?"

She grimaced. "We'll risk the sayada, then."

Getting onto the old sayada grounds was not the difficult part. "Reduced forces with the king gone," Aiden whispered. "Kerry doesn't see it as an important place to guard."

Igraine put a hand over her nose. "And the people use it as a privy?"

Aiden handed her a kerchief. "Those without homes sleep here. The people still come, even though the sayas are gone." He took her arm to steer her around a man huddled in a corner.

The man sat with his knees to his chin, head bowed low to keep the rain and cold off his face, a ragged blanket pulled tight around his shoulders. A pang went through her. *This is what your lover wrought with his coup,* she reminded herself. *If the sayas were still here, that man would have food, shelter, clothing. That's what I want, and if Braedan were here, the sayas might be back by now. But what if Kerry becomes king? What happens then?*

Aiden led her to a side door the sayas had used to allow rare after-hours guests in and out. He took off one glove and ran his hand over the door. "Burned," he whispered. "But the lock still holds." He pulled a small metal pick from one pocket in his cloak and put it into the lock. In a moment, he was rewarded with a click, and he gestured Igraine into the building proper.

"You're a man of many talents, Aiden," Igraine said.

He cleared his throat. "I came to King Braedan's banner a thief and a beggar. He promised that if I joined him, I'd never be hungry again. I remain his faithful servant—and yours."

She smiled. "Come this way," she said, tugging his arm. Faint light from the city drifted through the holes in the ceiling, but it was enough to allow them to pick their way toward the library. Once there, Igraine lifted her skirts over her feet to step over the toppled shelves, burned parchment, and scattered tables and chairs. "Back here." Aiden followed, and when they reached the far wall, Igraine put her hand on an untoppled shelf. "The latch is back here."

He found her hand in the dim light and felt for the latch. It opened with a quiet pop. Together, they pulled the shelf away from the wall and stepped into a stone corridor. "You seemed very certain of where that latch would be."

"I knew about it from Braedan." Her voice echoed off the stone. "He was familiar with a few sayas. They would sneak out through the library to meet him."

Aiden said nothing for a long moment. "Did he tell you which way to go from here?"

She sent up another quick prayer of thanks to the spirits for Aiden's sense of decorum. "I think we're on our own from here."

"We'll need a light." Aiden stepped back into the library. "I'll see what I can find in here."

Igraine tried to make out shapes in the faint light. "It's astounding that the library didn't burn."

"The king didn't want the library burned," Aiden said in an absent tone.

Igraine frowned. "You were here?"

"I was. After the king took the sayas to the castle, he instructed us to burn the rooms and the supplies—everything but the library."

"Why?"

The guard had disappeared into the darkness, but Igraine could hear his feet pushing aside papers, books, and furniture as he sought a lamp or torch. "Information. He knew the Taurin heir was housed here once. He thought there might be information about her in the library. He always intended to search it. From the look of things here, I'd say he did. I don't know if he found what he wanted."

Igraine picked her way through the room to a section marked as Kirok Mythology. The shelves had been ignored—probably, she thought, because there was no reason for Braedan to be concerned with anything about kirok mythology. Her fingers lingered on the spine of one book and made out the letters that spelled *Syrafi*. She swallowed hard. *I'd be a fool to take this. I'd be a fool not to.* She pulled it off the shelf and slipped it into her skirts.

Aiden found her a few moments later, oil lamp in hand. "It's not much, but it should last till we get to the catacombs under the castle where we can find torches," he said. He set the lamp on the floor and pulled out a piece of flint, struck it against his knife to produce sparks, and breathed out a long sigh when the old wick caught with a weak flame. He turned the wick up just a bit and held out a hand to Igraine.

She followed him into the dark corridor behind the hidden door. He pulled the door closed behind them, cutting off their last sliver of light from the city, and the latch clicked. "If my sense of direction isn't lying, the castle is this way," he said, and started walking along the dim corridor.

Igraine could only follow, trusting that Aiden's feet wouldn't lead them astray as she stumbled along behind him. He cleared cobwebs and rats for her, but she shuddered when something furry and warm skipped across her feet. She nearly bit her tongue to keep from crying out in surprise. *Never show all your cards,* she thought, remembering Rory's words years ago when he taught her to play some meaningless game of luck. She gritted her teeth and swallowed hard.

After several minutes, Aiden stopped. "The corridor branches off," he said. "Any ideas?"

"Braedan mentioned that some of the walls had paintings on them. Can you make anything out in this light?"

"Nothing."

Footsteps shuffled against stone in the distance, and Igraine froze. Her hand tightened around Aiden's. She sucked in a breath. Aiden squeezed her hand and let go. He gave her the lamp and drew his knife. "Who's there? Show yourself."

"Aiden? My lady, is that you?"

Nimue's voice drifted back to them on a whisper of stale air, and Igraine let out her breath. "Nimue, how on earth—"

"The guard who was supposed to stand watch came to your rooms, my lady," Nimue said, rounding a corner. Her face was cut into planes and lines by the shadows her torch cast over the walls. "He warned me that Chancellor Kerry's man switched duties with him. He was concerned about you—he hadn't seen you yet, and he wondered if you'd returned to your rooms. Lady Aislinn was abed, and the castle was quiet, so I came to see if I could find you myself."

"How on earth do you know about the catacombs?" Igraine asked.

The girl shrugged one shoulder. She looked herself again—young, hale, energetic, all traces of her disguise gone except the red hair. "I've done some reading about the castle history. When I didn't find you on the castle grounds, I thought I'd try this route. The legends say the Sidh carved these catacombs. Do you think it's true—that there really were Brae Sidh stone talents down here once?"

Igraine wanted to scoff, but the sincerity in the girl's voice stopped her. "I couldn't say," she finally said. "Nimue, I'm exhausted, and—"

"Oh, of course, my lady." She turned back the way she came. "Follow me. It's not far."

They wound their way through more dim corridors. Igraine noticed the gradual descent and then ascent as, she assumed, they went under the castle walls and entered the edge of the dungeons. "Must we go through here?" she asked, holding her sleeve to her nose as memories of her meetings with Logan rose.

"No, my lady. We skirt the edges of the dungeons. I found a path that will take us near the chambers the king used before his exile."

Igraine put a hand on Nimue's arm. "How did you—how do you know where he slept then?"

Nimue blinked in surprise. "Oh—forgive me, my lady. I just assumed they were his old chambers. They're very near the ones you use now."

Igraine's heart quickened. *Who is this girl? How long has she known Braedan?* "Nimue, were you ever—did you ever serve the sayada?"

"No, your highness. I was born and bred in the north, aye?"

Igraine blinked. "I'm sorry, Nimue, I . . . I think this strain is getting to me. I need to be abed."

"Yes, your highness."

Nimue turned away, and Igraine had to blink again. *By the spirits, I swear—I had only a bit of wine. Could that have been—no, it can't.*

But she swore that, for just a moment, the torchlight cast a shadow over two wings on Nimue's back.

CHAPTER TWENTY-EIGHT

> *The womb of the lioness will bless the three lands.*
> *— Tribal prophecy*

Mairead watched Connor's shadow disappear above the trees, the Morrag's cries echoing through the raven village. *He's gone. He's gone again. And now what?* She wiped hot tears with a fury. "Connor Mac Niall," she shouted. "Do not come back! Unless you are ready to be a real husband and father, do not ever come back!"

"My lady." Phinneas lay a firm hand on her shoulder. "There are wounded."

Gareth knelt in the snow cradling an unconscious Trypp against his chest. Letha knelt next to Trypp's left arm, wrapping cloths around the wound as quickly as they became soaked. A belt was cinched tight around the arm just above Trypp's elbow, and Trypp's arm—

Mairead stood paralyzed. *Trypp's arm is missing.* Her stomach lurched. "Oh, gods—Trypp—"

Letha looked up at her. "Traitha, fetch more cloths!"

Phinneas took over. "I'll do it." He disappeared into his own hut and returned with lengths of silk. "Lift the arm above his head. It will slow the bleeding."

Letha nodded, and Gareth helped her hold Trypp's arm.

Mairead could only watch, anger and fear and pain rising in her chest all at once. "How bad is it?"

"He lost the arm just below his elbow," Letha said.

Mairead clenched and unclenched her fists. *Be a leader. They want me to lead.* "What would you have me do?"

"Fetch water. More cloths."

Mairead ran to the hut she'd shared with Connor. She studiously ignored the upended baskets and destroyed bedding to look for linens and rags. She picked up a bucket of water and returned to kneel next to Letha. "Show me."

"Keep packing the cloths on," Letha said.

Bile rose in Mairead's throat as she wrapped another cloth around the stub. She turned her head away, blinking back tears.

"It is what we are raised for, traitha," Gareth said. "To protect you."

The bleeding slowed, gradually turning from a gush to an ooze. Trypp stirred and moaned occasionally, but he didn't speak. "Give him something to ease the pain," Gareth said.

"Not until he's replenished some of the lost fluids," Letha said. "Phinneas, may we move him to your hut?"

"Of course."

Gareth helped Wyll move Trypp to the hut. Letha and Phinneas knelt next to the wounded warrior. He writhed and moaned in pain. "Trypp, can you drink?" Letha asked.

Trypp managed a slight nod.

Letha fetched water and helped Trypp drink. She looked up at Mairead.

"We will care for him. You can go."

Mairead, Gareth, and Wyll walked outside. "What happened?" Gareth asked her.

"I don't know—I don't—he was sleeping, and then—" She babbled the story out in fits and spurts, and when she was done, both men let out a long breath. "Please tell me this has happened to one of you," she said to Wyll.

"I have never seen this, traitha," Wyll said. "We have our demons, our battles, our madness, but I don't know this."

"He says he hears her—hears her voice."

"I know," Wyll said. "That is unique to him. He is the First Raven, traitha. We thought—"

"You thought it was normal. You thought it normal for a man to try to kill his wife." She paced, overcome with restlessness, and tried to run through the thoughts swirling in her head. "Are either of you wounded?"

Gareth put a cloak around her. "Scrapes and bruises," he said. "You are well?"

"Yes. Phinneas—he did something to spirit me out of the tent when—" She shook her head at the memory. "When Connor tried to kill me."

Wyll put a hand on her arm. "Is this true?"

She shrugged his hand away and turned to him. "Is this what it is? What is meant by this prophecy—that a ravenmarked man will destroy the lion's child?"

"Traitha—"

Mairead stepped back. "And now you'll finish the job? You'll come after me, too—you'll try to kill me for my sins, just like your First Raven did?"

"No, we swore fealty to—"

"So did he!" she shouted. "He swore he would serve me all of his days, and then he tried to kill me—not once, not just tonight, but three times."

Wyll held up his hands. "Traitha, we—"

Mairead drew her knife. "You will not touch me, raven. Not today. Not ever."

From between the huts came a hiss, and Twitch emerged, tail flipping, ears flat on her head. Above, Grayfeather circled.

Wyll nodded. "As you wish it, traitha."

Mairead whirled to Gareth. "Prepare a litter for Trypp. We leave as soon as we are packed."

"You cannot leave, traitha," Wyll said. He spoke quietly, gently, and held his hands up in surrender, but the tone of his voice was certain and firm. "I am sorry. I know you do not trust us, and I know you are angry, and it is not in our nature to hold someone against her will, but you cannot leave. We cannot let the lions know where we are."

Mairead clenched and unclenched her fists over and over again. "You would hold me hostage?"

Wyll flinched at the words. "I am sorry," he repeated. "I wish I could let you go. But this is the will of the First Raven." He paused. "Your husband, traitha. He has ordered that anyone who enters the village without blindfold may not leave."

Mairead turned away to hide the tears brimming in her eyes. "He never said that to me."

"Perhaps he didn't intend to make you adhere to the requirement. Perhaps in his joy at seeing you, he just didn't think it important. Or perhaps he was waiting until you were mounted on horseback to request it. I don't know. All I know is the order he gave us."

Gareth put a hand on Mairead's shoulder. "If you do not let her go, the lions will search for her," he said to Wyll. "They will find you, and they will kill you to rescue her." He pointed at Twitch. "And if we cannot leave, our animals will. You cannot keep the cat and the hawk hostage."

"Perhaps not," Wyll conceded. "But if that is the case, we may have to kill them."

Gareth paled in the dim light.

Wyll took a deep breath. "Forgive me, traitha. Forgive me. I do not like this. But I cannot go against my First Raven. You must stay."

Letha emerged from the hut. "We can't leave now even if they would let us, Mairead. Trypp will need time to rest, and we must look to his wound to ensure it does not become septic." She gestured with her chin. "We are safe here, for now. These men will not harm you. They merely wish to remain hidden."

Mairead blinked back tears. "I will be in my—in Connor's hut," she said.

Back in the hut, she surveyed the damage. She picked up her torc and sat down on the sleeping mat, turning the torc over and over in her hands. Thoughts tumbled over each other, begging for a hearing—*you are not strong enough to hold the Morrag back—Connor would not wish you to leave the ravens—he didn't mean to hurt anyone—he tried to kill me—Trypp's arm—Gareth was right—what now? What's next?* She hid her face in her hands and wept. *Connor, I'm sorry I wasn't enough. I'm sorry.*

It was some time later when Gareth knocked on the door and called to her. "Mairead? May I enter?"

She wiped her eyes. "Come."

He entered the hut and knelt before her. "Letha sent me to tell you that Trypp is stable. The eunuch is watching him as well. The cut was clean, and they expect the arm to heal eventually."

"Heal. How does one regrow an arm, Gareth?"

"He can still fight. He fights with his right arm, not his left. Any day a man can return home to his wife and child and still swing a sword is a good day for a tribesman."

"But he's not home, is he? He's here, trapped because I had to seek the ravens."

He reached for her hand. "You could not know, traitha."

"I should have known. I should have seen."

"You saw only a man you loved. There is no shame in that."

She fought back new tears. "Are you saying that he isn't our enemy?" She gestured around the hut. "That they aren't enemies, that they aren't a threat to us or to your tribe? You were right, Gareth—you and the lions. These men are faithless betrayers, and now they are kidnappers."

His hand tightened on hers. "They are different, it's true, but I do not see faithlessness when I look at them, traitha. They seek to serve you just as the lions do."

"Serve me until when? Until the Morrag tells them to destroy us?" She didn't wait for him to answer. "I thought they were my army, but how can I trust them when they might turn against me? Maybe your prophecies were right—maybe they are here to destroy me." She took a deep breath. "It doesn't matter, because none of us will be alive for long if Connor has anything to say about it. We need to prepare for battle—for when he returns."

"What makes you think he'll return?"

Her stomach roiled. "We're still alive."

It didn't take long for Wyll and some of the other ravens to arrange a rotation for guarding her hut. Mairead couldn't bring herself to fight the decision. She merely curled up in a blanket to consider her options. *But there are none right now,* she thought. *I need Gareth and Letha to get back to Isfyrin, and Letha won't leave Trypp. Twitch won't leave Trypp, either. And even when he's ready to travel, do I want to risk more lives? For what purpose?* She finally ate a cold meal of dry meat and bread and fell onto her sleeping mat early that night. She buried her head in her elbow, inhaling Connor's scent that lingered on his tunic as she fell asleep.

In the morning, Gareth returned with Letha just as Mairead was finishing her morning meal. She poured tea for both of them, and they sat around the

small fire pit in her hut as Wyll stood guard outside. "This is the most privacy they will allow," Gareth said. "They are determined that you will not leave the raven village."

"How is Trypp?" Mairead asked.

"He has awakened off and on," Letha said. "We have told him about his arm. He bore the news well. His wound is . . . as well as can be expected."

"I am glad to hear it. I will visit him later today." She picked up her cup and took a deep breath. "There is something you should know, Gareth. I'm with child."

"A Faltian baby, due in autumn," Letha said.

"By the spirits," Gareth whispered. "What if he has his father's curse?"

Mairead put her hand over her belly. "I don't think that will happen. I believe it's a girl."

"But she could still be cursed with the magic, couldn't she? You have a warriormark—women should not have a warriormark."

"What are you suggesting, Gareth?" Letha asked.

He took a deep breath. "I do not like to say it, but if the lions see Mairead growing big with child, they will fear this child. And why shouldn't they? If this child is dangerous, like her father, why shouldn't we fear her? Even if she's not dangerous, what if she is cursed? What if she must bear this disease of the raven? I would not wish to burden a child or a mother with such an illness."

Mairead's hand tightened on her belly. "Then what would you have me do?"

He chewed his lip. "I don't know," he admitted. "There are women who take certain herbs to . . . expel a child early."

Mairead's blood ran cold, and Letha reached over to hold her arm. "Gareth, you know such a thing is not done in the tribes," Letha said.

"I know, and I have always thought that was right, but now—"

"But now, because of the threat of illness that this child may or may not have, you would suggest that I kill my child?" Mairead interrupted. "What if she is perfectly healthy? What about the purpose she is created for? She is my heir, Gareth—right now, the only heir I have. I would never think to hurt my child, boy or girl, illness or no illness, curse or no curse."

He opened his mouth, then closed it. "You are right, Mairead. I'm sorry. I don't know what I was thinking."

Mairead straightened her shoulders. "You are forgiven, but your question raises a difficult point. I have to assume we will return to Isfyrin eventually, and it's becoming impossible to hide my belly. I need to know—will this cause problems in the tribe?"

Letha folded her hands. "This would not normally cause problems. Children are celebrated in the tribe, and a woman without a husband is not shunned. But I fear that you will be different. If you tell these men that you wed Connor, you may put your child in danger. If you allow them to believe that you have no husband and refuse to say who the father is, you may become a trophy for one of the men who seeks power."

"Braun. I had considered that already." Mairead took a deep breath. "We need not worry yet. We are stuck here, in this village, until something changes."

"Then that is likely our first priority," Gareth said. "How do we get out of this village?"

Mairead bit her lip. "Perhaps Phinneas can help."

Gareth and Letha exchanged a look. "He's gone, Mairead," Gareth said.

"Gone? Where?"

"We don't know," Letha said. "I went to check on Trypp this morning, and the eunuch's things were packed and his hut nearly empty. He left instructions on how to care for Trypp, but he left no other word of his plans."

Mairead fought back the twisting of her stomach. She swallowed bile. "Then . . . we wait, I suppose," she said. *But for Connor or slavers or tribesmen? Who can say?*

CHAPTER TWENTY-NINE

Evil does not always announce itself.
Sometimes it comes quietly, on catpaws, with elegance and quiet authority.
— Journal of Culain Mac Niall

Emrys walked forward in the prince's throne room behind Alasdair Mac Mahon, stopping mere inches behind the slaver. "One city, delivered as promised," he said to Mac Mahon.

Mac Mahon seated himself on Henry's vacated throne. "And all for the price of a dozen men lost to the mountain when I have three thousand here, inside the city and ranged across my empire."

"You will reward the girl who made it possible, as promised."

Mac Mahon waved a hand. "Of course, as she wishes, whatever she wishes."

"She wishes to be an empress."

"You say she is pretty?" Mac Mahon's smile would have chilled Emrys' soul, if he still had one. "Then perhaps it's time for me to settle down and beget some heirs, yes?"

Emrys forced a smile. "I have met with the reconnaissance from the mountain. They returned with interesting news."

"Yes?"

"There are men in the mountains willing to sell their metals and gems. There is also a strong force of men willing to fight and defend the great mountain city. But I may be able to convince some of them to betray the city, and if it falls, the mountain will be ours."

"Our agreement remains—I receive the metals and stones I was promised, yes?"

"Of course." *What are metals and stones to a damned soul?*

Mac Mahon grinned. "There aren't many strongholds left now—Leiden, and a few ranches and villages—and then all of Culidar north of the Wilds will be in my control."

"Leiden will not be easy, my lord. When we came north, we assaulted her walls for several days and then moved on. The graymen are not easily defeated."

"I want Leiden."

His greed will destroy him. A little shudder of pleasure passed through Emrys at that thought. "Where is Henry?"

"In the prison."

"Have him brought here."

Mac Mahon pointed at a guard, who scurried away to do as he asked. The slaver turned back to Emrys. "What now?"

"I will take a larger force of men into the mountains and return later this spring with northern treasure."

"You need more men?" Mac Mahon frowned. "When I have only just taken this city? That seems imprudent."

Emrys folded his arms. "I need more men to defeat those on the mountain."

Mac Mahon leaned forward. "I have more than I had before, precious metals or no, and I have the strongest force on the northern plains. We need time to capture Leiden and build up our force, and then we can attack the mountain." He leaned back and folded his hands. "I propose that you bring me Leiden, and then you can have the men you want."

Emrys frowned. *The man becomes too strong. Time to show him what he is dealing with.* "Do you believe that I can't have another man sitting on that seat in a moment? Do you think I didn't have something to do with Henry's position?" He stepped closer to Mac Mahon, and the guards twitched. "These mountain men must be defeated, or you will hold your throne here for a season, at best."

Mac Mahon didn't blink or twitch. "Bring me Leiden," he said in a low, tense voice. "When Leiden is mine, I will give you the men you want."

The door opened behind Emrys, and two guards brought in a beaten and disheveled Henry. The former prince was stripped to the waist and bound, and his blond hair and beard were matted with blood and dirt from the battle and his nights in a cell. "Where's my sister?"

"Ask my friend," Mac Mahon said, gesturing.

Henry turned to Emrys. "You—how do you look so much like Connor?"

"Your sister discovered something more binding than sibling love, Henry," he said. "She preferred a title and crown and riches to protecting your throne."

The man flinched. "Elizabeth betrayed ...? I was a fool—I should have—"

Emrys stepped toward him. He put a bare hand on Henry's shoulder. "No time for regrets."

Henry started to sputter and wheeze, and then the pain of Emrys' touch drove him to his knees. Emrys drew his soul in slowly, patiently, savoring the meal and drawing strength from every transgression. Henry paled. He slumped and fell, twitching, to the floor. When the prince lay dead, Emrys turned back to Mac Mahon with a satisfied smile. "This is what awaits you," Emrys said, pointing. "Serve me, obey me, and this throne remains yours as long as you live. Defy me, and you will lie twitching on the ground while I feed on your every transgression. And you have many of them, Alasdair. It will take a very long time for me to finish you. Days, perhaps."

Mac Mahon closed his mouth and swallowed hard. "What would you have me do now?"

"Secure the city and set up guards, and then every man you can spare is to come with me to the mountains. Including all of the Nar Sidhe warriors we brought north."

"Madness," Mac Mahon whispered. "Very well. Take what you will."

Emrys slipped between the elements.

The tribesman was waiting for him at the appointed place. He jumped and drew his sword when Emrys appeared. "You bring news," Emrys said.

The man relaxed and lowered his sword. "You said to tell you if the outland raven bedded the girl. He has. They have wed."

Emrys could barely control the rage that welled up in his breast. *Enough to just have an emotion,* he thought. He tried to let his anger out slowly, subtly, so that the tribesman would not notice. "Where is he now? The raven?"

The tribesman shrugged. "He left. A spirit took him. I don't know where he is."

"Can you get close to her?"

"I can."

"Then kill her."

The man paled. "Kill her? She's just a girl—nothing, even with all these words and prophecies—she's—"

"She will be the death of your tribe if you do not kill her first."

The tribesman let out a long breath. "Very well."

Emrys crossed his arms. "The raven—you say a spirit took him?"

"It was like nothing I'd ever seen. He became the Morrag. He attacked several men, cut the arm off of one, tried to kill the girl ...." He shuddered. "He said he would cleanse the earth."

Emrys was tempted to shudder as well. He grimaced. "If you see him," he said. "You must kill him."

"We tried," the tribesman said. "We tried—several of us—we attacked. We barely got out with our lives. Even the Tal'Amuni—"

Emrys put a hand on his arm, and the man's voice caught as a fragment of pain stole a tiny piece of his soul. "Tal'Amuni?"

"Y-y-yes. A eunuch, they say. Even he could not stop the raven."

"Where is this Tal'Amuni now?"

The man shrugged. "He disappeared as well. No one saw him go."

Emrys turned away from the tribesman and crossed his arms. *The Tal'Amuni are in on this? If one of their half-men is here, they have more at stake than just a slaving empire. But what are they seeking?* "The Tal'Amuni lives," he said. "Spread the word. I want him alive."

"Yes, sire," the man said. Voices in the distance called his name, and the man stepped closer to Emrys. "I must go. Is there anything else?"

Emrys shook his head, and the man set a brisk walk toward the distant voices. Emrys remained, staring out in the direction of the plains, Isfyrin to the west, Tal'Amun to the east. *And I in the middle, wondering again what my Enemy is planning.* He slipped into the elements and returned to Galbragh to gather soldiers.

CHAPTER THIRTY

*Cuhail's warriors met Namha's demons with
the crash of a thousand seas and the breaking of a hundred worlds.
— Tribal poetry*

The inn was a welcome relief to Minerva after the bitterly cold journey from the wisdomkeeper's island. She winced as her nose thawed in the warmth of the common room. *The only part of me that's still warm is my palm,* she thought. As if on cue, the brand pulsed again.

Alfrig closed the door and stood next to her, shifting her weight back and forth between her feet in an attempt to warm herself. "More crowded than I expected."

Men huddled around most of the tables, all of them brooding over ale or oiska, speaking in hushed, urgent tones and casting dark glances toward their fellow men and the door. "I don't like this," Minerva mumbled to Alfrig. "There is darkness here."

Alfrig grunted, but said nothing more. She crossed the room to the inn-keeper, and Minerva followed. "A room and a meal," she said, tossing several coins onto the counter. He took the coins and gave her a key. "I am looking for someone—a tribesman with a marked face. Has he been here?"

"Aye. Staying in the room next to the one I just gave you, in fact. He's not here now—went out an hour ago or so."

Minerva's stomach twisted as Hrogarth's last words came to mind. *I will be merciful now, but if you ever return, Esma, you will die. I will not abide an oathbreaker in my village.*

The door opened, and Alfrig and Minerva both turned to see three people enter the inn. Two of them—a tribal woman and a tall, dark warrior—were unfamiliar to Minerva, but the third was unmistakable, even covered in furs. *I would know the eyes anywhere,* Minerva thought.

Alfrig took three steps toward him and stopped, crossed her arms, un-crossed them, and waited. Hrogarth caught her gaze and nearly leapt across tables to meet her, but then stopped just short of touching her. His hands twitched at his sides. The woman with him caught her breath on a sharp intake and started toward them, but Hrogarth motioned her back. "No, Grytha," he said. "This is between me and my wife." He lowered the furs on his head.

Alfrig gasped. "Your braids—why—"

"I am no longer fit to lead the nine," he said. His voice cracked. "Why did you lie to me? Why did you leave without telling me where you were going? Our daughter was not with child."

Alfrig flinched, but her voice held strong. "How did you find me? How—"

"The ravenmark drew me east. I came north to find you. To say goodbye." He pointed at Minerva. "You travel with her."

"She needed my help," Alfrig said. "I am still her traitha."

Hrogarth grunted. He looked at Minerva. "I told you I would not show mercy."

Minerva swallowed hard. "That is true, traitha."

"My wife still cares for you or she would not have lied to me."

"That is also true."

Hrogarth broke his gaze and turned back to Alfrig. He lifted one hand and removed his glove, reaching for Alfrig's face in one smooth motion. A tear rolled down Alfrig's cheek, and Hrogarth wiped it away with his thumb. He offered his wife a strained smile. "All is forgiven," he whispered.

A tiny cry escaped Alfrig's mouth, and she buried her face in her husband's chest and wrapped her arms tight around him. He enfolded her and buried his face near her neck. Minerva turned away. *They do not need us here. This is their moment.* At the same time, the ache returned, and she thought of her husband and those moments when the world disappeared but for the two of them, and she wished she could have such a love again. *But I think such things are past for me. I think my calling is elsewhere. Husbands and children are for other women, not for me. My chance died with him.*

A hand on her shoulder broke her from her reverie, and she turned to the tribal woman and Taurin who had entered the tavern with Hrogarth. "You are Esma?" the woman said.

"I am. Are you a guardian?"

"I am Grytha, guardian for the hound tribe. This is a Taurin who travels with us. Logan." The tall warrior removed his scarves and furs, but not his gloves. He nodded by way of greeting.

"Why are you here?" Minerva asked. "Why has Hrogarth left the nine?"

Grytha flinched, glanced at Hrogarth and Alfrig, and took a step closer to Minerva as she lowered her voice. "Hrogarth's second now leads the hound tribe, and the traithas will gather for the earth to choose his successor as traitha over the nine."

Hrogarth has left the nine? It was almost impossible for Minerva to imagine—the nine tribes of Taura led by anyone other than Hrogarth. *Can the tribes remain the tribes without Hrogarth over them?* "What happened?"

Grytha bit her lip. "Hrogarth is being called east. By the Morrag."

Minerva's stomach flipped, and her breath caught in her throat. She clenched her fist, and her palm burned in protest. *She's calling them. She's calling her warriors. No, Alshada—no! Not yet! It's not time—it can't be time for this!* She wanted to say all of these things aloud, to share the terror, fear, grief, anger with her guardian sister, but all she could eke out was a whispered, "the Morrag ...."

It was Logan's turn to flinch. He cleared his throat and shuffled his feet, and Grytha put one steadying hand on his arm. "These are tribal things," Grytha said, "and not meant for Taurin ears." She gestured around the common room. "Let us speak privately, with the trai—with Hrogarth and Alfrig."

Grytha turned to Alfrig and Hrogarth. They broke away from each other and followed Grytha. The guardian led them to a room in the back of the tavern and closed the door behind Logan.

Hrogarth and Alfrig sat next to each other on the small cot at one edge of the room, their hands linked tightly with interwoven fingers. Logan leaned next to the door, his posture the tense relaxation of a warrior on duty. Grytha stood in the center of the room. She gestured to Alfrig. "You've succeeded, traitha. You have found her."

"Only to say goodbye."

Alfrig did not seem surprised by his statement. "I knew this would come," she said, her voice unwavering. "I knew he would leave. This is not unexpected. The mark told me he was in trouble, that he sought me. It did not tell me why. Now I understand. He must go east, to the raven—to the one who calls her own to her side."

Hrogarth reached for Alfrig's hand and opened it to reveal her wisdommark. He traced the whorl. "It is, in some fashion, a relief. I regret only that I will not die near you and my family." He sighed and stood. "The Morrag grows stronger daily, and her First Raven awaits his warriors where fire and ice meet."

Minerva startled. *Where ice meets fire? But we've sent the heir to Albard—where ice and fire meet. Is this the same place? Did we put her in the midst of ravens?* She took a step toward Hrogarth. "Traitha—"

He turned to her. "You lost the right to call me that, oathbreaker."

Minerva stepped back. "Forgive me. It was habit, nothing more."

"What is it you wish to say?"

She considered all of the ears in the room—the king's man, the guardians, the ravenmarked warrior—and those who may be listening elsewhere, and she reconsidered. *The whole reason this began was because of the heir. We were to keep her safe. To speak of her now would be ill-considered. Do not further damage what you have been asked to protect.* "It's nothing. Forgive me for troubling you."

"I am curious, husband—why do you travel with a Taurin?" Alfrig asked.

"This man was the pretender king's guard. He traveled with us in hopes of finding his king."

"And have you found him?"

Hrogarth nodded. "The pretender king is here. He's inside the Dylan estate."

Alfrig turned to Logan. "Then you can return to your king and let Hrogarth go on? Grytha and I can return to the tribe alone."

Minerva watched Logan, Hrogarth, and Grytha exchange looks in the heavy silence that followed Alfrig's words. "He's in trouble," she said. "Your king. It's the Forbidden, isn't it?"

Logan turned to her. "How do you know?"

"I sensed it when we entered the city today," she said. "I sensed the same thing in Kiern, before your king and his duke and the wolf tribe battled each other. I was there. I saw him kill her the first time. I told him she would not give him quarter. She's found him, hasn't she?"

Logan nodded. "And we have spent the last two days trying to figure out how to get into the estate and free him of her grasp without loosing her on Taura."

"Hrogarth can defeat her," Alfrig said. "Hrogarth—"

"Alfrig," Hrogarth warned.

Alfrig straightened and turned to her husband. "They know what you are. You have no need to hide the mark from these people."

"That's not it," Logan said. "We fear that she is too strong for Hrogarth—that she will draw too many of the transgressions he bears into herself. If that happens, we have no other ravenmarked warriors to help defeat her, and she will be loosed on Taura."

"If I confront her—if she and I come to blows—and I fail, she will be unleashed on the world," Hrogarth said. "She will make rivers run with the blood of the innocent. She will burn the great forest to the ground, and she will level cities. She will open the chasm of Namha and join him in his reign of terror in this world. Together they will rule over this world and the next."

Minerva took a deep breath and spoke. "And if you do not fail? If you vanquish her?"

"I do not understand."

"All we can do is kill the host body she uses," she said. "We weaken her, but she will find another body and remain on Taura. You are the only one among us who can vanquish her for good. You at least have a better chance than we do. Why would you not try?"

Grytha stepped to Minerva's side—a symbolic gesture if nothing more. "Traitha, my sister speaks truth. You may win. You may yet do a great service to the tribes and to Taura."

Hrogarth shook his head. "She is still too strong for me. The risk—I am weak now. The madness grows stronger each day. I do not have the focus, concentration .... If the Morrag speaks at an inopportune time, I will be cast down, and the creature will use my transgressions to strengthen herself. And if she draws the transgressions borne by a raven into her spirit, she will become too powerful for any man or raven to gainsay. She will rule all."

"Husband," Alfrig said. He turned to her. "If you win, if you vanquish her, you rid the earth of her poison. The risk is worth it."

"You do not know—you can't know the weight I bear. The burden of the transgressions. And she can take them—all of them—the ones I bear for myself and the ones I bear for others."

"How can you bear another man's transgressions?" Minerva asked.

"I don't know," Hrogarth said. "But I do. I feel them—the weight of them—around me all the time. I am a conduit, a channel. And she can use me to take them into herself—to strengthen herself. I would spare you this pain, Alfrig. I would spare you this—this watching me become lost to the madness and agony of the Morrag."

She smiled. "Oh, my dearest warrior, I can bear the pain. I cannot bear thinking that if we could stop her—if you could stop her—that you would not even try for worry over me."

"If I lose—"

"Then you lose. The tribes have borne greater agonies than a loose demon. We will live."

Minerva looked at Logan. "Have you come up with any other plan that doesn't involve Hrogarth defeating the Forbidden?"

Logan shook his head. "Nothing that has a chance of working."

"So this is the best plan we have—Hrogarth confronting the Forbidden and breaking her spell over Braedan." Minerva looked at Hrogarth. "Who is to say, traitha, but that perhaps the One Hand created you and brought you to this place for just this purpose?"

"I told you not to call me that," he said, but his voice lacked conviction.

Minerva failed to suppress her smile. "Forgive me. Old habits."

Hrogarth bowed his head. When he lifted his face once more, it bore a resolve Minerva had never seen. "Very well. I will seek this woman, and I will help you free your king." He drew a knife and offered it to the guardians. "But you must promise me, both of you—you must swear to me one thing."

"Anything, traitha," Grytha said.

"If it comes to it—if you see that I am dying, that she will win, that she is using me to draw the transgressions of the world into herself—you must kill me."

The blade sat in his hands, the hilt offered to the first one who would take it. Grytha turned away.

Minerva took the hilt. "I promise," she said. "For the tribes and for Taura, I will not allow the demon to use you in this way."

CHAPTER THIRTY-ONE

The cries of the widow and orphan rise over consuming fires.
Through smoke and ashes, I weep over my city.
— Prophecy in the Syrafi Keep

Braedan stared at the blonde girl across the chess board, waiting. *Waiting.* The girl studied the board, her slender fingers hovering over a piece. *Waiting. That's all I do—wait.*

He'd never been particularly good at chess, but then, neither was she. Together, they managed to have some fairly interesting games. *An even match is better than being trounced,* he thought. *But still, I wait.*

The days went by, slow and studious, the way Mairead played chess. His men remained trapped by winter weather inside Duke Dylan's estate, and Duke Dylan remained imprisoned due to his refusal to swear fealty to Braedan. The Dylan estate was closed tight and guarded by Taurin soldiers, and Dylan's men were confined to their barracks and guarded around the clock.

The Taurins showed signs of strain. The effort of keeping Dylan's men and his household subdued required that they follow a watch schedule that didn't allow for long stretches of sleep. On top of the lack of sleep, the estate was now required to feed twice as many men on the same amount of food for an indefinite length of time. No one was allowed in or out of the gates, and the townsfolk were holed up in their own homes, studiously looking the other way while their duke and their king held a stand-off of wills.

This would be easier if Malcolm were here, Braedan thought. But Malcolm had betrayed him. Cerys said so. *Cerys said so. She had proof.* He touched the hilt of the sacred blade at his side. *I can't trust any of them—any of my guards. There's no one to trust. Except her.*

"Trouble, your majesty?"

He frowned. "Did you move?"

"Not yet." She picked up a piece and set it down a few squares away. "I believe you are defeated, your majesty."

He studied the board. "You're more devious than I would expect for a saya."

Her pixie-like face might have been carved in marble. "I was trained to be a queen, yes? Not a saya."

"Did you take the vows?"

The corner of her mouth tilted. "I could not be a queen if I had taken the vows, could I? I could not wed if I were sworn to chastity."

She never answers my questions directly. He poured wine and leaned back in his seat. She frowned. "You disapprove."

"You know my opinion already."

He did. She said he drank too much. She said he swore too much and slept too late and tried to control things that did not concern him, like the kirok. And while she never said it, he also knew she disapproved of his closeness to Cerys. She watched her words carefully around the healer, but Braedan never had the sense that she feared Cerys. She simply seemed to be playing a game of wills of her own. *A game I only see the surface of.*

For her part, Cerys had made no secret of her opinion about Mairead. She wanted Mairead and the rest of the sayas put to death immediately. "Treason," she whispered to him with increasing regularity. "They defy you, majesty, as did Duke Dylan." She would dress his wound every night, using the moment as a chance to tease him and tempt him into bed with her, and every night it grew more and more difficult to refuse her.

But when I fall asleep drunk, she has no chance of cajoling me into bed. He drank again, staring at Mairead over the rim of his goblet. "You are a very pretty girl, my lady," he said, not for the first time.

"You are kind, your majesty."

"How old are you, anyway?"

"Twenty, your majesty."

Twenty. Old enough for a marriage. As old as I expected her to be. But still, something nagged at him. The dark man had told him the Taurin heir was no longer on the island—that she'd managed to escape Braedan's hand early in his reign. *But he lied to me about other things. What if he lied about that? What if this is the heir, and what if I could secure my throne by wedding her?* But no—Igraine waited in the capitol—Igraine, with her sharp tongue and sharper wit and curves and red hair.

He pushed back from the table and stood. "You have my leave to return to your sisters."

Mairead stood and folded her hands before her. "If I may be bold for a moment, your majesty?"

"You may."

"You seek guidance. I see it on your face. You are confused about who to believe, how to act, and what your next move should be."

He scoffed. "So you would have me pray? You believe Alshada might help me reason out my difficulties?"

Her smile was a thin one. "Not Alshada, perhaps, but one of his agents?"

"One of the sayas."

"Perhaps."

"And you truly don't see the conflict of interests there, my lady? You're asking me to take advice from women I sent into exile. How can I trust what they might say any more than I trust what Cerys says? What Dylan says?" He stepped around the table. "The crown is both a shield and a target, and while I can trust no one, I must listen to everyone."

"Then listen to us as well, your majesty." A faint hint of desperation crept into her voice. She seemed to hear it, and some of her finely tuned composure faltered as red rose in her pale cheeks. "Forgive me, sire. I spoke out of turn."

He downed the rest of his wine and set his goblet down. The warm rush of the deep Esparan red spread down his hands and feet, and he poured more from the carafe on the table. He thought again what a lovely creature this little saya was. Her pale, straight hair hung unbound to frame her face with a lovely golden glow, and he twined a lock of it around one finger. "Everyone thinks my tastes run to redheads, but the truth is, I appreciate all beautiful women."

The red glow in her cheeks deepened. "Sire, I—"

"I am still in need of a wife."

She frowned. "I thought—your princess, sire. I ...." She cleared her throat and stepped back. Her legs bumped the chair, and she stumbled slightly. He caught her elbow. She put her hands on his arms to steady herself.

Braedan took advantage of the opportunity and pulled her closer, hands tightening on her upper arms. "You're playing a game that you are not equipped to play. You claim you are the long-lost heir to the throne. What possible reason could you have for claiming that? You have to know I will either kill you or woo you. If I wanted to kill you, you'd be dead by now. That leaves wooing you."

"Your majesty, I would not want to usurp Princess Igraine's place." Panic edged her voice.

"Do you know—my agreement with her was never formalized. And with the death of the Eiryan ambassador, there's no reason to think her father will agree to join our houses." He paused, giving her just a moment to think about the implications of what he said. "You could secure your position, my lady. It would be easy to do."

She took a deep breath and swallowed hard. A calm demeanor came over her, and she smiled.

Smiled.

"I am, of course, at your mercy," she said, her voice unwavering. "But your majesty would do well to think of what may happen should he deflower a noblewoman when he is promised to another." She lowered her voice. "Rest assured that I would not be quiet, your majesty."

He tightened his hands until she flinched, but to her credit, she didn't cry out. "A great risk."

"You already pointed out that you hold my life in your hands. Rape me if you must—take my virginity, my innocence. Try to secure your throne with my blood. Force me into a marriage of convenience." She paused. There was no tremor of fear, no hesitation in her voice when she spoke again. "But I assure you, *my lord,* I will not go quietly to any of those things."

He reflected again, as he had for the two weeks he'd known this girl, how hard it was to ruffle her for any length of time. He pushed her away and picked up his goblet again. "Go."

She didn't hesitate this time. She gathered her robes around her and left the room.

Braedan drained the goblet in one long swallow. *Bested by a silly girl,* he thought, and threw the goblet at the wall. His head throbbed. It always throbbed, but the throbbing was worse when he was sober. And when Mairead was gone. Whatever else she was, her presence soothed him. He sank back into a chair and buried his face in his hands. The wind howled outside, and all Braedan could hear were the whispers and taunts of a thousand spirits. He put his hands over his ears in a futile attempt to shut them out, but it did no good. The voices were inside his head, not outside. *The drink won't hide them. The girl can't hide them, not as she did. Edgar was right.*

The blade in his belt warmed, and he put a hand on it. In the days since he'd taken Dylan prisoner, the dreams that began at Duke Fingall's estate had only grown worse, and they encroached on his waking hours as well. At night he slept in short, restless bursts, awakened frequently by dreams of destruction and the cackle of a woman who promised vengeance and death. But when he woke, the echoes never entirely receded, and he would relive his transgressions in scenes that played in his head as clearly as the first moments he committed them.

Cerys brought on more madness whenever she was around. He would swear that she whispered suggestions to him. "Kill the duke," he heard her say as she tended a fire. "You do not need his support. Claim these lands for the crown. Gather men to your side and fight your way back to Torlach. With me beside you, you would not fail."

It was that last that prompted him to cross the room in three strides and yank her away from the fire. He spun her around to face him. "What did you say? What—"

But she blinked in innocence and shrugged. "I said nothing, majesty. Perhaps your shoulder—"

"My shoulder is fine." He pushed her away and slumped on his bed. "Go."

She brought him a goblet of wine, and he took it. Her fingers stroked his neck down to the shoulder. He wore only a loose undershirt, and she took advantage of it. "You could have infection," she murmured. "Sometimes such things happen even once the wound is thought healed. Let me look."

She removed his shirt and ran her fingers over the scar on his shoulder. Before long, her lips were against his neck, and once again, her voice was in his head. *With me by your side ....*

He pushed her away and stood. "Go."

There was a long pause, and for a moment, he feared her. But her eyes darted to the blade at his belt, and she finally curtsied. "As my lord commands."

The door closed, and Braedan collapsed on his bed. His dreams that night were full of Cerys' voice.

A knock jolted him out of memories of his past two weeks. "Your supper, my lord," called the guard.

He scrubbed his face with his hands and stood. "Come."

Everything happened so quickly that even once he had time to think it through, he couldn't separate the events into specific actions. There were men in the room in a rapid rush of boot steps, and without warning, his hands were held behind him and his mouth was gagged. One of the men shut the door and turned to him. He fought and pushed, struggling against the arms that held him tight on either side, trying to scream through the cloth, when the man who approached removed his helmet. "Majesty," Logan whispered. "It's me."

Braedan stopped struggling. The hands on his arms loosened.

Logan stepped closer. "I've been searching for weeks. If I lower your gag, will you speak with me without calling for help?"

Braedan nodded, and Logan pushed the gag down. "What are you doing here?" Braedan asked, not quite at a whisper. Logan motioned for quiet. "What's wrong? Where's Igraine?"

Logan flinched. "She is in Torlach." He cleared his throat. "Much has happened, your majesty. Your throne is in danger, your princess is in danger, and you are tarrying here, holding a Taurin duke hostage on his own estate."

"Igraine is in danger?"

Logan's jaw tightened. "She is. Your uncle will likely either send her home or imprison her."

Braedan took a deep breath. The blade warmed his skin through his tunic. *I dreamed of her death,* he thought. *I dreamed of her body abused and tortured and violated and hanging on the city gates, and now such a fate looms. How many other things that I have dreamed or envisioned will come true? And Cerys—what does she know of things to come? What has she done to me?* "Let me go," he said quietly.

The men holding him hesitated. "I have to be sure," Logan said.

"I will not attempt escape, I swear it," Braedan said. The hands on his arms loosened, and he pulled away from them to stand on his own. He stepped closer to Logan. "How did you find me?"

"I came with a tribesman and one of his earth guardians. Edgar said you came north, so I followed." He paused. "It was a risk, I grant you that."

Braedan put a hand on the hilt of the sacred blade. "Is the tribesman looking for this?"

"Not exactly. He was looking for his wife. But he gave you that blade, I believe."

"Hrogarth."

"Yes," Logan said. "Hrogarth."

Braedan let out a long sigh of relief. "Then if he's here, perhaps he can free me of this thing."

"He's not going to help you with anything until he knows what side you are on," said another voice.

Braedan turned to the man at his right.

Malcolm lowered his cowl. "You sent me away on nothing more than the word of a whore who whispers what you want to hear. I need to know, sire—

these people, the others, this country—we all need to know who you serve."

"I serve Taura," Braedan said.

"You did, once," Malcolm said. "Now you serve something else." He jutted his chin toward the door. "If she came through that door right now, what would you do? Would you join us, return to the throne, and serve Taura as you did before? Or would you fall at her feet and obey her?"

Braedan hesitated. *What would I do? I don't know.* "She said you betrayed me."

"She told you I went to Dylan. She told you I was Dylan's man, that I was planning to help him escape and return to Taura for help, and that I wanted to raise a force of men against you. And you believed her."

"I did," Braedan said.

Malcolm took a step toward the king. "I was your faithful servant for most of your years of exile. I helped you take Torlach and secure your throne. I saved your life at Salmon Springs. And you would treat me as a boot boy—as one not even worthy of walking behind you."

Braedan's stomach turned, and his chest constricted, but he forced the words out. "I had reason—"

"You had the word of a whore."

"You sound like a jilted lover."

Malcolm's mouth formed a grim line. "I had my taste of her, it's true. But only once. I couldn't ...." He turned away. "She made me see things."

Logan cleared his throat. "Majesty, we need to know—are you on the side of Taura, or are you on the side of your woman?"

Braedan knew he didn't mean Igraine. He touched the hilt of the sacred blade. "I am on the side of Taura."

"Then it's time you prove it," Logan said.

Braedan tensed. "You would speak so to your king?"

"When I once again serve a king, I will give him the respect he is due."

"You can't—"

Logan crossed the space between them and raised one fist. Braedan didn't have any time to react before the guard's gloved hand connected with his jaw. White sparks of pain shattered his vision, and he fell backward onto the cold stone floor, jarring his wounded shoulder in the process. He lay still for a moment, waiting for his vision to clear. Blood filled his mouth. He barely had time to spit before Logan wrapped one hand in his tunic and hauled him to his feet. "You listen to me, sire," he whispered. "Taura is waiting. She stands on a precipice. And every moment that you tarry here in a battle of wills with an obscure duke, listening to the whispers of a demon, you endanger the woman you claim to love the most—your own country."

"I don't—"

"*You will listen,*" Logan shouted. He shoved Braedan backward into Malcolm's hands. Malcolm held him by the elbows as Logan took another step forward, his mouth set in a fierce line and his forehead creased in anger. "The time for us to listen to you is gone. The time for you to search for obscure artifacts and lost heirs and whatever else you think will secure your throne is done. It is time for you to stop being a petulant child. It is time for you to stop playing at this throne business and start being a gods-forsaken *king.*"

Silence hung heavy in the room as the words sank into Braedan's consciousness. He couldn't think of what to say, how to respond. The entire left side of his face throbbed and stung, and he still tasted blood. He considered spitting, but swallowed the blood instead. "What do I need to do?"

Logan's face relaxed—not a lot, but enough for Braedan to see that he had responded in a way that would not earn him another punch. "You need to get out of this place. You need to apologize to Dylan, and you need to ride south and raise an army as you go. You may yet be able to save Torlach, Igraine, and your position if you go now." He crossed his arms. "The problem is that Cerys isn't going to let us leave without a fight. I need to know that you are willing to fight her."

"I don't understand."

Logan's jaw tightened again. "Cerys is not human. Her body is human, but her spirit is—"

Braedan's blood ran cold as he realized the truth, and he finished Logan's sentence. "—Is not. She's one of the Forbidden, isn't she? She's the woman I fought outside of Kiern—the one I killed with this blade." He touched the warm hilt again as he remembered what the guardians and Edgar had told him over and over. *She will not give me quarter. If I try to escape, if I refuse her, she will kill me, and she will kill me in the most painful of ways. The only question is, why has she not yet done so?* And then he realized—*the blade.* "This blade has been protecting me. That's why she hates it. That's why I'm not lost to her. The nightmares aren't threats—they're warnings of what will happen if I follow her."

"She will either use you for her own ends, or she will kill you," Logan said. "There is no other choice for her. And I do not hold out much hope of getting you out of this estate without a fight."

"I killed her once by accident—I don't know if I can do it again."

"You aren't the one who is supposed to kill her," Logan said. "That's for someone else." He took a deep breath. "Malcolm, gather the king's men, but do it discreetly. Start with those you trust most. And let Dylan and his men out of prison." Malcolm saluted and left the room.

"What is your plan?" Braedan asked. "Cerys will notice if our men suddenly start moving about like they're intent on mayhem."

"I'm hoping she does notice. I want her to come to get you, her prize, so that she can meet him." He pointed to the second man—the one who had not spoken since they entered the room.

Braedan turned, and the man removed his helmet to reveal a shaved head and the swirling blue lines Braedan had only seen once before, what seemed an age ago, in Torlach. "Traitha," he whispered.

Hrogarth inclined his head. There was a distinct humility and resignation about him that Braedan had not seen in their first encounter. "I see that the blade has kept you whole."

Braedan touched it, and it warmed under his palm. "Is that why you gave it to me? For protection?"

Hrogarth shrugged. "I had a vision. I was told to give it to you. I didn't know why. Apparently the earth had plans for you. She wanted you to have that."

Braedan grimaced. "It has not come without a price."

"Valor never does."

"Valor?"

"The king I met in Torlach was a boy—a child with nothing to recommend him except the fortune of an old Taurin surname. He needed some blooding. He needed to lose some blood and take some blood. He needed to understand that a chieftain—a true chieftain, a true protector—cannot hold that position without a warrior's heart. He had the position. He needed the heart." He put one hand on Braedan's injured shoulder. "You have bled on this ground. You have taken blood with a piece of Taura—that blade. You are bound to this land now as truly as I have ever been. It is your choice. Will you defend this land to your dying breath, or will you betray her to the demon who would destroy her?"

Braedan thought of the dreams and visions he had tolerated for so many weeks. He thought of Cerys' voice in his head—her whispers, her suggestions. He remembered the feel of her smooth, insistent hands on his shoulder, the way her body tempted him. He considered Mairead—the curious tilt of her head, the disapproving grim line of her mouth, the non-committal stare she would give when he rambled about the struggles of a king. But more than anything, he thought of Igraine. *I have been such a fool. I have nearly lost her—lost the only woman who has given me purpose, lost the kingdom I claim to love—for a fight over fealty and the temptation of a whore. I have been a fool. I have been a king of fools.* "I will defend this land," he said. "I will defend her to my dying breath."

"Not just your throne?" Hrogarth asked. "Not just your position? Will you defend your land even if it means you lose your princess, your throne, or your life?"

"Yes. To my last breath."

"Then I will defend you. I will engage the demon, and I will try to rid Taura of her poison."

"And if you don't?"

Hrogarth hesitated. "If I don't, you will have a very long fight ahead of you." He put the helmet back on his head.

Logan opened the wardrobe. Wordlessly, he began pulling out the king's battle dress. Braedan stood quietly as Logan dressed him as a squire would while Hrogarth watched. Logan said nothing, concentrating only on the layers of clothing and armor. "What happened in Torlach?" Braedan asked.

Logan hesitated. "There was an attack."

"On Igraine?"

His eyes remained fixed on the straps of Braedan's leather body armor. "And the sayas. The attackers were assassins. Igraine was shot—poisoned—but she survived. That night, there was another attack. They killed many of the sayas and kirons."

Braedan's blood ran cold. He put a hand on Logan's arm. The guard straightened to his full height. "Is Igraine all right?"

"She was when I left." He frowned and shot a glance at Hrogarth. "Majesty, I—" He sighed. "They said I did it. They arrested me. I confessed, but you must believe, I did not do it."

"But a confession means—"

"She helped me escape," Logan said. "She and Aiden and Cormac Rowan. Lord Rowan gave me a letter to give you. Hrogarth has it."

"Why does Hrogarth have it?"

The chieftain stepped forward and handed the letter to Braedan. "Your guard has sought sanctuary with the tribes these many weeks and months. I held this letter for him."

Braedan read the letter, thoughts of armor forgotten. *Logan and Igraine? It can't be true. They wouldn't ....* He held the letter out to Logan. "You know what this says?"

"I do."

"Is it true?"

Hrogarth cleared his throat. "I will wait outside."

When the door shut, Logan spoke quietly. "Igraine and I were friends, nothing more," he said. "It was not appropriate. I regret it. She was never anything more than a proper lady around me. But there was something ...."

"Yes?"

He sighed. "She helped me help sayas escape. I didn't agree with your decision to keep them prisoner. I was helping them escape slowly, one at a time. Igraine aided me."

"And that was all?"

Logan snorted a laugh. "All? Yes, all she did was help me disobey your orders, defy your commands, and betray you. You have every right to arrest me and execute me, my lord. I ask only that you wait until you are back in Torlach. I will not put up a fight, I swear it. I will go quietly to the chopping block as soon as you are back on your throne."

Braedan looked down at the letter again. "Who else knows of Cormac's accusations?"

"I don't know."

"Have you mentioned this to Malcolm? The others?"

Logan shook his head.

Braedan tore the letter into three large pieces, walked to the hearth, and tossed it into the fire.

Logan's mouth tightened. "You may need that. You may have needed it as proof against Cormac."

"Proof of what? That he allowed you to escape? Why would that bother me? I need you back at my side." He crossed his arms. "I only need to know one thing: do you love Igraine?"

"It does not matter. She adores you. She wants nothing more than to have you back."

"Do you love her?"

"I swear to you that I will never pursue her."

"Do you love her?"

Logan turned his head away. "Majesty, do not make me lie to you."

Braedan put a hand on Logan's shoulder. "You have been my most trusted guard since you joined me in Culidar. You have acted against me only because you saw the folly of my actions when I didn't. I am proud to count you as my ally and friend." He held out his bracers. "Now, finish helping me with this armor."

Logan took the bracers and started to lace one around Braedan's forearm, but they were interrupted by the sound of shouting in the corridor. Braedan snatched up his sword belt and buckled it around his hips. He drew the sacred dagger; it warmed his palm.

Hrogarth threw open the door. "They are coming," he shouted. "Quickly, get him out."

Logan grabbed Braedan's arm and put him between Hrogarth and himself. "Who's coming?" Logan said as they started running.

Hrogarth ran toward the kitchens, away from the shouting. "The demon and her people. Get the king away from here—get him to Alfrig and Grytha."

Braedan ran. "Who?"

"The tribal women—those who can take you to safety," Logan said.

They rounded a corner, heading toward the outside walls, when a woman's scream echoed all around them. "Mairead," Braedan whispered. "It sounded like her."

"Who?" Logan asked.

"The rightful Taurin heir."

Logan stopped running and turned toward the sound. "Hrogarth, which one do you want—the king or the girl?"

"Stay with your king. I will seek the girl." He started to run toward the scream, but stopped.

Standing in the corridor, her hand around the neck of the young saya who claimed to be the rightful Taurin heir, was Cerys in all her demonic glory. Mairead gasped and wheezed under her hand, and Cerys turned to the men. "Hector," she said. "I wondered when you would return."

Braedan wanted to say something, but Logan pushed past him and approached Cerys. "Aldora," he said. He drew his sword. "Your time is done."

CHAPTER THIRTY-TWO

Bonded by blood, she unites the people under one banner.
— Lion tribe prophecy

Days passed in the raven village with no real progress toward returning to Isfyrin. Mairead stayed in her hut most of the time, the guards outside carefully controlling her movements and visitors. She was allowed to venture into the raven village, but only with men on either side of her. Gareth and Letha were allowed to visit her, but only as long as the guards remained right outside the door.

After a few days, she was allowed to visit Trypp. The warrior was in good spirits, despite discomfort. "It's an arm," he said. "I can still hold a shield, if needs be, and I can still wield a sword and hold my wife and son. Any day a warrior can return home to his family is a good day."

It stung. Mairead forced a smile. "I am glad to hear you say such."

"Traitha, I am sorry," he said. "I didn't mean—"

"My loss should not prevent you from celebrating your life." She reached for his good arm. "I am glad I did not lose you, Trypp."

"Connor's madness is not directed at you, Mairead, and it's not your fault, and it's nothing you could stop." He took her hand. "Gareth told me of your news."

She tried to smile. "We think it's a girl."

He grinned. "You and Wytha might have to discuss a betrothal between our families."

Mairead laughed. "It's a bit early to consider that." She leaned down and kissed Trypp's forehead before returning to her hut. His words haunted her. *All a warrior can ask is to return home to his wife and son. But Connor, can you come back? Do you even want to? And do I want you back?*

The days continued to grow warmer, which prompted Mairead to question how long the ravens could hold them in the village. She cornered Wyll one day. "The lions will wonder where I am," she said. "And even if they don't want me back, they will be looking for Gareth, Trypp, and Letha. You can't keep us captive here for long—not if you want to remain hidden and safe."

"How can we know you won't reveal our village? Especially since you clearly don't trust us any longer."

"I can't find my way back. We came in the snow and ice, and it was night when we arrived. Everything looked different. Blindfold us and take us back to Isfyrin. Leave us within sight of the city. No one will search for you—we'll make sure of it. You have my word."

Wyll frowned. "I have to obey orders," he mumbled.

Later, though, Mairead noted that he spoke in quiet, muted tones to Osgar and some of the other ravens. They occasionally darted furtive glances in her direction, but no one mentioned taking her back to Isfyrin.

That night, Wyll and Osgar visited her as she ate supper with Letha in her hut. Gareth was with them, standing next to Wyll with a grim expression on his face. "We have reached a decision," Wyll said. "We will take you back to Isfyrin."

Palpable relief passed through Mairead's body. "I thank you," she said. "You have my word, Wyll. The lions will not find out where you are."

He and Osgar exchanged a glance. "No," he said. "They will not. Because

Gareth has volunteered to stay behind until your husband returns to decide what to do with him."

Mairead and Letha both stood. "What?" Mairead said. "Gareth, you—"

"Mairead," he said. "It is done. Trypp has a wife and son, and he needs to be home with them. Letha is your midwife. I have no ties—I can stay."

"But what of Elsbet?"

He shrugged. "We are young. We can wait. Tell her I will be home as soon as I am able."

"This is madness," Mairead said.

Letha put a hand on her arm. "No, this makes sense. You may not like it, traitha, but this gives you a chance to return to Isfyrin, and gives the ravens some assurance of safety." She paused. "Certainly I would wish for more trust between the tribe and these men, but I understand why it isn't there. This allows time for that trust to grow."

"How do we encourage trust if they keep one of our men?" Mairead asked.

"They are releasing three of us, Mairead. Gareth is well and whole. He will be fine." She turned to Wyll. "If even a hair of his head is harmed when he returns, though, know that the entire wrath of the Catspaw clan and her allies will be upon you."

Wyll inclined his head. "It is understood, guardian."

Mairead waved a hand in resignation. "It is astounding to me that you would all swear fealty and obedience and then make these arrangements behind my back."

"We knew you would not agree," Gareth said. "Traitha, this was my idea. You need to be home. So does Trypp. It was either me or Letha, and you and Trypp need Letha."

Mairead folded her arms. "How will we communicate? How will I know if Connor returns, either for good or for ill?"

"They've agreed to let Grayfeather take messages," Gareth said. "He has been granted passage."

Mairead grunted. "You've thought of everything, I suppose."

"Most everything, I hope."

"When will we leave?" Letha asked Wyll.

"In the morning. I've spoken with Trypp. He will be ready."

The following morning, Trypp met Mairead and Letha at the stable where their horses had been for almost a month. His arm was still in a sling and bound against his chest, but he had color and health in his cheeks. *He's practically cheerful.* "You are looking well, Trypp," she said.

"The promise of home can do wonders for a man's spirits." He held out the reins of her horse.

"Gareth can't be so happy."

Trypp frowned. "It is true, traitha, and I wish he were coming home, but I cannot be sad about seeing my wife and child."

Mairead took a deep breath and gestured to his arm. "What of that?"

"Wytha is a warrior's wife. She will understand."

Gareth arrived with Osgar, Wyll, and several other ravens. "They will allow me to go with you as far as the point where we let you go on alone," he said. "I'll send Grayfeather along with you."

"I still don't like this. I don't trust these men."

"Have we been abused at all since we've been here?" he said. "Aside from not allowing us to leave, they have treated us with nothing but respect and hospitality." He paused. "These are good men, Mairead," he said in a low voice. "They just want to remain safe and serve you."

She took the reins of her horse. "Let's go."

Wyll blindfolded Gareth, Letha, Trypp, and Mairead at the edge of the raven village, and then each one was told to mount his or her horse. The ravens took their reins and instructed them to just hold onto the horse's saddle. "We will lead you," Wyll said.

If Mairead had had any idea of where the raven village was in relation to Isfyrin when they left, all possibility of finding it again was completely gone by the time the ravens at last stopped their horses. Mairead pulled off her blindfold. "Those are not the gates we left from."

Trypp frowned. "This is the northern gate—near the Lionjaw clan."

"Why would you bring us here?" Mairead asked.

Osgar stared at the gate in longing. "So that you know what it is to be an outsider."

"Osgar," Wyll said in a warning tone. He turned to Mairead. "We only wanted to confuse you. We brought you north so we would not risk you seeing the way back to our village. We will not return the way we came, either." He pointed to the south. "You need only follow the wall, traitha. It will lead you to the right gate."

"You will be well?" Mairead asked Gareth.

He whistled and held out his arm, and Grayfeather flew down and alit. He murmured a few words to the hawk, then lifted his arm with a quick motion. Grayfeather hopped over to Mairead's shoulder. "Send him with word now and then, will you?"

"And you as well."

"Of course, if he visits." He forced a smile. "Tell Elsbet that I have not forgotten my promise."

"What promise?"

He grinned. "She will know."

Wyll gestured. "We will wait until you are out of sight," he said. He jutted his chin toward the south. "Go. The One Hand be with you."

Mairead turned her horse south. Trypp fell in on one side, Letha on the other. Letha glanced back several times. "Is he still watching you?" Mairead asked.

"I don't know what you mean," Letha said, facing forward once more.

"Wyll can't keep his eyes off you."

"He's been nothing but honorable," Letha said.

"That doesn't mean he wants things to stay that way," Trypp said. He snorted a laugh at Letha's glare. "I saw the way he looked at you, guardian. The man's thoughts are anything but pure."

Letha's face colored again. "This is none of your concern. Or yours, Mairead."

Mairead held up a hand. "We're just observing," she said. "But you should know—wedding a raven is not for the faint-hearted."

"Who said anything about wedding?" Letha said, but her voice lacked conviction.

They finally approached the gates near the Catspaw clan just as the setting sun cast golden shadows on the city walls. Trypp rode up to the gates and requested entrance, and word spread quickly that the Deliverer and her companions were found. They rode to Aerwyth and Hedwar's home, where they were greeted with tears and hugs. Wytha was there, the baby strapped to her back, and when she saw Trypp, she gave a tiny cry and ran to him as he dismounted. "What happened?" Wytha asked. "How did you—"

"A skirmish," Trypp said. "I am well."

"You aren't well."

He pulled her close to himself. "I can still swing a sword, Wytha, and I can still hold you and our son. I will be well."

She buried her face in his chest. "I was so worried—so afraid—and I missed you so much—"

Mairead swallowed hard, and her heart ached with both sadness for Trypp and for the missing piece of her own spirit. *I will likely never have that with Connor.*

Aerwyth took Mairead's hands. "Traitha, we feared for you—"

Hedwar put a hand on Mairead's back. "It's good to see you well, traitha."

"Where is Gareth?" Aerwyth asked, looking around the group.

Mairead forced a smile and swallowed hard. "There is much to tell you. Can we go inside?"

"Is he alive?"

"He is alive," Mairead said. "And he is whole. But there is much to tell you."

"Of course." Hedwar ushered them into the hut, and Aerwyth stoked the fire, prepared food and drink, and brought warm blankets for the group. Trypp sat near the fire, Wytha next to him and his son on his lap. "What accident did you meet, Trypp?" Hedwar asked.

"I will tell all," Mairead said. She removed her furs and outer layers.

Aerwyth gasped. "Mairead, you're with child," she said.

I suppose it has become fairly obvious. When she left the city weeks before, her belly had been easily hidden under layers of clothes, and the weather had been cold enough to justify more layers than she needed. Now, everything had changed. She had to belt her breeches under her belly, and her tunic had an obvious bulge. She passed a hand over the baby. "I am," she said, looking up at Aerwyth. "I bear the heir to the Taurin throne, the child of Duke Connor Mac Niall of Taura." She paused. "My husband."

The silence in the room was heavy and tense. Aerwyth just stared, and Mairead couldn't tell what Gareth's mother was thinking. Hedwar stood near Trypp, arms folded, a frown creasing his forehead. Trypp and Letha just waited.

Wytha was the first to move. She crossed the room and pulled Mairead into a warm embrace. "Health and blessings be to you and your child," she whispered. She held Mairead at arm's length and smiled. "This child is blessed to have you as mother."

The blessing broke the silence, and Aerwyth approached as well. "Health and blessings to you and your child," she whispered, arms around Mairead. "I only wish you had told me. I could have helped you know what to expect."

Mairead blinked back tears. "I feared what you might say. I feared—I know you hoped that Gareth and I would—"

"You feared for your babe? From me?" Aerwyth pulled back and held Mairead's shoulders. "Dearest Mairead, you are as my own daughter. A babe is a babe. I bear you no ill will. If the raven will honor you and raise your child, I'll hold none toward him, either."

Mairead's throat tightened, and she felt her mouth start to quiver. Aerwyth pulled her back into an embrace just as her tears started to fall.

"I will tell you all," Letha said. She sat and relayed the events of the previous weeks as Aerwyth and Wytha guided Mairead to a seat, brought her a blanket, and offered food and tea.

Hedwar listened with a grave expression, and when Letha was done, he turned to Mairead. "You've been with ravens all this time?" he asked.

"They were honorable. They seek only to serve me, Hedwar."

"Except when your husband tried to kill you and Trypp and my son. And when his men held you captive. And when they kept my son as a hostage." When she did not answer, he nodded once, firmly. "It is as we have said, traitha. He would destroy you. They would destroy you."

"The man who did this didn't intend to kill me," Trypp said. Everyone turned to him. He stood, wincing as he lifted his stump. "He didn't even intend to hurt me. He was caught up in something we can't understand, can't know. Your son and I defended the traitha, and for that, I was maimed. But he could have killed me." He paused. "In fact, I don't think he was really trying to hurt the traitha, either. I think he just wanted to escape before he hurt anyone. This was just a stupid accident." He gestured the stump again. "Perhaps this was recompense for my own sins."

"Trypp, don't—" Wytha said.

"Speak the truth? It was my fault a tribesman died. How do I know the Morrag doesn't want my blood for his death? Perhaps this was her vengeance—my punishment."

"You've made your recompense," Hedwar said. "You have no more debt to pay."

"Not in the tribe, but the Morrag's justice is not our own."

"No. It is not," Hedwar agreed. "And that is why we need to seek these ravens and recover my son."

"What?" Mairead stood. "Hedwar, no—we told them they would be safe, that we wouldn't seek them."

"They hold my son, Mairead!" He gestured to the mountain. "Whatever other foolishness passed between you and the raven, his men hold my son captive."

"He volunteered to stay."

"To save you!" He pressed the bridge of his nose and let out a deep breath. "I do not like this—I do not like going after any man, any group. I do not wish to hurt anyone. But my son is a bladed and blooded warrior of the lion tribe and my only heir. He is not an object to be passed around as a symbol of power."

Mairead's heart constricted in her chest, and her stomach twisted. "I understand. But do not expect my help in looking for them."

"You are bound—"

"Half of them swore fealty to me, Hedwar. And I swore to them as well—I swore they would be safe."

"That was not your promise to make."

"It was if you really believe I am who you think I am."

He opened his mouth to respond, stopped, and left the hut without another word.

Trypp put his hand on Mairead's shoulder. "You have the hawk," he whispered near her ear.

"I'm going to freshen up," Mairead said. She gathered her belongings and went to her room, where she sat at her desk and scratched out a quick letter to Gareth. *Your father intends to seek the ravens. Warn them. Find a safe place. Will seek you as soon as I can.* She rolled the note up and threw a cloak over herself.

Aerwyth was at her stove cooking and Trypp, Wytha, and Letha had all left the house by the time Mairead emerged from her room. Mairead sneaked out the front door.

Night had fallen, and the streets of Isfyrin were alight with oil lanterns. Signs of spring were all around the city. Families ate together with doors and windows open in an effort to enjoy the warming weather. A few early spring calves and lambs called for their mothers from pens and pastures. There was a warmth in the air that Mairead hadn't felt in months, and she inhaled deeply, savoring the hint of the season to come. The baby jumped and moved in her belly, and she smiled. *She knows this is home, too. Maeve will not be happy if this child becomes tribal.*

As Mairead expected, Grayfeather was perched on his stand outside Gareth's hut, his head tucked under his wing. She clucked her tongue to wake him, and he returned the noise as he lifted his head. She reached out to pat his wings. "I need you to fly," she said, holding up the small piece of parchment. "Can you fly at night?" He held out his leg, and she tied the parchment to it. "Take this to Gareth as soon as you can. Can you do that?" He chirped and tucked his head back under his wing. She stroked his back once more. "In the morning, then."

She turned to walk back to Aerwyth and Hedwar's hut and saw two figures talking in low tones on the path. She started to walk past, but one of them stood in her way. Instinct took over, and Mairead reached for a knife. The man swatted it out of her hand. "Someone wants to see you," he said, and his friend threw a blanket over her and picked her up in two massive, tree trunk arms.

Mairead tried to kick, tried to scream, but they were too quick. They spirited her into a space behind a hut and tied her legs, then took the blanket off her long enough to gag her and tie her hands. *One Hand, no—not again! Not again!* She grunted against the gag, trying to cry out, but one of them put a hand on her mouth and a hand over her belly. She felt the flat of the blade in his hand.

He put his mouth next to her ear. "Make one sound, and your whelp will not live to the city gates."

My baby. Gods, no! She squeezed her eyes against tears and nodded. The two men picked her up and started to run toward the gates. *Please, One Hand, let someone see—let someone know what they are doing!* But no one noticed. They ran behind huts and stayed in shadows and passed through pastures until they reached the gates.

"What kept you?" a new voice asked. Mairead heard the creak of a heavy door.

"We had to wait till she was alone."

"Did you have any trouble?"

"No." They passed through a small door. The men threw Mairead over the back of a horse and started to lead it through the forest outside of the city.

Mairead was acutely aware of the weight on her baby, and her entire torso ached with the pressure of the saddle pushing up against her belly and ribs. She shifted in an attempt to relax, but nothing was comfortable. She concentrated on just staying on the saddle and praying for rescue. *You sent Connor before. I think that's too much to expect. Can you send someone? Gareth, Wyll, someone? Please, One Hand—I cannot believe this is the end of things.*

In the distance, a lion screamed, and the men stopped. "What was that—a woman?"

They aren't tribal, she realized with a start. *One of them called Hedwar a "chieftain," and this one doesn't know the sound of a lion.* She waited, listening.

The lion screamed again. The sound sent a chill down Mairead's spine.

One of the men gave a low, nervous laugh. "Some kind of animal, I think," he said. "Probably a wild dog. I doubt it will bother us."

"We could get off the mountain if we dump her body here."

Mairead fought rising panic. *They intend to kill me? Now?*

"Not here. He wants it done near the raven village."

Mairead blinked back tears as they continued on their path. *They'll kill me near the ravens to set off a war, to make sure the tribe destroys the Morragmen. And my baby …. One Hand, help!*

She lost track of how long they walked, but she knew it was well into the night before they stopped. When they pulled her off the horse and set her on the ground near a tree, she could no longer see the lights of Isfyrin. Her body ached. She tried to recognize something—anything—that would give her an idea of where she was, but there was nothing, no hint of her location. *And even if I could find my way back, they have my feet bound.*

The scream echoed off the mountains again.

The men stood very still and listened. One of the horses whickered and stamped its feet. "I need to take a piss," one of them said. He walked away.

Mairead watched the other man. He tended the horses, but showed little or no interest in her. She struggled against the ropes binding her wrists and ankles, but they didn't budge. She tried to move the gag out of her mouth, but had no luck. Disappointed, she leaned back against the tree.

Several moments passed while they waited for the other man to return. The night was eerily quiet around them. Mairead heard nothing—not the whisper of an owl's wings or the scurry of a raccoon. Her hands turned cold. *That creature—the Forbidden. Did he find me here? And who betrayed me at the gate? Which gate did we go through? I just need to stay alive for a little while—a little while till they can come looking for me.* Another scream echoed through the trees.

The first man returned, lacing up his breeches as he walked. "Let's get out of here."

"Why?"

"That scream—whatever that is, it's coming closer." He hoisted Mairead to her feet. "We'll do it here."

"It's still too close—"

"Do you want to stay here and wait for that thing to attack?" He drew a dagger.

Mairead tugged against his grip and tried to scream around the gag. Her feet still bound, she couldn't gain purchase, and she pulled too hard and fell. The man swore. "Pick her up," he said to the other one. The other man held her arms, and the one with the dagger approached and trailed the flat of the blade down her cheek. She tried to lean away from him, but the man behind her held her steady. "I have no desire to drag this out," the man said. "This isn't to be torture. I can make this quick and relatively painless, or I can leave you lying here with a stab wound in your gut and let you die to the next predator that comes down the mountain. Your choice."

The only sound was Mairead's rapid breath against the gag. She shook her head as the man gripped her tunic in one hand and moved the knife down to her side, aiming the point between two ribs. *One Hand, no!* The point pierced her tunic—

The three horses suddenly reared and bolted away. "What the—" the man said, turning.

His words ended in a scream.

A shriek shattered the pre-dawn, and then a snarl and a blur. The man holding her arms put her between himself and the creature attacking his partner. She struggled against his grip, but before she could get away, a heavy object knocked her out of his arms. She fell into the moss and dirt as another scream ended with a snarl and the cracking of bone.

Mairead remained still, hoping that if the lion thought her dead, he would move on. She heard the massive feet come toward her, inching closer, then felt hot breath near her ear. A low rumble started in the cat's chest, and the lion lay down with its head next to hers.

Mairead didn't know whether to move or not. Her heart hammered against her ribs. With her face planted in the ground, she knew she would have to at least turn her head at some point so that she could get fresh air to breathe. *The cat will know I've moved. May as well finish it.* She finally rolled to her side, and the lion sat up. The golden eyes fixed a stare at Mairead. In the light of the rising sun, Mairead could just make out the shape of the massive animal. *This can't be happening,* she thought. She held out her hands to the lion, and the cat sniffed at the ropes before carefully, gingerly chewing on them until they fell off in a coiled pile.

Mairead pulled the gag off her mouth and rubbed at her cheeks where the cloth had bitten into them. She untied her ankles. The tip of the cat's tail twitched in a slow, thoughtful rhythm. Mairead considered her options. *They told me if I met a lion to scream and stand up tall, but ....* She couldn't. She froze, and her heart beat slow and easy. "Have you come for me?" she whispered.

The cat stood, stretched, and nudged Mairead's hand with her nose. Mairead lifted it and put her hand in the soft ruff around the cat's neck. A low rumble vibrated through the cat's throat. Mairead laughed. The cat walked behind her and molded her body to Mairead's. Her tail twined around Mairead's midsection. She rubbed against Mairead's shoulder with her massive head, took a step back, and lay down to wait, tail twitching.

Mairead sat up on her knees. "Is this my initiation? Did the earth send you? Are we bonded?" She put her hand out.

The cat licked Mairead's hand.

"They told me no one has bonded with a lion since the Breaking."

The cat blinked. She licked Mairead's hand again.

Mairead laughed at the rough tongue. She considered where she was. "The sun is rising over there, so that's east, but I don't know which gate they took me from. Should I go east or west to reach Isfyrin?" The cat offered no noise or suggestions. "I suppose we wait till full light, then."

When the sun crested the horizon, both Mairead and the cat stood and stretched. Mairead walked to the bodies and examined them. She pulled the hoods off both men, but there was nothing to identify them as anything more than slavers from the plains. She took two knives and a canteen that she found on their bodies, but couldn't find any food. "Everything must have been on their horses." She straightened to look around. "Which way?"

The cat made a low rumble in her throat. She started to pad westward, so Mairead followed.

Water was easy to find. Everywhere, snow and ice melted in the sun, and Mairead had no trouble drinking her fill without resorting to melting snow on her own. She refilled her canteen several times, but her stomach gnawed at her. *No supper, and I was up all night. And this babe needs food.* She was relieved that the baby still moved after the fall she had taken. Her body ached from bruises and shock, but at least the baby seemed fine. *She can survive a day or two without food. My body will take care of her. I've fasted longer at the sayada.*

Once, a kiron had visited from the Great Kirok in Aliom and told the sayas of the persecution faced by kirons in Sveklant. His words moved Mairead to prayer and fasting. She had lasted three days without food before the peace of Alshada had descended upon her and she had risen to break her fast.

But that was fasting in my own cell, with robes and candles and walls around me. And I didn't move for three days except to drink and use the chamber pot. This . . . And with a babe . . . . Her thoughts were beginning to wander, she realized. Her stomach was as nauseated as it was hungry, and bile rose in her throat. She stopped and heaved against the rocks nearby.

When she was done, she looked up to see the cat sitting a few feet in front of her, waiting with her tail curled around her paws. "It's the babe. Sometimes not eating makes me vomit. Do you know where we are?"

The cat stood, stretched, and kept walking. Mairead followed.

Between exhaustion, hunger, and frequent rests to ease the pregnancy-related discomforts, she made very poor time. She walked all day, following the cat the whole time, but when the sun started to set, she still didn't see Isfyrin. Mairead found a quiet grove where she made a bed of fir boughs and lay curled in a ball. The cat warmed her.

She woke to a dark, cloudy sky. In the distance, the horizon had just started to lighten with the rising of the sun. She stood, stretched, and followed the cat again.

She walked in the trees for hours. Late in the day, she stopped. Her head spun, and her legs shook. She sat. "I'm hungry," she said. "I shouldn't be so weak. It's the babe—it must be."

The cat came close and nudged her. The low rumbling growl in her chest soothed Mairead. "Is there to be some vision?" Mairead said, but her voice sounded far away. She curled up and slept.

She woke late, the deep black of a moonless night draping the mountain. She sat up, rubbed her face, and stood. She walked to the edge of an outcrop and looked down to the plains. The cat stood next to her. *Can't see the plains from here. It must be a dream.*

Light rose in the east, but in her dream state, Mairead knew it wasn't real sun. It increased, flared to life, and lit up the plains below. Mists coalesced into a cloudy shape of a lion, and the shape trampled a camp on the plains, flooding it with light even as the ground ran red with blood. A flock of black birds went behind the lion. A city fell to lions and ravens. Among the dead were faces of men she knew—*tribal men.* She knelt, her knees weak at the sight.

The light continued to rise, and it bathed the plains in a warm glow. The black birds remained in the sky, and from the west came a wolf shape, and from the east, a great bear. They joined the lion, and the plain blossomed again. Life teemed and flourished, and from the palace in Galbragh flew a new standard—the lion and wolf against a raven's wing.

Mairead watched, tears streaming. She lifted her face to the sky. *One Hand, guide me. Give me wisdom.*

She heard someone behind her and turned. The woman—the earthspirit from her vision—stepped toward her. She touched Mairead's face and then breathed out a long breath over her, and Mairead felt a flutter in her belly. She put her hand on it.

The crone touched Mairead's belly over her own hand. *Your womb will bless the three lands—a great king, a queen, and warriors. All of these shall come from your womb.*

A pang clutched at her spirit. "But my husband .... Will he be able to be a real father?"

Your husband will do all that is required.

It wasn't the answer Mairead wanted. "But—"

The earthspirit motioned for silence.

"No, wait—I have so many questions."

Ask, daughter.

"The ravens—can I trust them? What of the lions? How do I reunite the tribe? Is it right to go to the plains?"

She thought the earthspirit chuckled. *Daughter, your wisdom is greater than you realize. As for trust, do not trust a title or a name. Do not trust or distrust just because a man is a lion or a raven. Trust each man for himself. Some will prove themselves true; some will prove themselves untrue. As for the plains, the path will be made clear.* She took Mairead's hand and turned her.

Behind them, a pillar of fire twisted and writhed into the air. Mairead blinked; the heat warmed her face, but it didn't burn. The old woman gestured to the fire. *You must pass through.*

Mairead stepped back. "What—where did this—"

You must pass through.

Mairead took a deep breath. *This is a vision—this isn't real—this won't hurt.* But as she stepped forward, the flames licked at her feet and fingers, singeing her clothes. She smelled the burning leather and linen, and she forced down panic. Her feet moved too slowly, she thought. She stepped forward, forward, forward, but the fire didn't stop. She couldn't pass through. There was only fire, as far as she could see. Her clothes were gone, burned into ashes on the ground. She turned to go back, but there was only fire behind as well. She raised her hands and her face. *One Hand, show me the way.*

The fire faded behind her. She looked down at her skin, felt at her face, her hair, her legs. Her clothes were gone, but her body was unharmed. She knelt, clean and naked before the eyes of the forest.

The old woman was gone.

The cat joined Mairead, nudging at her hand with a moist nose. Mairead rubbed the cat's ribs and scratched her belly. "What's your name?" She paused. She'd half expected the cat to answer. "I suppose I should just find a name for you. I can't call you nothing." She laughed. "A lioness. I've bonded with a lioness."

The cat rumbled a low growl. A man with long straight hair tied back at his neck stepped out of the trees. Mairead stood, only vaguely aware that she was naked. *I should be afraid, embarrassed, ashamed, but I'm not.* The cat walked toward the man and wound around his knees. He reached down and scratched between the cat's ears, and then he straightened and held out a gleaming white robe.

"That's for me?"

"You're cleansed, daughter. And you're marked. Come into your power."

She stepped forward, and he draped the robe around her. She ran her hands over the fabric on her arms; finer than silk, it warmed her all the way down to her bones. *Even my toes are warm, even without boots.* "This is— what is this?" she asked, but he had gone.

Mairead knelt again. The cat sat in front of her. "My head," she said. "I need food. Will you help me find the city, Devyn? Can I call you Devyn?" The cat blinked and nuzzled Mairead's hand with her nose. "I'll assume that means yes. Let's find Isfyrin."

Mairead and the lioness walked until midday, and just as the sun stood at its peak, she saw smoke in the distance. As they came closer to the smoke, she paused, evaluating the camp from behind a tree. "The ravens," she said, realizing she recognized the clothing and stance of several of the men. "It's a raven camp." Devyn grumbled an answer.

As she entered the camp with the lioness next to her, the ravens stood. Gareth and Wyll met her, both of them gaping. "Your face," Gareth whispered.

"Am I marked?"

Gareth nodded.

Mairead touched her face. "I want to see it."

Wyll drew his sword and held it for her.

Gareth pointed. "The cat?"

"She is my companion and protector. I call her Devyn. She brought me safely back. Did Grayfeather reach you?"

"Yes. We split into several groups and scattered into the forest. There are ten of us here."

"Then you are all safe?"

"For the moment."

Mairead let out a sigh and examined herself as much as possible in the blade of Wyll's sword. She touched the swirling blue lines across her face. They were similar to Hedwar's, but thinner, more graceful, and looped with trailing lines that made her think of vines growing on the side of a stone building. "Am I accepted?"

"You are more than accepted," Wyll said. "These are the marks of a traitha. The marks of a chief traitha."

"How can you tell?"

He touched her face. "This—here—this is the symbol of chief traitha. Not even Hedwar or Wulf have this." He knelt. "You are more than accepted, warrior. You are traitha over the ravens."

Gareth knelt. "You are traitha over the lions as well. And you are my traitha."

"You've already sworn fealty to me, both of you. There is no need—"

"We swore fealty to a girl, an idea, and one in name only," Wyll said. "Now, we swear to a fulfillment of prophecy, a marked traitha." He raised his voice. "Men of the raven," he said. "Behold, the earthspirit has marked your new traitha. Bend your knee, for the prophecies are fulfilled this day, and the lioness has come."

Every man in that camp took a knee before her. When she told them to rise, they stood as one, and their cheer split the skies. Mairead looked up. *One Hand, thank you for these people. Make me worthy of leading them.*

CHAPTER THIRTY-THREE

Shed no tears for me, my heart,
For though my bones lie cold
My soul will feast with Syraf fair
And dance in streets of gold.
— Ancient Svek Song

Minerva waited with Grytha and Alfrig in the shelter of a guard shack at the gates of Dylan's estate. The wind swirled and howled around them, tearing at their cloaks and hoods. Minerva pulled her cloak tighter around her. *One Hand, keep them safe,* she prayed.

Hrogarth and Logan had insisted on leaving the women at the gate, much to Alfrig's dismay. She argued her case to her husband in no uncertain terms, but Hrogarth would not be moved. "You are too valuable to the tribes to risk losing you to the demon," he said. "I will not allow her to destroy the wisdomkeeper's heir."

Alfrig's jaw tightened at that, but she didn't respond. Minerva flinched. *If he knew what we'd found out on the sacred island, perhaps it would change his decision.* But Alfrig said nothing, and Minerva wondered if the guardian had changed her mind about taking her place on the sacred isle. *If Hrogarth dies, there will be nothing tying Alfrig to the mainland except her children. And it was never the children or grandchildren that made Alfrig hesitate—it was always Hrogarth.* Hope flared in her chest. *Perhaps I will not need to go—perhaps Alfrig can take her place. But then how will I rid myself of the earthspirit, especially with the Morrag rising?*

Grytha, for her part, had been silent during the exchange between Alfrig and Hrogarth, and she had been anxious and tense when Logan led Hrogarth through the gate. "Logan seems to know what he is doing," Minerva said. "I'm sure he'll be back."

Grytha sighed. "It is foolish. He is Taurin, I am tribal. He serves the king, I serve Hrogarth. He has shown no interest in me beyond what is necessary to stay alive in the tribes, and yet I wish nothing more than to stay with him."

"You would leave the tribe?"

Grytha turned to her. "I would," she whispered. "Tell me—is it as hard as it seems?"

Minerva's heart ached for the young woman. "It's as hard and as easy. Does he know how you feel?"

"No. Not yet."

Minerva's hand tightened on Grytha's shoulder. "Do not wait. He may be happy to learn of your affections."

"When he comes back," Grytha said.

The plan was simple. The men had captured a wagon of food from a near-by farm and tied the farmer up in a barn with the promise that they would return to set him free after delivering the food. Once through the gate, they would sneak into the manor house and follow Malcolm to the king's quarters. When he was safely freed of the estate and the demon was dead and banished, they would release the farmer and apologize to him, reunite with the women, and go their separate ways—Hrogarth to the east, the women to the tribes, and Braedan and his men to Torlach.

But something nagged at Minerva. Her brand itched and burned as it hadn't in months, and she found herself fidgeting and scratching her palm whenever Alfrig wasn't looking. The plan was simple, but Aldora wasn't a simple creature. *Who can say what she might know and foresee? Who can say if she might see them coming?*

Alfrig returned to the sheltered area. "Something is wrong."

"How do you know?" Minerva asked.

Alfrig frowned. "It's a feeling—a sense. The Morrag is restless, but so is the earthspirit."

"Yes," Grytha said. "I sense it, too. It's in the wind as well."

Minerva scratched at her palm through the glove. "Can we get through the gates?"

Alfrig stepped away. The streets around the manor house were deserted, all of the villagers having taken refuge indoors due to the storm. "No one ever goes in or out of this place in this weather," she grumbled.

Minerva started walking.

"Where are you going?" Grytha called.

I don't know. "Around the manor house. Perhaps we've missed something—a path, a hole—something." They fell in behind her, but she didn't stop or slow down for them. In the distance, she saw the outbuilding where Dylan kept the sayas, and she quickened her pace. She pointed. "That's where we need to go."

Alfrig trotted to keep up. "Why?"

"The sayas are there. We need to warn them."

"How will we get there?"

Minerva made a fist. *One Hand, I don't know what this is, but I am trusting.* She stopped her prayer. *I don't even know if you are here.* She turned to Alfrig and Grytha. "Those women were my sisters once—as you are both my sisters now. I owe it to them to help them."

"They rejected you," Alfrig said. "They branded you a witch and sent you away."

Minerva looked toward the outbuilding again and scratched her palm. "They need to know what's happening in the manor house. If the demon inside those walls is so determined to undo Braedan, a man who holds no particular faith and ascribes to no religion, how much more will she wish to destroy the servants of the god who would destroy her?"

"I will help you," Grytha said.

"As will I," Alfrig said.

The women ran on toward the back side of the manor. The wind hit them full in the face, tearing at their hoods and furs, pelting them with ice and snow. Minerva's face stung, and she squinted against the assault, trying to see where she was going. She put one hand on the wall around the manor house and used it to guide her path.

Her hand faltered. Minerva stopped. *A gap.* The servant gate at the back of the manor house hung open. Minerva inched inside just a bit, looking for guards. No one appeared. She motioned the other women through the gate.

"An open gate is not always a good sign," Alfrig said.

"The wind may have blown it open."

Alfrig grunted. "Is that the house?"

"Yes." They made their way toward the outbuilding along the wall, trying to stay in shadows and nooks, but there was no resistance and no evidence of guards. Minerva wondered if they just weren't watching during the storm. When they finally had no choice but to run across the open yard to the outbuilding, she was grateful she'd left her robes in the wisdomkeeper's cave. *Alshada, I wanted to honor you by keeping my robes, but perhaps that was a vanity you did not require.* She swallowed hard. *It may be that many of my actions are merely my own vanities.*

They gathered at the door of the outbuilding, all three winded and shivering with the biting cold. Minerva pounded on the door. "Sayas! Are you well?" No one came. She tried again, and then two more times.

At last, the door opened a small crack. The woman behind it gasped. "Minerva," she whispered. "You would return, now? After—"

"Are you well?" Minerva interrupted. "Are all of you accounted for? All of you well?"

"Yes. All but one—she is in the manor house. Why?"

"Which one?"

"Saya Vivian."

Minerva startled. "The decoy?"

"Yes. Braedan calls for her often. They play chess and dine together, she says. We believe as long as he thinks she is the heir, the heir is safe."

And if you all treat her as the heir and he believes she is the heir, she is in more danger than Braedan is. "Shut this door and do not open it for anyone but me," she said.

The woman's jaw tightened in indignation. "You have no rights here."

"This isn't about rights," Minerva shouted. "There is a demon in that manor house, and if you want to live—if you want Vivian to live—you will bar this door and fall to your knees in prayer."

For a moment, Minerva was sure she would argue again. "We will pray," she finally said. "Go. Help Vivian." The saya shut the door and locked it.

Minerva turned to Grytha and Alfrig. "There is one saya in the manor house."

"We should be in the manor house anyway," Alfrig said. "I cannot stay out here when my husband might need another sword."

They made their way through the storm, slipping on the cobbled paths several times. Minerva considered walking to the side on the grass, but with increasing ice and wind, she counted on the cobbled path to see where she was going. *Too easy to go astray if we get off the path.*

The kitchen entrance was unlocked when they arrived, and Minerva took the lead again. Grytha and Alfrig came behind, both drawing daggers out of their boots. Minerva frowned. "Is it time for that already?"

"It's always time for this," Alfrig said. "I won't be caught unaware in this place. The very air is taut."

"You will get no argument from me there," Minerva said. She drew her own small knife. It was barely a weapon—useful mainly for skinning small game or cleaning fish—but it was all she had. Her palm welcomed the feel of the knife with a warm pulse.

The kitchens were empty, and the halls had a deserted feel to them as the women started their search for Logan's party. "This is not right," Minerva whispered. "When I stayed here those three days, this house bustled with activity at all hours. The fires were always lit, and the kitchens were always working. This is not the way Dylan ran his estate."

"Perhaps the servants have run away with the conflict between Dylan and Braedan," Grytha said. "Gone to their own homes?"

"Many of them had no other home. They lived here."

They wound their way through corridors and halls with no resistance. As they reached the second floor of the manor, Alfrig hissed and stopped. "Hrogarth," she said, opening her palm. Grytha did the same. "He needs us."

"Can you find him?"

Alfrig took the lead. Minerva followed Grytha, the three of them at a brisk trot. They ran down a corridor and rounded a corner, and Alfrig held out an arm to stop everyone as a scream curdled the air. "The girl," she said.

Minerva's blood chilled. "It must be Saya Vivian."

Alfrig ran again. They rounded one more corner and stopped. "One Hand have mercy," Grytha whispered.

In the middle of the corridor stood a woman with long, full red hair and pale skin, wearing the simple attire of a serving girl. She wasn't especially beautiful; she was the kind of woman who would not recommend herself to many people based on appearance alone. Most men would likely pass her in the street without a glance, Minerva thought. *But her face ....* Minerva shuddered. *I am truly in the presence of evil.*

The woman stood tall, confident, drawn to her full height. There was a faint glow around her, and her face shone with power. Her eyes were red— *red*—and her mouth was curled into an ecstatic sneer. She had one arm extended, her hand locked tight around the throat of a girl who sputtered and kicked her feet. The woman had lifted the girl off the ground enough that her toes could be seen kicking beneath the edges of her robes. The demon's other hand was extended toward three men on the other side of her—Hrogarth, Logan, and Braedan. The woman turned toward the men. "Hector," she said. "I wondered when you would return."

Minerva's stomach lurched as all of her sayada lessons flooded back to her. *Aldora—Hector—these are creatures of legend. Alshada, is he truly what she says he is?*

Logan pushed past the men as he drew his sword. "Aldora, your time is done," he said, and ran toward her.

Grytha screamed, and at that moment, Braedan and Hrogarth seemed to notice the women. Hrogarth frowned, but Braedan merely cast them a confused glance before he drew his sword and a small blade.

The woman called Aldora dropped the girl and lifted her hands. "I call upon the fires of the earth and the chasm," she said. "By the power of my master, serve me now!" A ball of fire appeared in her hand, and she threw it at Logan.

He ducked to miss it. Minerva thought he would attack the woman, but instead, he kept the sword before him as a shield and shouldered Saya Vivian away from Aldora's hand. The girl fell unconscious to the ground, and Grytha ran to pull her away from the melee. "Hrogarth, now!" Logan shouted.

Hrogarth ran toward Aldora with his sword drawn. She laughed. "You come at me with puny blades when I command the very powers of the chasm?" she said. Another ball of fire flew toward the men, and she extended her other hand to shoot one at the women. Both missed their marks, but they succeeded in starting fires in the casements at either end of the corridor.

Minerva watched from where she crouched in hiding with Grytha and Saya Vivian. "Is she all right?" she asked.

"I think so," Grytha said. "She breathes. Her pulse is there, but it's very rapid. We will see what happens when she wakes."

"Watch her," Minerva said. She stood and returned to the corridor. Alfrig, Hrogarth, and Logan all danced around Aldora, watching as she drew in more of whatever demonic power she commanded. Braedan still stood behind the others, sword and dagger in hand. Minerva watched him, and she realized, suddenly, that Braedan was paralyzed into inaction, his eyes fixed on the woman's face. *He is drawn to her,* Minerva realized. *He sees her as beautiful. If he follows her* .... She started to creep around the confrontation in the center of the hall, making her way toward Braedan while the others focused on Aldora.

When Minerva reached the king, she tugged at his arm. He whirled to her. "What—Esma! What are you doing here?"

She slapped him, realizing too late that his face already bore a rising welt. "Majesty, do not look at her," she shouted.

He blinked several times. "I don't .... Oh, gods." He turned again and saw what he had been enamored of.

Minerva put her hands on his shoulders from behind. "She is evil, sire. It was she who tried to kill me in the forest outside of Kiern. It was she who you killed once before. You may choose, sire. You may choose to follow her, to serve that evil all your life, or you may choose the side of right and truth. You may choose to be a slave, or you may choose to be a *king*."

He stared too long, Minerva thought. The pull of the evil was strong. She could feel it drawing him. He took a step toward Aldora. Minerva tried to hold his shoulders, but he shook her hands away. *One Hand, no! Do not let him go! Please, save him!*

Logan saw Braedan walking toward the woman. He swung at her, but she waved his sword away with a negligent hand. "Sire—Braedan—no! Don't you see what she is? She does not want you—she wants Taura!"

But Braedan kept walking. Aldora turned toward him with a feral, hungry grin. "Come, my love. We can rule together. You will have your every desire."

The blade in Braedan's fist flared with blue light, surrounding his hand, but he seemed not to notice. He took another step toward Aldora.

Minerva's palm burned. She pulled her glove off. *It's now or never. Decide, woman. Decide—are you a coward, or are you a guardian of this place?* She clenched her fists. *Alshada, One Hand, give me wisdom. Give me strength.*

Alfrig approached Aldora with her dagger out, stepping toward the demon from behind, hand raised to stab the creature in the back. Aldora's concentration was fixed on Braedan, her hands outstretched as she beckoned him and he stepped closer to her. He dropped his sword, but the sacred dagger remained fixed in his hand. Logan started to run toward Braedan, and Hrogarth raised his sword to attack Aldora.

Minerva acted without thinking. She took three long strides toward Braedan, hands outstretched, so that her glowing palm reached him first. She grabbed his hand that held the sacred blade. He looked down, his face a jumble of confusion. She stood before him, blocking his view of Aldora. "No, sire," she said. "I will not allow you to destroy Taura." She raised her dagger—

"*NOOO!!*" Logan saw what was happening and raced to push Braedan out of the way, Aldora completely forgotten. The two men fell to one side, Logan holding Braedan down away from the view of Aldora.

Minerva turned to the demon, dagger still raised. "You will not destroy this land, demon," she shouted.

Aldora's grin widened. "We have met before, haven't we?" The demon stepped toward her, one hand out. "Do you recall our previous meeting? Such delicious transgressions, girl. Such a sweet soul, so tormented, so much shame and regret. Would you care to see again?"

She did remember. She remembered how her legs had turned to water when she saw the transgressions of her youth and remembered the sins committed before she came to the sayada. *Lust, greed, lies, anger . . . so much . . . so much against my people, my tribe. Alshada, how could you bear me? How could you tolerate my presence?*

A surge of righteous anger welled in her breast, and she tightened her jaw and grasped her tiny dagger tighter. She held up her hand and showed Aldora the glowing palm. "You will not take this land, demon," she repeated. "You have no power over me. I am not yours. *I am not yours!* I belong to the Maker of All Things, the One Hand who holds this world, Alshada, He of the Stars and Skies, and I will *NOT* bow to you, nor will I surrender!"

Aldora's eyes flashed red, redder, but there was a flinch—a pause, a hesitation—at the mention of Alshada. Minerva saw it, and she smiled. "This land is not yours, demon. This land will never be yours. Taura will never belong to you or Namha or any of the powers of the chasm."

At that moment, Alfrig's dagger connected with Aldora's side, but the demon moved at the last moment, and the dagger only grazed her. She screamed with pain and whirled on Alfrig. Her hand connected with Alfrig's throat, and Alfrig gasped and wheezed as Aldora pulled the soul out of Alfrig's body.

"*NOOO!*" Hrogarth's scream of agony shook the stones of the manor.

And then Braedan was there, rushing at Aldora with the sacred dagger before him. "I do not belong to you!" he shouted. "I will not surrender Taura to you!" He drew back to strike her with the dagger, but she brought the back of her hand across his left cheek. The blow sent him off his feet, flying to connect with the stone walls, where he fell in a slump.

Hrogarth rushed at Aldora, sword raised, as the demon dropped Alfrig's limp body to the floor. Hrogarth swung, and Aldora's arm came off over the body of his dead wife. Aldora screamed, but she didn't stop—she came at Hrogarth with her other arm, grasping the bare skin of his forearm. "You fight the one power you have no strength to overcome," he said, and Minerva heard the rasping voice of a woman over his own.

Aldora did flinch then. She dropped his arm and took a step back. "She is loosed," she whispered.

Hrogarth's feral grin matched her own as he advanced. "Vengeance is come. The raven is loosed." He raised his sword and brought it down in a sweeping arc that split her body in half from shoulder to hip.

Aldora's scream echoed around the halls of Dylan's manor house as her spirit rose in an inky black cloud. Hrogarth reached for the cloud with his warriormarked hand, and a fierce red glow emerged from the whorl on his palm. The shrieking grew louder, and as he pulled the inky cloud into his palm, Minerva realized she could hear the sounds of spirits in torment in Namha's chasm. She shuddered, but it seemed to her that Hrogarth almost gained strength from the process. He bowed his head and closed his eyes, whispering words she could not hear over the shrieking. The wind howled outside, and the shrieking howled inside, and Hrogarth sent Aldora back to the chasm where she belonged.

When it was over—when the shrieks finally faded and the cloud was completely gone—Hrogarth collapsed next to his wife's body. "Oh, my love," he whispered. Tears streamed uncontrolled down his cheeks. He buried his head against her chest. "Oh, my love." His shoulders shook with sobs.

Logan, Grytha, and Braedan emerged from shelter to stand over the chieftain. Braedan's face was a jumble of bruises and welts. Grytha knelt next to Hrogarth, her own face wet with tears. She put a hand on his shoulder and said nothing.

Braedan's face was pale and stricken with horror, grief, shock—a thousand things that Minerva could not name. "By the gods," he whispered.

Minerva turned to him. "No, not gods," she said. "One god. Alshada. Choose, sire. Choose this day which god you will serve—a god of your own making, or the one true god."

He still held the sacred blade in his hand. He opened his palm and looked down at the glowing animstone. "I am . . . not fit to lead this country. I am not a king."

Logan put a hand on his shoulder. "You are enough of a king for now."

"A king would not have allowed a creature like that to hold such sway over him."

Footsteps echoed in the hall and Malcolm arrived, trailing a contingent of Taurin and Starling's Cross men, all with weapons drawn. Duke Dylan was among them. They all took in the scene—bodies on the ground, a very shaken saya huddled against a wall, charred remains of casements on the outside walls—and Malcolm let out a long breath.

"By the Hand of Heaven," Dylan whispered.

Logan turned to Malcolm. "Have you established control?"

"Yes," Malcolm said. "Dylan's men are freed. The Taurins she had bewitched attacked us as we went, but we dispatched most of them with little trouble. The few who remain scattered in that terrible shrieking."

"Losses?"

"Minor. We have enough to leave here and return to Torlach."

Braedan turned to Dylan. "My lord," he said. He knelt. "My lord, you must accept my apology. I cannot hope to have your fealty, but if you would at least forgive me for the way I have treated you, I would be in your debt forever."

Dylan put a hand on Braedan's shoulder. "Come. Let's you and I have a drink and a talk." Braedan stood, and Malcolm fell in behind him as Dylan led the way.

Minerva knelt on the other side of Alfrig's body, across from Grytha and Hrogarth. "Hrogarth, I am so sorry," she said. Her voice broke over her own tears.

"You know what it is to lose your beloved."

"I do." She bit her lip. "Alfrig was always my traitha. Even when I was a saya, it was Alfrig's voice in my head—Alfrig's voice that guided me more often than I wanted to admit."

He chuckled and sniffed. "She had a resonance that could certainly embed itself in one's head," he said. Grytha laughed quietly. "She died a noble death. She died well. I mourn her, but I have never been more proud of her." He paused. "I wonder only who will take her place."

Minerva understood. Grytha frowned and passed a look between the two of them. "Her place?" she asked. "Traitha, I was her second in the tribe."

"Not among the hounds. On the sacred isle. It was Alfrig's fate to become the wisdomkeeper. Now ...."

"We have been to the wisdomkeeper," Minerva said. "She knows that Alfrig will not replace her." She hesitated. "I will be taking her place." *And like that, it is decided.*

Hrogarth nodded.

"You do not seem surprised."

"I am surprised by nothing anymore. She who guards the earth and her wisdom is not mine to gainsay. If she has chosen you, she has a reason."

"What will you do?" Grytha asked.

Hrogarth took Alfrig's hand in his. He leaned down and kissed her forehead. "I will bury my wife in this frozen ground," he said. "And then I will go east."

"To the raven?"

"Yes. I will submit to the Morrag and her First Raven." He looked at Logan. "I owe you an apology, Commander Mac Kendrick. I have treated you shamefully. I am sorry."

Logan's shoulders relaxed. "I thank you. And I am sorry for your loss. I also know what it is to lose my beloved."

Hrogarth scooped Alfrig into his arms and stood. "Grytha, will you help me return her to the earth?" Grytha followed him out of the corridor.

Minerva went to the saya, who still huddled on the floor near the place where Aldora had attacked her. "Are you well?"

"I will be."

"She's gone now. You may return to your sisters. I believe you will be safe there now."

The girl stood. "The king—he believes I am the rightful Taurin heir."

"Wait." Logan took a step forward. "You aren't the heir?"

"No," Vivian said. "I am not."

Logan let out a long breath. "Thank the gods."

"We sent decoys," Minerva explained.

"I knew about the decoys. I feared she was not one of them."

Minerva put a hand on Vivian's shoulder. "Go back to the sayas. Tell them all is well in the manor house, and thank them for their prayers."

Vivian touched head and heart and folded her hands. "Go with Alshada, saya."

Minerva returned the salutation, but she reflected that it no longer hurt her to do so. *I am tribal again.*

When Vivian had gone, Minerva turned to Logan. "Shall we join the king?"

He held up a hand. "You were a saya. You heard what Aldora called me. And yet you do not warn them. Why?"

She folded her hands before her. "They do not need to believe it true, do they?"

He opened his mouth and shut it again. He sighed and lowered his head. "I know I am damned," he said. "I have sought absolution, and there is none for one such as me. All I can hope for is to do some good before Alshada exacts his vengeance upon me and I pay the final price for my sins."

"There is always hope."

"Not for one such as I am."

Minerva put one hand on his arm. "You and I are more alike than you think."

He flinched away from her touch at first, but then allowed it. He gestured to the body on the floor. "She did have a flare for the dramatic, didn't she? The fire from the chasm? Red eyes? If she weren't so deadly, she'd be a bad joke. Aldora never did understand subtlety." He took a deep breath. "I'll clean this up. You tend to the king."

"What will you do with the body?"

"The body was just a shell—just a poor girl Aldora chose to house herself in for a time. I will bury her properly outside of the estate." He knelt in the corridor.

Minerva watched for a moment before she turned away to find the king. Her palm warmed, but it no longer itched, and the air had relaxed. She glanced out a casement and saw the edge of silver light in the distance. *There is always hope.*

CHAPTER THIRTY-FOUR

The false king rises. The heir waits.
— Prophecy in the Syrafi Keep

Braedan had never been so grateful for oiska in his life. He took the cup offered by Haldor Dylan, swallowed it in one gulp, and gave it back. "Another."

Dylan grunted. He poured another shot and stepped back. "Take it slow, lad. Ye've had a bit of a shock."

A bit of a shock? No, having an unexpected dinner guest is a bit of a shock. This was .... He stared at the cup of oiska. The surface of the liquid vibrated with the shaking of his hand. He put his other hand over it. *What have I stumbled into?*

"Are ye well, lad?"

Braedan nodded. "No," he corrected, looking up. "I'm not well. But I am. I don't know how to explain it."

Haldor Dylan sat across from him at the small table in Braedan's bedchamber. He set the oiska between them. "You have questions."

"Dozens. Hundreds. What was she?"

"Forbidden," Dylan said. "A creature of legend and myth. Bound to Namha."

Braedan held up a hand. "I know that. I've met her before. But what is she really? I mean, how could she have so much control over me?"

"Ye let her, lad. You let her into your head, heart. She goes where she is invited."

Braedan shuddered. He drank the second cup of oiska and put his elbows on the table. He buried his head in his hands. "I was such a fool," he whispered.

Dylan poured another cup of oiska for Braedan. "Aye," he said. "I'll not argue that. But ye've come through it unscathed, mostly. There is still time to repair the land. You have a second chance."

Braedan didn't respond. He couldn't look up, couldn't acknowledge Dylan's assessment. He could only think that if he hadn't started down the road to the throne, if he hadn't behaved like a spoiled child, Taura would not be such a mess. *This country is on the verge of war,* he thought. *My princess is in danger, my uncle threatens the throne, I have few dukes to back me, and I very nearly lost my soul to a creature who would use me to control the country I claim to love. There is no greater fool than I.*

Dylan said nothing. He just sat staring, waiting for Braedan. When Braedan drank again, Dylan poured more oiska. When Braedan shivered, Dylan built the fire up. When Braedan put his head all the way down on the table, Dylan reached over to pat his arm. "Mayhap it's time for bed. Ye've had a fair bit o' oiska. Let me help you."

Braedan didn't fight it when Dylan removed his armor and guided him to his bed. Dylan took Braedan's boots off and set them to one side, then covered Braedan with a blanket. "We'll talk again tomorrow, lad. Dream well."

Braedan's sleep was sound, but not dreamless. For the first time in months, though, he did not dream of destruction and death. When he woke, Malcolm was standing guard inside the door. Braedan sat up. "How long did I sleep?"

"Nearly a full day," Malcolm said. "Many have been by to check on you."

Braedan rubbed his face with both hands. "I dreamed."

"More of the same?"

Braedan stood. "Fetch the guardian—what's her name? Esma?"

"Yes."

"And Dylan, fetch him. And the other guardian. And Hrogarth, Logan. All of them."

"Yes, sire." He left the room.

Braedan used the privy, put on fresh clothes, and splashed water on his face and through his hair. By the time the others arrived, he was finishing his second cup of water and writing furiously on a piece of parchment. He put down his quill and stood. "I dreamed last night," he said. They all exchanged looks. "I dreamed like I have never dreamed before."

"You have been dreaming much lately," Malcolm said.

"No, it wasn't like that. This was different. There was a man. He was a warrior. He looked tribal, in a fashion. He was tall—very tall—and he had the bluest eyes I've ever seen. We were talking inside a cabin in the woods." He laughed and ran a hand through his hair. "I don't understand it. I can't explain it."

"Explain what?" Logan asked.

Braedan sat down. The dream was still so vivid. He thought that if he concentrated long enough, he might be able to reach out and touch the man's arm. He even lifted a hand in an attempt. "His voice was so real," he said. "Not like a dream—not that kind of real. Like we were sitting next to each other, having supper."

The room was full of nervous movements as the others listened.

"I am not mad, I swear to you. The man was . . . gods help me, but I think it was Alshada."

The others exchanged looks. "This is very well, sire, but how can we be certain?" Dylan said.

Braedan stood and paced. "I don't know. I don't know how to make you believe. I can only tell you that I was blind before that battle. I was a fool—a blind, hard-headed fool. I didn't see the truth of this world, the creatures who walk here, anything. I only saw what I wanted—what I thought I needed—Igraine, a throne, power, money, even Cerys—and all I needed was him—was his acceptance."

He had captured their attention now. He stopped pacing and turned to them. "He showed me all of my transgressions, but it was different. I wept, but there was comfort. He let me say I was sorry—he let me ask for peace—and then he gave it to me. The transgressions were gone."

"Gone?" Logan asked, his voice wistful.

"Gone." Braedan snapped his fingers. "He told me I have work to do. He sent me back here." He went to the table and picked up the parchment he'd been writing on. "I started making plans. We must return to Torlach—we have things—"

"A moment, sire," Dylan said, holding up a hand. He stood. "You assume that those you have wronged will forgive you, too. What of me? My household?"

Braedan lowered the parchment. "I am sorry, Dylan. I would do whatever you wish to make amends."

Dylan crossed the room. He held a hand out. "You wish to make amends? Be a king—a true king, a king we can follow."

Braedan clasped his arm and grinned. He turned to Hrogarth. "I would make amends with the tribe as well."

Hrogarth stood. "That is not for me to decide. I am no longer traitha over the nine. You will have to speak with the new traitha." He paused. "But if you go to him with the humility you have shown here today, you have a very good chance of being heard."

Braedan bowed. "I thank you."

"What would you have us do?" Logan asked.

Braedan took a deep breath. "We ride for Torlach tomorrow."

The guardian from Kiern stood. "Sire."

He pointed at her. "You were in Kiern."

She smiled. "I was."

"Esma, isn't it?"

"My tribal name is Esma. My Taurin name is Minerva. I answer to both."

"Then I shall call you Minerva. I am Taurin, after all."

She inclined her head. "You wondered in Kiern whether all that you had seen was real. What have you decided?"

"That everything I thought I knew was wrong."

Minerva tipped her head. "Not everything."

He thought for a moment. "That a king has more reason than anyone to seek truth. That I want history to remember me as a good man, not a powerful king. I want men to speak of how I restored things, not how I destroyed them."

"You once believed that you were your own man. You thought you could outsmart your own stupidity. Do you still believe that?"

He shook his head. "I do not deserve this country," he said. "I do not deserve this throne."

"That is true."

"But neither does my uncle. The best thing for Taura right now would be for me to return to Torlach and restore the regency—to hold the throne for the rightful heir." He frowned. "Where is she, anyway? Where is Mairead?"

Minerva bit her lip. "The girl you knew as Mairead is not the heir. Her name is Vivian. She is a decoy saya."

Braedan laughed. *Of course. Now it makes sense.* "That's why she would never really tell me anything of detail. She was hiding the fact that she isn't the one I thought she was." Minerva inclined her head, and Braedan crossed his arms. "Do you know where the real heir is? Is her name really Mairead?"

Minerva folded her hands before her. "Forgive me, sire, but I am not yet convinced enough of your conversion to share such details."

He waved her comments away with an idle hand. "They aren't important, anyway. The important thing is to get back to Torlach and establish the regency so that we can re-secure the throne for her and her progeny."

Minerva opened her mouth, took a breath, and then closed her mouth and stepped back.

"What is it? You may speak freely, guardian."

He didn't miss the tiny flinch when he called her "guardian." She took a deep breath. "I dreamed last night, too."

The room waited.

Minerva's chest rose and fell rapidly, her face flushed, and Braedan thought her hands shook. "I dreamed . . . I dreamed of a king."

Braedan took a step toward her. "A king?"

"I didn't see his face. I saw his legacy. I saw a great battle for Torlach, for Taura itself. I saw a false king on a throne, and then I saw the rightful king take his place. I saw him take the throne from a path paved with the blood of patriots who died to give it to him. I saw children of his line reuniting the three lands. And I saw his queen, and she was ...." She bit her lip. "It was not your princess, sire. It was the heir. The real heir. And I dreamed that you had decided the throne would be hers, that you determined to deliver it to her."

Braedan turned away. *Not Igraine. But perhaps not me, either. A faceless king, and a queen who is alive even now, waiting to have children for her line. My legacy? Or another man's? Who can say?* He took a deep breath. "The throne is not mine," he said. "I know this. I am ready to give up any claim I have to it. I will protect and defend it to the best of my ability, and I will do everything I can to give it over to the rightful king or queen, whoever that may be."

He heard Minerva moving around behind him, and he turned around. She went to the hearth and pulled out a piece of charcoal. She approached him. "Give me the sacred dagger."

He drew the blade and handed it to her.

"Kneel."

He didn't think to question it. He knelt before her.

"Now give me your weapon hand."

He held out his hand.

Logan stepped forward. "What are you—"

Minerva silenced him with a look. "Braedan Mac Corin, you have shown yourself worthy in battle. You have borne wounds in defense of Taura. You have fought without regard to your own safety. This blade testifies to your bond with Taura through blood and earth. Do you swear now to uphold the laws and government of the Taurin monarchy? Do you swear to uphold and defend the interests of Taura against all enemies, whether in her boundaries or without? Do you swear to defend the Raven Throne to your dying breath?"

Braedan thought the whole room held its breath. "I swear it."

She took his hand and turned it palm up. The animstone in the dagger's hilt glowed a bright blue when she sliced a shallow cut on his palm. He resisted the urge to hiss and bore the sting without flinching. Minerva rubbed her thumb across the blood on the blade. She painted a mark on Braedan's forehead, then took the charcoal in her hand and painted another mark over the first. "I anoint you Braedan, King of Taura, first of your name, Defender, Keeper of the Raven Throne, Ally of the Nine Tribes, and Protector of the Kirok. Long may you reign, and long may your descendants carry your legacy."

Braedan could not move. The weight of her words and actions held him pinned to the floor on his knees. *Alshada, I am not worthy of this*, he thought.

But Minerva wasn't finished. She closed Braedan's wounded hand, then put a hand on his head. "Rise, sire, and take your throne."

Braedan stood, and as he did so, Minerva knelt and bowed her head. He was about to protest, but Dylan stepped next to Minerva and knelt. He lifted his sword across both palms in offering. "You have my fealty and my sword, your majesty."

Logan and Malcolm came next. They knelt next to Braedan and pledged swords to him. Finally, Hrogarth approached. He didn't kneel, but he drew a blade and held it to Braedan, hilt first. "The first time we exchanged blades, I expected that the next thing we exchanged would be blows. I am glad that we have another opportunity to exchange blades."

Braedan drew a dagger from his boot and exchanged it with Hrogarth. "You may not be traitha over the nine, but you will always be my ally."

"My guardian will carry a message of what happened here back to the nine," Hrogarth said. "I cannot promise their allegiance, but I can promise you a hearing."

"It is more than I have a right to expect," Braedan said.

Hrogarth turned to the others. "I must bid you all farewell. My wife is buried, and my call is in the east. I can no longer hold the call at bay. The raven is loosed, and the First Raven will need my sword." He turned to Grytha. "Tell the hounds what happened here. Do not let my wife die in vain. And tell the traithas of the new Taurin king."

"I will, traitha."

He looked at Minerva. "The wisdomkeeper could do worse than you, girl," he said. "I will remember you all to the One Hand." He turned and left the room, and Braedan knew he would never see Hrogarth again.

Braedan looked at the small circle of people kneeling before him. "Rise, friends," he said. "Please."

They stood. "I expect we need some oiska, aye?" Dylan said. "I'll fetch it." He stepped out of the room.

Braedan leaned close to Minerva. "I hope you know what you're doing."

Her face held an otherworldly aura, and when she spoke, there was an additional resonance to it that he did not recall from previous interactions. "The One Hand knows all," she said. "He brought me here for this moment, as he brought you. His will be done."

"What is his will?" Logan asked.

Minerva turned to him. "We cannot see all, hidden one, but all are subject to him—to his good and perfect will." Logan flinched. Minerva held out her hand, revealing the blue glow of her own guardian's mark. "I dreamed of you as well, hidden one. He is not finished with you. He wishes you to know that he sees you, and he knows you."

Logan turned away. "That's not much comfort."

Minerva spread her hands. "I am called home now."

"Home?" Grytha asked.

"To the wisdomkeeper. She has work for me. I will return when she is finished with me."

"What about the sacred blade?" Braedan asked.

"The blade allowed me to take your blood with it. I have freed you from the bond. The blade is bonded to me now."

The relief Braedan felt was palpable. "I thank you. You have done me a great service."

"Not as great a service as you will do for Taura." She did not wait for a response, but left the room with a gait filled at once with humility and power.

Braedan let out a breath he thought he'd been holding for hours. Logan turned to him as Malcolm stood. "Well?" Logan said. "What's next?"

Braedan looked out his window. Two thousand years of Taurin history stared back, demanding his allegiance and his service. *This throne is not mine. Anointing or no, coronation or no, this is not my title. I only hold it for the one who will be greater than I am. But while I hold it, I will honor it.* "We ride for Torlach. We save my betrothed, and we secure the throne for the rightful Taurin heir."

CHAPTER THIRTY-FIVE

> *Syrafi illusions have been said to fool even the Evil One himself.*
> — *Tal'Aster teaching*

Spring in Torlach brought only restlessness to Igraine's spirit. The weather remained cold and wet for weeks, and she found herself relegated to her chambers with only knitting and embroidery to keep her company. She usually chose embroidery; her mother's voice rang constantly in her head, reminding her that "knitting is for common women." *Yes, Mother, by all means, let me use one small needle to create ridiculous designs on tapestries for no other reason than boredom.* She felt useless and impotent, and there was little to encourage her.

The winter had brought no further word of Braedan's whereabouts, and Kerry had all but formally declared his nephew dead and claimed the throne. Children were still disappearing, and on the shores of Culidar, a mysterious army of red-dyed men amassed, claiming the mythic title of Nar Sidhe. They took longboats into the channel to harass ships trying to reach Torlach. Merchants chose to port in the south more and more, preferring the swampy journey north with wagons and horses to savages with grappling hooks and swords.

Igraine had few formal duties anymore. Her many letters to the kirok were still unanswered, and Kerry had goaded her into so many arguments in court that she no longer had enough authority to be taken seriously. Her every attempt at reading law was scrutinized and discussed. She couldn't even go riding because of the weather. She sat in her chambers and read kirok books, embroidered, and wrote long letters to Braedan that she couldn't send. *And even if I could send them, there's no guarantee he would receive them. Gods, Braedan—are you still alive? Where are you?*

Nimue's time had become almost entirely consumed by Lady Aislinn, and she could send only occasional messages to Igraine through Aiden. Aiden became Igraine's only reliable source of information. He had grown close to one of Aislinn's maids, and the girl believed he hated Igraine. The details she shared with the guard always made it to Igraine's ears.

One morning, Igraine finished dressing and entered her study to find Aiden waiting for her. "You didn't escort me to supper last night. 'Twas another fine evening with your lady?" she asked.

His face reddened. He cleared his throat. "The kirok has arrived, highness."

She sat and laced her fingers in her lap. "Now. After all these months."

"Yes, highness. And it appears they are closely allied with the chancellor."

"Why do you say that?"

"They bring word from Espara—from Lady Ilyssa's family. The lady has died."

Igraine let out a long breath. "If Kerry's wife is dead, he'll be wedding Aislinn within the month."

"Yes, highness." Aiden paused. "Aislinn refuses to take any more of the herbs. She is trying to conceive."

"Does Kerry know?"

He shrugged. "It could be that it will take some time for her to conceive— she didn't conceive with her first husband."

"But he refused to bed her often. She did tell me that much months ago, when she first came here." Igraine thought. "Kerry has never formally revoked my position as ambassador. Only a regent or king can do that, and he's still only chancellor. He can't really keep me from meeting with the kirons."

"No, but he can arrest you for disobeying him."

"I'm not disobeying him. He's given me no orders concerning the kirok. I want to be in that room."

"They plan to meet after the midday meal. There's also to be a state banquet tonight where Kerry will speak and honor the elders."

"Thank you, Aiden."

Igraine asked her maid Gwyn to alert her as soon as the kirons arrived at the castle, but she need not have worried. The commotion from the courtyard was enough notice. Kerry had arranged for bells and trumpets to announce the kirons, and kirok flags flew next to Taurin. Igraine stepped outside to look down from a balcony and saw Kerry in full livery with a dress sword at his side. Cormac hovered behind him wearing similar finery.

A contingent of Taurin guards escorted a full, formal guard of kirok soldiers in blue, black, and gold. The men parted as a carriage entered the courtyard and pulled to a halt before Kerry. The footman helped three men out of the carriage—two in long blue robes of high-ranking elders and another in the brown robes of a scribe. Kerry greeted all of them with a low bow and escorted them into the castle.

Igraine turned away from the spectacle and took Aiden's arm. "Stay close to me today," she said. "I may need you."

"Of course, my lady, but the chancellor watches me, too. I worry ...."

"Yes?"

He frowned. "He's been sending the few men I could trust away on fool's errands. There may be some men loyal to Braedan in Kiern, but there's no way to know."

"What do you know of the new duke there—Connor Mac Niall?"

"Not much, highness. He's been rather quiet on the issue of the crown and the regency. I'm not sure he's even arrived to claim his holdings yet. I only know his reputation—that he's a rake with women and deadly with a sword."

She was quiet, her mind turning. *If I wanted to convince Duke Mac Niall to support Braedan—or at least to withhold his support from Kerry—what would I have to give up?* "Which dukes on the table still support the king?" she whispered.

Aiden was quiet as a servant walked by. "I don't know," he said. "We know Seannan supports the chancellor, and Dylan in the north is very quiet on the whole succession. The others—it's hard to say which way they'll be swayed."

"There is still much respect for the Mac Niall name," Igraine said. "If we could convince Duke Mac Niall to support Braedan, might we convince the other dukes?"

"It's hard to say, my lady." He paused again. "But it's worth a try."

She took a deep breath as they arrived at the door to the small audience hall. "Much will depend on what happens today, I suppose," she said. Aiden opened the door, and Igraine entered with her chin high.

Chancellor Kerry, the two elders, and the scribe all turned. "My lady," Kerry said with a strangled edge. "I did not think to see you today."

She curtsied. "I have ever intended to fulfill the duties the king gave me, my lord."

One of the elders set down his goblet and folded his hands. "This is the princess I've heard so much about, I assume? Igraine Mac Roy? I thought you said you'd revoked her title as ambassador to the kirok."

Igraine blinked. "Have I misunderstood Taurin law? Only a king or regent can make such a change to an appointment. Unless you've been made regent without my knowledge, chancellor, I think I'm still within my rights to attend this meeting."

The other elder stepped forward, and his hands formed the old greeting she remembered from the sayada—hand to forehead, then heart, then folded before him. "Your highness, I am Prelate Leo d'Antris, aide to High Prelate Johanan. I'm not certain you would remember, but we met once, many years ago, in your father's home."

The man had grayed considerably, and his tanned features were lined with age now, but she remembered him from her childhood. "Spirits, it is you," she said. He held out his hand, and she took it, curtsied, and kissed his ring. "It's been years. I was so young."

He smiled. "I was there with the High Prelate to commission the kirok in Maghara. How is your fair city, highness?"

"Maghara was well when last I saw it," she said. "It's been many months, and I fear I've had little news from my parents. The harbor here has been volatile." She held back news of Ian's presence on the island.

"That is very true," he said. "Even our ships were harried by the savages."

She smiled. "Well, I'm certain my betrothed will put an end to it when he returns to Torlach." The elders and Kerry exchanged a look, but she pretended not to see. She gestured. "But don't let me prattle on while we neglect your fellows. Please, introduce me."

"This is Elder Elias." He pointed to a large, fair-skinned man. "And this is Kiron Ygan." He gestured to another man, slight, with the brown skin and round face of Tal'Amun.

Igraine looked at Ygan's folded hands. They had the scars of a man who did more than read scrolls aloud on kirok feast days. "'Tis a pleasure to have kirons in the castle," she said. "I welcome you in the name of Alshada." She gestured. "Please, let us sit and discuss why you are truly here."

Kerry's frown deepened, but he didn't object. He and the other men sat at the small table, and Igraine took a goblet of wine from a servant. The girl curtsied and scurried away.

Leo gave Igraine a thin smile. "I see you've forsaken your vows, highness."

She put her goblet down. "I never took them. I was still undecided when the sayada was overtaken."

"Ah," Leo said. He leaned forward. "Undecided. Unlike the poor women you allowed to be taken under arrest."

"I did all I could to save them, Prelate. I had only their safety in mind when I came to the castle."

"Only their safety?" Leo laughed. "My lady, forgive me, but that's hard to believe. You very neatly insinuated yourself into a position that no noblewoman should have, and then managed to parlay that into a betrothal that your father has not yet approved."

Igraine sat up straighter. "I fail to see why my position in King Braedan's court is at issue. I assure you, Prelate, I had every intention of seeing the sayas and the kirons to safety. I'd hoped to hear from the kirok sooner. You can't blame their deaths on me. The kirok is the one that failed to respond."

"I question your loyalties, my lady," Leo said. "A woman who gets herself out of a tricky place, only to turn her position to her advantage while her sisters languish—it's something I must question. Do you truly have the kirok's interests at heart? Or the king's? Or only your own?"

Igraine sipped her wine again. "I am ambassador to the kirok first. I have the king's interests and yours at heart, Prelate. I intend to be as impartial in our dealings as I am able, but since I work for his majesty, you need to expect that I will err on the side of Taura."

"I can represent Taura's interests, thank you, highness," Kerry said. "And I fail to see how the kirok could respect you as a representative, my lady, when you clearly don't follow their teachings."

She straightened. "And you, my lord? Let's discuss the Lady Aislinn, shall we?"

He feigned a sad expression. "Unfortunately, as it turns out, I've had no need to remain faithful for several months. Prelate Leo brought word today— my wife died in her father's home almost a year ago." Kerry shrugged. "A pity, but we weren't close. Her sanity trod a thin line. And since we had no children and my nephew was my heir, I'll need to remarry soon. I'm not a young man. The Lady Aislinn will be a good match for me. She's young and hale and can surely provide many sons."

Leo lifted his goblet to Kerry. "And may I offer congratulations, my lord? May we celebrate the end of our meetings with a wedding?"

Igraine's heart pounded in frantic desperation against her ribs. She licked her lips. "The end of these meetings? We've only just started."

Kerry unrolled a piece of parchment. "I've been negotiating with the kirok for many months now, highness. Everything is already settled. The elders will rebuild in the city and countryside."

"And what will you be getting, then?"

"Support for my coronation."

Igraine remained upright only by sheer force of her will. She straightened her shoulders and lifted her chin. "You told Braedan to keep religion out of the affairs of state," she whispered.

He shrugged. "I've had a change of heart. The good Prelate Leo has helped me see the light of Alshada's truth."

Leo turned a cool gaze toward Kerry. "Let's not pretend this is any more than it is."

"And what is it?" Igraine asked.

"An alliance of convenience. A pragmatic move on the part of the kirok—a way to return to Taura and move about freely," Leo said. "We have no illusions of Chancellor Kerry's allegiance to the kirok or Alshada, but we will support him as long as he allows the kirok to rebuild and spread the truth of Alshada to the people."

"I could have done that," Igraine said. "I was working with Braedan—I had him convinced—"

Leo shrugged. "We treated with the one who wrote to us."

Her hands burned cold with realization. She turned to Kerry. "You've intercepted my every communication with the kirok since I came here, haven't you? You've planned this all along."

He stood. "I believe our meeting is over. Your guard may escort you back to your rooms." He motioned Aiden forward.

Aiden hesitated. "Your highness?"

Igraine stood. "Is this prison, then? It's finally come to this—that you'll be keeping me in my rooms?"

"Prison is a very unpleasant way to look at it, your highness," Kerry said. "Think of it as a way to ensure your health and safety until you are able to return to Eirya."

Her mouth tightened. "I want to see the Eiryan ambassador. Send for Rory Nolan."

"Of course. I'll have him escorted to your study as soon as possible."

She returned to her chambers with Aiden and paced and fidgeted until the knock finally came an hour later. She adjusted her skirts and hair and turned to the door. "Come." Aiden opened the door, and Rory entered. "Thank you, Aiden." The guard closed the door, and Igraine turned to Rory. "Thank you for coming."

"I confess—this isn't what I expected," he said, one hand resting on the sword at his side. He was dressed in leather and wool and wore a small insignia of his house on one breast. "You look well."

She waved away his comments. "What are they saying about Braedan in the city?"

"Everyone assumes he's dead," he said.

She blinked back the sting of tears. "And Aislinn—what do they say about her?"

"They pity her—the sweet, young widow of the king's cousin. They speak of how he took the throne and then ran away, and how Chancellor Kerry is the best thing to happen since Regent Fergus." He paused. "You can't blame them, Igraine—there is fear all over the city. The children, this army in Culidar .... I can see the fires from my ship, and they grow brighter each night. I've very nearly returned to Eirya several times."

She turned away from him and sat down. "People see instability and they have no one to turn to for reassurance because until today, the kirok was gone at Braedan's order. Of course they would be angry with him, and now Kerry swoops in to save everyone—take care of everyone. This is exactly how he wanted it—he kept me from my duties, intercepted my letters, and got rid of Braedan. He wants the throne, and I'd not be surprised if he had his own wife murdered so he can marry Aislinn."

Rory approached behind her. He put a hand on her shoulder. "Igraine—come back to Eirya. We can leave tomorrow. This doesn't need to be your battle. The king is dead—"

"He's not dead!" She shook off his hand and stood. *Gods, Braedan—please be alive!* "He's not, Rory. Don't you think if he were, Kerry would be certain to parade his body before the entire country? The only reason he's not taken the throne faster is that he can't prove Braedan is dead. He moves slowly so that it won't matter if Braedan is alive or not—if he's alive and he returns to find his uncle with a firm grip on the throne, Kerry will have the support to have him exiled, imprisoned, or killed. If he's dead, then Kerry has nothing to worry about."

Rory frowned and folded his arms. "All right. Let's assume the king is alive and unable to contact you. Why do you stay here, Igraine? In the castle? What can you possibly do when the chancellor chips away at every bit of power you managed to eke away from Braedan?"

She turned away again. "Go away, Rory."

"Answer me."

She took a deep breath. "I'm trying to hold his throne. I believe in him—in what he offers Taura. Kerry is not a good man. He has only his own interests in mind. Braedan thinks of Taura first."

"And what of you, eh? You think only of your own interests, don't you? Wanting to be ambassador, legal advisor, queen—"

"I never wanted the throne," she said, whirling around. "Never. He talked me into it—Braedan did—and I accepted because I loved him. Love him."

"And now he's gone. And month after month goes by, and you have nothing to count on."

"You're an ass, Rory."

"At least I'm an honest one." He stepped toward her. "I know you cling to this hope that he's alive, and I understand. But know this, Igraine—I'm waiting, and when you're ready to admit that he's gone, I'll still be waiting."

"Waiting." She scoffed. "You liar. You wait for nothing but the next whore who spreads her legs for a few coppers."

"I haven't been a kiron since I arrived, that's certain, but I'm not offering any whore a title or a family as I am you." He paused. "At least come stay with me, in the ambassador's house. You can bring your guard and your ladies."

She sat down again and crossed her arms. *I might have more freedom at his house.* "I'll consider it."

"Truly?"

"Yes." She took off her circlet. "Kerry is having a banquet tonight for the elders. You've been invited, haven't you?"

A muscle twitched in his jaw. "I have."

"Well, you'll need a guest. Kerry won't turn away a foreign royal on the arm of a foreign ambassador. Will you let me be your guest?"

He made a sweeping gesture. "As you wish, your highness. I'll go home to prepare." He bent and kissed the top of her head. "Grainy, listen—whatever else happens, know I do love you. Always."

She took his hand and smiled up at him. "Thank you, Rory."

When he left the room, she sent for Cormac. He arrived quickly, as if he'd been waiting for her summons, and bowed. "Your highness."

She smiled. "Have a seat." He sat across from her, and she arranged her skirts and folded her hands in her lap. "It's been some time since we sent Logan away. Tell me truly, Cormac. Have you heard anything from him?"

"No, I'm sorry." He paused. "I think we must assume the king is dead."

She swallowed the sting of tears in her throat. "Will you be supporting Kerry in his bid for the throne, then?"

"I will."

"What did he offer you?"

"My lady?"

"He must have offered you something. Just a few months ago, you would rather have died than see Kerry on the Raven Throne."

"Things have changed, it's true."

A long moment of silence hovered around them. *He won't tell me. My days of influence are over. He believes Braedan dead and allies himself with power. There's nothing left for me here.* "Thank you, Cormac," Igraine said. "You may go."

"Of course, my lady." Cormac stood and left the room.

Igraine called for a bath and took her time preparing for the banquet. Her thoughts were a jumble. *Everyone believes Braedan dead. Cormac has allied himself with Kerry. The kirok and Kerry make their own treaty without my help. There is nothing left here for me.* Tears stung her eyes. *What else is there? I can wait until the kirok returns to Taura and become a saya again, but would they have me? I can't take vows I don't believe in. I can return to Eirya, but my father will have me wed to Rory the moment we step onto the docks. And there's still the question of this mysterious power that I may have. My mother could tell me more, but I would have to return to Eirya for that.* She swallowed over a lump in her throat. *There's nothing left for me here in the castle. If I went home ....*

When Aiden brought word that Rory had arrived, she took a deep breath and prepared herself for what she would have to do that night. She met the ambassador in the foyer of the ballroom, where other arriving nobles milled about waiting for the chancellor to arrive.

Rory was dressed in his Eiryan livery, a gold cord around one shoulder to indicate his rank and his hair bound at his neck. He smiled and bent to kiss her cheek. "You look beautiful, as always, your highness."

She took his hands and returned the smile and the kiss. "You are as charming as ever, my lord."

He put her hand on his arm, and they approached the hall. The steward paled when he saw Igraine. "Your highness—I was told you wouldn't be attending tonight."

"Her highness is attending as my guest," Rory said. "You'll be letting her in, aye?"

"Of course, my lord." He turned to those already assembled and announced them. "Duke Riordan Nolan of Falcon Heights, Ambassador representing His Majesty, King Cedric Mac Roy of Eirya, and his guest, Igraine Mac Roy, Princess Royale of Eirya."

Kerry's face hardened into stone from his place in the center of the dais. To his right sat Aislinn Seannan and to his left, Prelate Leo. Kerry stood and descended to meet them. "My lord Nolan," he said, his voice strained. "I did not expect you to bring a guest."

"Let it not be said I'd ever leave a beautiful royal lady alone in her chambers when there are festivities afoot," Rory said. He patted Igraine's hand.

Kerry gave Igraine a tight smile. "It's just as well. You should be here to hear everything."

She returned the smile. "I'd not miss it."

The steward seated Rory and Igraine at the far end of the table on the dais, and the courses started to arrive. Igraine picked at her food while Rory ate and drank his fill. He leaned over to her and whispered, "You don't enjoy the pork?"

She shrugged. "I've little appetite."

Rory took her hand.

She smiled up at him. "I may have been too hasty all those years ago. Perhaps I should let you have another chance."

He blinked, surprised. "Truly?"

She shrugged.

He lifted her hand and kissed it. "We have much to discuss later, then."

Kerry raised his goblet and stood, and the steward pounded the floor to get everyone's attention. "Good evening, my lords and ladies. I thank you all for attending tonight. We are grateful you're here to help us welcome back the kirok to Taurin shores."

A smattering of polite applause echoed off the walls, and Kerry smiled. "It's no secret that my nephew had a rather tense relationship with the kirok. Ambassador Mac Roy was of little help to the kirok elders, I fear, and I had to take over her position to make headway."

Igraine's hand tightened around Rory's under the table. "Steady, love," he whispered.

Kerry continued. "In times like these, the presence of the kirok is more important than ever. The teachers provide hope, encouragement, and guidance to all of us, but especially to the least among us. With a horde looming across the channel and children disappearing from homes and streets, there has never been a more vital need for the kirok to minister to us. Therefore, I'm pleased to announce that within the month, kiroks all over the island will undergo restoration. In addition, I am turning over all interactions with the kirok to my seneschal, Lord Cormac Rowan. He will personally oversee the restoration efforts at the sayada."

The applause was louder that time, and the elders raised their goblets to Cormac. He returned the gesture.

Kerry continued. "Unfortunately, the return of the kirok doesn't solve our biggest problem as a nation—that of our lack of leadership. It's been months since I received word from my nephew, and as chancellor, I do not have the authority I need to lead Taura as it deserves. Therefore, I've called a meeting of the Table of Councilors, and I'll be seeking to replace my nephew as king. As soon as a quorum of dukes arrives in Torlach, meetings will begin."

There was a quiet, nervous applause, and murmurs fluttered through the room. Kerry gestured them down. "Now, I know this is a surprise for most of you," he said. "And it's a risk, I'm sure, as you know I have no heir but my nephew. But often, bad news precedes good. I've received word that my wife, the Lady Ilyssa, has passed on in Espara. While this is sad news, it does free me to announce that I will wed the Lady Aislinn Seannan." He held out his hand and lifted Aislinn to her feet, and she blushed properly. "The lady is the picture of breeding and proper noble behavior, and I'm sure that, in time, she'll provide the Raven Throne with many heirs."

The applause then grew louder, and Kerry bent to kiss Aislinn's cheek and then seated her again. He lifted his goblet to the crowd. "Now, I implore you, return to your meal and enjoy. This day marks a new beginning in Taurin history—a restoration of prosperity and peace that, with Alshada's blessing, will continue for millennia."

The nobles toasted him in response, including Rory. Igraine raised her goblet, but said nothing. *He knows he's won,* she thought. She drank, set down her goblet, and leaned over to Rory. "A word outside?"

He set his goblet down. "Of course. Are you ready to leave?"

"I was ready an hour ago, but I needed to hear all of that."

He stood and went to Kerry's side, leaned over, and spoke with the chancellor at length. Kerry nodded, and Rory returned to Igraine. He held out his hand and helped her to her feet. They left the hall amid flutters of conversation and speculation.

Once in the foyer, Igraine's composure started to fade. She called Aiden over. "Aiden, go tell my ladies to start packing my things," she said. "And be sure to let Nimue know that I expect her to accompany me."

"Of course, my lady." He paused. "Where will they be accompanying you?"

"To the ambassador's house. I'll be staying there until he concludes his business here, and then I'll be returning to Eirya."

Aiden opened his mouth, closed it, and bowed. "Yes, my lady. I'll begin at once." He walked away.

Rory led Igraine outside and called for his carriage. He led her to a quiet bench where they could wait. "This reminds me of our first night," he said. "After your parents' party."

"Don't be thinking you'll woo me with memories, Rory. I have enough poor ones of you as well."

He laughed. One big hand reached up under her hair to cup the back of her head. "And what would it take to woo you back into my bed, then?"

"Rory," she started, then sighed. "I've grown so much since we were together before. We were children. I've grown pragmatic. And it would seem there is little for me here. At least you and I are compatible in many ways."

"We are."

She held up a hand. "But—there is much you don't know about me."

"I have time," he said. He lifted her hand to his mouth and kissed it. "Anything I don't know about you now is something I want to learn."

She forced a smile. "Can you give me any assurance of faithfulness? Anything?"

"I'll try. That's the best I can do."

Rory won't be faithful, but at least I'll have Eirya. And he'll provide well for me, and he'll be kind. At least we'll have that much. In Eirya, perhaps I'll find answers to this blood inside me. And I can take in any bastards he might find and raise them as my own. It's not the life I wanted, but it's the life I'll get to have. "All right. I'll return to Eirya with you."

"And?"

She sighed. *He's right. Braedan must be dead. I would have heard more than just a fleeting note by now if he were alive.* She held back tears. "If my father will allow it, yes. I'll marry you."

CHAPTER THIRTY-SIX

The blood of the lioness binds.
Justice returns to the land.
— Second Book of the Wisdomkeepers

Gareth brought spare clothes and provided Mairead a tent to change. Devyn kept watch. When Mairead emerged with her folded robe, the cat stood and fell in step next to her as she walked with Gareth. "What happened?" he asked. "How did you come to be out here?"

She told him the story. "They were plainsmen," she said. "They did not speak as tribesmen. But someone at one of the gates of Isfyrin is in league with someone who wishes me dead."

She stumbled, and he caught her arm. "How long has it been since you ate?"

"Two days. I think. It was a bit unclear."

"I think the earthspirit made sure you would have an initiation," Gareth said. "It would have been nice if you hadn't been with child." He put an arm around her waist and led her to the fire, where he gave her flatbread and some small bits of pheasant and brewed tea for her.

Wyll sat next to them. "Have you seen any other ravens or lions?" he asked.

"No one. You're the first people I've seen in two days. Have you seen any lions in the forest?"

"Grayfeather searches the skies, but he has brought us no signs of them," Gareth said. "We keep moving, but we're watching for them."

"And if you find them?" she asked. "What do you intend to do about your father?"

He shrugged. "I don't think I'm much of a Catspaw anymore. I'm not a raven, either. I'm sworn to you, traitha. In every way I can be."

She smiled and touched his arm. "Perhaps you are the one who will betray."

He frowned.

"Your prophecy—one to wed, one to fall, one to betray. You betray your birth to follow me and camp with the ravens."

He tipped his head in consideration. "I suppose that could be," he mused. "I'm still confused about who will marry, though, especially since you have wed the raven."

"As with so many prophecies, I'm sure we'll know when we look back."

When she had eaten, she gathered the ravens around her to discuss strategy and planning. She looked around the circle of men and saw hesitation, distrust, even fear on their faces. She sat down and laced her fingers together. "I owe you an apology," she said. "All of you. When my husband was taken, I was afraid. I feared for my life, the life of my child, the safety of my companions .... I feared that one of you—all of you—would be as violent as Connor—Ulfrich—was that day."

"What changed?" Wyll asked.

She gestured to her face. "This changed. I had a vision. The earth showed me that you will fight with me—that we will fight with the lions. The ravens, the lions, the wolf from the west, the bear from the east—we will fight together, and I will lead you."

Wyll inclined his head. "You are forgiven, traitha." There were murmurs and nods of agreement around the circle of men.

Mairead smiled at them. "Thank you." She took a deep breath. "When I left Isfyrin, Gareth's father was planning to gather a force and descend on your village to rescue his son," she said. "But with my disappearance, that may have changed—I don't know. What I do know is that I intend to make my stand with you. So what I want to know from you is, where do you want to make your stand?"

They shifted nervous feet. Wyll cleared his throat. "I'm . . . we're not sure what you mean, traitha."

"Where would Connor tell you to make your stand? What would he say?" She stood and gestured to the mountain. "This is as much your home as it is home to the lions. It's time you claim it as such. Where will you draw a line and tell the lions, 'no more. You will come no farther'?"

Wyll exchanged glances with a few men and cleared his throat. "Our village," he said. "It's not much, but it's ours." The men around the fire agreed.

Mairead stood. "Then we will gather the ravens and return there. And I will stand between you and the lions, if I must." She paused. "My husband made you a promise, and he could not keep it. I will keep it for him. I will make my stand with you. I will lead you."

"The ravenmaster," Wyll said. "It's as the eunuch said—you are the ravenmaster." He stood. "We make our stand in the village. Let's gather up the ravens and go home."

They broke camp and mounted horses. Gareth insisted that Mairead take his, and she did not argue. The rest was welcome. Devyn padded next to her, and the horses seemed not to even notice her. "It's an odd thing about the companions," Gareth said. "There is something about them that eases the spirits of our livestock."

"Perhaps they have their own marks."

He turned to Wyll. "How will we call in the other ravens?"

"I'm not certain," Wyll admitted.

"We can send Grayfeather to search for them," Gareth suggested. "He can take a message."

They decided to return to the raven village first. Gareth told Mairead it was two days away from where she had found them. "How did I end up so far from Isfyrin and the raven village?" she asked.

He shrugged. "In your vision, it's hard to say where you were led. There are boys who start their vision quests two days from the city and end up taking seven days to return. The mountain can be confusing. Men have starved to death an hour's walk from the city."

When they stopped to camp, Mairead found herself so tired that she could only stay awake long enough to eat a short meal and retire to the small tent Gareth provided for her. When she woke the next day, he showed her a small piece of woven cloth. "Grayfeather brought it this morning," he said. "The ravens don't use much woven cloth—they don't have weavers. This was from a lion. He's trying to tell me they're close."

Mairead finished tying off a fresh braid. "Any sign of other ravens?"

"No. We should reach the village by mid-afternoon, though. Might be a few of them there." He paused. "How do you feel today? Rested?"

"I'm well, Gareth. I just needed a good night's sleep."

"The marks—I can't look away from them."

She touched her face. The skin was still smooth to the touch. There was no indication of the tattooing—no rough skin, welts, soreness. "I wonder what Connor will say," she said, then winced. "I mean, if—"

"I know." Gareth put a hand on her arm. "I don't think he's dead. And I don't think he'll be back to kill us. I think he's just wrestling with her."

"What if she wins?"

"She won't."

Mairead knew he only said it because she wanted to hear it, but the words were a comfort anyway. "I didn't think I could take him back if he left, but I think I've realized this is part of what he is. I don't get to have the village life. I will always be wed to a warrior, and that means living with someone who comes and goes. So if he comes back, I will welcome him." She let out a long breath and forced a smile. She put a hand on her belly. "I hope he hurries. I want him to be here before the babe comes."

They mounted and rode toward the raven village. Gareth's estimation proved correct, and the sun was about halfway through its downward path when they arrived. Everything was as they had left it, Wyll noted. He kicked at the dirt near the communal fire pit. "They didn't even disturb the ashes."

"If they've even been here," Gareth said.

Wyll grunted. "It does stay fairly hidden."

When Mairead had been in the village previously, the snow had been heavy on the trees. When she left, she'd been blindfolded. Now, really examining the space for the first time, she could see how it would be hard to find. Set at the bottom of a culvert, surrounded by thick trees and difficult terrain, the location would not be tempting for men to investigate. The ravens had constructed small guard platforms in the trees and disguised them in forest colors. Quivers of arrows were tied to tree trunks all around, and the men had surrounded the village with camouflaged pikes.

She found Wyll and Gareth just as Gareth was tying a piece of parchment to Grayfeather's leg. He stroked the bird's head and spoke quietly to him. Grayfeather chirped in response and then took wing. "How does he understand you?" she asked.

"I don't know. None of us know. They just seem to know what we're saying—and sometimes even what we don't say." He pointed to Devyn. "Have you spoken much with her yet?"

Mairead scratched the cat's head. Devyn sat on her haunches and rubbed Mairead's thigh. A low, rumbling purr shook Mairead's leg. "Not much. A bit as I walked. She answers sometimes—little noises, purrs, chirps. I don't really know what to do with her."

Gareth shrugged. "You don't have to do much. They just seem to know what we need. But if you ask her to help with something, she probably will."

I wonder if she could find Connor. Surely she knows the mountain better than any of us. She put the thought away for the time and helped unpack the horses.

It was just before supper that Mairead finally found the courage to return to the hut she had shared with Connor. Gareth went with her, but she held up a hand at the door. "I need to do this," she said. "I need to face being without him."

Gareth put a hand on her shoulder. "If you need me ...."

She smiled. "You are as much a brother to me as any man could be." He squeezed her shoulder and walked away.

She opened the door to the hut, and Devyn walked in as if she already knew the place. Mairead followed her. She rested a hand on her belly and sighed. Devyn stretched out on the ground near the fire pit. Mairead sat next to her and buried a hand in her fur. "And so we start again," she whispered.

It was mid-morning the next day when the first group of ravens returned. Mairead welcomed them, and to a man, they swore fealty to her once they saw her marks. The same thing happened later in the day when the second group returned, and again when the third and fourth groups arrived.

Mairead retreated to her hut at that point and dug through Connor's things until she found the small polished plate he used when he shaved. She held it up to her face and traced the lines that swirled from over her left eye down her left cheek and disappeared under the edge of her tunic. Compared to Hedwar's mark, hers was thin and graceful, but determined. The lines were continuous and unbroken from eyebrow to shoulder. They twisted and looped into knots and whorls that always resolved and continued. *You are chosen, marked, bought, and blooded. You will lead these people into their inheritance. But at what cost?*

There was a commotion outside again, and Mairead straightened, expecting more of the ravens. "Mairead," Gareth called. He knocked on her door as she stood. "Quickly, come."

She picked up a bow and quiver and followed him out of the hut. "What is it?"

"Lions."

Her stomach twisted. "Here?"

He ran toward the edge of the village. "They followed the last group. It's my father."

Mairead ran as fast as her growing belly would allow, following Gareth to the edge of the village.

They had dismounted by the time Mairead and Gareth arrived. Wyll and the other ravens held them at sword point, and two dozen lions stood with hands raised in peace. Hedwar and Trypp were in the front of the group. Behind them, she saw Braun and Wulf.

Trypp and Hedwar both turned when they heard her approach. Hedwar gasped. "Mairead," he whispered. "Your mark."

She stopped in front of him. "I had a vision of the earth. The One Hand marked me."

He nodded. "It's—"

"Unheard of," Trypp said. His arm was still bandaged, but he no longer had it bound against his chest. He stepped toward her and bowed. "Traitha," he greeted.

She could not help but smile. "Trypp, you must never bow."

He straightened. "It is because you say so that I will bow until my dying day," he said. He looked at Devyn, who had planted herself right next to Mairead's right leg. "Who is this?"

"Devyn. My companion."

Trypp whistled, and Twitch padded out of the trees. She edged over to Devyn, who appraised her with her steady, golden stare. Twitch slunk in, head down, and at last, Devyn lowered her head, too. They bumped noses, Twitch rolled over, and Devyn started to purr.

"I guess they like each other," Trypp said.

"Good news," Mairead said.

"We do not desire to hurt you men," Hedwar said. "We only came for my son. We need him back in Isfyrin. We will let you live in peace here if you will release him."

There were angry murmurs behind her, but Mairead held up her hand. "You will *let* us? What right have you to dictate our freedom?"

"That's not—"

"You cast these men aside because of fear," she said. "What right have you to tell them where they can live?" She waited while her words sank in. "These men were cast out of your tribe the moment they were marked. They had no choice. They did not ask for the mark or the exile, but it's what they received. Are they now to receive more they did not ask for? Persecution, destruction, death?"

"No," Hedwar said. "I do not wish to hurt these men."

"But there are those among you who would," Mairead said. "Other clans, other men in your clan—there are threats everywhere. What will you do with them? How will we live in the shadow of Isfyrin with that kind of hatred toward us?"

"'*We?*'" Trypp asked. "Are you part of this village now?"

She looked at the lions before her and turned to look at the ravens behind. *The city is home, but this is home, too. Because this is where Connor is and where he'll return if he comes back. And wherever my husband is, there is my home.* "I am," she said.

Trypp didn't wait a single moment. He turned to Hedwar and removed a dagger from his boot. "You gave me this when you accepted me into your clan," he said. "When I had no other clan, you gave me one and let me serve my earthbonded parents until they died. But I hear how you talk—you and the other lions. I hear your fears and your prejudices and your assumptions, and I know you make decisions based on your fluid interpretations of vague prophecies." He dropped the dagger on the ground. "I will no longer be part of it. I will no longer be a lion."

Gareth gasped. "Trypp, no."

"Shut it, Catspaw," he said, but there was a note of affection in the tone. He pointed at Mairead. "This woman is braver than any lion I've ever met. Her husband, a raven, threatened her life, and yet she came back to the raven village and made her stand with them. She is more outcast than any of us— outlander, foreign, a woman with a warriormark—and she doesn't let it change her. She is a woman—no, she is a leader, a warrior, worth following." He stepped back and crossed his arms. "I make my stand with her."

"And what of your wife and child?" Hedwar asked.

Trypp shrugged in his easy way. "Wytha was hoping for a change of scenery."

Hedwar turned to Gareth. "And you? Are you staying here?"

"My place is serving my traitha, Father. You taught me that." He stepped closer to Mairead. "She is my traitha now."

Hedwar let out a long breath. "I did not intend—"

"What did you intend?" Wyll asked. "You say you only want your son back, but you brought this force. What were your intentions, Catspaw?"

Wulf stepped out of the crowd, Braun close behind him. "We intend to kick you off the mountain."

Mairead drew her sword. "Try."

Wulf chortled. "Try to best a silly girl with fake marks? With pleasure." He stepped forward, drawing his sword.

"No, wait!" Hedwar stepped between them. "We need time. The council—"

"The council has spoken too much," Wulf shouted. "It's time for action."

"No!" Hedwar started to draw his own sword. "Wulf, stand down!"

No one moved for a long moment. At last, Wulf sheathed his sword and crossed his arms. "For now."

Hedwar turned back to Gareth, Mairead, and Trypp. "We will discuss this as a council. I will return in a few days. Is that all right?"

Mairead inclined her head. "I hope that we will be friends, traitha."

Hedwar gave her a small bow. "As do I, traitha." He motioned the lions to back away, and they all mounted their horses and rode westward, Hedwar bringing up the rear.

Gareth and Mairead turned to Trypp. "Wytha is anxious for a change of scenery?" Gareth said.

Trypp shrugged. "She'll be fine. She doesn't get attached to things." He turned to the village. "So, traitha. Where can I build?"

The ravens continued to file back into the village over the next several days. Almost all of them knelt and swore fealty to Mairead the moment they saw her marks. Predictably, there were some who chose not to swear, but Mairead thought their resolve had faded a bit. Devyn's presence seemed to make a lot of knees wobble. Aelfred, in particular, eyed the cat with a mixture of fear and admiration. "I did not know that anyone could bond with a lioness," he admitted. "For an outlander, and a woman, I would never have thought …."

Mairead waited, but he never finished his sentence. "The cat isn't going anywhere," she said. "I hope you won't, either."

"I won't," he said. "I cannot call you traitha yet, but I intend to stay."

Osgar returned with a small group of men who had been dissenters. Mairead thought he appeared to be in very ill health. His face was pale, and his hands seemed affected by palsy. He held them tight at his back so that she could not see them when he greeted her, but she noticed the shaking later when he drank near the fire. Devyn's ears flattened when she saw Osgar, and she drew her lips back to reveal a hint of a white tooth when he came close to her. Mairead leaned down later and whispered to Devyn. "He is not a threat, Devyn," she said. "He is just a sick, tired, broken man." But Devyn gave a low rumble in her throat that was most assuredly not a purr.

The lions returned a few days later, but Hedwar approached without the other men at first. He motioned behind him. "I brought visitors," he said, and Wytha, Letha, and Elsbet rode up to the village.

Trypp ran to his wife and helped her dismount. Elsbet gave a tiny cry and leapt out of her saddle into Gareth's arms. Mairead watched them as Letha dismounted and approached her. "How are you?" the guardian asked.

Mairead shrugged. "I am well."

"They told me about the marks, but I did not believe it. I have never seen the like, and I have seen countless men and women marked." She pointed at her own, which were like smoky curls rising in a haphazard, disconnected pattern up her face. "Mine are very like most guardians, and you can see on Hedwar and Wulf what a traitha's marks look like. Yours are like a combination of both guardian and traitha."

"I hope this show of good faith means something," Hedwar said. "These women wanted to come. Wytha intends to stay."

Gareth pulled away from Elsbet. "What about you?"

She bit her lip. "Gareth, this is not your home. This is not my home. I am a lion, not a raven. You are no raven. Please, come back to the city."

Gareth's face was a storm of emotion. "Elsbet, I—"

"You made me promises," she said. "Did those mean nothing?"

Gareth ran a hand through his braids and let out a long breath. "I made those promises before I knew these men."

"And these men are more important than I am? Than the woman you promised to wed?"

"We can still be wed. Letha would marry us—you can live here."

"I am a lion, Gareth. I am no raven." She turned back to her horse, mounted, and rode away.

Gareth started to walk after her, but stopped. He turned to Hedwar. "Father—"

"If you made her a promise of marriage, you owe her something, Gareth," he said. "You must either marry her or release her to wed another."

"I hold you no ill will if you leave, Gareth," Mairead said. She put a hand on his arm. "You have a home, a family, an inheritance in the city. If you need to go, go."

He stared after Elsbet for a long time, then turned to his father. "I will decide by tomorrow," he said. "Tell her that. Tell her to expect my answer tomorrow."

"We will return tomorrow, Elsbet and I and the council members. We will talk these things through." Hedwar mounted and rode away.

Letha stayed. She picked up her pack just as Wyll arrived. He stopped and bowed to her. "Guardian," he greeted. "You are well come to our village."

She fought a smile. "I thank you," she said. "I thought you might have a suggestion for where I could stay?"

"So you intend to stay?"

"I do. The traitha will need a midwife. And you may be connected to the earthspirit, but you are no midwife."

Wyll grinned. "True. Well, yes. I can think of a couple of places where you could stay. Would you like to talk them over?"

"I would." Wyll held out a hand, and Letha gave him her horse's reins and fell in step next to him.

Gareth brooded that afternoon and evening, and no amount of reassurance from Mairead could convince him he would be forgiven if he left for Isfyrin. He finally told her goodnight and retired to a tent near Wyll's hut. Mairead returned to Connor's hut and lay down on her mat with Devyn next to her. She scratched the cat idly for some time, thinking. At last, she sat up and found one of Connor's tunics. She knelt next to Devyn's head. "Gareth says you might help me if I ask it," she said. She put the tunic near Devyn's nose. "This belonged to Connor. Do you think you could find him if you followed that scent?"

The cat sat up, yawned, and stood. She nudged Mairead's hand and squeezed her eyes shut as Mairead scratched behind her ears. Devyn leaned forward and licked Mairead's cheek with a rough tongue, and Mairead laughed. "Yes, it's all right. Go look for him. I am safe here. I'm surrounded by guards." The cat gave a series of chirps and went to the door. Mairead opened it and let her out into the night. "Hurry back," she whispered. She returned to her mat and lay down to sleep.

She woke with a jolt before dawn. Frantic voices and shouting outside her hut drove her to her feet, and she pulled on breeches, boots, and sword as quickly as possible. She grabbed her bow and quiver on the way out the door.

Gareth met her outside. "Plainsmen," he shouted. His sword was already in his hand. "Get to safety."

Mairead drew her sword. "No, I fight."

"The babe—"

"I will not break my promise, Gareth!" she shouted. "I stand with these men."

And with that, the battle was joined.

They came over the edge of the culvert in a wave of red paint and incoherent screaming. Mairead stumbled for a moment. *Dear One Hand, save my people,* she prayed. She saw Gareth and Trypp run into the melee. "For the ravens!" she shouted. "For the lions and for the One Hand!" She nocked an arrow and started firing as fast as she could. One, two, five men fell to her arrows, but there were too many more. She used all of her arrows and then grabbed another handful from one of the quivers placed around the village, firing again as soon as she could.

Something knocked her into the ground, hard, and a foot held her shoulder down. Instinct kicked in, and Mairead twisted her body to bring an elbow back into the side of the man's knee. He swore and stumbled backward. It was enough for her to sit up and draw a dagger. When he came toward her again, she was ready. She ducked under the sword and brought her dagger up into his side once, twice, three times. He fell to the ground, and she sliced his throat and moved on to the next arrows.

The sounds and smells of the battle threatened to overwhelm her senses, but she inhaled a deep breath and nocked another arrow. *Nock, aim, fire. Nock, aim, fire.* Over and over, she picked the men off one at a time until she was out of arrows again, and then she drew her sword and ran into the battle.

Gareth saw her and ran to her side. "Get out of here! Cover us with your bow!"

"I did—ran out of arrows." She slashed and parried, fighting clumsily, hoping just to keep one or two men away from the raven village. "Go get your father."

"He won't—"

"He will to protect you!"

Gareth paused and whistled. Grayfeather circled overhead. "Get my father," he shouted. The bird circled once more and flew west.

Mairead gritted her jaw and redoubled her efforts, fighting back-to-back with Gareth as they slashed, stabbed, parried, pushed the horde back. Trypp was there, shield over his missing arm, sword slashing from his right hand. Twitch darted in and out of the battle, biting and snarling and scratching. The ravens fought tirelessly, never pausing, never hesitating, as they pushed the intruders back, back, away from the edge of their village. They formed a perimeter around the village and guarded their boundaries with grim determination, but the horde continued to come in waves. "We'll never beat them back without your father," Mairead said to Gareth during a pause to catch her breath.

"We can't count on his help. We'll have to try."

And then, just as she despaired of any success at all, she heard pounding hooves and a horn and the shouting of dozens of men. The lions rushed in from the side of the horde, slashing, shouting, screaming victory over those who had come up the mountain uninvited. In that moment, there were no lions and no ravens—there were only men of the mountain who were defending their homes. Mairead's spirit soared, and she shouted her own defiance and returned to the battle.

It took half of the day, but they pushed the horde back down the mountain into retreat. The lions formed a perimeter with their remaining men, and the ravens pulled those unable to fight into the center of the village.

Mairead called a meeting of the leaders and trusted advisors. Hedwar, Wulf, and Braun joined them. "Who are they?" she asked.

For once, Wulf didn't respond by berating her. "They were plainsmen, to be sure, but those red marks—I've never seen those before."

"Connor has told me, and I have heard, that the Nar Sidhe have red marks like those," Mairead said. "But if they were Nar Sidhe, why did they not use their magic against us?"

No one could offer an answer for that. "We might be able to find more clues if we examine the bodies, traitha," Wyll said.

"You?" Wulf said. "What of the lions?"

Wyll turned a cool eye toward him. "You are welcome to join us, Lionjaw. But since our men have more experience and contact with plainsmen, you might find we know more about what they look like than you do."

Mairead stifled a yawn. She covered her mouth. "Forgive me," she said. "I fear the day has caught up with me. I'll be in my hut resting." She turned to go.

Gareth followed her and stopped her with a hand on her arm. "Mairead," he said. "May we speak?"

"Of course."

He lowered his voice. "Tomorrow, I am going to return to the lions."

Mairead's stomach twisted, but she forced a smile. "I understand, Gareth."

"I will still count you my tribal sister."

"And I count you my brother." She put a hand on his arm. "You aren't betraying me, Gareth. You are just choosing what's right for you."

He let out a long breath. "I am glad you understand. And I hope we will work together to bring the ravens home to the tribe."

Mairead gestured around. "Don't you see? This is home. They are home. And so am I."

"Traitha," Osgar called.

Mairead and Gareth turned as the raven approached. "What is it?" Mairead asked.

He held out a skin. "A drink? It would seem there is no better time to drink together than in the wake of a victory."

She smiled. "One drink." She took the skin and drank a small mouthful. She pulled her furs tighter around her. Her shoulders ached from the fighting, and she felt heavy and bone-weary. "I thank you."

He tipped his head to consider her. "Your marks—they are very convincing."

Mairead put a hand on her face. "I'm still getting used to them. And to this role. I fear I'll fail the ravens and the lions."

"You didn't fail them today."

She reached for his arm. "Osgar, it has ever been my intention to bring you into the tribe again. What the lions have done to you is wrong."

"It wasn't wrong," he said, so quietly that Mairead had to strain to hear him. He gave her the skin again. "The One Hand knew what we were. What we are. So did the lions."

She took the skin. "No. I don't believe that. You are only what the One Hand made you. He has a purpose for you."

"What do you think you are?" Gareth asked.

Osgar turned away without responding. "Do you know—I was a Lionjaw, once."

"You were?"

"It seems so long ago. But I remember that knowledge—that feeling of . . . *rightness*. Of knowing that we had something special, divine, powerful—something that the other clans didn't have. Lead the Lionjaws, and you lead the tribe."

Gareth frowned. "Some would say that about the Catspaws."

"Perhaps all the clans feel that way," Mairead said. "But perhaps the time for clan division is gone. Perhaps it's time for the tribe to unite as lions, not as different clans."

Osgar's jaw tightened. He tucked the skin inside his furs. "Come. I want to show you something." He walked toward the forest.

Mairead started to follow, but Gareth put a hand on her arm. "Be careful," he whispered.

"What is it?"

"Just a sense. Something isn't right."

"Then come with me." She followed Osgar, Gareth close at her heel. She picked her way over the path Osgar had made in the undergrowth. "Osgar? What is it?"

Behind her, Mairead heard shouting, screaming, the sounds of attack. She stopped. "Osgar, the village—we need to go back." She turned—

—and came face to face with the dark man from the plains.

Gods. He looks so much like Connor. Gareth drew a sword and swung at the dark man, but the man parried effortlessly. "Mairead, run!" Gareth shouted.

Mairead tried to take a long step away from Osgar, but he wrapped one arm around her shoulders and chest. She felt a solid "thud" in her back, then the eruption of a thousand pinpricks of pain. She tried to scream, but only a wheeze emerged. Warmth ran in a flood down her back. Her legs went cold, weak, and she collapsed. The baby scrambled in her belly. "What . . . what did you . . . do?"

Osgar looked down at her, his dagger dripping with her blood. "Destroyed the idol of the lion tribe."

Mairead couldn't fight, couldn't move. Life drained out of her. *My baby . . . Connor . . . Is this how it ends? Bleeding out on the forest floor?* Mairead tried to keep her eyes open, tried to focus. She whispered the spells Letha had taught her as her palm warmed. *Trypp, Letha—I need you!*

The dark man spared a glance as he fought Gareth. "It is not done until she is dead."

Panic struck Mairead's chest. *He will kill me and the baby, and then he will have nothing stopping him from destroying Taura and Culidar.*

And then, the familiar warm tickle of the Sidh healing started to pass through her. The bleeding slowed as braids started to pass through her wounds, binding, connecting, sealing. *But how? The baby?*

Osgar crouched next to her. "Why are you still alive? You defy death at every turn. I betray you to the lions, to the plainsmen, even to this creature, and you still live."

Mairead's head spun. *Oh gods—my baby.* She folded her arms over her belly. "No—don't hurt—don't take—"

Osgar drew a blade—

A crash in the brush—the clash of sword on sword— "Mairead!"

Trypp. She forced her eyes open and watched in the dim light as Wyll, Trypp, and Letha rushed into the clearing. "Help . . . baby . . . ." *Light . . . why is there so much light?*

Wyll roared and rushed at Osgar, and the raven went down in a single fierce swing. Trypp ran toward the Forbidden and Gareth. Mairead watched through blurred vision as Gareth swung in a broad, overhand arc. In a move so quick she wasn't sure she saw it, the dark man blocked Gareth's swing with his own sword and plunged his other hand toward Gareth.

Gareth fell.

"No!" Trypp's voice echoed over the trees.

The dark man bent and stabbed once more. Trypp swung his sword, but it whistled through empty air.

The dark man was gone.

Trypp knelt next to Gareth. "No. No. No. Not you—not you—it should have been me. Not you." His head bowed onto his friend's chest, and his shoulders shook, and above the trees, Grayfeather cried in mourning.

Warmth flooded Mairead's legs, and pain convulsed through her belly, and she moaned. "Letha . . . my baby . . . ."

Letha was there. "Wyll—help."

Gentle arms picked her up. "Hang on, traitha. Hang on."

But she knew—she knew as the spasms ravaged her spine and her belly. *My baby is gone. Connor—where are you?*

CHAPTER THIRTY-SEVEN

There is no evil that can destroy that which the One Hand keeps.
– Second Book of the Wisdomkeepers

Minerva pulled her coracle out of the shallow waves and turned it over under shelter of a large rock. She straightened and knuckled her back. The short journey across the choppy water between the Taurin mainland and the Ragged Isles had been easier than expected, but she felt Alfrig's absence keenly. *And not just because she wasn't there to help row,* she thought, blinking back more tears. She swiped her eyes. *No time to waste on tears. Alfrig would not wish it.* She smiled. *Or perhaps she would tolerate grief. She was not, after all, the woman I remembered.*

Hrogarth had surprised Minerva when they buried Alfrig. It was not an easy or short task in the dead of winter with frozen northern ground, but they at last managed a shallow grave. The wind and ice had, mercifully, held off for a few hours, and they lowered the linen-wrapped body into the grave. Hrogarth had wound strands of ivy around one of Alfrig's daggers, and he placed the dagger over her chest. He touched her head once more and nodded before stepping back. Logan, Malcolm, and the other Taurin men filled the hole and then stacked large rocks over the mound of earth.

When the task was complete, Hrogarth knelt next to the monument and put one hand on the stones. He bowed his head, and his shoulders shook. Grytha moved forward to comfort him, but he waved her away and looked up.

He's laughing, Minerva realized. "Traitha?"

His deep, hearty laugh rumbled up from his chest and filled the air. He finally wiped his eyes, but the tears were ones of joy, not sorrow. "Forgive me," he said. "Forgive me. I do not wish to make light of her passing. But I remember a moment when we were first wed. I was an ass—selfish, brash, foolish, such a typical young warrior. I thought I knew everything. I even thought I knew the best way to prepare food. She taught me a lesson I never forgot."

"What was that?" Grytha asked softly.

"She boiled boot leather and told me it was jerky."

Malcolm snorted a laugh and quickly caught himself. He inclined his head. "Forgive me, my lord."

Hrogarth shook his head. "No, you should laugh. She was sneaky. She put it in my pack when I went hunting, knowing I would likely have some that night when the light would disguise what it looked like. I pulled it out of my pack and tried to take a bite. I couldn't tear it free, no matter how hard I tried. I nearly broke a tooth. In the morning, I looked more closely and figured out what she'd done."

"What did you do?" Minerva asked.

He sighed. "I went home and admitted my foolishness, and I never told her how to prepare food again. I never went hungry again, either. She cared for me well. She raised three strong warriors and three powerful guardians while she served the tribe as guardian. She guided young women in the initiation and tattooed countless boys after the hunt. She could weave and sing and cook as easily as hunt and skin an animal." He put both hands on the stones as his voice cracked, and he bowed his head. "She was my whole life. She was the reason I had to go home every night. Now ...."

Minerva knelt next to him and folded her hands in her lap. "Traitha, there is still much to live for. We still need you. We need your sword and your leadership more than ever."

He shook his head. "War belongs to younger men."

She put a hand on his shoulder. "Aldora was not the last threat to this island, traitha. War is coming, here and across the channel. Dark forces are rising. I know you feel it."

"The bird doesn't let me forget."

"Then you have to help defeat them," Minerva said. She tightened her hand on his shoulder. "Traitha, we need you still. Do not abandon us."

He took a deep breath and let it out, and his shoulders bowed inward. "I don't know. I am so tired. I wish to rest."

She leaned toward him. "Alfrig will wait."

He turned to her, his face streaked with silent tears. He nodded slowly and closed his eyes. Another tear rolled down one cheek. "She always waited. Always." He leaned toward the stones and pressed his lips to the monument. "Rest, my love," he whispered. "I will join you when my work is done."

It was the next day that Braedan summoned all of them to his room to share his dreams. Hrogarth's announcement that he would go east to join the First Raven was a relief to Minerva. *We all are called to something in this fight,* she thought. *He is a raven. Braedan is a king. Alfrig was a sacrifice. And I ....*

She rubbed her tattooed palm and frowned as she started toward the path to the wisdomkeeper's cave. *What am I? Can I still be so unsure?* The dreams she had the night before Braedan summoned them were vivid and unmistakable in their imagery. She knew—to the very core of her being—that Braedan *must* be crowned king. She *knew* it. And yet now, as she prepared to take her place with the wisdomkeeper, she questioned it again. *What if it was all a mistake? What if it didn't mean what I thought? One Hand, show me the way.*

She picked her way along the path until she reached the entrance to the wisdomkeeper's cave. "Great Mother?" she called.

Shuffling footsteps echoed in the distance, scraping closer and closer. "Esma," she called. "You are well come."

She doesn't ask about Alfrig. Minerva stepped into the cave, the warmth bringing instant relief from the bitter chill outside. She walked gingerly until her eyes adjusted, then walked faster as the faint light and shadows resolved into the shape of the crone. "I bring news," she said.

The crone grunted, her milky eyes holding the depths of eons of knowledge. "Likely nothing my dreams have not revealed. But come. We will share tea and discuss." She turned and led Minerva into the cavern.

The aroma of a richly seasoned soup filled Minerva's nose as they entered the wisdomkeeper's living area. The wisdomkeeper stirred the contents of a bubbling cauldron. "Your friends have visited again?" Minerva asked.

The old woman cackled. "Dried beans, jerky, potatoes from the cellar."

Minerva smiled. "You knew I was coming."

The old woman laughed again.

Minerva sat down as the crone ladled soup into a bowl and prepared two cups of tea from a separate kettle. "Thank you," she said when the crone passed her a cup.

The wisdomkeeper grunted a response and sat across from Minerva. She took a long drink. Minerva reflected that it seemed neither of them wanted to bring up the reason Minerva returned alone. The crone ate several bites of soup, drank another swallow of tea, and sighed. She put down her cup. "How did it happen?"

Minerva set down her bowl and spoon. "The Forbidden creature, Aldora. She did it. She took Alfrig's soul."

The crone let out a long sigh and bowed her head for some time. Minerva waited. "No," she whispered. "Her soul is not consumed. It was merely . . . separated from her."

"How?"

"The creatures have some sway over souls. It is a power we cannot fight or resist. But those who are covered by the One Hand will not lose their souls to the Forbidden. They will merely be killed, not destroyed."

Minerva frowned. "I still don't understand."

The crone sighed. "This is a mystery," she said. Her tone suggested that even she couldn't explain the difference. "It is one which the One Hand has not chosen to reveal yet. Perhaps when his Chosen One comes, these things will be made clear."

"Then you think Alfrig is safe? That her spirit survives in the world beyond this one?"

The crone nodded. "I believe the One Hand cares for those who have served him in this world. Evil cannot destroy that which belongs to the One Hand."

It was some measure of relief. Minerva let out a long breath. "He gave me dreams," she said.

"I have dreamed as well."

"Did you dream of a king of Taura?"

The crone nodded. "And more. You were right to crown the usurper. He is no longer a usurper. He is now the one who is bonded to Taura. His blood protects this land."

Minerva rubbed the palm of her hand. It tingled at the crone's words. "What of the queen? His queen, the one I saw in my dream?"

"She is not his queen. She has taken another husband."

"Another husband?" Minerva shook her head. "Mairead has wed? How—"

"She has taken the First Raven to be her husband. She has already conceived."

Minerva's stomach plummeted. "This . . . this can't be right, Great Mother. I told him—I anointed him. I told him I saw a king and queen—not his princess, but queen who would bear children to reign in Taura. If she has wed another and conceived a child, how will his line continue?"

"The One Hand reveals only as much as he wishes," the wisdomkeeper said, and Minerva thought she sounded frustrated. "To serve him in this place will require you to become satisfied with ambiguity."

Minerva stood and paced, rubbing her hand. "Then this may have been for naught? Anointing him? Encouraging him to take his throne? It may be worthless?"

"Not for naught," the crone said. "His blood and the anointing provide protection for this land. The earth would not have allowed the anointing if she did not have a purpose for it." She paused. "What are his intentions?"

Minerva sighed. She closed her eyes. "He intends to return to Torlach to reclaim his throne. He intends to call the people to him as he rides south, and he says he will take back the throne and hold it for the rightful heir."

The crone grunted. "And you? What will you do?"

Minerva hesitated. "I was so certain a few days ago," she whispered. "Right after I anointed Braedan, I was certain I should return here to learn from you, to take your place. And now, when the decision must be made, I find my feet frozen in a place of indecision."

The wisdomkeeper laughed—not a cackle this time, but a low, gentle chuckle of understanding. "Oh, child. You think too much."

Minerva frowned. "When did thought become a sin?"

The crone held up a hand. "Not a sin. But you allow your thoughts too much power."

"I did not know such was possible."

The crone stood and crossed the cavern to Minerva. She lifted Minerva's hand and removed her glove to reveal the blue light from her tattoo. "What do you want, child?"

Minerva didn't hesitate. "To serve the One Hand and bring glory to him."

"And do you think he cares where you do that?"

Minerva opened her mouth, closed it, and sighed. "I don't know."

The crone touched Minerva's forehead. "He gave you a mind, Esma, but not for the purpose of paralyzing you." She touched Minerva's breastbone. "He gave you a heart, but not for the purpose of leading you astray." She lifted Minerva's hand and turned it into a fist. "And he gave you strength, but not for the purpose of crushing the weak. He wishes you to use these things—your mind, your heart, your strength—together. You, Esma—you use your mind so much that you silence your heart and crush your own strength."

"Then what am I to do?" Minerva whispered.

The crone smiled. "Let your mind quiet for a time. Rest here. Heal your heart and restore your strength, and perhaps you will find the One Hand's purpose for you."

Minerva thought of Braedan and the Taurin men. *I could help him. I could go to Torlach with them, tell the Taurins that he is indeed anointed king. Perhaps the sayas might even listen now.* "I am tired," she said.

"Then stay. Rest. This place is one of ease for your spirit."

Minerva nodded. She rubbed her palm again. "I will stay." *For now.*

CHAPTER THIRTY-EIGHT

The One Hand belongs to no man and every man.
— Tal'Aster wisdom

When the Morrag finally alit, Connor had no idea where he was or how far she had flown. He was only aware that he occupied some place inside of the corporeal form she liked to take—the coalescing ravens who formed her undulating, winged body. As the ravens came together, he realized that he stared out of her black bird eyes and spoke with the croaking voice he'd only ever heard directed at him twice before. *We've merged,* he thought, and oddly, there was some level of relieved sadness to it. *Thank the gods. It's finally over.* And then a pang of loss—*Mairead. I wanted to spend a lifetime with you. Please don't hate me.*

He hadn't wanted to kill her. He hadn't wanted to kill any of them. Once he realized there was no holding the Morrag back, he'd only wanted to leave— to fly away—before anyone was hurt. But then the lions and the ravens and even that foolish, ridiculous eunuch had tried to stop him. *If they'd just let me go—if they'd just let me leave—* He could see it as an oddly distant memory. *Trypp, my friend, I am so sorry.*

There was fear and relief, but there was also anger. That part of him that still held some humanity resented the Morrag for her words and her choices— for threatening Mairead, for hurting Trypp, for determining that he could no longer have anything resembling a human life. *I never asked for this. I never wanted this. I only wanted a life of my own, without duty or obligation. And then I just wanted my wife. And now, this—now you would take everything from me and turn me into this murdering, angry demon.*

The bird eyes shifted in that odd, jerking motion he'd seen from ravens before. She'd landed outside a small cabin surrounded by trees and snow-covered mountains and hills. Nearby was a small, iced-over pond, and snow fell lightly.

"Master!"

It was the raven's voice—the Morrag—but although Connor heard and felt it as a guttural croaking caw, he understood it as the word—*Master. Who is she calling? She has a master? What about the earthspirit?*

Another croak. "Master!"

The cabin door opened, and a man stepped out and folded his arms in front of his chest. The man had a ruddy, stern face, but kind blue eyes. He wore leather breeches and jerkin, just like Connor, but he had a rough, homespun tunic under the jerkin. His hair was long, dark, straight, and tied back at the neck. "You're early."

Connor sensed her mouth open in a scream of righteous agony. "No!" Her arms (*wings*) flapped in frustration. "It is time. My sister cries out for justice. The enemy's hand stains your fields. Let me go, my Master. Let me avenge my sister. Let me avenge you."

Connor didn't know what he expected the man to do, but it was not what he eventually did. He stood with his arms crossed, stoic, unmoving, until the last echoes of the Morrag's scream finally ceased to bounce across the mountains, and then he stepped toward Connor with a gentle, purposeful stride. He put one hand on her shoulder. "Let the man go."

She screamed again. "No! He is mine! You promised he would avenge me. You promised he would cleanse the earth."

"You heard the promise you wished to hear. This is not the man you were promised."

But she's been telling me for years—I would avenge her—I would cleanse the earth. Connor grasped at the faint hope the exchange offered. *What if she was wrong? Gods, was she wrong?*

Another shriek, this one full of the anger and despair of untold eons. She went to her knees. "Please—Master, please—give me this man! He may yet avenge me. Please, Master, let me be reunited with my sister. *Let me be whole again!*"

The man's face held such sadness and pain that Connor almost wished he could voluntarily give himself up for the Morrag's purposes. *You fool!* his dying vestiges of humanity cried out in his head. *This is a chance! This is hope! This man may yet release you—may yet allow you to go back to Mairead!* But there was a hollowness to the hope. Despite the love he held for his wife, despite the desire to live out her days with her, he longed for what the Morrag wanted, too—*justice. To have justice—to finally know that all the wrongs have been corrected.* And there was fear, too—that if he returned to Mairead, it would only be a matter of time before the Morrag took him again. *Only a matter of time before I destroy my village, my friends, my people, my own wife.*

He sensed the man's will and determination—a will that resisted persuasion because it saw more than the supplicant saw, a determination that would see resolve despite the pain it might bring in the present. The man placed a heavy hand on the Morrag's head. "I know," he said in a firm, unwavering, tender voice. "I know. But you are early. Your time is not yet come."

The shriek of despair that emerged from the Morrag's throat—the shriek of despair that Connor enjoined—rose from deep inside the very bowels of the earth and continued higher than the heavens. It echoed around and around the quiet vale in which she'd landed, and the weight of it shook the mountains and earth. The frozen pond cracked, and Connor watched the cabin roil at its base.

Through it all, the man stood still.

When the Morrag's scream at last died, she collapsed in a sobbing heap of black feathers.

And Connor wept with her.

They wept together, and Connor couldn't tell how long it lasted. She wept for the vast ages of death and destruction and evil and pain the earth had suffered. She wept for her sister—for the life of the earth, for the energy that brought spring and summer and held autumn and winter at bay, for the wounds her sister had borne because of the curse of men's feet on the earth. Connor shared her grief. *I have seen the curse. I've watched the curse spill out on a dry desert and a snow-covered field. I've borne the curse on my own body, and I've inflicted the curse on others. I am more accursed than all of those men. I am king of the damned.*

The man's heavy hand pressed on Connor's shoulder. "Rise," he said. "She has released you."

Connor lifted his head (*human—not bird—human eyes, not bird eyes—hands, not talons or wings*). "Wha—"

"She has released you." The man knelt before him. "She has gone. You are free."

Connor sat up. "Human." *My voice—it's normal.* "I'm human."

The man shrugged. "Half, anyway."

"I was in the hut—I was dreaming—my wife was—" Connor stopped and buried his face in his hands. "Oh, gods—my wife." *She will never take me back—not now.*

The man clapped him on the shoulder. "Come into the cabin," he said. "You need some rest and refreshment."

Connor stood on shaking legs that felt, somehow, unsteady or unreal. *I was expecting a bird's legs.* His head reeled. "Who are you?"

The man was equal to Connor in size and build. The sword strapped on his hips was a broad, two-handed thing—massive in length and likely matching in weight, Connor thought. The man rested one hand on the hilt. "I should ask you the same. What are you—Taurin? Tribal? Sidh? You seem confused."

Connor frowned. "How do you know I'm Sidh?"

"It's around you—the colors of your talents."

That made Connor's skin prick. "Talents. No one knows that but my mother. How did you—"

"The colors are around you." His gaze remained steady on Connor's face. "You haven't answered yet: who are you?"

Connor's jaw tightened. "I think you already know." He gestured to the cabin. "This is your house?"

"One of them. Come in and eat." He opened the door and ushered Connor through. "Take off your boots."

Connor did as he was asked. A large piece of beef roasted over the fire, and the drippings sizzled and hissed on the coals below. Connor turned back to see the man at his larder preparing flatbread. His hands were rough and scarred, but strong. "How do you come to live out here?" Connor asked. "Do you belong to the lion tribe?"

"I belong to all of the tribes. Sit down. I'll bring you wine."

Connor sat. "No wine. I don't have the stomach for it."

"Try this vintage." The man spoke with a kind of gentle authority that defied resistance. He gave Connor a goblet. "Drink. It will warm you."

Connor drank, and sweet warmth traveled down his throat and into his stomach. "This is really good," he said. "Esparan?"

"No," the man said. "It's from a vineyard in the land I'm from."

"Where is that?"

"I doubt you would have heard of it." He pulled the beef from the fire, sliced a thick slab, and put it on a trencher in front of Connor, along with a large piece of flatbread. "Eat. You look like you've been hungry for days."

Connor's mouth watered. "I haven't been hungry lately, but this smells fantastic."

The man sat next to him. "Eat."

"Won't you eat?"

"I've already eaten."

Connor ate the first slice of meat, then a second, then a third, and four pieces of flatbread. He finally finished his food and leaned back in his chair. "I thank you for your hospitality," he said. "Is that it? Am I free?"

"What is it you wish to return to?"

Connor hesitated. He turned the goblet in his hand. "My wife. And my men."

"Noble things to return to," the man acknowledged. "And yet you hesitate."

Connor stared down at his goblet and tried to conjure words. None came. At last, the man spoke. "It's night already," he said. "Sleep here tonight."

It seemed like the best suggestion Connor had heard in a very long time. He was suddenly very sleepy. He yawned. "You are a kind host, sir," he said. "Can I ask your name?"

"Tomorrow." He pointed at the small cot in the one-room cabin. "Take the bed."

Connor was too tired to argue. He fell onto the cot and into the deepest, most restful sleep he had known in many years.

He woke to the smell of fish cooking over the fire. There was no sign of the man. Connor stood, taking the chance to look around the cabin. It was a remarkably simple place. One wall held the small hearth, warm coals smoldering under a spit of trout. The cot sat against the wall near the hearth; above it were several shelves of bound books. There were scrolls, too, and several small carvings of animals and people. He picked up a wolf carving. The workmanship was the best he'd ever seen; detailed and proportioned, the carving showed a bushy male wolf baying at the moon, and Connor thought he could almost hear the howl.

He put the wolf back on the shelf and turned toward the door. On the wall, the man had hung pegs for his various implements—ax, several knives, bow and quiver, fishing pole. His sword leaned against the wall next to the door. Connor reached out to put a hand around the hilt, but the door opened.

The man stood on the threshold with a sackful of wood for the fire slung in a carrier over his shoulder. He still wore the same clothes. "You presume much."

Connor stepped away from the sword. *I feel like a boy caught with a handful of sweets at supper.* "I was admiring the craftsmanship. It looks heavy."

A smirk creased the stern expression. "It is." He put down the wood near the hearth. "I'm the only man who can lift it."

Connor scoffed. "We're of a size. You think I can't pick it up?"

The man gestured. "Go on. Try it." He crossed his arms.

Connor put one hand on the hilt, but the sword didn't budge. He put both hands on it and all of his weight behind the effort, but he may as well have tried to lift a mountain. He backed away. "That's no ordinary steel."

The man laughed. He went to the fire and removed the fish. "These are done." He put one on a trencher. He took more flatbread from the fire, tore a piece in half, and offered one half to Connor. He took a fish for his own trencher and kept the other piece of the bread. He poured water for both of them, and they started to eat. "So, you've had a night to sleep. Tell me what happened to you—how you came to be at my door."

You already know how it happened, Connor thought, but he knew, somehow, that he couldn't say that. He had to speak what happened. *And yet, I can't.* "I don't know." Connor paused. "The Morrag. She took me. Claimed me." He took a deep breath. "I still don't know your name."

The man smiled. "Don't you?"

"You seem familiar, but I don't remember ever meeting you before."

"It will come to you in time," the man said. He gestured to Connor's sword. "You're good with a blade?"

"Passably good."

The man grunted. "I've heard otherwise, Connor Mac Niall."

Connor frowned. "You know my name?"

"Your reputation precedes you. I've heard of a half-man, half-Sidh warrior who hires his sword to the highest bidder and bests any man who challenges him."

The words landed like tiny darts on Connor's spirit, and he shuddered. "I don't hire myself out anymore," he said. "And I've been bested."

"Why don't you hire yourself out?"

He already knows why. Connor couldn't say how he knew—he just *knew.* The man only asked these questions because he wanted Connor to say the answers aloud. And Connor, despite his hesitation, continued to oblige. "I met a woman. She gave me something bigger than money to fight for."

"What's that?"

"Justice. Freedom. Liberty. Restoration."

The man's lips tilted into a crooked grin. "You would make your father proud, no doubt."

Connor laughed, soft. "I don't know. I struggle to be half the man he was. Don't misunderstand—he taught me everything he could. But I could never be like him."

"No, of course not. Your father was an administrator. You're a warrior."

Connor shrugged. "My father was a noble leader. I'm just a jackass with a sword."

The man stood and sorted through some wood at his hearth. He sat down and started to carve. "The blade is a useful tool. It can bring death. It can save a life. Sometimes, it can take something raw and through destruction create something beautiful. It depends on the hand of the wielder."

Connor watched the man's practiced, artistic hands chip and carve away at the wood. Eventually, the head and shoulders of a man rose from the block.

"Do you have someone in mind?"

"Yes." He chipped and carved. "Tell me what happened in the raven village."

Connor watched the man's hands move the knife over the wood. "The Morrag took me. She's been threatening for weeks, and she finally did it. I think I tried to kill—tried to kill my wife." The words hurt to say.

The man didn't stop carving. He waited.

Connor swallowed hard, looking down at the floor. "Because the Morrag wanted me to. She wanted me to kill them. All of them. She insisted they should die."

"What did you want?"

"I didn't want to hurt them—any of them."

"But you saw their transgressions?"

Connor took a deep breath. "Yes. But I couldn't be sure. The Morrag wanted their blood, but I can't be sure of anything—if I should trust her or not."

The man stopped carving. "The magic. The avenging raven."

"She demanded justice. I felt it. She wanted their blood. Mairead's blood." He paused. "Would you defend her—this demon?"

"No," the man said. "Not defend her. Help you understand that she didn't lie." He tipped his head to one side. "Tell me—what does she tell you about me?"

Connor frowned. *Nothing.* "Who are you?"

"Someone who has a vested interest in your success."

"Success at what?"

"Your role in the prophecies."

"Can you see the future?" he asked.

"Why would you want to know the future?"

He hesitated. "My wife. Our child. Will she be cursed? With this?"

"You want to know if the child will be ravenmarked? Or burdened with these talents? I don't think that's your real question."

"No, it's not."

The man folded his arms. "I have seen the future, and I know the path all three of you will walk. I could tell you about your child—I could tell you exactly what the child's destiny is—but I don't think you really want to know that. I think you want to know if you can be a good father."

Blood on the snow .... "I've done so many things. I've hurt so many people." He took a deep breath. "I'm not designed to be a father. I'm only designed to kill."

"What are you missing?"

"I don't know. That's what I keep trying to figure out." Connor fell silent and watched the man return to his carving. "I should repay your hospitality. Is there something I can do around your cabin? Some work you need done?"

The man smiled. He stood. "I would love nothing more than to spend the day working side by side with you. Come."

They worked together all day with few words. Connor carried wood, cooked, made small repairs, fished, and did whatever else the man asked him to do. There was a resigned peace to it—as if helping the man met some kind of obligation. That night, Connor watched as the masterful hands carved the small statue. Legs and feet emerged; the carved man knelt, a sword before him, point on the ground. A cloak billowed behind him in waves that appeared one at a time. He still had no face, but he was muscular, and there was a ferocity about the statue, even though the sword point was down.

Connor read a few passages from a book of King Aiden's songs. King Aiden had the soul of a bard, it was said. He had written poem after poem in service and praise to Alshada. He had fought battle after battle, killed man after man, and when all seemed hopeless—when he knew that he and his wife were riding into their final battle, when he knew he would never see his son again—he wrote words of hope: "My soul cries out for Alshada, for my God. Though you slay me, yet will I hope in you."

Connor watched the fire. "I don't think I have that kind of faith."

"If you knew you were going to die, what would you rather have faith in?"

Connor couldn't answer that. He went to bed restless and slept fitfully. All night, he heard the man chipping away at the statue, and though he had found it soothing before, now it was painful.

When morning dawned, Connor stared at the food the man put before him in disinterest. "Not hungry," the man said, but it wasn't really a question.

Connor shook his head.

The man sat down next to him. "Are you ready to go back?"

Connor let out a long breath. "How can one who is destined to kill have any peace?" he whispered.

The man put one hand on his shoulder. "The blade brings death, but it can also bring life to those it defends," he said. "Could you not be the blade that brings life to those who cannot defend themselves?"

"What about the next moment I have to choose between mercy and justice?"

"What do you fear?"

Connor buried his face in his hands. "I see so many things. I know what I am—what I've done—but I see the memories and crimes of other men. I see so much pain. I see crimes committed in the name of religions I have never heard of. I see the brutality of wars in countries I don't recognize. I hear the voices of men, women, children hurting each other, taking peace from the world with every angry, foolish word that falls from their mouths. It's bad enough to recall my own sins—far worse to be burdened with the sins of others. How can I bear these voices, these sins in my head and remain sane?"

"Tell me about the babe."

Connor couldn't look up. He knew the man wasn't referring to Mairead's babe. "She was a camp girl. She told us she was with child. I feared it was mine—I've never wanted to burden a child with what I am. I feared it would be ravenmarked. Phinneas says the mark doesn't pass in the blood, but I didn't know—I couldn't be certain. I told her to expel her child. I gave her the herbs to do it, and I walked away. I found her the next day in a field, bleeding. She'd taken the herbs and miscarried, as I wished, but she wept. She regretted it. She didn't want to live without her babe. She was already bleeding to death— she'd cut her arms open. She . . . begged me . . . ." He sniffed. "She begged me to end it. Her last words were whispers. 'End it' is all she said." He took a deep breath and shuddered. "I should have helped her—I should have summoned my mother or taken her back to the camp or .... All I see now is my dagger pulsing with her last heartbeat. I pulled the dagger out, and she died."

The only sound in the room was the crackle of the fire and the uncomfortable scraping of Connor's boots on the floor. "They were innocent," Connor whispered. "Her babe was innocent. And I killed that babe, and because she begged for death, I killed her. I buried her and I buried what I did. She was a camp girl—no family, no ties to anyone. No one even knew where she came from. There were more, and no one missed her. But I knew then what I was."

"What are you?"

"A murderer."

"Irredeemable?"

"A man without peace. A man who deserves death. And she was just one. How many others have I needlessly killed? How many other innocents have suffered at my hand?" Connor sighed. "Mairead doesn't know my past—what I did. I'm a coward. I should have acknowledged that baby. I should have given that girl money and sent her away, at least."

"Even if the baby wasn't your child?"

"Does that matter? I bedded the girl. It was as much mine as anyone else's. She only wanted a life with a child and a man to take care of her." He sighed again. "I was an ass—a foolish, miserable ass. I thought so many times of taking my own life, but I could never do it. I dove into so many battles with a death wish, begging death to find me, and it never would." He wiped tears from his cheeks. "I wanted to die. I lived as I chose, and I waited for the raven or death. And then I met Mairead."

The man went to the fire, picked up the carving he'd been working on, and set it on the table in front of Connor.

The practiced hands had carved Connor in exquisite detail, down to the tattoos on his arms and the knotwork on his sword. "You finished it," he said quietly.

"No," the man said. "Not yet. It won't be finished for many years."

Connor picked up the statue. "How many more trials will I face? How much more chipping and carving can one person's soul endure?"

"You were not called to live a safe life, Connor Mac Niall. You were called to live a useful one. Such a calling requires much carving." He put a hand on Connor's arm. "It is fortunate for you that I am a master carver."

"Are you saying that girl, that babe, all those other things were just there to carve me into what you want?"

"No. I'm saying I can redeem your mistakes and make them something beautiful."

Connor bowed his head. "I am not worthy to be here. I have been such a fool—such an ass, so cruel, so angry and bitter." He paused. "I don't know if I can change."

"You want to know what your purpose is—what you are supposed to do." He glanced at the sword near the door. "What is the purpose of your sword?"

"To protect and defend the people in my care," Connor said without hesitating.

"Do you think you could do that for me?"

Connor was quiet for a long time. "How can I make amends for that girl? For the villages I destroyed during the war? For all those other things?"

"You can't."

"I suppose I knew that. But—"

"You can do good—you can help Mairead achieve her goals—but nothing will erase those things you've already done." He paused. "At least, not in this world."

And now we come to it. Connor took a deep breath. "I've known," he said. "I've always known. I've always known in my head that you are who you say you are, but I thought if I just left you alone, you would leave me alone. I could not bend my knee to you, because I knew you would want more from me than I was willing to give."

"And now?"

"I want to go back."

"I won't stop you."

Connor knelt at the man's feet. He bowed his head. "But I can't go back until you forgive me. Until I know you have forgiven me for my crimes—for rejecting you, for harming the innocent, and for being my own god."

One scarred hand touched his head. "I forgive you, Connor Mac Niall."

All of the women he'd ever bedded, all the money he'd amassed, all the drink he'd ever consumed, all of the magic he'd ever channeled—none of those pleasures could compare to the flood of peace that consumed his spirit in that touch. He shuddered and let out a long, relieved sigh. His body crumpled into a heap. "If I had known—if I had known it would be like this," he whispered. The weight, the burden of his crimes melted away, and the voices of the past fell silent. But the biggest change—the most welcome change—was the silence of the Morrag.

The silence of the Morrag. She's gone. She's not in my head. "Where is she?"

"She no longer controls you," the man said.

"I don't understand," Connor said. "I thought my submission to her was required. I thought I had to give in to her to be her raven."

The man smiled. "And who do you think she must submit to?" He crouched. "I have placed my protection over your mind and heart, and she can no longer take you without your permission. But do not give her permission, Connor. She will take it. Do not open the door to that anger again."

"Then how do I train my men? How do we acknowledge what we are without succumbing to madness?"

"She still has some sway over this world until the curse upon the earth is lifted. She will continue to demand that her ravens bring death to everyone. It is up to you and your men to remind her that there is room for mercy." He smiled. "The most important lesson you can teach your men, First Raven, is mercy."

"Much forgiveness is expected of those who have been forgiven much."

"This is the beginning of wisdom," the man said. He straightened. "Are you ready to return?"

Connor remained on his knees. It seemed right that he should continue to bow. "Show me your face."

"My face?"

"Your real face. Show me who you really are."

The man chuckled. "You demand a sign?"

"No, not a sign. A memory. Something to think about when I start to doubt that this really happened."

He said nothing. Connor watched, waiting for an answer, and realized the face above him was changing, breaking apart, glowing into a vision of such bright and terrible beauty that he could not keep his eyes open. Even when he closed them, the light shone through his eyelids. Even when he covered his face, the light penetrated. An odd metallic odor and taste filled his nose and mouth, growing stronger by the moment.

This is what it is to be touched by Alshada.

When the touch faded, Connor lifted his head. He lay in an earth shrine not far from the raven village. The sun was setting in the distance. He felt full, sated, and content.

And for the first time in months, his mind was quiet. *No Morrag. No voices or memories that aren't mine. Just peace.*

A pair of sad golden eyes watched him. He scrambled to standing, and the lion padded out of the bushes. He took a step forward. "Are you part of this?"

The lion came forward and nudged his hand. She turned away and glanced back at him, took a few more steps and glanced back, and kept walking.

Connor fell in step next to her.

CHAPTER THIRTY-NINE

The Morrag defends her land.
— The First Book of the Wisdomkeepers

Connor followed the cat back to the raven camp at a slow lope. Periodically, she stopped and looked back to make sure he followed, ducking back into the brush again when he got close. As they approached the village, Connor realized what he was smelling—*smoke. Mairead.* He drew his sword. "Where is she? What's happened?"

The cat rumbled a growl and broke into a run.

Connor tipped his head and listened. *An attack.* He ran next to the cat.

The ravens were engaged in battle with dozens of men in leathers and red ink. Elemental braids rose above the battle, and he saw one of his raven brothers bound in air and stabbed through the heart. *Nar Sidhe.* He raced into the melee, conjuring elemental talent as he ran, flicking away the opposing braids when he saw them. He slashed, struck, stabbed, parried. "For the

Morragmen!" he shouted. "For the raven! For the lions!"

A ripple of recognition wound through the Morragmen, and one by one, they saw him. Hope, determination, new ferocity rose on their faces, and they redoubled their efforts to drive the Nar Sidhe back. "For the Morragmen! For the raven! For the lions!"

Connor fought through the horde, looking for the familiar blonde braid, seeing nothing, fighting, slashing until his arm ached, and fighting on and on as the raven village burned behind him. The lion was a golden blur next to him, and one enemy at a time, the tide started to turn.

When the ravens and lions clearly had the upper hand, Connor found one of the ravens. "Where is she? Mairead?"

"She was in the village," he said.

He looked at the cat. "Can you take me to her?"

The cat ran, and Connor followed.

A few huts on the far side of the village still stood. Connor's was one of them. Wyll stood outside Connor's hut. "Traitha," he said, his voice tight. He put a hand on Connor's arm. "She lives, but ...."

Connor pushed him aside and entered the hut. Letha sat on the floor on her knees next to a very pale and still Mairead. "They stabbed her. She barely lived. Your babe healed her, but it ...." She took a deep breath. "I think it was too much for her. The baby is dead. Mairead miscarried."

Connor fell to his knees next to Letha. *Gods, my child.* "Mairead?" he whispered.

"She's alive, but barely. She lost a lot of blood between the wound and the miscarriage." She busied herself with mixing herbs in a bowl.

Connor looked at Wyll and Trypp. "Who did this to her?"

"Osgar," Wyll said. "I killed him."

"Where is Gareth?"

"Gareth is dead." Wyll's voice was tight, pained, wooden. "The creature—the Forbidden—he was in league with Osgar. The creature killed Gareth and disappeared before Trypp could reach him."

Mairead moaned. "Connor." Her voice was breathy, faded. "The babe ...."

Connor stroked her forehead. "I'm here, Mairead. My love. I'm here." He looked up again. "She should be in the city. This place won't stand."

"I agree," Wyll said. "But she defied the lions and stood with us—with the ravens—and the lions will never let us into Isfyrin."

The door opened, and Hedwar and Braun entered. Hedwar's face was twisted in anguished grief, and Braun's mouth was pulled into a grimace. Trypp gestured toward Mairead. "She nearly died," he said to the other men.

"And she miscarried her child. For these—for the ravens. Now can we accept them back into our tribe?"

Hedwar looked at Braun, and Braun nodded. "Yes," Hedwar said, his voice cracking. "For Mairead, and for my son." He turned and walked from the hut.

Connor stared at Braun. "My father is dead," Braun said. "I speak for him now, and I say the ravens belong in Isfyrin. Can you take her there? At least until she heals?"

Connor nodded. "Where should I take her?" he asked Letha.

"We can go to the sick hut. Wyll, prepare a litter."

"No need," Connor said. "I can take her. And you."

"How?"

"On the Sidh braids." He stood. "Do you trust me?"

"Yes. Take me first so that I can prepare what she needs, then come back here and fetch her."

He wrapped himself and Letha in braids of earth and pulled them both down into the ground. She stiffened in his arms, and he sensed fear rising in her body. He transported them to the sick hut, and he pulled back the braids around her and set her down. Her hands twitched for a moment as if wanting to check her body, but then she took a deep breath. "Go get Mairead. I'll be ready when you're back."

He returned to the hut in the raven camp and picked up Mairead's limp body. *Please, Mairead—please—hold on. I love you.* In moments, he was placing her on a mat in the sick hut.

Letha knelt next to her. "She will want to see the baby."

It stabbed deep into his spirit. He nodded. "I'll be back soon."

He returned to his hut in the raven village and found the baby's body wrapped in rags and laid in a basket. He picked up the bundle, and grief welled deep inside him. He opened the rags to see the body. Everything was perfectly formed and impossibly tiny, the perfect eyes closed, the rosebud mouth open in death as if she wished to speak. He picked up the tiny hands and examined the fingers. "Gods," he whispered. He knelt. "My child. My little girl. I'm sorry."

Braids of air touched his cheek. Maeve alit in the hut. Tears streamed down her face. "Oh, Connor."

Connor held out his hands to her. "Your heir," he said, his voice cracking.

"Gods." Her voice caught on a sob, and she took the babe. Even her petite hands dwarfed the little bundle. "Oh, Connor. I'm sorry. I'm so sorry." She sniffed. "Where's Mairead?"

"With the midwife in Isfyrin."

They both traveled to Isfyrin and knelt next to Mairead in the sick hut. "How is she?" Connor asked.

Letha cast a quick glance at Maeve, then turned back to her patient. "The bleeding is slowing. I think she will live, provided she doesn't develop an infection in her wound or her womb."

He couldn't speak. He could only take Mairead's hand and bow next to her, lost in thoughts and remorse and desperate prayer. *One Hand, save her.*

The hours blurred together into snatches of conversation, sleep, and minimal meals. He heard Letha and Maeve discuss Mairead's condition, and Maeve offered Sidh healers. He remembered one of the Sidh midwives arriving and passing the talents through Mairead's body, but pronouncing her as healed as she could be. "I can do nothing more for her," the healer said. "She will live, in time. Her body will replace her blood and elements. The stab wound is as repaired as even I could do. It will just take time."

Connor nodded. "How did the baby heal her?"

The healer shrugged. "I do not know, truly. I would not have known such a thing were possible. But it is not surprising that the act killed her. Such a wound would drain even an experienced healer. The baby likely replaced Mairead's elements with her own, not knowing it would kill her."

Connor nodded and sniffed. "What if I never get the chance to be a real father again?"

Maeve put a hand on his arm. "She is young and healthy. She will conceive again, surely."

But you never did. What if this baby was my one chance? "I'm not even sure she'll have me back. I don't know if she can forgive me leaving again."

Maeve hesitated a long time. "May we speak outside, Connor?"

He nodded. They dismissed the Sidh healer and stepped outside. "There is another of her blood," Maeve said in a low voice. "I don't know where—I only know he's somewhere on Taura. He is her half-brother. Her father was the heir, and the father sired a son on a second wife."

Connor swallowed hard. "If she can't have children, he will have to."

"And he is in as much danger as she is. Right now, he and Mairead are the only two who can possibly carry the relics. If the Forbidden keep trying to kill Mairead, it means that either they've abandoned hope of retrieving the relics, or they've found someone else to carry them. I can't believe they've given up on that quest."

"If you find him, tell me. I'll bring him here. I'll keep him safe."

"Be careful. It could be that he's in league with them."

Connor grunted an agreement. "It's hard for me to believe anyone related to Mairead wouldn't have a pure heart."

"They weren't raised together," Maeve reminded him. "We have no idea what this boy is like. He could be another Osgar."

"Fair point."

She returned to the Sidh village shortly after that, promising to visit Mairead when she could.

There were other sad tidings as well. Trypp came to the hut to see Mairead, his face wan and haggard. "Gareth's parents are preparing his body," he said. "It was senseless—stupid. There was no reason for it."

"Men die. He was trying to save Mairead. He died with honor."

Trypp let out a long breath. "It should have been me. I'm the one who had more to pay for. He was too good—his parents' only son—and now—"

Connor looked up at him. "You've never said—what happened on the hunt where your friend died?"

Trypp looked away. "I killed him. I thought he was the stag, and I loosed my arrow. It hit him right through the neck. He bled out in my arms."

Connor swallowed over a lump in his throat. "It was an accident."

"It was foolishness. I was too eager. I rushed my shot. I should have paid more attention. I saw it was him as soon as the arrow left my bow, but—" He broke off, and tension melted out of him. He leaned against the wall of the hut. "I will not rest until that thing that killed Gareth is dead."

Connor couldn't say anything, but he thought of the tiny babe, and his chest tightened. *Neither will I.* Trypp started to leave, and Connor stood. "Trypp, wait." The tribesman stopped and turned to Connor. Connor took a deep breath. "I am sorry."

Trypp held out his stump of an arm. "For this?"

Connor nodded. "I did not mean to. I didn't want to hurt any of you. She wanted you all dead, but I was fighting her. I was trying to get away, trying to—"

"Save it," Trypp said. "I don't need your explanation. I knew what was happening. I lived, which is likely more than I deserve."

Connor let out a long sigh. "We are tribesmen."

Trypp nodded.

"I owe you everything," Connor said. He gestured to Mairead. "You and Gareth and Wyll—if you hadn't been there, she would be dead. I owe you my life. I am in your debt."

Trypp inclined his head. "I will likely need to call in that favor eventually."

Connor grinned. "I hope you will."

Trypp put his remaining hand on Connor's shoulder. "I forgive you, my friend."

Mairead passed in and out of sleep all night, sometimes mumbling, sometimes crying softly. Letha changed her bedding and the cloths between her legs and wiped down her skin with warm rags. Connor left her side only when he had to relieve himself. Devyn padded into the hut right after the gates opened in the morning, Wyll close behind her. He knelt next to Connor as Devyn stretched out beside Mairead. "How is she?"

"Alive. She lost a lot of blood."

Wyll sighed. "Then we wait."

Later in the morning, Maeve alit in the hut. "I need to show you something. Can you leave her for a bit?"

He told Letha he would be back soon and followed Maeve into the air high above the city. She led him toward the plains and stopped above Galbragh. *The Forbidden waits there,* she said in his head.

He felt himself frown inside the braids. *In Galbragh? What about Henry?*

He's dead. Alasdair Mac Mahon has installed himself as leader here. He calls himself an emperor. He's taken Henry's sister to wife.

Connor stared down at the city. There were signs of fortifications, and the Forbidden's army had encamped just outside the city walls. *So this army ....*

This army prepares to go up the mountain against the tribe. The one you already fought was just a test of your strength—a skirmish to evaluate your defenses. And there's another army twice this size on the western shore of Culidar. That army prepares to enter Taura. The wards around the Sidh village and the island weaken, and these Nar Sidhe are growing stronger daily.

His stomach twisted. *Are the enchantments that weak now?*

They weaken, but slowly. The prayers of the sayas still ring, and with the new peace between the tribes and the Sidh, the wards around the village are holding. But there is something else. She paused. *Do you know the amasidh?*

His blood chilled. *Gods.*

They are making more of them. They kill children with unquickened blood and make their talismans and distribute them to their army. The people in Taura are terrified. They see only grisly murders of children. They don't realize the children all have some small amount of Sidh blood. Pain tensed her voice.

He hesitated. *I don't know how to help, Mother. I need to be with Mairead.*

As you should be, for now. But we will need you in Taura soon. You are a duke, or will be if Braedan regains his throne. Taura will need your blood, your power, and your title.

He watched the army for a moment, and then he saw him—the Forbidden. The creature looked up, seeming to sense their presence. A cold sneer twisted his mouth.

Connor's fists clenched in recognition. *Mother—do you see it?*

She gasped. *It's like looking at your father.*

As if he'd heard, the creature below them mouthed one word: "Brother."

Righteous rage grew in Connor's chest. He reined it in, and when Maeve flitted north again toward the tribe, Connor swooped down, drew up braids of stone, and twisted them into scathing cords that wound around the creature's body. The Forbidden one hissed, and the Nar Sidhe around him turned and watched the braids, but Connor disappeared before they could attack him. *Next time, I won't stop,* he thought. *I'll lash you until your very sinews lay smoking in the night air.*

Maeve waited in Letha's hut. "Do not *ever* do that again," she said in a low, scolding tone. "You *idiot!* Do you realize what could have happened if they'd seen your braids?"

"He needed a message." Connor folded his arms. "Go back to Taura. I'll come when I can—as soon as Mairead is all right."

She relaxed, let out a breath, and took his hands. Then she pulled him into a sudden embrace and held him for a moment. "Whatever else you are, you are still my son," she whispered. "I don't want to lose you."

He put his arms around her. "I know. Don't worry. I'll be fine. I don't think the One Hand is finished with me yet."

She drew away and knelt next to Mairead. She brushed the hair back from Mairead's face. "Tattoos and lions. Gods." She bowed her head and kissed Mairead's forehead. "We will talk soon, daughter," she whispered. She stood, wove braids around herself, and returned to Taura.

Connor sat down again and watched Mairead's chest rise and fall in sleep. He twirled her hair around one finger. "I promise you," he said. "He will pay for what he did. I will send him back to the chasm myself." He took her hand and raised it to his lips. "I'm here, Mairead. He'll never get close to you again—not if I can do anything about it."

CHAPTER FORTY

A new tapestry is woven in the blood of battle.
— Second Book of the Wisdomkeepers

She woke to pain and emptiness. Devyn's warmth comforted her, and her rough tongue licked Mairead's cheek.

"Mairead," a quiet voice said.

She moaned at the ache in her belly and between her legs.

"Mairead, are you waking?"

Connor. She tried to swallow, but her throat ached with dry pain. She coughed, and the tightening spasm sent a rush of warm wetness between her legs onto a wad of cloth. She reached for her belly. *My baby.* She licked dry lips. "You're here."

He kissed her hand, and something moist fell on her knuckles. "I'm here."

She opened her eyes. "Just you? Or is she here, too?"

"The Morrag is still here. She'll be here till the end of the world. But she's not in my head anymore." He paused. "How long was I gone?"

"Weeks. Where were you?"

"It's a long story, but I was with the One Hand. I think."

"The One Hand?"

"I can't think of a better explanation. She took me to him. She wanted him to allow her to loose me on the world. He wouldn't let her." He held her hand up to his mouth again.

"There was a creature—one of the Forbidden. He was with Osgar. They—" Memories tumbled back. "They killed Gareth." She gasped a sob. "And our baby."

He helped her sit up and pulled her into his arms. "I know." He drew away. "I brought her body from the raven village. Do you want to see her?"

Mairead nodded, and he picked up a small bundle and put it in her hands. She unwrapped the rags to stare down at the translucent skin and perfectly formed body. "Never to suckle her," she whispered. "Never to hear her call me 'Mama' or brush her hair or listen to her laugh while you ...." Sobs welled up, and she cradled the baby's body next to her chest. "I'm sorry, Connor."

"You have no need to be sorry. This was not your doing." He put strong, comforting arms around her and rested his lips against her head. "I'm sorry, Mairead. Saying I'm sorry is so inadequate. I should have been here. I should have been stronger than the Morrag. I should have bent my knee to the One Hand sooner—years ago—I should have—" His voice broke again, and he stopped and composed himself.

Mairead leaned into his chest and cried, and Connor's silent tears wet her hair.

When she was spent, she wiped her eyes. She kissed their daughter one more time and rewrapped her body. "She should have a name. We should bury her with a name."

Connor nodded. "What do you want to name her?"

"Gritta."

He took the baby's body. "Gritta. Very well. We'll bury her tomorrow."

Mairead nodded and lay down again. "There's so much to do."

"You need to rest now. When you're better, I want to take you to Espara."

"I can't—there are duties—"

"Just for a little while. Just for a short holiday. I've figured out how to take another person with me in the braids, so travel won't take long. The sun will be good for you." He hesitated. "If you will have me back, that is."

Have him back. She took a deep breath. "I will honor my commitment," she said, "but I'm going to need time."

"You will have it."

She sighed and laced her fingers with his. "For good or for ill, we are wed. I am committed to being your wife until my dying breath. And I still need you—not just for myself, but for this army and this land."

He covered her hand with his. "We will have some work to do, I think."

"Yes." She lay quiet for a moment, enjoying the comfort of his hand. "Tell me one thing."

"Anything."

"When she took you, you flew at me and croaked. Was that her or you?"

"It was me. I was trying to tell you that I love you. I wanted to say it one more time. But she had control of me, and I couldn't. My voice was gone."

She closed her eyes. "I thought I could be enough—that I could keep her from you."

"I wanted you to be enough, too," he said quietly. "I didn't want to bend my knee to him. But he was—is—the only thing that will keep me in balance and keep her out of my head." He lifted her hand to his mouth again. "But you need to know, Mairead—I do love you. And if I ever leave again, it will only be because something bigger than us—than our marriage—requires it."

She sighed. "What good is it to be the ravenmaster if I can't control the raven?"

He shrugged. "I think we misunderstood the title. You are our traitha—our leader—but you are more. You are our example. When you face trials, your first response is to pray to the One Hand. And you understand mercy. The ravens need to learn that. Mercy and forgiveness are the keys to keeping the madness away."

Can I still turn to the One Hand first—now that I've lost and gained a husband, lost a brother, lost a child? Will I still understand mercy when I have to look into the eyes of a raven or a plainsman? She blinked back tears. "This—this war, this land, these goals—I'm just a piece of the puzzle. I'm not even the most important piece. You are."

"I'm not—"

"You are, Connor. Alshada, the One Hand, he could use any other woman to do my part. You are the piece we can't do without."

"But we can't do without you, either. Your blood, your strength—they are as important as mine." He kissed her forehead. "You should sleep."

"That would be nice." Sleep overtook her, and Devyn's warm, comforting purr settled her.

Braun and the other elders came to see her later that day. All of them knelt and pledged their allegiance, and when the others left, Braun remained. "My father died in the battle for the raven village," he said.

It made her stomach twist. "Braun, I am sorry."

"We were not close. I do not mourn deeply. The earth has chosen another to be traitha in my clan. I came to tell you that I am free to serve you now in whatever way you require."

"Why now?"

He wet his lips. "Because of your marks and your lion, but also because I watched you fight. I watched you defend that village as if it were your own."

"It was my own."

"Even the Forbidden couldn't kill you. You are marked—you are our traitha."

"Did you wed your woman, Braun?"

"The day after my father died."

Three men. Gareth fell. Trypp betrayed the tribe to follow me. Braun married. She reached for his hand. "I accept your fealty."

He blew out a breath. "Thank you, traitha." He left the hut.

Letha sat next to her. "Be careful. He is not a man to be trusted."

Mairead chewed her lip. "I think I trust him more than most. I had to win his fealty, Letha. He did not give it till it was earned."

"And if he betrays you? If he becomes an oathbreaker?"

"We are all oathbreakers, Letha. We all deserve death."

The next day, they buried the baby in a tiny box under a tree in one of the city's earth shrines. When they had buried her, Aerwyth and Hedwar helped Mairead to the place where they had buried their son, and she knelt next to the grave and mourned her friend. "My brother," she whispered. "He was as a brother to me. The only brother I've ever known."

When she stood, Connor had an odd expression on his face. "What is it?" she asked.

"Nothing. Another day. When you're stronger."

"Tell me."

"When you're stronger."

She couldn't fight with him.

Aerwyth put an arm around her. "If you are well, Mairead, Hedwar and I would like to show you something." She looked at Connor. "Your husband, too."

Mairead nodded, and Aerwyth guided her through the village to a hut she recognized from the perch outside. They stopped. "Why are we here?" Mairead asked.

Aerwyth took her hands. "Hedwar and I would like you to have this hut. We have no need of it, and Gareth had no heirs." Hedwar opened the door, and Aerwyth guided Mairead inside.

Mairead fought back the sting of tears as she stepped through the door. "Oh, Aerwyth . . . I don't know . . ." She turned to Connor. "I thought we would go back to the raven village."

"The village is mostly gone," Connor said. "The plainsmen burned it. And if the lions will let us live here, we will all be safer until we can kick these bastards off the mountain for good. I will chafe inside these walls if it means you are safe."

"Gareth served you with all his heart," Aerwyth said. "He loved you as a sister. If you swear to remember him, we want you to have his hut."

As a sister. She turned to them. "I loved him as a brother, and he died protecting me. I promise you: if I ever have a son, he will bear Gareth's name in the tribe. He will have a Taurin name first, but he will be a lion, and his name in the tribe will be Gareth."

Hedwar inclined his head. "You honor us, traitha."

She stepped toward them both. "And you will no longer call me traitha. If you would have it, I would wish you to call me 'daughter.'"

Silence fell in the hut. Connor put one hand on her shoulder. "I wish it, too."

"I have no mother or father," Mairead said. "And I took your only child from you. I beg you—take me as your child. I will vow to care for you until death separates us."

Aerwyth pulled Mairead into an embrace. "My daughter," she whispered. "I will take you as my earthbonded daughter. You will be known as Mairead Catspaw, bonded with Ulfrich Wolfbrother."

Hedwar put his hands on both womens' backs. "We vow as well. We will protect and shelter and guide you as parents until we return to the earthspirit and the One Hand."

Branded as traitha, adopted as daughter. I have become a lion. I have a home. Mairead clung to Aerwyth and sobbed, and Connor rubbed her back, and Hedwar put his head against hers and Aerwyth's, and Mairead grieved in the embrace of her family.

After Aerwyth and Hedwar left the hut, Mairead curled up in a bear pelt while Connor prepared some supper for them. A flutter of wings and a sharp cry outside nudged her out of her thoughts. "Grayfeather." She stood and went to the perch outside Gareth's hut.

Grayfeather ruffled his feathers and tipped his head. She smiled and held out an arm. He alit on it. "I've missed you," she said.

He pecked at her hair, but it seemed half-hearted. She stroked his wings and back. "Do you miss him?"

He chirped, quiet, and blinked at her.

"He was a good man. You served him well."

The bird nudged her with his beak and gave a low trill in his throat.

"I have no need of you. If you wish to stay, I would take you, but if you wish to go, you are free."

The bird clicked his beak and squawked.

Mairead stroked his back again. "Do you want to go?"

He rifled his feathers and stretched up, nearly lifting from her arm.

She smiled. "Then go. And know you are always welcome here."

She lifted her arm, and Grayfeather took wing. He soared above her for a moment, turned on a current of air, then faded to a tiny speck in the distance.

She pulled the bear pelt tighter and turned back to the hut.

Connor waited at the door. "Hungry?"

"I think so."

He guided her into the hut, and Devyn warmed her legs while she ate, and the warm spring night fell around the village.

EPILOGUE

By the blood of the thousand unquickened shall the island be made our own.
— Nar Sidhe prophecy

The odors of sulfur and decay assaulted Emrys when he entered the cave. Bachi was already there, his wrecked face twisted in a rictus of rapt delight. "He waits for you," he said. "He has news."

Emrys suppressed a grimace. *News.* It could mean anything from the conquest of Taura to the return of the Syrafi. Bachi's excitement came from the anticipation of seeing their master. He didn't care if the news was good or bad—he received as much pleasure from pain as he did from reward. *They are one and the same to a mind as twisted as his.* "Do you know what kind of news?"

Bachi shook his head. "My forces have not crossed the channel yet. Have you had any luck?"

Emrys swallowed hard. "Only moderate."

Bachi was about to respond when a flare of fire from the sulfur pit interrupted. "My remaining faithful servants," said a voice. "You come with news, and I have some for you."

Bachi fell to his knees as soon as the voice split the silence. He pressed his face to the ground and mumbled incoherently. Emrys watched, frowning, then turned to the pit. "I have news, Master," he said. "The woman's child is dead. I've succeeded in killing her line."

"Well done," the spirit voice said. "But if she and the raven are still bedding each other, your work was in vain."

"She and the raven may not reconcile. He left her for some time, and she suggested she would not take him back into her bed."

The voice didn't respond at first, as if it were thinking. "This is well," it finally said. "But as long as they are both alive, there is the possibility of reconciliation."

Emrys clenched his fists. "What do you wish me to do, Master? Kill them on my own? Wait for you? I cannot touch them still. The raven was able to stab her, but it's clear that the One Hand still protects them."

His voice retreated as if in a long tunnel. "I have seen her city fall, and I have seen the plains running red with the blood of lions. The bear lumbers from the east, and the raven fades into the west. The age of empires is coming."

Emrys' mind worked quickly around the words. *Age of empires. Mine?*

Aldora's? His? And who is the bear? "Taura is fading?"

"The time of the bloodied hill approaches. Torlach will fall, and my faithful servant will sit upon the broken throne."

Emrys stepped closer, ignoring the prostrate Bachi. "There is none more faithful than I, Master. I have done all that you ask. I have not overstepped as Aldora did, and I have not fallen to the greed of my brother."

"Nor have you betrayed me as your other brother did. This I know. You have indeed been faithful, Ohmin. You will receive your reward in full."

The briefest gratitude fluttered in Emrys' breast, but he could not bow yet. He wet his lips. "Master, please tell me—will I have to share again? Will I share my reward with Aldora?"

The voice that came back was full of the most chilling joy Emrys had ever heard. "My beloved has received her reward in full. We are reunited, and she sits as my queen in my realm. When I return to my seat in the world above, she will rule here."

Bachi looked up at that. "Master, you promised—you swore that I—"

"There is yet room for you here, faithful one. Take care not to fall to the raven, or you will discover the place I have prepared for you all too soon."

Actual fear flickered across Bachi's face, and he lowered himself to the ground once more. "Yes, Master," he whispered. "I will do all you command."

"Continue as you have been, faithful one. Taura's fears will destroy her from the inside out, and you will receive your reward next to Ohmin when he takes the place I have for him."

"And you, Master?" Bachi asked. "When will you reclaim your seat?"

"When all has come to pass—when the First Raven is destroyed and his woman and her line are gone, when the bear has overrun the lion and the shining isle has fallen into the sea—then will my reign be made manifest among those who remain. Then will the One Hand depart that world, and I will become judge and ruler over all."

He promises this over and over, as he has promised since time began, and every time, we fall for it. We do this again and again, and each time, Alshada's people rise once more. Emrys chewed his lip and folded his arms. *But this time, things are different. This time, Aldora is gone, and the First Raven rises. Perhaps this time, we will finish the people of Alshada once and for all.* He knelt and lowered his head to the ground. "Bless us for this work, Master."

The pain of Namha's touch washed over them, and Bachi's screams of rabid delight filled Emrys' ears.

BRONWYN ALIT outside Maeve's hut at sunset, as usual. Maeve was waiting. She stood from her perch on a fallen log to greet Bronwyn with a small hug.

The Syraf held Maeve at arm's length, frowning. "You've been crying."

"My son's wife." Maeve shook her head. "No, my daughter-in-law. Their child died. She gave birth to a dead child. A girl." She composed herself. "My heir."

Bronwyn's face was a jumble of emotions—everything from shock to grief to anger. "I did not know, Maeve. I am so sorry. I did not know that she was even with child."

"But you knew they had wed?"

"I heard rumors. I have had other duties of late." She bit her lip. "The wisdomkeeper has anointed Braedan. He is King of Taura."

Maeve's legs went weak. She let out a long breath and sat. "By the spirits."

Bronwyn sat next to her. "The heir—your daughter-in-law—she still carries the blood of her ancestors. Ronan Kerry will make a legal bid for the monarchy. And Braedan has the blessing of the earthspirit. There are three good claimants to the throne. This will come to blood."

"What should I do?"

"The only thing you can do right now is care for the Sidh and carry messages to your son."

"Has the One Hand withdrawn his hand yet?"

Bronwyn raised an eyebrow and gave a crooked grin. "The One Hand?"

Maeve bit off a curse. "I have spent much time with Edgar of late."

"Clearly," Bronwyn said. "No, he has not withdrawn his hand from Taura. But the day draws ever closer. And the more Nar Sidhe amassed in the channel and on the shore of Culidar, the more Taurin blood will be shed when he does withdraw his hand." She paused. "We need a leader, Maeve. We need Connor."

"He will not come—not now, not while he and his wife are grieving."

"He will do as he is bid to do."

Maeve bit her lip. "I will ask. But I cannot promise anything."

"It is all I ask." Bronwyn stood, shimmered into her owl form, and flew away.

Maeve entered her hut just as Edgar knocked on the door. "Maeve?"

She smiled. *He still knocks, even though he could just come in.* She opened the door for him. "When will you learn to just open the door?" she asked.

"This isn't my house. I'll stop knocking when it's my house."

Maeve laughed. "Your house. You can't own anything in the Sidh village."

"I could own your heart. I hope."

She twined her arms around his neck. "You already do." She traced the marks on his face. In the days after Hrogarth's departure, the traithas had gathered for the earth to choose a new chief traitha. After two days and nights, Edgar had emerged with new marks—new shapes and symbols on his face that indicated his new rank as traitha over the nine. "I still can't get used to this."

"Neither can I."

"You bear your new responsibilities well."

"It's easier now that all the traithas went home." He wrapped his arms around her waist. "Besides, now I have more time for you again."

She kissed him. "There is news from Culidar. Mairead's baby died. She's had a stillbirth."

Edgar let out a long breath. "Gods, Maeve. I am so sorry."

She blinked back tears. "It is the cycle of life, yes?"

"That doesn't make it easy." He pulled her close and buried his face in her hair. "I wish I could help."

She relaxed against his chest. "You do."

He kissed her neck. "Do you fear for an heir?"

"I do. But I find myself more sad for Mairead and Connor than afraid I won't have an heir." She pulled away from him. "It was unexpected, anyway. I don't know that they will have another child with the same power. Perhaps my heir will come from someone else. The One Hand obviously has something in mind."

"Then you've finally abandoned the notion that your heir will have to be a pureblood Sidh?"

She sighed. "I suppose I have. She'll have to have some Sidh blood, but if Mairead could conceive a child so powerful, perhaps the purity of the blood isn't as important as I thought."

Edgar pushed her hair back from her cheek. "Perhaps the One Hand intends your heir will come from you."

She scoffed and turned away. "You know that's not possible."

"Sidh women are able to have children all their lives, yes?"

"Yes, but you know why I can't have another child."

"Have you ever been seen by a tribal midwife? An earth guardian?"

"No, but—"

"Then how do you know they can't help you?"

Maeve turned back. "Edgar, I can't give you a child. If that's what you want from me ...." She let the thought trail away.

He took her hands. "Maeve, I love you. I will be with you as long as you will have me, whether you can give me a child or not. But I think we should try. I think there's a chance."

"What makes you say so?"

His grin made her knees weak. "A hunch."

"A child would need more than this arrangement we have. I won't raise another child the way I raised Connor—sharing him between two homes."

"True. A child needs a home with both parents."

"You can't live here."

"And you won't live in the tribe."

She bit her lip. "What if I would?"

"Would you?"

She lifted one shoulder.

"I might have room in my hut for a wife and child."

A wife. Could I? Maeve took a deep breath. "I don't know how it would work. I don't know—"

He kissed her. "Marry me."

A family. I've had a lover and a son, and now could I have a family? "Yes."

Edgar scooped her into his arms and buried his face near her neck. "You will not regret it," he whispered. "I will do everything to make you happy. I swear it."

Maeve leaned back and kissed him. "You already have."

A BRIEF HISTORY OF THE THREE LANDS

By Xinias Ja'aster

(Excerpt from the introduction.)

It is a peculiarity of brevity that it often contradicts itself—that is, that those things which profess brevity may, in fact, be the longest. Certainly an attempt to record the annals of three of the largest empires history has produced cannot possibly be accomplished in anything resembling brevity. Nonetheless, my emperor has requested that I apply my meager skill to the task, and I am ever his faithful and humble servant.

There have been three significant turning points in the history of the three lands. It is these which I will endeavor to examine in greater detail in this volume. Each turning point has its own array of socioeconomic, political, geological, religious, and cultural backgrounds, causes, and influences. However, for purposes of an introduction, I shall provide merely a brief overview of these influences.

It is important to acknowledge that all of these events are preceded by the creation of the world and the three races—humans, Sidh, and Syrafi. Such things should go without saying, but as I know pedants will take delight in pointing out the obvious, I will endeavor to answer them now rather than later.

The Breaking of the World

Our first point is one that came even before the lands were three—when the vast continent we now call Culidar included Taurin and Eiryan lands, along with a host of smaller principalities long submerged. It is unclear precisely how long the battle for control of the earth and its inhabitants continued before the Breaking. Based on ancestry of the Taurin heir I constructed from our records, I can safely say the Breaking probably occurred sometime between Year of Creation 3875 and 4018. We know the earliest records that mention the Taurin throne appear in approximately 4022, and those records include the assumption of some years of power.

It is clear from ancient writings (including the Books of the Wisdomkeepers) that the two magical races had split before the Breaking occurred. There was a rebellion among the Syrafi at some point long lost to the annals of time, and many Syrafi chose to mate with humans at the bidding of their leader, Namha. Those Syrafi who followed Namha were cursed with the darkness of the chasm[1], which resulted in their physical change from white to black. Namha gave them the name Ferimin, which means "destroyer" in the ancient language of the three lands. The offspring of the Ferimin and the humans they seduced became the Forbidden Ones who fought in the battle over the land of Culidar. While we do not know how many Forbidden there were originally, it was clear after the Breaking that only four of the "soultainted" remained unbanished.

---

[1] We must note that "chasm," in this case, refers to a place outside of this current world. It is not a literal chasm as one might find on a mountain, but rather the deep supernatural darkness that exists in a place outside of the All-Seeing Lord's presence.

The Sidh also split into two factions, though it's not clear if there was a particular event that caused the split or if it was simply a rebellion of the unwillingly led. The Sidh queens have ever been secretive and guarded with information about their people, and it has been my impression they do not wish to suggest a failure of leadership may have led to the split. In any case, the movement of the Nar Sidhe was an undercurrent of unrest before the battle for the continent, though it did not come to fruition until the moment of the Breaking.

As for humanity, there have always been those who were willing to live rough in the most inhospitable places and those for whom such a life bears no appeal. Prior to the Breaking, men had started to form cities and towns, and other men had retreated to the forests and mountains to live rough on the land. These rugged people formed ten tribes. It is unclear when these tribes took guardianship of the terrestrial magic. While their annals record a moment of acceptance after the death of their greatest warrior, it is likely they had already taken some responsibility for guarding the balance between life and death. Indeed, the curse already upon the earth would necessitate such; the very presence of Namha and his followers on this mortal coil would require guardians to keep the spirits of the earth bound until the appropriate time. Additionally, we know there were ravenmarked warriors who appeared in the tribes before the Breaking, indicating the presence and activity of the Morrag.

These great tribes had formed an intricate—if primitive by Eastern standards—society long before the Breaking. The peoples established settlements across the vast arable lands and thick forests of what is now Taura all the way across the northern part of current Culidar and into the northern mountain plateaus. Indeed, the people group was poised on the very edge of empire when Namha moved against them with his army at his back.

The following pages will go into greater detail about the war that led to the Breaking, but for now, it is important to note several major results of the Breaking:

1) The Breaking itself: It would be difficult to estimate the magnitude, scope, and destruction caused by the All-Seeing Lord's cataclysmic destruction of the Western side of the great continent. And it has been posited that "breaking" is an inaccurate name for what occurred. It was not, in fact, a breaking of the land, but rather a sudden submersion of the low-lying lands of the west. This event resulted in the creation of the channel between Taura and the continent, the Eiryan island, and the Ragged Isles in the north. It is important to note, however, that the

channel appears to be deeper than such a submersion can account for.[2]

2) The division of the tribes: The sudden inrush of water forced the tribes to split into two factions. Those trapped on the continent retreated to the mountain plateaus of the north. Those remaining on Taura retreated to the forests and formed the nine tribes of modern Taura.

3) The creation of the reliquary: It fell to the newly crowned Queen of Taura, the warrior Cuhail's widow, to gather and protect the relics of the battle. She took the jar that held the dying tears of the Syrafi chieftain, the animstone worn by the first Sidh queen, and the sword her own husband wielded until his death and asked the new Sidh queen to construct a stone chest to hold the items. When the chest was completed, upon orders from the Syrafi, the Sidh queen hid the reliquary until such a time as it would be needed again. The relics remain hidden to this day.

4) The destruction of the ravenmarked: It is speculated now that Cuhail, the first King of Taura and a tribal warrior as well, was, in fact, marked by the Morrag. Researchers posit that no mere mortal could have fought as he did, and he famously led a contingent of ravenmarked warriors against Namha and his Forbidden Ones (which is, of course, what caused his death). Time and poetry give birth to legends, and no one can say with certainty whether Cuhail bore the ravenmark. His elite warriors, however, did bear the mark, and upon the victory over Namha and his Forbidden Ones, the ravenmarked men were unable to return to society. It is an oft-forgotten footnote in tribal history, existing mainly in whispers, but there was a time when the tribal chieftains led their own warriors to kill the ravenmarked among them. The chieftains justified the act with a "greater good" argument—that is, they claimed to save countless lives by killing men who were determined to cleanse the earth by wiping it clean of human taint.[3]

The Svek Invasion

Within one hundred years or so of the Breaking, the government of Taura had

---

2 Some suggest the channel is, in fact, "broken" at the bottom—that is, that much of the sea that submerged the low lying parts of the continent actually came from a vast aquifer that suddenly burst open. The most ardent supporters of this view even suggest that the "crack" is still open, still constantly pushing fresh water up through salt deposits. Of course, without divers who can truly investigate such claims, we will likely never know exactly how deep the channel goes or whether new waters are constantly springing up from its depths.

3 The implications for modern tribesmen and warriors is clear and does not need to be discussed here. Time will tell how current events play out. It is the position of this historian, however, that the early chieftains took a route of expedience that could have been avoided.

established itself and stabilized the newly formed island. Cuhail's widow, Queen Emyr, quickly took control of the chieftains and lords who had served under her husband. She established a seat of government on the hill that is now Torlach and sent cartographers to redraw the maps of the lands. As soon as he came of age, her son, Culain I, took the throne, and for one thousand years, the Cuhail Dynasty held the Raven Throne under the rule of a largely competent and talented group of monarchs.[4]

Under the reign of Cuhail's Dynasty, Taura expanded east to Culidar and west to what is now Eirya. The Taurin kings brought order, peace, and prosperity to the wildest edges of Culidar. Under the banner of the Raven Throne, the continent experienced relative peace for nearly one thousand years. It was a time of architecture, trade, and learning. The famed University of Leiden was founded in 4317, and it stood for six hundred years as a shining beacon of egalitarian education. Along Haman's Road, commerce flourished, and through cooperative efforts, the principalities through which the road passed shared the responsibility of keeping it clean and safe.

On its western boundary, Taura made peace with the tribes and sent explorers beyond the western shores to settle what is now Eirya. Those few humans who had been trapped on the far isle after the Breaking had joined together to form small villages and cities. The Taurins brought government, but those already in Eirya proved difficult to govern. The people were an independent, unruly lot connected only by similar backgrounds who had formed uneasy alliances and truces that could only loosely be called a "government." Through superior power, the Taurin government was able to bring the Eiryan peasants to heel. Though the Eiryans put up little struggle, an undercurrent of disunity simmered for hundreds of years until the legendary Boru the Usurper led the uprising that threw a Taurin government weakened by invasion and war off the Eiryan island. Boru's reign was short and bloody, but his successor, Lughaid the Unifier, ushered in decades of peace and growth from which Eirya would emerge a growing world power. Though the earliest days of formal civilization on Eirya are worth mentioning, the small island did not play a significant role in the politics and future of the lands until well after the Svek Invasion was repelled.

---

4 The unfortunate reign of King Dougal (r. 4823 – 4827) is still widely regarded as a very poor joke perpetrated on an unsuspecting populace by an old and entrenched Table of Councilors. Dougal's first act as king was to put forth a proposal to build a vast seawall and use tariff income from trading partners to pay for it. The Table finally forced the king's abdication when he suggested that he keep his bloodlines pure by wedding his own daughter (as his wife had fled the country long before he took the throne). Most Taurin historians are reluctant to speak of the reign at all; as a result, some of the most accurate information we have about Dougal is from the bawdy songs of a wandering troubadour named Nathanael the Morose.

The first reference we see to the Taurin Empire or the "Empire of the Three Lands" is in the mid-4400s with the publication of *The Annals of the Taurin Kings* in YC[5] 4462. The author, a devout kiron named Padraig Black-finger,[6] was the personal and favored scribe of King Conchobar the Wise, a man who managed to temper his quest for empire with a passion for education, open commerce, and personal liberty. The 73-year reign of King Conchobar (4453 – 4526) ushered in the greatest period of peace, prosperity, and expansion the world has seen before or since.[7]

The era of prosperity and growth came to an end in the year 4954, with the invasion of Svek warriors from the continent. The Svek—and others, it should be noted—have long labored under the assumption they are the legendary third land of the "three lands." This is debateable, at best, and patently false, at worst. However, the rising independence of the Eiryan kingdom in the late Fifth Millennium and the modern Eiryan insistence that it has been and always shall be an independent state does give credence to the Svek view.

Under the great warrior Eirik Gunvald, also known as the Northern Bear, so called because of his size and his attire made of bearskins, Svek warriors crossed over the northern channel between Culidar and the Ragged Isles in mid-winter, 4954. The invasion took the young Queen Brenna of Taura and her dukes by surprise, and by spring, the Svek warriors—men who were not untrained in cold combat conditions—had conquered the upper third of Taura. Unable to secure the timely aid of the Eiryan king or the nine tribes, Brenna and her young husband, Aiden, rode to their fate in late spring that year, both of them cut down by the Svek in the Battle of Salmon Springs.

The Taurin Empire ended that day, and the country itself would have died as well but for a series of events orchestrated by a few very wise men and women:

1) The aid of the nine tribes: Faced with the possibility of losing their great forest, the nine traithas of the Taurin tribes at last banded together to come to the aid of the remaining Taurin dukes who fought to repel the Svek invaders.

2) The leadership of the first Duke Mac Niall of Kiern: The first Duke Mac Niall, Lugh, was a commander in the royal army. When he saw his king and queen cut down, he rose up and took leadership of the army, negotiated with the nine tribes, and led the Taurin army north to push the invaders back. The

---

5 Year of Creation
6 His hands were reportedly stained permanently black as a result of years of writing.
7 With apologies to my own emperor and his predecessors who have occupied the Throne of the Nine Seas.

Battle of Salmon Springs was a turning point, but not the one the Svek hoped for. It was, in fact, the moment when a Taurin national identity was formed in the blood of its fallen king and queen, and the cry of "for the Raven Throne" was branded that day into the national consciousness.

3) The rumored assistance of the Brae Sidh: It has never been proven, but legends persist that the Brae Sidh queen and her people emerged from their hiding place in the great forest of Taura to use elemental magic against the Svek.

4) The survival of the offspring of Brenna and Aiden: Duke Lugh Mac Niall (so titled by the first Regent Fergus after the battle) is rumored to have hidden the infant son of King Aiden and Queen Brenna in a breadbasket and spirited him away to the care of a young family in the south of Taura.

5) The formation of the Table of Councilors and the Regency: Once the Svek were pushed back to Culidar and the Taurin Empire broken, it fell to the surviving lords, officers, and religious leaders to form a new government. Thirteen men emerged as dukes from those first talks, and one of them, Duke Fergus Mac Corin, was chosen to serve as regent. Duke Mac Niall asked for land in the north, and in gratitude for his wartime service, the duke was given not only vast tracts of northern land, but also the responsibility to treat with the tribes and act as an unbreakable line of defense against future invaders.

The collapse of the Taurin Empire and retreat of the Svek resulted in the rise of Eiryan independence and the encroachment of disorder and chaos across the Wilds of Culidar. In the aftermath of the Svek war, the Taurin government simply did not have the resources to maintain a presence in either Eirya or Culidar. A spirit of nationalism and isolationism rose as well, and for more than six hundred years, Taura remained a subdued participant in the world economy while a series of regents held the throne until a suitable candidate for the monarchy could be found.

The Restoration of the Monarchy

The third major turning point in the history of Taura is not yet complete. While it's impossible to say how this moment in history will ultimately affect the course of Taura, Culidar, the Svek territories, the tribes, or Eirya, it is clear that current events will have a profound impact on the future of all the lands and, indeed, the broader global economy and political structure.

Rumblings of dissatisfaction with the Taurin Regency began decades ago, sometime around the close of the sixth millennium, with the ascension of

Fergus II to the Regency of the Raven Throne. Fergus Mac Corin was an unpopular choice among the thirteen dukes of the Taurin Table of Councilors. He had, at best, the support of seven dukes, one of them his own brother-in-law, and he had the vocal opposition of several dukes under the leadership of Duke Culain Mac Niall of Kiern. Mac Niall's opposition to Fergus continued unabated (but for a period of grief after the death of his wife) for nearly twenty-five years. Outside analysts think it likely that Taura was moving quickly toward civil war when the simmering rebellion was ruthlessly squashed in 5987 by Fergus and his ally, Duke Sean Mac Rian of Fox Hill. Duke Mac Niall and his family were killed, and the duke's name was attainted and his lands and title forfeited by royal decree. The duke's son, Connor Mac Niall, fled Taura, and the Mac Niall holdings were given to Sean Mac Rian as reward for his assistance in securing the regency.

But the regency was not to last. In 5995, an ailing Regent Fergus attempted to pass on the regency to a distant nephew of House Mac Corin. However, Daron Mac Corin had little support among the remaining twelve dukes of the Table of Councilors, and Duke Ronan Kerry, Fergus' estranged brother-in-law, was able to convince the Table to back the exiled Prince Braedan Mac Corin for king. In a single night, Braedan's forces crossed Cuhail's Channel and took the throne from Fergus, established a tenuous hold on the throne, and installed Braedan as king. Fergus died of his illness, and Daron was beheaded.

As the events subsequent to this coup have been documented elsewhere, and as these events are still unfolding on Taura and in Culidar and Sveklant, I will leave this introduction with a few observations about the key international parties involved:

1) Eirya: Under the rule of King Cedric Mac Roy, Eirya has seen some of the greatest economic growth and political stability in its history. Mac Roy is strong and healthy, and with three sons and four grandsons, there is no questioning his line of succession. Mac Roy is intelligent and skilled at trade and commerce, and under normal circumstances, he would likely be in an ideal position to take advantage of Taurin instability and improve his nation's fortunes at Taura's expense. However, Mac Roy's daughter, Princess Royale Igraine, remains on Taura in potentially dangerous circumstances, and it is therefore unlikely Mac Roy will do anything to damage relations with Taura until his daughter is safely on Eiryan soil.

2) Sveklant: Though the Svek remain largely decentralized, recent years have seen the consolidation of several tribes and families into larger, more powerful principalities. One prince in particular, Niklaus Gottschalk, styles himself King Niklaus the First. His seat of power has begun to consolidate around

the town of Albard, near the ambiguous border between Culidar and Sveklant. While it remains to be seen if the rise of men such as Gottschalk will influence events in the west overall, there is no question that the rising strength of Svek princes poses deep concerns for Culidar's future.

3) Culidar: Culidar remains largely under the control of slaving empires, traders, and self-styled princes. Vast portions of the Wilds are under no rule at all, and there is some evidence that the barbarians of the Nar Sidhe territory are emerging from their self-imposed restraint to attempt to control the more arable and fertile soil of Culidar. There is a certain inevitability to government in Culidar—whether slavers, princes, or barbarians, the vast lands are largely untamable and the peoples mostly uncontrollable. It is highly unlikely any prince, warrior, king, or other force could bring order—even a tyrannical order—to such a place.

4) Taura: Despite its quiet and unassuming nature over the past several hundred years, Taura remains a hingepin on which history turns. Should the Taurin government fall into chaos, it is likely the ripples of such a major event will cascade through history for thousands of years. Should the government remain intact under Braedan Mac Corin, or if some other prince, king, or regent should restore stability, it is likely Taura will rise to prominence once again.

(Here ends the excerpt. My lord shall receive the completed history when current events have brought themselves to completion. I remain, as always, your humble servant.)

CHARACTER INDEX

Aiden: Castle guard, loyal to King Braedan

Aldora/Cerys: One of the Forbidden

Alfrig: Wife to Hrogarth, earth guardian for the hound tribe, chief earth guardian over the nine tribes

Brannon, Elizabeth: Henry's sister, betrothed to Alasdair Mac Mahon

Brannon, Henry: Prince of Galbragh

Bronwyn: Syrafi warrior, friend of and messenger to Queen Maeve

Catspaw, Aerwyth: Wife of Hedwar, mother to Gareth

Catspaw, Gareth: Warrior of the lion tribe and Catspaw clan

Catspaw, Hedwar: Warrior of the lion tribe, traitha of the Catspaw clan, father of Gareth

Catspaw, Letha: Earth guardian for the Catspaw clan

Dylan, Haldor: Duke of Starling's Cross

Elkbane, Wyll: Outcast raven

Elsbet: Betrothed to Gareth Catspaw

Emrys: One of the Forbidden; in current bodily form, the illegitimate child of Culain Mac Niall and half brother of Connor Mac Niall, though his spirit is thousands of years old.

Farrell, Jamie: Duke of Willow Heights

Fingall, Cameron: Duke of Salmon Springs

Goldeneye, Trypp: Warrior of the lion tribe and Catspaw clan

Goldeneye, Wytha: Wife to Trypp

Grytha: Earth guardian for the hound tribe

Hrogarth: Traitha of the hound tribe, chief traitha over the nine tribes

Ja'aster, Phinneas: Chief Eunuch to His Imperial Majesty, the High King of the Eastern Seas, Tal Ja'al the Tenth

Kerry, Ronan: Lord High Chancellor and Duke of Stone Coast. Uncle to Braedan Mac Corin.

Kyath: Hrogarth's second in the hound tribe

Lionjaw, Braun: Warrior of the lion tribe and Lionjaw clan

Lionjaw, Osgar: Outcast raven

Mac Corin, Braedan: King of Taura. Son of Fergus Mac Corin, Regent of Taura. Betrothed to Igraine Mac Roy of Eirya.

Mac Kendrick, Logan: A Taurin guard, prisoner of Hrogarth. Also called Hector, one of the Forbidden, by Aldora.

Mac Mahon, Alasdair: Slaver on the plains of Culidar

Mac Niall, Connor: Ulfrich Wolfbrother, Duke of Kiern, husband to Mairead Mac Niall, First Raven

Mac Niall, Mairead: Heir to the Taurin throne, prophesied deliverer of the lion tribe, wife to Connor Mac Niall

Mac Roy, Ian: Third son of King Cedric Mac Roy of Eirya.

Mac Roy, Igraine: Fourth and youngest child of King Cedric Mac Roy of Eirya. Betrothed to Braedan Mac Corin. Former Taurin Ambassador to the Great Kirok and legal advisor to the Raven Throne.

Malcolm: Taurin soldier and personal guard to King Braedan

Minerva/Esma: Former saya, former earth guardian

Namha: The Great Adversary of Humanity

Nedra: Earth guardian for the wolf tribe

Nolan, Riordan (Rory): Duke of Falcon Heights, former lover of Igraine Mac Roy. Current Ambassador to Taura representing the Eiryan crown.

Seannan, Aislinn: Widow of Daron Mac Corin, cousin to Braedan, beheaded in Braedan's coup. Currently betrothed to Lord High Chancellor Ronan

Kerry.

SilverAir, Maeve: Mother to Duke Connor Mac Niall, Queen of the Brae Sidh, lover of Edgar Wolfbrother.

Wisdomkeeper: Also known as the Great Mother or the nameless crone. The keeper of all earth wisdom on Taura.

Wolfbrother, Edgar: Traitha of the wolf tribe, lover of Queen Maeve

GLOSSARY

Aliom: The seat of the Great Kirok, Aliom is not a kingdom of its own, but a small city-state located on the edge of the Esparan Empire. It answers to no king or kingdom and is controlled by Prelate Johanan.

Alshada: Sometimes called the One Hand, sometimes called the Creator, Alshada is the main god of the kirok in Aliom. Some say he is the only god; others say he is one of many.

animstone: Pieces of gray, translucent stone from the Syrafi Keep that have the power to suppress blood magic when worn by Syrafi, Ferimin, Brae Sidh, or Nar Sidhe. The origin of this stone is unclear. Some say it may be a remainder of a world created before this one; others think it is matter from a distant star. The Brae Sidh queen wears one in her crown, and it appears she is the only exception to the rule of suppression. She is able to use the stone to augment her power.

Brae Sidh: Pronounced *"bray shee,"* these are the "hidden folk" who live deep in the great forest on the Taurin Isle. They were created in the first days of the world as Alshada's workers. Each Sidh is born with one of three talents—air, water, or stone. At Alshada's instruction, they formed the geography and weather patterns of the earth in the earliest days. They are ruled by a queen, and humans can come and go from their village, but only during sunset or sunrise when the veil between the village and the human world is thinnest. They now live hidden under enchantments and surrounded by the tribal people.

codagha: The web of magic that binds the Brae Sidh queen to her people. She can sense where they are or if they are hurt. Through the *codagha,* she can bind the will of a Sidh to her own, but this is seen as abhorrent and only a last resort for someone who is a criminal or lost to madness. There is an unwritten agreement that the queens will respect the privacy of their people.

Ferimin: The dark counterparts of the Syrafi. They split from the Syrafi after being seduced by the fallen Syrafi, Namha, with promises of great pleasure and power. When they left the service of Alshada, they were tainted and tarnished, and now they can only shapeshift into giant crows. They are still immortal, but can be banished to Namha's prison by tribesmen with the warriormark. If they are not banished, they can take over a human body and possess it, but they lose the ability to shapeshift. They can still create illusions, however, and they are still persuasive and able to tempt humans into great folly.

Forbidden: Creatures born from the union of Syrafi with humans. The humanity taints the Syrafi magic, but the creatures are still immortal. They can steal souls and are strengthened by the transgressions of humans. They can travel between the elements, appearing all around the world in a blink. When their human bodies die, they find new bodies to inhabit. They can only be completely destroyed by one of the ravenmarked. Limits: When a human is protected by Alshada, the Forbidden cannot act on that person directly—he or she must send something else. They cannot act against Brae Sidh magic, and those who know how to use the earth magic can weave spells that keep the Forbidden away.

Great Kirok: The main religious power in the western world, seated in Aliom and dedicated to the service of Alshada. It is governed currently by Prelate Johanan, who has served for twenty years.

kirok: The name for any of the smaller individual groups of worshippers of Alshada throughout the known world. Run by men known as kirons.

kiron: A priest bound to the Great Kirok in Aliom. They belong to one of several different orders, among them the Order of Sai Johan (itinerant preachers) and the Order of Sai Cyphus (permanent kirons).

The Morrag: The personification of the avenging spirit of the earth. The Morrag uses ravens to take the shape of a woman. She marks men for her service by branding them with a raven feather on the thigh. When she calls them to kill, they are driven to exact justice in her name.

Nar Sidhe: Formerly part of the Brae Sidh, the Nar Sidhe followed Namha in the earliest days of the world and split apart from the Brae Sidh to take up residence in Culidar. They live in the southern forest of the country on the border between Culidar and the Esparan Empire. They are ruthless about attacking merchants and nobles who pass through their territory. Their presence at the southern edge of Culidar is one of the reasons for the poverty in the country. Only a handful of very capable freelances are able to escort merchants through Nar Sidhe territory. Unlike the Brae Sidh, who have remained fairly insular and still have dark features, the Nar Sidhe have spent a thousand years capturing women and men to breed with, and they have diluted their blood enough that they look very much like most of the people in Culidar.

The Rending: The separation of the Sidh into Brae Sidh and Nar Sidhe. When those who followed Namha left the Sidh, the damage to the *codagha* was so extensive that it killed the Sidh queen.

sayada: The home of the sisters of the Order of Sai Atena. There are few sayadas left; the largest, the one on the Taurin Isle, was destroyed when King Braedan overthrew the regency.

sayana/saya: Sisters of the Order of Sai Atena. They are sworn to uphold wisdom, devotion, and service to Alshada mainly through study of the ancient scriptures and service to the poor. The sayanas are leaders of the sayas.

Syrafi: Beings created to serve Alshada as warriors. They are immortal and able to shapeshift into the form of giant white owls. In human form, they are unique and distinct in appearance. They can also cast very realistic and elaborate illusions, and they have unusually persuasive speech.

Syrafi Keep: The earthly home of the Syrafi in the most northern mountains of the world, before the great ice seas and beyond the edge of Sveklant. The keep is surrounded by magic and impossible for humans to see. Sidh can go into the Keep, but once accepted, they can never return to the human world.

talents: The magic of the Brae Sidh and Nar Sidhe. There are three talents— air, water, and stone. The Sidh speak of braiding elements; to others with Sidh blood, the magic will look like colored braids. Air appears as shades of violet; water appears as shades of blue and green; stone appears as orange and brown and other earth tones. Only those with Sidh blood can see the braids.

ABOUT THE AUTHOR

Amy Rose Davis is an independent fantasy author. She lives with her husband, Bryce, and their children in Oregon. She likes coffee, chocolate, red wine, whiskey, dogs, cats, the color green, new pencils, her girlfriends, and camping, among other things. She is as likely to watch *300* as *Becoming Jane*.

Bloodbonded is Amy's second published novel and the second book of *The Taurin Chronicles*. Book three, *Unquickened,* is forthcoming.

Connect with Amy online:
Facebook: http://www.facebook.com/amyrosedaviswriter
Blog: http://www.amyrosedavis.com